THE LIVERPOOL PACKET

© 2001, Andrew M. Hajducki

This first edition published in 2023 by

Anoetica Publishing Ltd, Edinburgh

Printed in the UK on sustainably sourced paper.

Front cover features the original painting
"Sunrise, Liverpool Waterfront" by artist Roy Munday

ISBN: 978-1-3999-4171-6

Other works by Andrew M. Hajducki available on ANOETICA:

DOG KENNEL HILL (Crime Fiction)

MINOR SAINTS AND FERTILE SOILS (Poetry)

A JOURNEY IN WALES AND THE WELSH MARSHES (Travelogue)

THE
LIVERPOOL
PACKET

ANDREW M. HAJDUCKI

ANOETICA

FOREWORD

I can still remember sitting on the upper deck of an open top bus on a blustery day in April, huddling from the wind as the sights of Liverpool drifted by. If our driver had a script he was supposed to follow, he'd long since abandoned it in favour of his own, refreshingly honest commentary, peppered with finest Scouse humour. As we passed the Tate, he piped up with, 'Now here we have one of the best collections of modern art in the country – if you like that sort of thing, which I don't cause it's a bunch of bloody rubbish!'

It was the Easter break and I was fifteen. I'd only ever passed through Liverpool before to catch a ferry to the Isle of Man one summer, a holiday no doubt chosen by my dad on account of the antiquated modes of transport still in everyday use there. Where else, after all, can you still see commuters and schoolkids boarding a Victorian tram in the morning, or housewives returning home by steam train with their shopping bags?

This time I was accompanying him to the city itself to research locations for a crime novel he was writing. We stayed in The Blundellsands Hotel, a fine building which, although it still stands, has now been converted into flats. It is located in the Northern suburb of Crosby, where the protagonist, Christopher Kingstone, now a QC living in London, grew up and where he now returns to search for clues that might lead to his cousin's killer, all the while untangling the mysteries of his own past and trying to suppress his yearning for long-lost teenage crush Ros.

Over the course of a week we did a few of the usual touristy things such as a trip on the Magical Mystery Bus, but for the most part we walked around residential and industrial areas, wandering up side streets and back alleys, chatting to anyone that looked friendly enough and getting a feel for the place. We caught a ferry to Birkenhead and on return (after, as I recall, a meal of chips liberally sprinkled with salt and vinegar and possibly served with a pickled onion), I remember him musing that Liverpool is best seen from the river.

I don't know why my father ever chose the 'Pool as the setting for his debut novel, although it's clear that it must have left an indelible impression on him. A casual reader would be forgiven for assuming that the author was a Scouser himself, as some of the more poetic passages read like a love letter to the city, but perhaps it's easier for an outsider to feel the essence of a place.

That poetic eye for the world – he wrote many of his own poems which were compiled into an anthology entitled *Minor Saints and Fertile Soils* – comes across in the colourful way in which he paints the finer details of Christopher's thoughts and observations.

Those who knew him may notice other similarities between the author and his central character - both are QCs of similar age, divorced (when the book was written) and with the same taste in music. Both have a romantic, idealistic and innocent side, balanced by a sharp, cynical and rather catty sense of humour. But as he was at pains to point out, it is a work of fiction and the writer and his creation are not one and the same. That said I do recall a number of times where a certain Christopher Kingstone ordered pizzas to our address or made restaurant bookings, though this was less a case of blurred identities than a ploy to avoid the rigmarole of having to spell out our unpronounceable Polish surname over the phone.

Born in South London in 1952, Andrew Michael Hajducki dreamed of becoming a writer, but when the time came to choose a career, the law seemed a more reliable profession. After completing his undergraduate studies at Downing College, Cambridge, he trained as an English barrister at Gray's Inn in London before moving to Edinburgh, where my siblings and I were raised, and forging a career as a Scottish advocate and later QC. At one point he flirted with the idea of politics, standing as a Liberal candidate for Edinburgh South where he came a close second place, ahead of the Tories. He was also an avid adventurer and hillwalker who spent much of his life exploring the far flung corners of the country, usually with a collie dog in tow.

The ambition to write never faded however, and by the time he began work on *The Liverpool Packet* he'd already published three volumes of railway history and two legal textbooks. But it was literature that held a special appeal and he poured a great deal of time and love into his fiction debut which took a good couple of years to research and write. Yet when it was completed he didn't attempt to pursue a publisher, despite protestations from friends and family that it was more than worthy of a proper release – as one friend is quoted as saying, 'It's a hell of a lot better than many books I've paid good money for!' However, in a strange case of life imitating art, a chance meeting with his own long lost teenage crush culminated in his second marriage to artist Kate, with whom he remained for the rest of his life.

Whether he was shy of public scrutiny or simply lacked the time and energy to attempt to forge a name for himself in a new and highly competitive field when his existing occupation was demanding enough, I am not certain. Nonetheless he didn't give up there and went about plotting a follow-up by the name of *Greenwinter*, although this ultimately never came to pass.

The following decade saw him pen five more railway titles and several new editions of his legal works, but it was only as retirement was drawing imminent and more free time was once again bestowed upon him, that Andrew set his sights back onto fiction. He booked himself into a writer's retreat in Yorkshire and returned to his childhood stomping ground of South London to begin researching his next novel, a crime thriller set in the 1950s amongst a backdrop of protests against capital punishment, which was intended to kickstart a hard-earned retirement spent hiking and writing.

Alas fate had other plans in mind, and the last years of his life were spent in a long drawn out battle with illness. Nevertheless he kept his momentum going until the very end, completing his second and final novel, *Dog Kennel Hill*, named after the area in Camberwell, just months before his death in 2021.

His output may have been modest but Andrew's works of fiction are wonderfully composed, fast paced and entertaining yet thoughtful and introspective, and give a tantalising glimpse at his creative style.

It is with great excitement that we welcome this long overdue and posthumously published first edition of *The Liverpool Packet*, beautifully brought to life by artist Roy Mundie's evocative painting of the Mersey at sunrise, a perfect match to the mood of the novel. Re-reading it again now, I am delighted to say it has lost nothing of its impact in the intervening decades, although much else may have changed. It is a pleasure to finally see it deservedly in print, a mere twenty-two years after he wrote it and two years after he died – a new record for lateness even by Andrew's standards – timekeeping never was his greatest strength.

David A. Hajducki, Edinburgh, 2023

'I never said it was possible, I only said it was true.'
– Charles Richet

I

As the last lees of day were filtering through the still warm city, Ros and I turned the corner into Riego Street and stopped outside the first house on the left.

'Are you sure...?'

'Sure of what – that we're actually invited to the party or that we've just made it all up?'

'I don't know, but I just thought...'

'Oh, don't be so bloody wet, Chris! Do you really think that if your cousin hadn't wanted us to come...?'

I shrugged and remained silent as Ros pressed the bell and gently mouthed the word 'prat' in my direction.

But nothing happened and the plaintive tones of Sandy Denny singing 'Who Knows Where The Time Goes?' continued to float along the front of the shabby Georgian terrace and a well-fed tabby cat with a scarlet collar and a look of utter contempt appeared from up the basement stairs and with an effortless movement of its tail sent an empty milk bottle clattering down to the deserted depths below.

Somewhere in the distance a car horn sounded and a dog barked as if conditioned to reply but still there was no response from anyone in No. 16 and the scuffed door remained resolutely shut. I tried for a moment to forget that I had been the one who had skulked behind Ros all the way along Hope Street, complaining bitterly that, 'I don't see why we have to go to April's sodding party in the first place and anyway her kind of thing is not really my scene', before Ros looked at me in complete despair.

'Well what is your scene then, Chris – I mean, have you actually got a scene at all?'

I felt justifiably miffed – now was surely the time to prove that Ros was wrong and to assert that I did have a scene, even though I couldn't for the life of me say what it was. And because of this slight, I decided to take a more positive role so I hit the bell push as hard as I could, using a lot more anger than I had expected.

We were both taken aback by the sound of an urgent electric clamour from within and wondered what to do next. There was now enough sound to waken the dead, though in the graveyard at the end of the street the deceased remained in their ordered places and nothing seemed to stir. The tabby cat looked up, stopped rubbing its head on the basement gate and took off startled as the door was noisily flung open to reveal a small blonde in a purple t-shirt that proclaimed her avowed intent to 'Save the Indigenous Peoples of the World'.

A few seconds passed and the blonde raised an eyebrow while the bell continued to ring. Then, standing up to her full height of five foot two and a half, she eyed the pair of us dolefully.

'Bloody Hell Fire!' was her succinct comment. I decided instantly that I could have cut her Darwen accent in half with a butter knife and, particularly liking the way that she made 'Fye-arr' into two long-drawn out syllables, I catalogued the phrase for possible future use. She said nothing more, while I considered asking her which of the particular indigenous peoples of the world she was proposing to save and from what fate that might possibly be awaiting them. But I saw from both her demeanour and the expression on my girlfriend's face that this would be chancing my luck so I merely stood my ground while twitching nervously.

It was Ros, as unfazed as ever, who merely gave a warm smile to the diminutive eco-warrior and greeted her with a friendly, 'Hello there.'

The blonde softened slightly and, obviously considering that Ros was not a complete tosser like me, changed her look from hostile to one of decided indifference and signalled with a casual flick of her hair that we were to follow her into the house. Having got as far as the hallway, she then stopped abruptly and ran a critical glance over the pair of us, taking in all of our essential details. Apparently satisfied with this non-verbal interrogation, she flounced off and above the noise of the still ringing bell I heard an unknown male voice asking, 'Who the hell were they pair you just let in?'

The blonde shrugged and replied in cool tones, 'Oh, no one important. Just a couple of dumb looking kids!'

Before I could protest at us being so summarily dismissed, the door of the front room, apparently a forbidden pleasure zone so far as a couple of dumb looking kids like us were concerned, opened and the blonde disappeared inside and we were again left on our own. As my eyes became accustomed to the feeble light on the stairs I managed to trace the bell wire back to its cracked Bakelite socket that almost seemed to predate the invention of domestic electricity and pulled on the exposed wire with a violent tug, there being no other obvious way of silencing the bell. As I did so there was a loud snap and a desultory flash and the wire came away from the wall with a shower of plaster dust while the offending socket broke in two. The discordant jangling ceased and I turned to Ros who gave me a shrug and a vaguely sardonic look to suggest 'whatever'.

I duly returned the arm that she was holding. Then, feeling that it was the right time to say something, anything at all to break the tension, I said, 'You're looking good tonight, Ros, very good, if I might be bold enough to say so.'

She smiled at this somewhat feeble compliment and replied, 'You might well be bold enough to say that, kind sir', and then paused and added, 'Even if you are behaving like a complete ridiculous fool at the moment.'

Ridiculous fool or not, I thought she may have blushed slightly at my clumsy compliment, but to be honest in that primeval thirty-watt dim, I couldn't really be sure of anything that I saw. But yes, she was looking good tonight, good in a pretty ethnic way, 'ethnic' being a word that I had only just discovered but was anxious to use as much as possible even if I didn't really understand what it meant. But I decided that at the moment it was a most fitting word for her, what with her long hair flowing over the cream coloured milkmaid smock which she had only bought this very afternoon from one of the traders in the market, a would-be hipster known to all as 'Dekko the Deal'. I thought that this dubious merchant prince seemed to believe more in the exploitation of the peoples of his home town rather than in saving them but my musing was interrupted by a call from above the hall.

'Oh, hi there, you two!'

The chatelaine of the house, April's best friend Gillian Ainsdale, came floating into view. Tall, with a commanding presence, Gill was, in her own view at least, the self-styled leader of the local radical bourgeoisie and counter culture – in matter of fact she was undoubtedly bourgeois but radical she was not and the only counters of culture she knew were those of the better (or at least the more expensive) fashion stores in the city. I found people like Gill completely ludicrous especially as she claimed to have a burning social conscience which, so far as I could see, only extended to a refusal to buy (then unacceptable) Cape apples and other politically tainted fruits, and of boycotting the services of the High Street banks that she probably didn't use anyway.

A chic anarchist for the sake of it, I couldn't stand Gill, if the truth be known. I was a first-time Labour voter still imbued with my father's post-war socialism and felt that Gill's decidedly fake feminist stance made her even more half-baked than people thought she was already. God, what a political pain in the bum I must have seemed back then but the fact that Gill was both rich to boot and fashionably dressed had only fuelled my feelings of personal inadequacy – particularly when I had just committed such a blatant act of vandalism in her home.

'Oh, never mind that stupid bell. I'm sure it needed mending anyway.'

I doubted if it had before my attack but it certainly did now. An uneven strip of wallpaper with the wire attached dangled loose hung beside the bin-tacked posters of those three contemporary icons of our city, Comrades Che, Lenin and Lennon. In the exalted company of those undoubted true lefties, I felt suitably humbled and for a moment felt prepared to overlook the many faults of Gillian Ainsdale, even though I still thought that she was nothing but a mouldy old hypocrite – unlike, of course, somebody such as myself.

Ros, sensing perhaps that the cause of my immediate discomfort was probably due to the severed wire rather than Gill's absurd posturing, laughed and even managed to do so in that annoying, trilling manner that she specially reserved for pissing me off – which it invariably did. Gill, seeing my awkwardness and misreading its cause, smiled in a tolerant and even more annoying way than Ros as if about to infer, 'Men, what are they like?' before she conducted us down the uncarpeted stone stairs to the kitchen.

Here things were definitely in full party swing with paper lanterns in a vaguely faux-Chinese and tangled riff-raff way with tinsel strung along the waxed pine shelves which bent under the weight of jars full of wild rice, healthy pulses and other macrobiotic delights of the now so distant 1970s. On the wall was a blackboard on which had been chalked in mauve scrawl, 'Milk 2 pints', 'Remember the leccy bill', 'Free the Liverpool Two', and an even more irrelevant, 'Don't forget that Shezzie loves you an' all', but being uninterested in their shopping list, electricity bill, the notorious Two or whoever Shezzie might be, I moved on.

In the centre of the room was a table covered with a patterned green oilcloth, a lacklustre display of cheap European wines in gaudy litre-and-a-half bottles, several outsize opened tins of rapidly turning flat pale ale and, on a large plate, illuminated by a pair of tatty flickering candles stuck in old beer bottles, an array of French sticks (the term baguette not having penetrated even our most cosmopolitan of cities at that time). I eyed disdainfully the unappetising army of wilted grapefruits bristling hedgehog-like with cubes of tinned pineapple and multicoloured cheddar and beside them an untouched bowl of wrinkled olives that had passed away from old age long before leaving their native shores – shores which, knowing Gill, would certainly not have been those of the then-hated Greek colonels.

I sighed and at last felt relaxed and prepared to look more tolerantly on the company. I was now definitely of the view that the level of sophistication in the house was about the same as that of my schoolfriend who sometimes gate-crashed parties in far off Crosby. I realised that I was no longer worried about having to mix with and be dazzled by Gill and April's oh-so brilliant university friends who, being a year or two older and more wordly than us ,would have shunned both Ros and myself. I fondly leant over towards her and, giving her a peck on the cheek, told her with as much confidence as I could muster, that I was going off to find her something more interesting to drink. Dismissing the Castello-del-something-or-other muck that I had abstracted from my father's wine cellar – a humble cupboard under our stairs where the hoover was kept – I tried to dispel any notion that I was a penniless juvenile skinflint with no taste in fine wine by taking hold of what I imagined to be an infinitely more sophisticated carafe of a then-popular Californian red. Pleased with my choice of fine wine in someone else's donated Co-op carrier bag, I was about to pour a tasting glass when I was stopped in my tracks.

'Chris, lovely to see you here! And how's life treating you these days?'

The greeting was from none other than my cousin April in a long skirt, flamboyant blouse and faintly ridiculous display of beads and bangles of all sizes and colours under the sun. I turned round, but before I could answer her question, a bearded desperado in a spotted bandana and virulent brothel creepers abruptly called her away. As she left, she waived her arm and blew me an extravagant kiss before departing with a 'Catch you later', a well played Pink Floyd album and a tray of home-baked hash brownies which, knowing April, would definitely have had the emphasis on the hash element.

'Up to her usual tricks, I see.'

I had now been joined by her younger brother, my cousin Ben who asked how I had done in my recent A-levels. I wanted to tell him jocularly that they had been, 'a piece of cake and not of the hash variety that your sister likes', but, not believing myself either with regard to the examinations or the hash brownies, I instead settled on, 'Well you know what they're like of course', and then added to this sanguine and world-weary remark, 'But I really do wish I hadn't left everything to the very last minute.'

Ben merely chuckled. 'You're a man after my own heart – unlike some girlie swats that I could name'. Whether or not this was a direct and malicious reference to April or even to Ros I never found out because then he suddenly announced in a loud whisper, 'Oh, my God! He's absolutely gorgeous!' and trounced across the room towards a startled youth sailing by in a rather fetching tangerine coloured shirt.

'Ah, dear boy and what brings one such as you to this jolly occasion?' Knowing Ben's modus operandi of old, I went off to find Ros again.

This time, however, I was disappointed for she was deep in conversation with a man whose impeccable clothing and air of seamless self-assurance meant that he probably had some unlikely posh name that was enough to send a scruffy boy like me in to a paroxysm of envy and spite. I almost entertained the thought that I would have to be more charitable in future but then remembered reading somewhere the theory that when meeting a person for the first time it takes on average less than four seconds for us to sum them up and decide whether they were friend or foe, I made up my mind there and then. In this case the dislike didn't take as long as four seconds, it was instantaneous and mutual.

As 'Mr Perfect-trousers', as I so kindly dubbed him, took the drinks out of my hands, he grunted something insincere and continued to monopolise Ros, oblivious of the fact that I, and not he, was the one that she was supposed to be with. I hovered around feeling (to use one of Ben's favourite phrases) about as welcome as a pork sausage at a bar-mitzvah, while the smooth one expounded upon the theme of Emily Bronte, Free Spirit and the Zeitgeist of something-or-other. I felt despair – how could she possibly put up with such arrant claptrap, Ros of all people? Then, just as I was planning to chime in with some crass remark about Wuthering Heights (a novel I had not then read but had certainly intended to read when I had the time), I decided to challenge his asinine comment about the bleak moors above Haworth moulding the sisters taste to a fine austerity of vision (whatever that waffle might really mean) so I came out with what I imagined was an apposite quote.

'The sky is darkening around me, the wild winds coldly blow...'

'Wrong Bronte, I believe old chap.'

'No, it bloody well isn't', and then, almost imperceptibly, 'old chap yourself'. But since I wasn't really sure if he might have been correct in this cruel rebuff, I remembered one of my teachers who liked to say when he was marking school tests, 'Ingenious, but no marks.' I could have used this to shut my tormentor up but I wisely decided to say nothing further. But then, anxious again to seem as though I was an intellectual after all and not wishing the creep to have the last word, I made what I imagined to be a meaningful but derisive snort in his ear. My rival merely turned his head away so as to entirely block my view.

Outraged both by this deliberate negation of my skill in serious literary criticism, and more obviously the fact that Ros apparently preferred his company rather than mine, I spent a minute or two addressing the back of his carefully constructed hairstyle with a satisfying silent mantra of, 'Bullshit, complete bullshit' until, beginning to feel self-conscious, I decided to drift away in search of more congenial company, preferably of the female variety.

I had narrowed the field of possibilities down to two. The first was a sultry brunette in a dark red dress, who was so stunning that I rightly felt that she would be unlikely to deign to even speak to a mere mortal like me. The second however was the girl standing behind her. I approached number two, a plump but jolly-looking girl with frizzy, mousey hair and a pleasant blouse a good size too big even for her and, throwing caution to the wind, I told her that my name was Simeon, that I was a second-year mathematician at the Uni and that my farming family came from a village near Bath. Twiddling her oversized CND pendant and running her hand through her curious hair, she told me that she was a theology student from Cannock way, that she respected all animals and children and that she had always been fascinated by quadratic equations and, 'things of that nature'.

I hesitated for a moment, wondering what the genus of things like quadratic equations might encompass, then

I launched into a lecture on some recent developments in quantum theory, omitting to tell her that the sum total of my knowledge had been culled from a newspaper article which I had half-read on the toilet at home and had fairly obviously failed to understand a word of. I soon found myself too far out and not waving but drowning. I hoped that the girl would not ask me anything about modern farming methods, those damned quadratic equations, villages near Bath or, for that matter, anything else that I was supposed to have knowledge of but clearly knew bugger all about.

Ros, detaching herself from the charms of her deft yet most irritating companion, wandered over to join us. After whispering to me that, 'You're right you know Chris, it was Emily Bronte who wrote that poem', she politely asked my new companion as to the identity of her new friend and was met with a gleeful reply. 'Oh, he's Simeon of course, but you're just having me on because I know who you are anyway – you're Fiona, his half-sister – the one who likes hang-gliding, Anglo-Saxon literature and judo. He's told me all about you.'

'Has he now?' asked Fiona alias Ros and then, giving the frizzy-haired one that horribly irritating all-girls-together wink-wink routine, dragged me away with the comment, 'Martial arts, medieval waffle and hang-gliding, whatever next? You see, he can't really help it – he's a serial liar though, to be frank, madness runs in our family and Simeon here talks complete crap most of the time, particularly when he's got a drink or two inside him – as he clearly has today.'

Understandably confused, the girl from Cannock, probably doubting whether I had been sincere in anything at all, drifted away. Ros then gave me one of her 'enigmatic' looks.

'Only your half-sister, eh? Do I look like I'm one half of anyone's sister?'

I shrugged and said, 'Well, you know how it is...'

'No, Chris, I don't know how it is. You'll have to tell me some time.' Then she smiled wearily and shook her head. 'Why on earth do you always tell fibs to people, Chris? I mean you're not alone in that but why don't men, or should it be boys, ever grow out of the trait of telling porkies at parties?'

I took the last question to be a rhetorical one. I was about to protest that drink and talking complete crap were, in my case, only in part unrelated but, deciding not to stand up for myself or my sadly misunderstood sex, I said no more. Ros shook her head and abruptly turned round to made her way back to the bouffant-haired creep who I noted with pleasure appeared to be displaying rampant dandruff and, even better, the beginnings of male pattern baldness.

As he continued on his boring discourse on the Brontes that I had so impolitely dismissed, I decided that I could stand it no more so I set off again, this time with a bottle of sub-Rioca 'Yates Wine Lodge Bargain of the Week, Perfect with almost anything.'

Reaching the hall I noticed that the door of the front room was still barred to dumb-looking kids such as us so I began to make my way up the stairway to heaven to where a recorded voice was soulfully singing that she was awaiting the angels of Avalon and possibly an Eastern glow as well.

I pushed open a door and found myself in the living room which, apart from the red and green glow from the

12

monstrous hi-fi in the corner, was in darkness. I sat down on one of the extravagant floor cushions, poured a drink and grabbed a handful of crisps to see if the wine really did live up to its boast of being perfect with almost everything. I grimaced and came to the regretful conclusion that it did not.

Then, through the enforced gloom of the room, I became conscious of a huddled figure who was aimlessly rocking himself to-and-fro with the music. Dressed in clothes that appeared to be made out of some shiny and hideous silvery material, he was an odd-ball even for this particular house and I noticed that he was also wearing the sort of large cowboy hat that you saw only at country music evenings at pubs on the outskirts of Bolton.

'Mr Clint Eastwood, I presume?'

At this he jumped up, causing one of the giant speakers to sway violently, and began to mutter something about me being a real smart arse and that he would not dream of letting a complete half-wit like me have any of his ace Jamaican Gold.

'Steady on, Lone Ranger, I wasn't asking for any...'

'I don't care what you were doing. Just get lost, can't you? – I met enough of your lot in the hospital so all I can say is why don't you just go on and stick your...?'

Turning down his hostile invitation to attempt something both physically distasteful and biologically impossible, I sloped off back down the veritable stairway to heaven and went to the kitchen for something more palatable to drink. By the time I returned to the living room with some inexpensive but pleasant Pinot noir Burgundy, the place was now full of people who had drifted in. The now seemingly revived Ranger was having a conversation with the heavy curtains about the fact that his motorbike was needing some sort of expensive repairs and this was all due to the fault of some other person for reasons which I could not even attempt to follow even if I had been stone-cold sober. I turned away from him and the music, which had now been turned up. As 'Can't Get No Satisfaction' was grinding to an end, I heard a familiar voice.

'Hi, Chris - or is it still Simeon?' I ignored this remark and waited for Ros to come over to me .

'Fancy a bop then, Fiona my dearest half sister?'

'Honestly, Chris, where do you get your chat-up lines from? "Fancy a Bop" indeed.' Then she kicked off her clogs and as we began to dance energetically, or bop if you prefer, to Virginia Plain, I caught sight of the small blonde from Darwin who laughed and began to mime a ringing bell which she then promptly pretended to break in half. Temporarily distracted, I trod on the feet of my girlfriend even more than usual, and waited for her to sigh, 'Really, Chris, you've got about as much sense of rhythm as, well I don't know what...'

I ignored this and asked, 'Why were you talking to that smarmy fancy-panted creep all the time?'

'Ha! Jealous are you now? You're a good one to talk, telling Little Miss Dumpling over there that I was even half related to you.'

As we entered into a grudgingly engaged truce, Ben, separated for a moment from tangerine-shirt, bounced up and asked if he could display his ballroom talents with my charming lady friend. Not altogether unwillingly, I relinquished her battered toes to him and went off to find more drink. Just then I stumbled upon a bored looking Gill and took the opportunity of asking if she had seen April recently. Usually my voluble female cousin was the life and soul of such occasions who I thought had the ability to make even the most recalcitrant guest enjoy the proceedings. But where was she now? Gill had no idea and seemed disinterested so I went back to sound out Ben but he was of no help either, suggesting sourly that his sister was, 'probably getting stoned and dropping acid in some dark place with her boyfriend Barry Leemings, although why she even associates with that complete treg beats me.'

Having no answer to the treg question, I decided that I would have to go off and look for April myself, even if only to prove the malevolent Ben wrong in relation to the matter of her use of various controlled substances. I climbed the stairs slowly, 'Dark Side of the Moon' emanating from a closed bedroom door as I passed the landing and continued on up to the top storey when I caught sight of April through the open door of her room. She was sitting on the end of her bed with her head in her hands and crying in quiet desperation. The scent from a half-smoked roach drifted lazily upwards to the open skylight and, as Jimi Hendrix crooned softly in the background, I sat down beside her and put my arm on her shoulder.

'April, what's wrong? Are you all right?'

She made no reply but began to wipe her eyes with a grubby paper napkin.

'And why are you grieving over Goldengrove unleaving?'

She lifted her face and through a mask of tear-streaked mascara gave me an unconvincing smile.

'That's very poetic of you, Chris.'

I thought that reference would go down well.

'I just thought that you were...'

'Don't bother yourself to think about me, little cousin. I'm fine, just fine and anyway it's really nothing for you to be worried about. Just a surfeit of joss-sticks and bad beer, I'm sure.'

I thought she looked tired and clearly defeated and then I noticed the bruises starting to form on her bare arm and I knew that there was something for me to be worried about and that joss-sticks and bad beer didn't enter into it. There was a gap of some seconds and then she said sorrowfully, 'He really didn't mean to do it, you know.'

'Didn't really mean to what?'

''Cause the bruises, I mean.'

There was no need to enquire as to who 'he' was for Barry Leemings, dressed in a bad-taste checked jacket and looking disconcertingly like his brother, the Lone Ranger, had come in to the room and was staring at us both. I took my arm off her shoulder and April continued, 'It was just an accident and...'

Her voice trailed off as Barry turned a withering look on me. 'Yeah, that's right. You heard her. It was an accident. No big deal and anyway it's no business of yours.'

He was looking straight at me and I felt intimidated and unsure of what to do or say next.

'It is my business because she's my cousin, after all.'

'I know perfectly well who you are, Christopher.' The fact that I was her cousin apparently cut no ice with him and he just looked unconcerned so I added, 'April, do you want me to stay or...?'

She shook her head and added another smile that made me feel as though I was standing beside the freezer cabinets in a supermarket aisle. I took the hint and, closing the door quietly behind me, began to walk down the stairs before stopping and trying to make sense of what I had just seen.

The trouble, as I saw it, was that I liked April for all her faults. I always had and I suppose that I looked up to her and admired her cool, her style, and the fact that she was so clever despite constantly smoking dope like it was going out of fashion and displaying a masterly skill at messing up her own life, and other people's as well. And yet she had always been good to me when I was younger and had excelled in getting me out of scrapes with carefully thought-out excuses and lies to exculpate me in the eyes of my mother and my less-forgiving aunt Maura. Now that April was in some kind of scrape herself I couldn't just leave her there, so with a misplaced sense of duty and very little enthusiasm, I began to retrace my steps to her room when I heard raised voices through the closed door.

'No, I won't! Just bloody well leave me alone, will you? I can't stand it!'

'Don't you use that little lost girl tone with me! I know where you're getting it from.'

'Where I get it from and what I do with it is nothing to do with you, can't you see?'

Then their voices were lowered and I put my ear to the door just in time to hear Barry say in an uncharacteristically wheedling manner something about, 'Well, if not for my sake, then...' I missed the next bit but then he began to shout.

'Look April, I won't let you take that damned stuff any more!'

'You won't let me – you! Who the bloody hell do you think that you are anyway?'

17

'Someone better than a spoilt little bitch like you, April Kingston.'

'I may be a spoilt little bitch but you're a bloody two-faced cheap bastard! You're not fit to tell anyone anything.'

There was a pause and then I heard April shout, 'No, Barry please stop doing that! Don't do it, I tell you.' As I stepped back from the door there was the sound of a hollow bang and I heard glass shattering.

'Slag, I'll kill you for that.'

April screamed. I leapt forward, grabbing the battered door knob with such force that the remaining screw holding it in place fell out. I swore, hesitated for a second and then launched myself at the door. As my shoulder made contact with the splintering wood, the latch gave way and I was catapulted onto the threadbare carpet.

I looked up and it was like a freeze-frame from one of those B-pictures that I always enjoyed at the cinema when I was young. April was cowering by the window and Barry was advancing on her, brandishing a curved piece of broken mirror shaped like a gleaming scimitar. On the floor, and where it had apparently landed after being thrown, lay the remains of a bottle of nail varnish whose contents were now slowly seeping in an angry fuchsia lake across an old dhurrie rug that had seen better days. With about as much dignity as I could muster, I came to my feet.

'Leave her alone!'

He slowly swung round. 'Or what? Just because you went to an expensive school just like her doesn't mean that you can lord it over me, posh boy.'

'Just leave her alone, can't you.'

'Go and get lost Sonny Jim, it's got sod all to do with you anyway so just keep your nose out of it.'

'No I won't. If anyone's going to be killed it's not her, it's you, complete cretin that you are!'

He had several inches and more than several pounds on me and I was terrified by my own unsustainable boldness. In a single dextrous movement I kicked the piece of broken mirror out of his hand and attempted, indeed succeeded, in landing my fist in the middle of his face. I felt a pain in my wrist as he staggered backwards, lost his footing on the dhurrie, and fell heavily over the edge of the bed frame. And it was then that I lost the advantage for he slowly got to his feet, obviously winded if not wounded. There being nothing else I could do, I hit him again. There was a lull before the storm broke and in the silence I could hear quite clearly the lyrics of the song being played in the room below, 'All that you love, all that you hate.'

Then Barry dragged me to the floor and began to punch and kick me systematically while I tried to protect myself by curling up in a foetal position. I lay there and hoped that the cavalry would come to my rescue before I was well and truly done for. I had almost given up when, out of the corner of my eye, I saw that the noise had attracted an audience.

As Barry was about to pin me down again and deliver the final blow, he noticed that we had company.

'Bloody hell fire! The shit's really hit the fan big time now. Trust the kid to spoil things by getting into a fight.'

The small blonde continued to stare at us while Barry swore under his breath. Then, sensing that he could put me in the wrong without even really trying, he laughed. 'It's all over folks! Don't worry there's nothing to get all worked up about. Young Christopher and I were just having a bit of a lark about but now he's blown it by going a bit too far.'

'You bloody liar! I had to 'cause you were about to...'

I stopped, conscious of all the searching faces and seeing the blood tricking from the wound on my hand, my courage failed completely.

'It don't look like much of a lark to me, you couple o' daft buggers.' the blonde said and then added, 'It looked as though you were having a right scrap over a girl rather than just mucking about.'

Someone sniggered and the situation began to defuse itself for everyone except me. She considered matters carefully. 'Tell you one thing, though. It makes a right good party, does a punch-up.'

There was a ripple of agreement as I shamefacedly squeezed past the increasing number of onlookers. No one seemed to be looking at me, but all glances were directed at the still crying April. I felt that it was definitely time for me to leave and bounding down the stairs two at a time, I stumbled and collided with the Lone Ranger, causing him to let go of his spliff and his remaining five leaves left. He glared at me but I kept on in my flight, ignoring his fond farewell of, 'Have a nice day, asshole.' I hobbled to the front door where, to the sounds of 'Bye, Bye, Miss American Pie', I began to scrabble with undoing the lock when I realised that someone was calling out my name. But I was in no mood to stop now. I just wanted the leave the house and kept on running as best I could, battling against the pain from my leg, my utter humiliation and my burst pride.

I confined to limp up the road until I reached the corner of Riego Street and halted while the raindrops fell in a herringbone-pattern beneath the yellow sodium lamps. I felt nauseous, tired and, above all else, like an idiot. 'Trust the kid to spoil things', and, 'It's got sod all to do with you', kept reverberating though my head. Then I felt a tap on my sore shoulder and I winced.

'Chris, wait...'

It was Ros and my humiliation was complete. Was she too going to blame me for spoiling things and getting into a fight? I turned and noticed something red had oozed out of the wound on my injured hand and landed on the front of her new smock. I looked at her, distressed and dishevelled as we both were and once again I thought that she was still looking pretty good that evening.

'You know for a pacifist you can certainly land a mean right-hander. I think you cracked his cheek bone – I hope so, anyway. But you need to get seen to and have your hand bandaged without any further delay.' Then she began to cry and I put my arm round her and realised that, being Ros, she was bound to take my side without asking. I felt the rain on our upturned faces, I wanted to cry and explain what had happened to her, even though I had no real explanation to offer.

'I thought that he was going to kill April.'

'You probably did but...'

'But what?'

I knew that she was probably going to come out with something about it only having been a lover's tiff, just a silly argument that people in love have and I was going to say that it was no wonder then that women get abused when they're always making excuses for the Barry Leemings of this world. But she didn't, and I didn't, and she just kissed me.

'It doesn't matter now, Chris, it really doesn't. It's all over and we're out of the action.'

'Exit pursued by a bear, eh!' But this wasn't our A-level set text, *A Winter's Tale* and thankfully nobody was following us now.

'I think you were right, though.'

'Right about what?'

'About stopping him from threatening or hurting April any more.' At least Ros agreed with me about that.

'Come on, let's take you home Chris, before your mum and dad find out about the fight and go completely spare. Come on, I've still got a few bob left on me and can probably stretch to pay the fare home as long as we don't give a tip.'

'She is kind as she is fair.'

'Drop the Shakespeare drivel. Can't you ever stop going on a bit, Chris? Just, for once, be quiet.'

She murmured something else under her breath, and began carefully counting out the pound notes and the loose change.

I followed her advice, keen to just get home quickly and avoid any further misadventures. So, as the rain continued to gently fall, we managed to hail a passing taxi and, as we lurched away along the uneven roads of the still vibrant night city, I held her hand tightly and said nothing further. Perhaps I was just too young and had too little experience of life to understand how women could enter into doomed relationships that were dosed with threats of sporadic violence. It seemed as if, as I grew older, I was slowly discovering that everything was more complex than I had ever thought of in my wildest dreams.

I was ashamed both of April's vulnerability and of my own stupidity. As Ros cuddled up to me on the back seat of the taxi and shivered in her wet and completely ruined top, I ruefully thought that this was the end of a day that we would both probably want to forget. Not having the benefit of hindsight I didn't realise then that it was also the last time that I would ever see my cousin April alive.

2

It was now more than forty years after that party in Riego Street, and I was back at work in London. It was a Thursday morning towards the end of the Hilary term, the courts were in session and our chambers were almost deserted. A shaft of sunlight carelessly spread itself across the large desk at which I was sitting with a cup of fresh coffee in one hand and a sheaf of papers in the other. Surrounded by well-thumbed books, pink legal tape and an overwhelming air of respectability, I was staring vacantly at the print of a once-notorious double murderer hanging as crookedly on the wall as he had probably been hanged on the scaffold more than a century or so before. It was a quiet morning and with a start I realised that I was lost in pleasing but shallow dreams about Jessica Goodchild, a solicitor with whom I was due to have a conference in a couple of hours.

I watched as a scrawny metropolitan pigeon picked at some discarded biscuit crumbs on the windowsill then I rose from my chair and went over to view the languid world outside. Little was happening on the bright morning in legal Holborn and I smiled appreciatively at the neat square of houses outside that were stuck in a time warp only partially dispelled by flashy parked cars of overpaid counsel and undeserving solicitors. As I observed, the presence of a swarthy man appeared from the building opposite carrying a clapped-out computer monitor and dropped it with a crash into an empty skip.

There was a brief silence before the calm was broken by a hesitant knock on the door which heralded the appearance of Gary, twenty-four going on fifty-four. I scowled at him for time was no longer on my side.

'Excuse me, Mr. K, I'm sorry to trouble you when you're so busy, but...'

I studied his face but could see no trace of irony. I waited to hear the reason he was going to further interrupt my thoughts but he just stood there intently.

'What is it then, Gary?' Given my assistant clerk's feigned humility I felt anxious to actually get him to the point.

'Well, umm, there's a registered packet here for you, sir, and I've signed for it and I thought...' He looked lost for something to add as I clearly was still looking annoyed by having been disturbed. 'I thought that you should have it right away. It seems to be something urgent by its nature and, possibly of a private nature so to speak, so I took the liberty of not opening it myself, of course, but...'

He trailed off, waiting for some sort of feedback from me. I reflected on how this negative liberty of him not reading the contents of the packet had probably been forced on him by John, our grizzled head clerk. Gary's natural curiosity extended to examining all of our correspondence, whether personal or otherwise, and supplementing this by going through the waste bins in search of clues as to the minor mysteries and peccadilloes of our lives.

Gary then grudgingly handed over a large padded envelope which he clearly suspected of containing something of a reprehensible nature that he could later have used in evidence against me. Seeing that I was not going to give him the satisfaction of being present when the mysterious packet was opened and thus being deprived of a share in its forbidden secrets, he sidled out with a laboured sigh of disapproval.

I watched him leave and pondered upon the curious mixture of subservience and cheek which had both amused and irritated me since he had become our underclerk several months before. As the door closed, I glanced down at the packet with its neat printed label addressed to 'Christopher Kingston, Esq., Q.C., Bell's Inn Chambers, EC4' followed by a full post code and, underneath, the handwritten words 'Personal and Confidential' underlined in red. It was probably just junk mail such as an invitation to buy some over-priced product, subscribe to a learned journal or to give money to some worthy but boring charity. It was unlikely to be work because most of that came electronically but because of the way it was so enigmatically labelled I did not put it straight into the wastepaper bin. Anyway I was busy, or supposed to be busy at any rate and whatever it was would have to wait. Happily ignorant of the effect which the contents of the packet would have on my life, I dropped it, unopened, into my briefcase.

Then I picked up another of the large box files boldly marked in a firm hand 'Glenbreen Trading Co v Baltic-Estonia Steam Navigation Ltd.' and wondered if the firm hand that wrote this might have been the delightful Jessica Goodchild's. Not for the first time that day I thought that sometimes my job could be so boring that I could scream. 'Imagine a watch calibrated in guineas', my pupil master would have said in those circumstances when he was talking about some really tedious day in court but even the thought of seeing

Jessica soon or the unpaid fees mounting up in the case did little to alleviate the feelings of complete alienation from work and the law in general. I drank more coffee, the universal panacea for lawyers under stress, and feeling sufficiently high from all the caffeine that was working its way round my system, opened the file.

For a few minutes or so I gazed into space, trying to convince myself that I was actually concentrating properly and even getting somewhere in the task of trying to understand the strange fate of the cargo of the Heracleides IV. Then I wrote down some notes in the impressive hard-bound notebook that I kept for awkward clients and difficult conferences and felt that however sketchy those notes might be, I would at least have something before me should my bluff be called.

But the more I read of the papers, the more I became convinced that I would never understand what the damn case was really about. The cargo was undoubtedly a complete write-off as a result of a severe soaking in the Channel. But its value, which changed with each barely credible affidavit now littering my desk, was a matter apparently known only to God and to Patrick Aloysius Tierney, the sole director and guiding light of the Glenbreen Trading Company. One thing, however, was quite clear and that was that I had to have a convincing grasp of all of the issues involved since Mr Tierney was to be in attendance. If I was to become better acquainted with Ms. Goodchild, which I sincerely hoped that I would be, I reckoned a good showing to Tierney was at least one step along that path. 'Please the client and you please the solicitor', was an old maxim that, once learnt, was often forgotten.

As it happened, the case conference was a great success. Tierney turned out to be an intelligent and likeable character who poured forth, at considerable length and in sometimes mind-blowing detail, explanations for all of the various and apparently irreconcilable differences between the written pleadings and their all too fleeting shadows of reality. As I listened I began to have some sympathy for Michael Shalday, the junior who had drafted the claim, but that sympathy did not extend to wishing that he was present here today. Not wanting him to cramp my style with the gorgeous Jessica, I was uncharitably glad that he was stuck out in the wilderness at Snaresbrook Crown Court making, no doubt, a jurisprudential mountain out of a road traffic accident molehill. I smiled at the thought of all of the trouble that I had gone to in making sure that John had diverted the Snaresbrook brief to Michael on the pretext that, 'a little crime never hurt no-one, Mr. S. and it's good for your career development too, if I might say.'

Tierney, taking my smile to be an encouragement, began to bang on about the case, outlining the facts with great precision, the various previous dealings between the parties and an explanation as to how the whole matter had ended in tears for all except their legal advisors. And as I listened I was left wondering what conceivable reason other than tax avoidance Tierney might have had in sending goods in what, according to him, was a down-at-heel little coaster that was rather grandly named after a philosopher chum of Plato (in an explanation provided in parenthesis by our client during his ramblings). The owners of the ship had their offices in what Tierney dryly described as the 'unfashionable part of Sunderland' to which he added a quiet chuckle and added, 'And I trust we'll not have to visit them there', a sentiment that both counsel and solicitor both agreed upon. Time passed and, as we waded through proofs of evidence, emails, bills of lading, metrological reports and other irrelevancies, I felt as much at sea as the Heracleides IV must have been when she encountered adverse weather somewhere south-south-west of St. Catherine's Point.

With my impressively oversized but sadly leaking fountain pen, I made a note to discuss matters again with Michael Shalday so that the next time I was to meet with Tierney I could more-or-less pass off as my own his undoubtedly better understanding of both the facts of the case and the law which might be applied to them.

Our client was clearly enjoying himself and the best part of an hour was largely occupied by his frequent observations on our apparent strengths, or more realistically, the absence of strength in our opponent's position and the undoubtedly sound case for us. It was apparently a disappointment for him to announce, after consulting his watch with a great flourish, that, 'I think we've gone through everything that we need to at this stage so if you'll excuse me I have another urgent appointment elsewhere', and added, somewhat inconsequentially, 'Time waiteth for no man, not even myself, you see?' Then, after complimenting me on the management of the case so far, he added for the benefit of my instructing agent that, 'I have every faith in Mr Kingston and his handling of this whole sorry affair in which I find myself inextricably mixed up.'

I waited to see what Jessica's reaction would be but she merely smiled and commented that all the pleadings seemed to be in order, the documents lodged and that arrangements had been made for the pre-trial review hearing in two weeks' time in which she would be making an approach to the other side to sound them out in relation to any settlement proposals that the insurers might be willing to make.

'We're very obliged to you for your help, Mr Kingston', she said, ignoring the fact that I had barely had a chance to get any comments in while Tierney pontificated, then swept out behind the client. Following at a discreet distance, I heard Tierney say to John, who unlike himself was a man of few words, that I was, 'a most capable fellow, yes, most capable, and doesn't waste time with unnecessary chatter unlike some of his colleagues.' While I quietly agreed with that view I heard him trumpet to someone else, 'Well, hello there my friend and how is life treating you these days? Grand, I trust, grand.'

I looked out into the corridor to see who he had been addressing and was surprised to see that he had buttonholed a bemused Henry Atterson, our pompous head of chambers. He had been leaving his room to meet up with his usual stodgy pals for lunch at his usual venue and was in danger of having an interruption to that staid schedule. Henry, a well-known bore and the author of *Atterson on Commercial Rent Review Clauses* (a little bought but much quoted work which will be vastly improved in the second edition, hopefully bringing in something more tangible than the miserable royalties of the first), had been stopped in his tracks by this unexpected greeting from Tierney. Never socially adroit at the best of times, he was reduced to muttering something even more trite than usual while Tierney beamed and proceeded to vigorously pat him on the back. At this Henry was visibly outraged but before he could think of anything to say the Irishman had gone, leaving behind only his umbrella and the faint smell of the stubby unlit panatellas that he had been playing with during the conference.

Checking that the coast was clear and giving me a puzzled look, Henry then left in a furtive manner so as to avoid Tierney and, savouring the general air of bonhomie so often absent in our chambers, I went over to the clerk's room. My instructing solicitor was making some arrangements with John while Gary, eager to seem important or more plausibly eager to eavesdrop, lurked around in the background. With some difficulty, I managed to resist the entirely reasonable temptation to give him a stiff kicking then and there. Instead I calmed down and waited until Jessica was free.

John had reminded me that I had a conference booked with a Mr George Hennessey in Leeds at three-thirty, 'Copyright matter. There's no written brief but he wants advice on something that has been troubling him greatly so he is coming down to see you in person. He's a retired police inspector turned successful crime novelist you know though he's rather abrupt – I spoke to him on the phone and he's, well to put it mildly, plain speaking, as Yorkshire folk often are.'

I wondered how abrupt and plain speaking, or possibly more accurately just plain rude, this Mr Hennessey from Leeds actually was but I would have to forego the pleasure, until later in the day, of getting the measure of him. Conscious that time waiteth for no man as Tierney had been anxious to impress upon me, I signalled to Jessica to come out into the plush carpeted hall, and as nonchalantly as I could manage, timidly told her I was about to go for something to eat and asked if she might like to join me. I was sure that she would refuse and say that she did not normally have time for lunch but a few minutes later we were on our way to a small Italian restaurant in a side turning off Fetter Lane.

We settled down at the last available table, a rickety affair in the corner covered with the obligatory red gingham cloth and surrounded by an artistic display of Chianti bottles and seemingly mummified, but probably plastic, pizza toppings.

'I think our Mr Tierney's taken quite a shine to you.'

'He seems to have, doesn't he? Bit surprising though, considering that I haven't actually got much idea of what this action is even about, let alone how we're going to win it, if it ever comes to trial.'

She laughed at such a degree of frankness unbecoming of senior counsel and added that neither had she, but that Tierney was the sort of client who wanted his legal team to fight hard despite the absence of any coherent instructions – a fact that was not altogether unusual to us as lawyers.

'As he said to me on the way, it's not the winning of the case that counts, it's the taking part. The facts are unimportant, he says.'

'Most normal people would regard the thought of taking part in a legal action when they neither know or even care about the facts about as enticing as catching leprosy. But, you know, I can't help feeling that Tierney really seems a bit of an unlikely litigant. Have you done any work for him before this?'

'Quite a bit really. I remember a planning appeal of his which we lost, a mega disaster actually because he didn't get permission for the greyhound track complex that he had set his heart on and rather a lot of money too.

But he just shrugged and said that it was a case of, 'Well we won most of the points so you could say, as the great surgeon is reported to have once remarked, 'The operation was a great success but unfortunately the patient died'.' Tell you one thing, though, Tierney's no fool. He's a good businessman and, more to the point, has piles of cash and pays us on time.'

'What, a client who pays his solicitor on time? That's a new one on me! Tell me, though, why does he put on that "plain man of the people" Irish nonsense?'

'What, the "him with two sons in the Jesuits" routine?'

I nodded and waited until she dropped the unconvincing Dublin brogue.

'I'm not really sure why Tierney does that, the exaggerated Irish-isms I mean, because he's really quite a wise cookie. Made a bomb from property development before the last recession hit and he's still rumoured to have fingers in every cherry pie from here to God-knows-where. I've always thought that Glenbreen Trading lark is just a front, a sort of hobby with financial implications, because he must be well past retirement age and I gather that he's still loaded even now.'

'So why does he still bother with Glenbreen?'

'Because he enjoys it and because he's obsessed about paying, or not paying, tax – not that that makes him all that different from any other businessman I've come across. He's always going on about marginal rates and avoidance provisions and how in his eyes H.M. Revenue and Customs are public enemy number two, number one I gather being a combination of our present government, the last ones, Mrs Thatcher and the late Mr Hitler all rolled into one. I've heard it so often from him now that I could recite his rantings in my sleep. But anyway, Christopher, why are you asking me all about Tierney when I think that you know him already?'

'I don't know him from Adam – I'd never even heard of him let alone met him before.'

'Well, that's strange! He asked for you to be personally instructed in this case. Said that he and your family go back a long way. I think that he mentioned something about having done business with an uncle of yours in the past.'

'That would have been Gerald as I don't have any other uncles but I don't remember him ever having said anything about anyone called Tierney. Mind you, I can't very well ask him now as he died a few months ago.'

'I'm sorry about your uncle, dying that is. I suppose there must have been some connection there that you don't know about. Oh bother, I think we'd better order now – that waiter over there is getting impatient and I don't want him to turn nasty. Just look at him - he looks like an extra from a horror film.'

Over the tagliatelle al funghi we chatted further about both the case and our rather larger than life client before the conversation gradually shifted to other topics such as how she had just been made a full equity partner in her firm, the type of commercial work she specialised in, shipping cases in general and the more interesting foibles of other barristers that she regularly instructed. In other words it degenerated into the kind of incidental gossip that lawyers all over the world delight in. And as we were talking I thought, in a not obviously lustful way, that Jessica was looking very comely with her small but shapely form clothed in a well-cut charcoal grey suit over a white silk blouse and her shoulder-length dark hair which was neatly trimmed and swept pleasingly around

34

the pretty oval of her face. I reckoned that she was in her late thirties or perhaps early forties, probably unmarried, because of her apparent devotion to her career or unsuitability of possible suitors. At least so far as I was concerned, she was about as unattainable as any woman who I have been brave enough to attempt to chat up in recent years.

Then over a sadly disappointing zabaglione I cross-examined her and elicited that she was a Londoner by birth, that her parents were retired school teachers like mine, she had an 2.1 from Southampton, enjoyed foreign travel and, most importantly of all, that following the end of a long and increasingly undramatic relationship with a college law lecturer called Bernard, she now lived in a large flat near to West Hampstead tube station with a Burmese cat called Miranda.

In return I told her that I was separated and now about to get divorced, had a son who had fled the nest some years ago and a daughter of eighteen who lived with me in my smart rented flat in Bermondsey. I added that I had a lifetime's obsession with collecting books in unmanageable numbers and that, like her, I enjoyed most but not necessarily all kinds of jazz. Wisely I decided against claiming to match her interest in opera since even I couldn't be confident of my ability to carry that one off knowing little if anything about Mozart and Verdi or any other such wallas. I also pertinently omitted to mention the fact that, being definitely a dog-orientated person, I actually liked cats as well.

It was getting on for ten past two when the waiter diffidently presented us with two insipid double espressos and an already overstretched bill. As soon as he had gone, I summoned up the courage to address Jessica directly by her first name and asked her if she was interested in coming with me to hear Jan Garbarek, one of my heroes, play at the Festival Hall the following week.

'I really like him too, in fact I've got one of his albums lurking around somewhere so it would be great to hear him in person if I could, but sadly Christopher, your timing's a bit off.' I resited the temptation to ask why so she added an explanation. 'You see I'm going to Switzerland tomorrow for ten days.'

'On business?'

'Not exactly. We're off to Murren actually – it's in the Bernese Oberland. We're going for some late skiing at the end of the season.'

'Who's we?' I let the mask slip and hoped that I didn't sound too inquisitive.

Oh, just a group of us who meet up there every year and have done since our days at the College of Law, partners included.' My face must have betrayed me because Jessica smiled, lent over the table and touched my wrist lightly, allaying my fears that she might have only been humouring me. 'Listen, Christopher, I didn't mean to snub you when...' I chose to wait so that she'd be forced to spell it out. 'Well... when you're so obviously asking me out on a date.'

I said nothing and she smiled and added, 'So don't worry, I'll be back in ten days and perhaps we'll arrange something more definite then. I'd like that. I'll leave a message on your phone.'

I mumbled that I hoped we would meet up again soon and I thought to myself that I would like that as well.

'I've enjoyed this lunch, Christopher, and well, um... thank you. Right, I need to get back to the office now and

I believe you need to get ready to see that next client of yours. So good bye for now.'

She shook my hand then blushed and, being male and thus easily embarrassed in such situations, so did I.

We parted company at the corner of Fleet Street and Chancery Lane and, as I made my way back to chambers to prepare for the meeting with the egregious Mr Hennessey, I considered her words with the care that one would have employed had they appeared in a conveyancing writ, while at the same time trying to fathom out her body language – the latter skill, according to my daughter, not being one of my strong points. My preliminary conclusion, perhaps not so difficult to discern, was that she seemed to like me but then I could have guessed as much without the analysis. Then the sun, having been hidden behind the watery London clouds, chose this moment to break out in a brief display of solidarity. I realised that I was now in a much happier frame of mind, helped, no doubt, by the best part of a bottle of Barolo which I had unwisely consumed while Jessica had stuck to her virtuous mineral water. I really needed now to get my thoughts in order so that I could deal with Hennessey and his copyright problems rather than continuing to think about Jessica.

So in an attempt to avoid sliding into mawkishness (a tendency which both my daughter and my estranged wife were united in attributing to me), I began to count out loud in not very convincing French, to the obvious alarm of two Japanese tourists who, under the mistaken impression that the old Public Records Office was Westminster Abbey, were attempting to photograph it from every angle without stepping into the stream of passing traffic.

'Quatre vingt quatre, quatre vingt cinq...'

And, as I smugly told myself by the time I got to quatre vingt six, at long last life was beginning to look up again.

3

That evening, as I was turning the key in the lock, Kirsty's voice greeted me.

'Hi, Dad! I've made your tea. It's in the oven and a bit over-cooked. It's not one of my best but I hope it's still edible. I'm on my way out to meet Alan. We're going to the cinema to see that new film about how women eventually got what they wanted – I mean the vote, of course. I'll be back at twelve or so and, oh, thanks again for letting me have they car. You didn't forget, did you?'

I actually had forgotten all about it but didn't intend to admit this to Kirsty. She had probably worked it out for herself though as she just laughed.

'Don't worry. I promise to drive carefully, return myself and the car in one piece and not have anything to drink. I'll give your regards to the suffragettes and I'll try not to be too radical and bolshy afterwards. Not that I'd ever be like that, of course. Anyway, bye then Dad.'

And, like a small-scale but determined tornado, my daughter was gone.

I went into the living room and stood in front of the big picture window, the main reason why I had rented this high-tech and decidedly not-me modern, two-bedroomed apartment. Below my gaze was the long sweep of river that formed the Pool of London where once ships from every nation had congregated while waiting to berth at the busy wharves amidst a confusion of tugs, lighters and barges. Now the river was almost deserted and the bustling ships had gone for good.

As I watched the ripples of gold on the water I thought, not for the first time, that this was indeed a far cry from the house in Wickham Road where I had once lived with Francesca and where our children Ed and Kirsty had grown up. I was temporarily lost in thought. That house had been an almost perfect home with a perfect garden, perfect carpets, perfect designer kitchen, in fact perfect bloody everything except for a less than perfect relationship with my perfect wife or at least I thought it had all been perfect until she, perhaps with good reason, had tired of me and left. Roland Rat, or whatever his name is, was welcome to her so far as I was concerned and it served that cocksure accountant right for abandoning his charming family in Upper Norwood for my wife. I was well shot of dear Francesca, or at least I had convinced myself that I was, which is perhaps, all things considered, not quite the same thing.

I felt tears in my eyes as I stayed purposefully looking out of the window for some time, thinking of my childhood and of the long evenings when I would stand with my dog on the beach at Blundellsands. There I watched the summer sun setting and waiting patiently for the incoming tide which would bring with it a great procession of ships passing in and out of the Mersey, another great trading river of England. Then, before the dusk would gather itself up into the lengthening shadows and whispering night, I would happily make my way home with Meg, where my mother would have supper waiting for us in the warm house and my father would be fretting over his crossword or the remains of yesterday's news in the paper and my mother would be fussing over him.

I sighed and picked up a discarded denim jacket, a used mug and an overflowing ring file marked 'Kirsty L. Kingston, J.A.G.S., Geography Notes – Do Not Touch'. How very precise, how very like Kirsty! I smiled and couldn't help thinking that whatever other attributes my daughter might have, she could generate more debris in a single afternoon than I could in a whole month, As I tidied up I tried to ignore the torn up scraps of paper and rejected reminder strips but I found it more difficult to fail to notice the empty cigarette pack lying on the carpet. Obviously my continuing campaign on the evils of smoking was making little headway with the twin assaults based on science and moral persuasion falling upon stony ground. 'Persistent little brat', and I thought as I went into the kitchen that maybe I'll have to resort to plain old cash bribery instead.

I returned with a tray of overcooked lasagne and thought that I was having pasta for the second time today – what has my life come to? I picked up the remote and turned on the Channel Four News. A chubby and serious man who resembled an overgrown coypu was informing me of the government's strategy for dealing with the threat of international terrorism and difficulties caused by leaving the European community and the general global financial crisis. As he singularly failed to engage my attention on either subject, I felt I would like to get a book down to browse through and then I remembered the unopened packet in my briefcase. Oh well, something to read other than the cereal box left over from breakfast. Who knows, it might even be interesting to peruse while I ate – another bad habit that Kirsty has picked up from me.

As I held the packet up to the light I noticed, for the first time, the smudged Liverpool L2 post-mark. At least it wasn't likely to be a brochure from one of those idiots who were trying to interest me in 'Why not invest in a West-End live theatrical production!' Why not indeed? Apart from a lack of the readies and the fact that I had not yet fallen off my trolley.

I pulled the covering letter out of the packet and saw that it was typed on a heavy linen wove paper and embossed in dark blue script, 'Runciman, Dewfold & Davies', a prestigious legal firm in Tithebarn Street in that city and whom I knew had once been my Uncle Gerald's family solicitors. Out of habit, I looked down the list of partners to see who 'Our Ref: LRD' was and worked out that it was an individual called L. Rupert Dewfold. Rupert, indeed! The name meant nothing to me and anyway what did that L stand for? I began to read the letter.

Dear Mr Kingston,

We apologize for troubling you but in our capacity as executors of your late uncle, Gerald William Kingston (deceased), we were instructed by him to pass to you, at a not earlier than the end of the six month period immediately following upon the date of his death, the enclosed sealed envelope, the contents of which we should stress, are completely unknown to us.

We would be obliged if you would accordingly sign and return at your earliest convenience the enclosed receipt therefore. Should you require any further assistance that we can provide you with, then please do not hesitate to contact us with your requirements.

Yours sincerely...

The corporate squiggle looked like a cross between the horns of a Jacob's sheep and a misshapen ring doughnut but at least the letter was short and to the point unlike many solicitor's efforts which I have seen in my time. The enclosed envelope referred to was large, plain and devoid of any markings. It reminded me of one of those brightly painted Russian dolls that Kirsty used to play with when she was young for inside there were three further envelopes.

Two of them were white, slightly smaller than that which the covering letter was in and were identical to each other and the third was a little brown Manila envelope of the type that wages were once paid in when men were men and money was counted in pounds, shillings and pence.

I held up the Manila one first and examined it. There was something inside which rattled about and, after carefully prising apart the gunned flap, I poured the contents out into the palm of my hand. As I held them up, the fine gold chain and cross caught the light and seemed to shimmer with an iridescence of their own and with a start I remembered where I had seen them before. How could I forget? They had been April's and she had been wearing them on the day of the party. Gingerly returning the cross and chain to their resting place, I felt uncomfortable and sad, for the very thought of even handling them now somehow repulsed me.

The two white envelopes clearly contained documents of some sort and, impatiently fetching a cup of ghastly instant coffee which I would normally have turned down, I sat down at the dining table and opened up the first of them. Its contents were few: a handful of press cuttings and a handwritten letter written on azure notepaper. The letter, I noted, was in my late uncle's distinctive black italic hand, still recognisable despite the clear imperfections caused by the pain and suffering of his last illness.

When I stop and look back on it, my uncle was one of the rocks upon which my life was built. My father's elder brother, he had started his working life in the Mersey shipyards when they were still flourishing and served his apprenticeship there. My bookish grandfather had never approved of apprenticeships, since he had always regarded practical skills with a sort of envious Luddite suspicion. But his time in the yards had undoubtedly given Gerald the chance to acquire a sound and thorough knowledge of marine engineering, something which he could not have learned from books alone, whatever my grandfather might had thought. Unfortunately his time in the shipyards had also given him the opportunity to ingest deadly quantities of the insidious asbestos dust that had hung around the fabricating sheds and inside the engine rooms of the ships that he and his workmates had helped to build.

Then, at my grandfather's insistence, Gerald had gone to university in Manchester and there he learned all there was to know about marine engineering but more importantly had met Maura, his wife to be. She had been a fine art undergraduate and I can still remember him telling me how she was, 'a great imperious lioness of a woman who totally caught hold of my heart and still held it to this very day'.

By the end of the fifties my uncle was already the director of his own boat-building company specialising in hand-crafted small sea-going craft and I had always thought, when I saw him messing about with dinghies, yachts and cruisers, that he was one of those rare but happy breed of individuals who could truly boast that their work was also their hobby. I wondered how many lawyers could truly say that and then, sadly, thought that there were probably quite a few.

Gerald, and the overbearing Maura, had lived with their children, April and Ben, in what I had always thought to be a rather grand house a few streets away from my parent's more modest terraced home. My bookish teacher father and his more practical brother were particularly close but they had always seemed to enjoy each other's company in spite of the elaborately staged annual arguments which usually ended in a verbal stalemate while we chewed over Maura's over-laced Christmas pudding and looked for the supposedly lucky silver threepenny bits wrapped up in their greaseproof shrouds.

One of my earliest memories of Gerald is of him jovial and extrovert at a family gathering, performing much to my delight some sort of trick with tumblers and disappearing playing cards, while Ben and April, who had seen it all a hundred times before, sat tight with a superior air about them while their young cousin was so easily amused. Gerald was indulgent towards me and one of the things that I particularly liked was that he always seemed to have time to stop whatever he was doing and listen patiently to childish tales about my daily doings. When I was older he would talk to me as a grown-up and I felt both flattered and honoured that he, alone among the adults in my family, wanted to treat me as an equal and as a person of some consequence rather than as the rather precocious kid that I undoubtedly was.

I was very fond of him and even after April's death, when things between us were never quite the same again, we still regularly kept in touch. I would occasionally drop in to see him and Maura in their new home on the edge of Chester and we would exchange the odd letter and card in which he would question me about the progress of my daughter Kirsty who, it rather sadly seemed to me, was something of a substitute for his own dead daughter.

Then, on a Sunday evening in the autumn of last year, I unexpectedly heard from Maura. At first she was almost incoherent on the phone but eventually she managed to blurt out that the chest pains which my uncle had been complaining of for several months were not due to angina and old age, as his doctor had confidently opined, but were classic symptoms of mesothelioma – an incurable asbestos-related cancer of the pleura that had developed over the years asymptomatically but which now sadly left him with only weeks in which to live increasingly painfully and die even more dreadfully. I was so stunned by the news that the very next day I travelled north and made my way up the path to the front door of their large bungalow, fearful in all honesty because I had no idea of what to expect, far less of what even to say.

I was met at the door by a subdued Maura. She hailed me, half-heartedly, as 'Topher', the name by which I had called myself when I was two years old and which, despite my protests, she alone had continued to use ever since. After a brief exchange of words and with a warning not to tire him out, I was ushered by my aunt into a darkened room where, propped up by pillows and surrounded by the smell, stuffiness and paraphernalia of the terminally ill, sat my uncle.

I tried hard not to show my shock at seeing him there, somehow shrunken in size in his now gigantic pyjamas and all of the time struggling for breath. His face was grey and gaunt and his voice, which in my memory had always been so rich and confident in tone, was now reduced to little more than a monotonous falsetto wheeze. That he had courage was obvious and I tried not to show that I felt sorry for him.

He greeted me and seemed strangely cheerful. Perhaps he had already resigned himself to the certain knowledge that his end would be a degrading one for he had seen enough of his friends die of the same disease to be without any comforting illusions to the contrary. Maybe his faith, which he had acquired by marriage and now professed with the cynicism which only a true convert can adopt, genuinely sustained him but then what did I, a lapsed Anglican, know about such things? Gerald had once said to me that his religion might be regarded as an unsatisfactory one for the living but a bloody good one for the dying, and it now seemed that he was putting that faith to practical use.

We talked together in pleasant generalities about our families and my work. I noted with relief that we both pointedly avoided any reference to the future which I, but not he, would be facing. Then, having sent Maura out of the room to make a cup of tea for me (he by that time being beyond even such innocent refreshment), his whole manner changed.

'Christopher, my boy, there's something I need to discuss with you and I don't want Maura to hear so please just listen to me and don't butt in.'

I sat down beside him and waited for him to continue.

47

'It's something that I have not felt fit to burden you with in the past.'

My curiosity aroused, I waited to see what he was wanting to discuss with me.

'It's about April...'

Tears welled up in his tired and by now almost colourless eyes and I wondered if his mind was wandering with the effects of the drugs that he was on. He must have seen this reflected in the way in which I was looking at him, for he chuckled throatily and coughed before taking a quick blast from his inhaler.

'Don't worry, I haven't fallen off my perch yet even though I will soon enough.'

He stopped again and waited as if to gather his thoughts or strength, before continuing in little more than a hoarse whisper.

'I know that April has been dead for many years now. I know that as a fact, Christopher, even if in my heart I've never really accepted it. Her death came as a very great shock to me and to be honest I've never got over it.'

He took a deep breath and coughed before going on.

'But please listen to me and listen very carefully. There's something that I want you to do and I want you to do it both for my sake and well for hers too.'

Again he hesitated, as if searching for the right words. How could any father accept the death of the daughter he had much loved and who had met such a pointless death, I wondered?

'Christopher I'm not going to say very much now, because it wouldn't be fair to either of us and anyway everything's such a great physical effort for me now. As you can see that I've not got long left now.'

I wanted to say something consoling like, 'You'll get better soon', or, 'You're getting the best of care', but the first was not true and the second was pointless and hardly helpful. How is it that it's so difficult to say anything that has any meaning to a person who is dying even though you are personally affected? Instead I kept my silence before he continued.

'Once I've gone, I want you to carry out a task in my and April's memory. You can either do it or refuse and it'll be your choice. I don't suppose that I'll ever know one way or the other.'

He paused and looked at me with affection.

'I trust you, Christopher, to think hard about whether or not you'll do what I ask and I'm sure that, whatever you decide to do, it'll be the right thing.'

I wondered what he was talking about. Why all the mystery if it was going to be something involving his ashes or some other small act of remembrance like tending to his or April's grave? I was tempted just to agree to anything so as to give the poor old sod peace of mind but something, perhaps my innate stubbornness or suspicious legal mind, caused me to resist. Maybe it was just that I respected Gerald too much to pander to him and give the easy and expected reply.

'What exactly do you want me to do?'

Instead of replying he laughed, and this set off another bought of wheezing.

'Always the cautious lawyer! You'll know soon enough, my boy. Please just promise me that you'll give my request serious consideration, no more, no less.'

We never discussed it further for Maura had silently re-entered the room and was looking at me with an uncomprehending but hostile stare as if in some way I was personally to blame for her husband's fatal illness. Gerald, his brief rally at an end, slumped back into the well-plumped pillows and I realised that the moment had passed irretrievably. I leant over and touched his shoulder gently but Gerald was already drifting into an untroubled, and no doubt well medicated sleep.

And, as it happened, this was the last occasion on which I ever saw him for, barely three weeks later and in the early hours of a wet and windy Tuesday morning, he died fortified by the Rites of the Holy Church that he believed in and a kindly administered final dose of NHS morphine.

I missed him then and I am not ashamed to admit that I still miss him even now.

I used the remote to switch the television off before beginning to slowly read over his letter to me.

Dear Christopher,
You have always been more of a son to me than Benedict ever has been...

Which, I thought, was rather hard on my cousin Ben who could no more have helped the fact that he had never really hit it off with his father than the fact that he was gay although I had always, perhaps wrongly, suspected that Aunt Maura had been responsible for both of these conditions.

By the time that you read this, I will already have been dead for half a year now.

I wondered if that had been strange to Gerald, writing that sentence down when he was still alive and very much

50

aware of his fate. What thoughts must have been going through his mind at that time and can any of us really get our heads round the notion that the world will continue unabated and unchanged beyond our own miserable demise?

I am now at peace with myself and my Maker but my darling April is not, and never can be, until the right thing is done and her death is both explained and avenged.

Explained I understood, but avenged? Surely this was a job for the God that he purported to believe in.

I am placing my trust in you, Christopher, not only because you were her cousin but because you are a good person and also a man of the law. As such you will understand something which I cannot – the meaning of the words "justice" and "truth". April and I had the benefit of neither.

I shut my eyes and momentarily considered whether the concepts of truth and justice meant any more to me than they had done to him. Were they a reality or merely an illusion? All that came into my mind was the figure of Libra, blindfolded and holding the sword of retribution in one hand and the scales of justice in the other. A hackneyed image perhaps but then I was not a criminal lawyer and had never had to present the stark facts to twelve good men and true, all anxiously searching the face of the accused to ensure that he received a verdict from them that they could both understand and live with. Perhaps my friend Gavin was right when he said that a criminal trial was like a twenty-first century morality play in a courtroom such as the Old Bailey and any connection between reality and what happened in the charade played out for several days before confused members of a recently summoned jury who hoped that they would soon be able to return home to their family life was a tenuous one. I hoped that his words to me were wrong but rather suspected that he was right. Turning to the next sheet of his letter, I read on.

My request is a simple one and yet it may also be one of the hardest things that you have ever been asked to undertake. I want you, Christopher, to discover and expose whoever it was that killed my beautiful daughter April. I am in no doubt that she was murdered – how could it have been otherwise when she died in such a violent manner? That is beyond doubt and I want to make it clear that I want no retribution or bloodshed, no vengeance or recompense. My only desire is that the world will at last know the truth how April died and who it was that killed her and ruined our lives, all those years ago. And if you are asking why it should be you that I am asking? You were the one who found her and therefore it is only fitting that you should be the one who will find her killer. You, and you alone, must bring an end to this whole business.

But why should I? It wasn't my business to rake over the embers of the long dead past and anyway why couldn't Ben or Maura do it? After all they were much closer to April than I had ever been. Why, for that matter, had Gerald waited more than forty years before doing anything himself?

The truth may well be unpalatable but it cannot be hidden away for ever. The Almighty knows what really happened but I want April's killer to get his or her just deserts here on earth.

Undoubtedly the truth, any truth for that matter, might well be unpalatable but as for just deserts what did he mean? Now I was beginning to suspect that my uncle really had fallen off his perch by the time he had written the letter, especially with all the religious language and references to the unimaginable. To be fair he always had been a bit on the mad side. Nonetheless, something within me stopped me from ripping it up, however tempting that might have seemed.

Before my final illness overtook me, I fully intended to undertake the task myself but I am now too weak, too confused and my time is too short. I need to prepare myself for what lies ahead on my own journey. Please, Christopher, accept this challenge and do as I ask as there is no one else that I could or should ask. I pray that you will be successful in this, the last thing that I will ever request of you. May the Living God give you the grace and strength that you will need and may He always guide you throughout your life .

Your loving uncle,
Gerald.

I halted and, wanting to do something to break the spell, carried the untouched instant coffee back into the kitchen and poured it down the drain. I watched it disappear in a frothy gurgle, poured myself a glass of

Saint Émilion wine, returned to my chair and picked up the letter again,

P.S. – The enclosed papers may help. Twentyman has retired and lives in Aidensbrook Road, New Brighton. You can find his number in the Liverpool phone book. Please keep all of this to yourself and whatever you do, do not say anything to your parents or to Maura.

I laid it aside and studied the flimsy sheets headed 'LANCASHIRE CONSTABULARY – Statement of Witness'. These primitive photostats now looked like antiquarian manuscripts that the Xerox machine had consigned to the technological graveyard and I was sure that I already knew what was in one of them.

My name is Christopher Kingston, and I am making this statement of my own free will...

And maybe the curling pieces of paper that I was now holding contained the truth or at least the truth insofar as I had ever known it. They were, I supposed, the last limp testament to the day upon which April had died and I had been forced, however reluctantly, to enter into the uncertain moral labyrinth of adulthood, however pretentious that might sound. I sighed once again, and as I did so the years began to slip away from me like the dark ebb-tide of the Mersey on a moonless night.

4

The fifth of August in that far of year had, in many ways, been an unremarkable day – the usual twenty-four hours or so that happened to fall midway through the summer bank holiday weekend when the television forecast of sunny periods with scattered showers had conspired to shorten the queues of cars heading out to Blackpool, Morecambe and the Lake District. It was, coincidentally, also the day upon which Ros turned eighteen years of age and the day on which April met her end. Not surprisingly, it was those events rather than the more newsworthy troubles in Northern Ireland, an unexpected strike at British Leyland, the unceasing problems of unrest in a central African republic and the prison riots at Pankhurst, which have stayed in my memory.

Early on that auspicious morning I crept downstairs in my socks and was silently but enthusiastically greeted by my faithful border collie Meg. She and I both were thankful that the forecast seemed to be erroneous for the sun was already out in full force and no trace of any dark clouds were visible. As Meg crunched her biscuits, I ate my cornflakes and wondered whether it was too early to phone Ros. After all it was just before eight on a Sunday morning and so far as I could tell all creatures were silent, and all mortals at rest.

I skimmed through my parents' Observer that had arrived with a thump on the doormat with the tuneless whistling of the paperboy and then summoned up the courage to call the familiar number hoping that the soft burr as the dial rotated would not wake my mother and father. The phone was answered almost immediately by her brother Graham.

'Oh, hi there Chris! You haven't forgotten about the celebrations tonight have you? Good, well just make sure that you're back by eight at the latest and the friends and family will all have gathered by then. Remember though it's supposed to be a surprise so don't say anything about it to her.'

'Anything about what?' Ros broke into the conversation. I avoided answering her question and told her that I'd be round within the hour and she seemed pleased when I told her where we were going.

'I've always wanted to go to the Witch Country and see where old Ma Chattox and Demdike and the others lived', she said, and added that some time she would have to borrow *Mist Over Peddle* again. I smiled, thinking of the carefully selected first edition of that work ('complete with dust-jacket, near mint, £2.50') which I had found in a slightly foxed second-hand bookshop near to my school and had proudly bought as one of the three presents that she would be getting from me that day.

By the time that I had taken Meg for a walk in the little park just round the corner and finished wrapping the presents, it was almost time to go. I gulped down a cup of coffee and once again carefully checked over my vehicle, a tatty blue Bedford van which despite its age and appearance, was nevertheless my pride and joy. Remembering to top up the slowly leaking radiator, I made sure that I had an extra bottle of water with me just in case. The Handsome Beast, as Ros liked to call the van, had been bought by me out of all of my holiday earnings for all of fifty pounds. The seller, an overweight builder in Litherland, told me in no uncertain way that to buy such a fine specimen elsewhere, 'would be like giving yer penny to the monkey', a phrase which I took to mean that I was getting a bargain but perhaps I had misunderstood him as judging by the amount of oil the Beast burned, it seemed to me that I was the one who may have been the monkey. But at least the van was mine, all mine, and I guarded it with the fierce proprietorial air that only one's first real transport can engender, however woeful or crappy that vehicle is.

Quarter of an hour later, and in a small cloud of black smoke, we were pulling away from the kerb in Church Avenue. Ros, who had been waiting for me at her front gate with a carrier bag full of carefully selected picnic things and a head full of equally carefully selected songs of Nick Drake, was bursting to tell me about a novel that she had just read and how one of the main characters in it closely resembled her – or at least was in some way a little bit like her. I smiled indulgently but was only half-listening while thinking to myself that at last things were beginning to work out and that perhaps this time we could actually accomplish a complete journey in The Beast without mechanical troubles causing us to break down and have to summon the help of the R.A.C.

As we drove through the harvest-scented summer countryside, a warm breeze flowed through the open doors and Ros, her hair blowing back into her eyes, started on her favourite lines from Hazey Jane II. As I listened to her singing the familiar words, which ever since I have always associated with Ros and that enchanted time, I took in the vibrant colours of everything we passed by. The flower-encrusted banks, the hedgerows in a hundred shades of green, the scattered flowers and even the mottled brown walls and the patchy tarmac lanes which led towards the brooding bulk of Pendle Hill. All of these and more registered with me and I knew that on this auspicious day I would have no doubts and worries about anything and that all I wanted was just to be there with Ros.

Both of us were beginning to feel hungry and just before noon we had our sandwiches on the banks of a pebble-bedded stream near to the bucolically named village of Barley while Meg splashed around aimlessly. Then, having our flask of tea, we sat down and looked over the well used one-inch map, a familiar pose for both of us as we shared a real liking for the Ordnance Survey and its world of bench marks, contour lines, rights-of-way, and windmills (disused). Indeed Ros was the only girl that I ever knew who took such a positive delight in the seventh series (revised). But then, as she once told me, she had been well-tutored by an eccentric geography teacher at school who had always maintained that if she taught her pupils how to read the O.S. map properly, there was a good chance that it might be able to save their marriages.

As we wallowed on the grass by the dappled, shimmering water I gazed at Ros and I knew that she was content, utterly content and that she, too, wanted this day never to end.

After a few minutes we gathered our things up and I repacked my old canvas haversack that had shared many an adventure with Meg and I in the past and had reached the status of an old companion. We then set out to energetically ascend the path up towards the hill. But it was a steep climb and just as our legs were beginning to tire and Meg was becoming markedly less enthusiastic than before, we reached the summit and halted. Ros and I stared at each other in an approving way.

She was always a bit of an eccentric dresser and as we stood on the hill I took in her bright Laura Ashley skirt, the white cotton rugby shirt that had once belonged to me but which she had now firmly adopted as her own, her long scarf of many colours and a wide brimmed new straw hat that she had bought the previous day from the lugubrious Dekko the Deal. Her now much favoured outfit was nicely set off by a string of large malachite beads which she felt always brought her luck wherever she was. What however, most strongly stuck in my mind now when thinking of Ros on that memorable day was her long tousled tumbling hair. When caught by the rays of the noon sun, it displayed a striking tint which, being both tawny with a suggestion of auburn, seemed to defy any description that I could put on it. Many years later, I spoke to my friend Gavin that the hue of her hair would remain indelibly etched into the febrile colour chart of my mind, to which he remarked that if I could still feel that way that I must have been truly out of my mind or perhaps just truly in love. I had no answer other than to agree on both counts.

From the summit of the hill Ros began to point out all of the landmarks that could be seen, remarking that it was wonderful how the map had come to life. Animated by the subtle beauties of the verdant pastel shades of high summer, I watched in silence as she confidently picked out the landmarks – the huddled roofs of Clitheroe, the wooded line of the Ribble valley, the rain-threatened Forest of Bowland and, barely discernable in the distance, the beckoning peaks of Ingleborough, Pen-y-ghent and Whernside. When the lesson had ended, I was content to place a rounded stone on top of the small growing cairn that others had placed there before walking away hand-in-hand until we stretched out on the cool flanks of the hill, Meg joining us in our contemplations.

For a time neither of us said anything as we looked up at the cloud-scarred sky. A large bird, a hawk or raptor of some sort, languidly circled high overhead, and gentle wind stirred the long grass that cushioned us. In perfect comfort, we were at peace with the world as it was.

Then I spoke. 'Cumulonimbus.'

'No it isn't.'

'Ros, must you always disagree with whatever I say?'

She laughed. 'Only when I know what I'm talking about and you clearly don't!'

She may have been right about the clouds but, hell, I didn't care enough to quibble and there was no need to pick a pointless argument. We looked up at the all-embracing sky and then both laughed at the ridiculousness of it all.

'Well if you want to, then you'll have to catch me first.' And I did and after that she turned her face away and carefully began to look towards the west and the unseen sea.

'Chris, will things always be like this, for us I mean?'

I stroked her hair and said that I hoped that they would but already an inner voice was telling me that one day that there might have to be an end to all of this, probably sooner rather than later, but I chose to ignore such intrusive thoughts.

We remained on the hill for a while wrapped in our thoughts before the sun, as if begrudging our happiness, disappeared behind the clouds. It was becoming cold and as Ros righted her shirt collar and pulled down the brim of her hat, we both wished that we hadn't left our raincoats back on the seats in the waiting Beast.

'Time to go', I said and Ros nodded in agreement.

As we crossed the fence and began to make our way down the path, Meg strained at her lead and the sheep eyed us warily. It seemed somehow as though the magic of the day had left us and that in some way our relationship had been checked and found wanting.

But, back in the village, the sun reappeared and stayed with us for the rest of that long afternoon, while the Bedford van struggled up and down the gradients in a mood of compliant complaint, its primitive shakes and rattling confirming that I had probably been done by the corpulent construction engineer from Litherland. But what did that matter now? Ros, her hand on my knee, was singing lines from Hazey Jane once again and even though I struggled with the column mounted gear lever and had to change a wheel on the road coming down to Newchurch-in-Pendle, I felt optimistic. Surely life could only get better.

Tea was taken in an establishment close by and Ros had a fit of giggles when I insisted on giving a tuneless rendition of 'Happy Birthday' to her, despite the glares of the only people present, two elderly couples who clearly thought that I was nowt but a long-haired lout and that Ros, in her strangely assorted garb, was a brazen hussy or worse. Maybe I was being hard on these old folks and maybe life had just defeated them in the way that it eventually defeats all of us when the enthusiasm of youth wears off. I suppose that if my daughter Kirsty were to hear me talking like this now she would either try to jolly me up or decide that I had finally 'gone Upminster' – a condition that she would laboriously explain to me was akin to being 'a few stops beyond Barking.'

A little after six, we headed back towards Whalley and the sinking sun. By this time we had begun a pointless argument about whether the Lancashire witches had received a fair trial and I remember being very defensive of the lawyers of that time, a view no doubt coloured by the fact that I had already decided that I wanted to read law myself at university and was therefore unable to admit to anyone, even Ros, that justice (as I later learnt to my cost) could sometimes be fallible.

The discussion had fizzled out after we had disagreed about almost everything. We reached the traffic lights at Ormskirk when out of the blue, Ros asked me if I would mind calling at Gerald and Maura's house to collect the new Fairport album which Ben had borrowed a few days before. Without thinking, I agreed. Why not? And yet it was this one simple request, so banal and commonplace as to be completely unremarkable, which proved to be so disastrous for us both. If only she had forgotten about it, if only she hadn't lent the bloody album to Ben in the first place.

Twenty minutes later, we pulled into Serpentine Drive and I dragged the squawking handbrake on.

'Hang on a minute, Ros.'

'I might as well come too.'

'It's not really necessary but if you want to...'

We climbed out of the van and I gave Meg a pat and told her to remain on guard. 'Just stay. Good girl, we'll be back soon.'

And with that, the stage was set.

I rang the front door bell and waited. Ros said that it was no good, there was nobody in and we could always come back another time. We looked up at the windows and thought that maybe she was right but I, being too clever as usual, said no that it was fine because the back door was never locked and that Ben had probably left the album out for us anyway. I was now conscious of the passage of time and of my promise to deliver Ros home in enough time to change for the family birthday. Moments later, we were creeping around the side of the house unseen and Ros was laughing at the thought of being mistaken for a burglar by a nosy neighbour, a category of persons who, unusually for the Blundellsands streets, seemed to be conspicuously absent that evening.

'No one can see us anyway, we're hidden by the hedge', I said to reassure her. The entrance to the back door was through a small conservatory which Gerald had built himself a few years earlier in a tasteful faux-Victorian style. He had been proud of this work and indeed he should have been for it was an attractive structure with slender spandrels, leaded lights and a floor laid with old encaustic tiles in a green and white fleur-de-lis pattern which Maura, in her gushing way, claimed were 'very pretty and genuine Minton.' She omitted to say that they were probably nothing of the sort, having been bought as a job lot from an old Welsh chapel in Wavertree that one of her brothers had purchased 'for a song', but perhaps with regard for the piety of Maura, 'bought for a hymn' would have been a more appropriate description.

As we approached the conservatory door I noticed that it was ajar by a few inches and as I pushed it open something furry and black shot out past us. It was Dusky, their amiable doggie who had once turned up as a hungry and uninvited guest on their doorstep and stayed with them ever since. I wondered what had startled Dusky so much and then I found out.

Something was wrong, badly wrong. In the stifling heat a bluebottle was buzzing frantically in a manic way and seemed to be circling like a demented wartime pilot hovering over its target. I then noticed a substance – dark, coagulating and unmistakable, which had spread out over the would-be Minton tiles. It was blood and I saw that it had come from April who was lying face downwards with her left leg folded beneath her and her arms awkwardly splayed out in a pose which reminded me of the gaudy crucifixion picture in a cheap missal which she had once shown to me when we were children.

I already knew that she was dead. The blood matted on her once honey-coloured hair told me that she was already beyond any possible redemption. It was all so obscene and yet at the same time so remarkably peaceful, as if her unseen spirit had already broken free and departed this life. Without knowing why, I felt compelled to do something, anything, so I put my hand on her shoulder and turned her over, carefully averting my gaze from the gash on her forehead and the look in her startled unbelieving eyes. I felt her pulse, desperate to be proved wrong, but there was no movement and I tried to fight back the fear that was beginning to engulf me. It was only then, that the enormity of it all grabbed me and I knew that I had seen a corpse for the very first time in my life and I was literally staring death in the face.

I began to retch and a stifled scream came from right behind me. I turned abruptly – I had forgotten Ros. She stood there and was breathing in short, sharp gasps interspersed with demonic sobs and at first I thought that she was saying my name until I realised that the words were actually a forlorn rendition of 'Oh, Christ! Oh, Christ!' I grabbed hold of her and pushed her head down on to my chest but she broke free and gaped, open mouthed, at April. I could feel her trembling all over and then, in a strangled and unreal voice, she started to whisper.

'Is she...?'

I nodded, and she became silent.

A full minute passed and then an unbearable panic overtook us both and we took to our heels and ran straight out of the gate and into the road. There was a sudden high-pitched wail of brakes and a dull thud and I thought for a moment that there had been a second death and that it had been Ros that time until I heard her shouting abuse at the unseen driver and, with a sigh of relief, I knew that she was all right. She came back towards me and collapsed on the pavement, unhurt but shaken, and I knelt down and held her so tightly that her hat fell off and lay on the road.

'Oh, Chris...' I was still unsure if she was calling on me or the Almighty now but it was clearly the former. 'Chris, just do something!' Then I felt her body stiffen as she arched her back and began to fight back like a trapped animal and I staggered backwards as she struck me hard in the chest with her elbow. 'Chris, leave me alone – just let go of me!'

I was transfixed and she went on in the same small scared voice. 'We must phone for the ambulance or police or a doctor or something... For God's sake hurry.' She grabbed my arm and dragged me up the front path of the house next door where Toby Ainsdale, in his customary neat tweed jacket and brown twill trousers, was already standing at his door having heard, no doubt, the commotion in the street outside. He looked alarmed as Ros dropped like a disciple at his feet and without a word I pushed past the two of them into his house before seeing his phone on the hall table.

I clumsily seized the instrument and it fell off with a crash, entangling me in the corded flex before I dialled the first of the three nines. A reassuringly Scouse female voice answered me and I gabbled out some sort of message about finding my cousin dead on the floor and I needed an ambulance and police before collapsing like a spent force on the carpet. The girl on the other end of the line was calm and asked me, 'Where exactly are you calling from and how is the injured person?'

'She's my cousin and I've just found her but she's not injured, she's dead.' But I couldn't speak any further as I was choking with tears and I handed the receiver over to Toby without saying anything and hunched myself in a corner of the wall, rocking back and forth as I overheard him giving the girl the address and telling them to go round to the back door. I then became conscious of Toby's distraught wife Elvira being present and I was aware that Ros had remained silent, stunned by shock.

When he'd hung the phone up, Toby helped me up and motioned me over to the couch in the living room where their rather daft wolfhound Rufus leapt upon me and tried to lick my face. I suppose that in his own way he was trying to console me. Toby pushed Rufus away and then went to put his arm round his wife's shoulder in reassurance. Ros came and sat beside me and I put my arm around her, cuddling her tightly and closed my eyes. I'd already had enough, more than enough, and a lot more than I could possibly cope with for one day.

Gently Toby said to Ros and I, 'I can't imagine what you two have just been through– how truly awful and ghastly a thing to see! I am so, so very sorry for you and your family. Oh God, how terrible, poor April. She was such a lovely girl.' Then he turned to Elvira, tears welling in his eyes.

'Look after Chris and Ros could you? Make them some tea or something and try to calm them down before the Police arrive. I'll go next door to see whether there is anything I can do for April but it doesn't sound as if there is. Oh Christ, Maura and Gerald will de devastated. They're both away for the day. We'll have to break the news to them before they arrive home and, oh, my God, that it all should have all turned out like this.'

Nothing further needed to be said and even though I offered to assist Toby he merely shook his head and told both of us to wait together in his house while Elvira made us cups of tea.

And after that I have no real recollection of anything until I got into the back of the police car with Ros jammed into the seat beside me and we were taken to the old police station in Crosby where we were separated and told that we would be questioned.

'Where have you taken Ros to now and what the hell have you done to her?' I asked but received no answer. I was placed on a battered tubular chair in what seemed to me to be a particularly cold and sunless room devoid of any decoration other than a scar faced clock with its loud shuttling tick on the wall and some peeling official notices about the need to lock your car before leaving it unattended and to report any householders illegally using their lawn sprinklers in the water shortages.

I waited patiently in silence until eventually a large and florid-faced man entered. 'I am,' he announced with a flourish, 'D.I. Inspector Twentyman – that's Detective Inspector, that is. You have my sympathies, lad, but I'll need to take a statement from you after we have sorted out some paperwork first. Is that OK?'

Twentyman took my absence of a reply for a positive answer and after a wait of several minutes, he returned and began to take some sheets of paper out of the drawer. The phone rang and he answered it with some measured replies of, 'Yes, I see. Thank you and you can tell them that I won't be needing anything further from them until later. Get yourself back to the station soon to help with the paperwork.'

'Just the constable still at the house making sure that no-one interferes with the scene', he explained to me. Just then there was a violent disturbance in the adjoining room with some frenzied shouting and language that even a navvy would have hesitated to use. With surprise, I realised that the offender was none other than Ros. Her outburst seemed to be directed against someone, presumably a policeman, who was insisting that she be taken home to her parents while I was to be kept in for further questioning.

'Leave her alone, can't you!' I demanded as Twentyman left the room and returned after a few seconds with a thin and rather miserable-looking man who seemed to be the Inspector's side-kick. Presumably the thin man had attempted to pacify Ros, but to no avail because he appeared to have lost his temper with her in an approach which did not seem to be particularly well tailored to a teenage girl who had just seen a dead body for the first time, I heard him say, 'Flippin' heck if she

68

doesn't stop that performance and bloody carry on, leave and go straight home with the female officer right now, she'll be done for a breach of the peace, so help me!'

The Inspector took all of this in without comment and then looked at me in a not unfriendly way and merely shrugged his shoulders. 'Don't hurt her!' I said with force even though I felt so subdued that I could hardly raise my voice beyond being barely audible.

'What do you think we're bloody like, son? He's never hurt your girlfriend – never touched her at all. She went completely berserk when he tried to even talk to her. Just told her to keep calm. She just went at him like a bloody spitfire! And if anyone was in danger of being hurt it wasn't her.'

'She's upset and still in shock', I added, perhaps necessarily.

'Maybe so. I can accept that right enough. But still...'

He said nothing further but thought about it and then smiled disarmingly and added, 'Quite a spirited lass, your girlfriend Rosamund is.'

'She doesn't usually swear', I added – as though that would make any difference.

'Aye, that's as maybe but she's using choice language today – surprisingly course language for a well-brought up young miss like her. Why, she just said to DC Laing that he were not but a 'big lanky bar steward', only she used a more vulgar word than that, and what she said he could do to himself were nobody's business!'

He chuckled and shook his head in mock disapproval as the one who I thought Ros had been directing the vituperation at walked back into the room. 'And do you know what? He is a big lanky something or other an' all.'

Laing then went over to him and whispered something in his ear and his smile slowly faded.

'Let her go, for the present. We want to make sure that the lass is well out of here and with her mum and dad as soon as possible – it was her birthday evidently, so treat her with special care. Some bloody birthday that turned out to be. We can check everything out later if we need to.'

He beckoned to me to sit down beside the big wooden table and took the seat at the other side. 'Now then, Christopher lad, no more buggering about like a fart in a bottle as me old man would say. Let's get on with the business in hand or we'll be here all sodding Sunday night and its already dark outside. It's near on ten o'clock already and some of us are intending to go to bed before tomorrow dawns – you too lad, I imagine. You look completely shot out.'

He smiled again, for he could see that I had been overawed by his brusque nature. 'Keep calm, lad and don't worry any more about your little Miss Albright, she'll be OK, Trust me. Just make sure that you tell us everything about your cousin and how you found her. I understand that the lass and you were out on a jaunt for her birthday and...' Then he looked up at the big clock up on the wall, as if it might provide some inspiration.

'Right then, seven fifty six p.m. as near as makes no difference and it's still the bloody fifth of August today. Keep on, as we don't want to be here till the sixth, no bloody chance! So just start at the beginning and finish at the end. We can ask nowt but that.'

He produced a cheap ball pen and began writing while speaking the words at the same time.

'My name is Christopher Kingstone, blah, blah, blah, I've already got the sodding details of all of that!' He glanced up at me and stopped his erratic course across the boldly lined paper. Then he pushed the mug of stale tea back across the table and poised the pen in mid-air.

'It's your turn, lad. In your own words then.'

And now all of this seemed as irrelevant to me now as the other nuggets of history which our lazy tobacco-stained form-master, Mr Rossiter, had tried to enthuse us with in the drowsy afternoons that dragged on and on until 3.45, when he invariably came out with his favourite quote that, 'It was the best of times, it was the worse of times', when we all wondered what that had to do with anything at all. Then we'd all have to wait until Rossiter fussily gathered up his books and said, 'Well that's all until next week', before the bell liberated us into the infinitely more exciting world that lay beyond the school gates. I still remember that teacher as though it was yesterday but did I really remember everything that had happened the day that April had died. Was I sure that I had told Twentyman everything that had taken place that evening more than forty years ago in the Police station at Crosby station on that summer evening?

*****

I turned to the other large envelope and tipped out its contents on to the table – a collection of cuttings from the Echo and the Post and the paper that I remember Gerald reading every morning over his toast and lime marmalade, his favourite Daily Telegraph. I scanned them quickly and picked one at random.

71

Next to a paragraph headed 'Dock Clerks vote to Return to Work', was a brief item headed 'Young Woman Found Dead at Home'. I started to read on to see what had been reported of the momentous day.

The body of Liverpool University English Literature student April Kingston (22), was found last night at her parent's home in the well-to-do suburb of Crosby Blundellsands. A police spokesman said that she appeared to have been savagely attacked with an unknown weapon some time during the early afternoon and that they were treating the case as one of murder. An appeal is being made for any persons who were in the vicinity of Serpentine Drive between 1 and 8 p.m. yesterday and who saw anything at all unusual to come forward.

A neighbour, architect Toby Ainsdale (49), said that the whole district had been shocked by this senseless and brutal killing and that he hoped that the vagrant or burglar responsible for it would be caught as soon as possible. He added that April had been a lovely girl and that everyone's sympathies lay with the Kingston family in their sad loss. Anyone with any information is urged to contact the CID at Crosby or their local police station as soon as possible. A reward of £500 has been offered for information leading to an arrest.

I paused. £500 was a lot of money even now – and in those days it was certainly a hell of a lot of money. Who, I wondered, had put up that sum and why? I couldn't find anything to suggest that a press conference had been arranged but was that something that the papers would have bothered to report then? I was surprised how stark

72

and unemotional it had all seemed and there had been no account of the part that Ros and I had played in the finding of her body. But then I supposed that it was hardly the sort of thing that you would have wanted a mention for and at that time I had more pressing concerns on my mind than worrying about any lack of public recognition.

I could easily imagine the inhabitants of the 'well-to-do suburb' reading the news over their starched tablecloths and commenting upon how dreadful it was that there were criminal types and psychopaths roaming their streets and how despite the ever-increasing domestic rates burden the police never seemed to do anything about stopping them. And, if April had not been my cousin, perhaps I too would have thought this.

A paragraph in Monday's Echo then caught my eye.

Crosby police are anxious to interview Barry John Leemings (22), a postgraduate student believed to be living in the Walton area of the city, in connection with the death of local girl April Kingston. See page 6.

There was no page six included in the bundle I had received but I knew that Barry Leeming had himself died shortly days later in a motorbike crash and that the trail had gone cold and that no one, whether Barry or anyone else had ever been charged with April's death.

I picked up another cutting, this time dated several weeks later. The article featured a picture of 'Gerald, grieving father of the pretty 22-year old', and a load of old tosh, ending with a purportedly direct quote from my uncle even though I was sure that the reporter had put the words into his head.

April's mother and I miss her terribly, She was a bright young girl with everything to live for. I believe that whoever attacked her intended to kill her. I would ask anyone who is shielding this person to come forward. He, or she, is out there and must be caught and brought to Justice. We are now increasing the award for any information that helps to apprehend April's killer to £2,000.

*****

I was still pouring over the packet and its contents and the fact that I had lost track of Ros since then when I heard Kirsty come in. I gathered the papers into a neat bundle and tried to assume the look of a disapproving father.

'Sorry Dad. I know it's a bit later than I said but we couldn't get in to the earlier showing and...' She stopped in mid-sentence, puzzled by my lack of response.

'Dad, are you alright?'

I nodded and then, because she was obviously expecting it, added in a testy and rather unconvincing manner, added disapprovingly, 'You ought to have phoned when you knew you weren't going to make it in for twelve. I was worried.'

She smiled in a way that she knew would win me over, said something about the battery on her mobile phone being flat and gave me a peck on the cheek. Then, assuming that the papers on the floor were something to do with my work, she looked concerned.'

'You know, Dad, you should get a life – go out more often, I mean. Maybe to one of those jazz evenings that you used to enjoy with Gavin and meet people and...'

She paused dramatically. 'You might even meet a new woman.'

I smiled and wondered what the reaction of my fiercely concerned daughter would be when, and if, I ever brought Jessica home to meet her,

'I wasn't actually working tonight, Kirsty. I was just reading through some family papers that have been sent to me. Something important has come up.' She looked puzzled. 'I might need to go up to Liverpool for a few days to sort matters out.'

'What sort of matters, mein vater?'

'Oh, just something to do with uncle Gerald's death and his will. Nothing important.'

She nodded, and seemed to swallow this half-truth.

'That case about a seed potato contract that I told you about – you probably don't remember me telling you about it at all. Well the case has settled so I don't have to spend wasted days with a calculator and a cold compress wondering about bloody seed potatoes in Lincolnshire. So as I've got nothing else urgent on, I just thought that I would go up for a few days next week. You don't mind, do you? You could always go and stay with your mum. She's been asking to see you.'

'No thanks, I'd rather not go there. I can't stand that Roland character. He's a complete dork. Patronises me the whole time and thinks that he can buy me off by bunging the odd twenty-quid note. What an idiot he is. I can't for the life of me see what mum sees in him.'

I tried not to smile but Kirsty's assessment of any replacement was, so far as I was concerned, very astute.

'I can't very well leave you here on your own.'

She chuckled and said, 'I'm a big girl now and it would be great to have the flat to myself as I've get lots to do for the exams and there would be no distractions with you away. Hey, chill out I'm not going to have any wild parties, take drugs, trash the place or...' she lowered her voice to a conspiratorial whisper '...or move Alan in or do anything you might disapprove of.' I laughed and had to concede that Kirsty was rather more worldly than I had been at her age or even now and probably had more common sense than I was ever likely to have.

'I suppose that you could always phone your mum if there was any problem.' Not, as I thought, that Fran would be much use if there was, given her current obsession with spending time with the dork-like Roland.

'I will do, Pops, but listen. How's about me coming up to be with you on Saturday morning and staying for the weekend? You're always banging on about how great the 'Pool is and I haven't been there for absolute yonks. Sophie at school told me that the Tate Northern's really great and that there's some fab shops around. I could go all sixties retro, Cavern, Merseybeat an' all that.'

I was about to tell her that my Liverpool had changed a lot since the Sixties and probably never was like she had imagined it to have been even then. But I was impressed by her cod Scouse accent, honed from countless episodes of her favourite soap which she watched while she was supposed to be doing homework and I thought, yes, why not? It had been years since we had been back there together and it would make a welcome break from the grim task that I had decided, against my better judgment, that I was going to do for Gerald.

5

It was a little after five and, in deference to the long-standing tradition in our chambers, we were having our usual Friday evening soiree in Henry Atterson's room. As I cast my eye over my colleagues, it occurred to me that I worked with a collection of palpable eccentrics and malcontents and that for some inexplicable reason, I really quite liked most of them. And, as always, the wine, a cheeky little Chablis which John had bought at a considerable discount from one of his many acquaintances 'in the trade' and passed to us with his customarily modest mark-up, was surprisingly good.

There was, it seeded, a light-hearted mood among the dozen or so members present, helped no doubt by the sudden and belated arrival of Spring that afternoon and unsurprisingly most of the conversation revolved around the forthcoming Easter vacation. Henry was sounding off about his bijou residence in far-famed Patterdale and just as I walked in he was advising Sabrina Watkins in booming tones that she was welcome to come up for a week to sample the beauties of spring in the Lake District and see how magnificent the daffodils were. Sabrina, the newest and probably most nubile tenant in our chambers, was a recent Oxford graduate of impeccable if somewhat haughty tastes and as I watched she politely but firmly gave Henry the heave-ho. I couldn't blame her, for although he had the reputation of being a lecherous old goat, his wife Dilwys was even more insufferable, possibly as a result of having had to live with Henry for so long.

'Henry, can I asked you something?' I said, without any idea of what it was that I was going to ask but I knew that this was the time to help Sabrina make her escape. But Henry took the chance to address me before I could ask him anything.

'Ah, Christopher! I saw that you were having a conference with that Tierney chappie the other day.'

Sabrina, suitably grateful, managed to make good her escape and Henry, oblivious as usual to any slight, began to address me in hectoring tones.

'I didn't know you were acquainted with him, Henry.'

'I am indeed but only, you understand, in a strictly business capacity.'

'Do you mean that you've acted for him?'

'Good heavens, no! Why the dishonesty shimmers off the man like the heat off a summer road! I would most certainly not represent someone like him. That would be more than I could stand! No, in case you were unaware of it Christopher, your Mr Tierney has a reputation for being one of the great litigators de nos jours. The truth of the matter is that I once did a case for some poor chap that was at the receiving end of one of his writs. Absolute balls-up it was and we won quite handsomely, though I say it myself.'

There were no half-measures with Henry whether it came to ordering spirits at someone else's expense or in praising his own efforts in one of his 'most fascinating cases I just happened to be in' histories which he endlessly recounted to anyone who hadn't the foresight to be elsewhere. I began to wonder on whose side the 'absolute balls-up' had been and then realised that he was still talking.

'...and, of course, he loves to sue all and sundry does Tierney but, strange thing is, he never seems to bear grudges.'

'Unlike you', I thought.

'You know after that case that I was telling you about he came up to me and started going on about where the best fishing rivers in Ireland were. Then without as much as a by-your-leave the damned fellow suggested that I might like to go with him on a fishing holiday and he could coach me into how to tie a cast on the Owencarrow or some such water. Do you know, he only wanted my company in darkest Donegal. What an extraordinary chap he is, most peculiar and, come to think of it, as daft as a proverbial brush.'

I couldn't help feeling that this particular definition fairly accurately summed up Henry himself and wondered why he didn't have more success with fishing, given his ability to bore almost anything to death. He continued on his set subject unabated, and as the concept of time seemed to have been temporarily suspended, I was forced to make the occasional terse comment to keep awake. I returned to the planet just as Henry began to launch into a denunciation of one of the Benchers of his Inn who wilfully, maliciously and without due cause had failed to invite Dilwys and himself to a champagne reception in honour of some visiting Panamanian lawyers.

'Bloody cheek and do you know Christopher, the worst thing about it was that it was a bloody good beano, or so I heard afterwards.' Surely no one still used words like 'beano' in this post-modern age but as I looked at

Henry and studied his face carefully, I could see no sign that he was not taking himself entirely seriously. In desperation, I waived to Gavin Teviotdale to come over and bail me out.

Gavin was, and is, one of my best friends and had been ever since we had both been pupils here in these chambers back in the late seventies. He had never been able to take the full majesty of the law seriously either and this, together with his almost wholly misplaced sense of humour, endeared me to him from the moment that we had first met. The only senior counsel in our chambers to specialise in criminal law, Gavin had a slightly raffish and disreputable air about him, despite his obvious ability to win difficult cases by the application of sound legal principles and common sense. A combination so unusual that it often seemed to go above the heads of the appeal court judges (or so he claimed). He had been swapping banter with Jennifer Collman, our family law and trusts guru with whom I had been earlier discussing aspects of the Heraclides IV affair.

Jenny, a large and congenial Yorkshire lass who was both extremely loud and, on occasions, extremely sensitive, was emitting stentorian hoots as Gavin recounted one of his racy and possibly true autobiographical tales. Being Gavin's, their emphasis was on the vulgar and sexist. Remarks suitable for few, if any, social gatherings such as this. But Jenny was always amused by Gavin's tales of the unlikely and her laughter reverberated around the room like the echo of a demented banshee, causing Henry to frown and thus look even more preposterous than he usually did.

Eventually Jennifer drifted away to chat with others and Gavin, after a few more jests, came straight to the point by asking me the identity of 'that charming little solicitrix that was in chambers the other day'. I suspected that he had already made enquiries of her in the clerks room but I told him her name anyway and by my manner attempted to show that Jessica Goodchild was of little consequence to me. Gavin, however, knew me all too well and offered to intercede with her on my behalf. I politely declined, having a pretty shrewd idea of the forth of intercession that he had in mind, and rapidly turned the situation around by enquiring after the health of Julia, his fecund and attractive, in a rather earth-motherly sort of way, wife.

This seemed to trigger off a long spate of venom about his bank manager, the connection apparently being that Julia had just redecorated their rambling Tunbridge Wells house by the use of a skilful but prolonged raid on their current account. This had led to what he described as 'a temporary stall in the progress of his cash flow situation', and in consequence, the bank turning nasty. I began to lose track as he went on to detail how their five children (all of whom, when they were younger, fondly called me 'Uncle Chris') near as we were to the season of goodwill would probably starve as a result and that there would be no money left to buy his only daughter the rather expensive horse that he had rashly promised her. After a litany of university fees and the need to properly support his first grandchild (at this point I resisted butting in to intimate that he should get his good-for-nothing son-in-law to face up to his responsibilities on that score), I suggested that it was perhaps all the fault of the Legal Aid authorities who should pay him the balance of the huge sums that they owed. He cheered up at this, saying that, 'It usually was, but hell it's only money after all and who cares?'

'Perhaps you should sue them', I said, 'and then it would be a case of biting the hand that fails to feed you.'

He ignored this quip and then admitted that the real reason he was so annoyed today was that he had just been given a kicking in the criminal appeal court on 'another bloody human rights issue that they don't, or won't, understand.' His explanation was cut short by Jennifer who had returned in majesty with the oily Michael Shalway in tow.

Michael was flushed with his success at Snaresbrook ('waited all day but got him off with only a hundred pounds and four penalty points') and I felt marginally less guilty about having sent him out to further reaches of the Central Line in the first place. Jennifer, however, was clearly bursting to tell us something and intervened before Michael could elaborate on his day in the far-flung Orient.

'Is it true, about Henry, I mean?'

'What, that he might actually have a brain?'

'Shush, Gavin, keep your voice down! He may be stupid but he's not totally deaf.' The idea of Jennifer trying to keep the peace amused me. Then Michael Shalway spoke.

'Well, I did hear in the robing room at Snaresbrook that there's a rumour doing the rounds that Henry has been having discussions with the Judicial Appointments Commission and I was told that our very own Gary claims to have seen a rather important letter.'

'He would, bloody little creep that he is. I have a suspicion he steams open all the 'confidential' envelopes we get.'

'Jennifer, shut up for a moment! Michael, are you really telling us – do you actually mean that... no, it couldn't be. It's too ridiculous a thought and Henry's not exactly in with the spirit of the times, is he?'

Michael Shalway grinned, obviously anxious to spill the beans. 'Yep, it's true! It is the age of equality and inclusion but I've done a bit of rootling about and my sources, which must remain confidential of course, are entirely reliable. All right Gavin, before you say anything I admit that it's my uncle Giles who just happens to be a judge himself. But anyway he's confirmed that Henry's definitely been appointed to the High Court bench. So it looks as if we'll all have the chance to appear before him – it'll be a sort of Russian roulette in the daily list, I suppose.'

'Hells Bells, that can't be true? I heard the rumour too but thought that it was only a sick joke. I reckon I'll just have to go and ask Henry myself.'

Even Gavin was appalled at Jennifer's lack of discretion but before he could stop her, she was striding across the room and bellowing loudly. 'Henry, I hear that congratulations are in order.'

Henry was clearly flustered. 'Er, well, it's not actually been announced yet but well, damn it, I was going to make a formal announcement to you all soon. Yes, all right, since I clearly can't keep anything quiet round here. Ladies and Gentlemen, I take up my appointment on the bench in May.'

'You are a dark horse, Henry', said Jennifer and, amidst the general hubbub of congratulations which followed, I distinctly heard Gavin say, 'More like an grey ass', a remark I felt a distinct possibility that Henry had also caught.

'I suppose that will mean we'll have to choose a new head of chambers', remarked Michael Shalway rather obviously.

'Almost anyone would be better than Henry', added Gavin maliciously. 'What do you think, Chris?'

'You knew that I've never been interested in internal chambers politics', I said. Which was perfectly true and I was uniquely qualified to make this point since I was the only person in chambers who would now admit to the fact that I had voted for Henry last time round, even if I couldn't remember why.

Gavin then remarked that Henry was 'the meanest fool in Christendom', and, 'unfit to run a beerhouse', although the logic of the latter escaped me. I remembered the last showdown we had in chambers, a disagreement between Henry and John over whether certain mail should go out by first or second class post – the dispute had arisen after Henry had interfered with the franking machine and caused John to waste a valuable afternoon trying in vain to fix it again. Good old Henry, I thought, and then it occurred to me that 'good riddance to the old pretender' was perhaps a more appropriate sentiment at this particular time.

The Chablis and the banter were beginning to run out when shortly before six the others announced that they were adjourning to the pub to plot out who they would wish to occupy the throne in the post-Henry era. I felt, somewhat churlishly, that I had had enough of both the wine and the company and besides I was getting peckish so I told them that I was sorry but that I had to go home without delay. On my way out the reptilian Gary, no doubt cheered up by the fact that several of us were showing signs of moderate intoxication and thus proving ourselves to be human or at least less teetotal and puritan than himself, emerged from the clerk's room and scuttled over to me like a sycophantic crab.

'Sorry to trouble you Mr K, but, um, there was a message from Ms. Goodchild to say that she will be sending you a further bundle of papers in the Glenbreen case for the week after next.'

I briefly studied the leering moon-like face and wondered if he knew that I had designs on Jessica or if he was merely displaying the powers of a true clairvoyant. Perhaps he had conferred with that damned red-haired assistant clerk Mandy in the chambers next door who, I was sure, had been lurking around in the vicinity of the Italian restaurant the previous day in order to spy on me. John always claimed that ginger-nut knew everything that was going on for miles around including things that she had no business to know. Just my luck to find out that she was a bosom pal of Gary. I decided, perhaps unwisely, against firmly planting my shoe on Gary's posterior and, with only the slightest hint of sarcasm, thanked him sincerely for the information while resolving to have a word as soon as possible with John about Gary's career progression.

Hurrying down the steps, I replaced the violent thoughts of what I would have liked to do with Gary with the rather more pleasurable ones of what, given the chance, I would like to do with Jessica. Gavin was standing outside waiting for me.

'Come on, Chris. Don't be a party pooper! We're all off to the Black Friar for a pint.'

I hesitated and my resolve failed so that minutes later we were seated in a darkened corner of that exuberant art-nouveau establishment. I listened as

Jennifer gave out her robust if not altogether tactful thoughts about the succession to King Henry the Inept, whom she picturesquely described in rapid sequence as being 'a braggart, a Scaramouch and a poltroon', apparently all in one go.

'Must you always be such a walking thesaurus, Jenny?'

'As long as your sure that it's a walking thesaurus you're calling me and not a walking something else, I don't mind. You know how I like using words, Gavin, and so should you, too. The English language is, after all, the stock-in-trade of us at the Bar even when we're in such an advanced stage of vinolency as this.'

The discussion about the new head of chambers continued and I quickly became bored. I didn't really care who they wanted to choose and besides nobody even went through the motions of asking me for my view. I smiled, and remembered that, according to Gavin, I was totally clueless and had sod all influence in chambers anyway. Pick who they damn well want, I thought, but don't involve me.

I tuned in to a conversation at the next table. Two young counsel were having an animated discussion about an expert witness who seemed to specialise in traffic prediction at planning inquiries. 'He's very strange. You know that bushy beard he has? Well, the last time I was leading him in chief, I swear that he had a large and very dead bumble bee caught up in his beard and I couldn't concentrate on the script because I just wanted to ask him if the question was one of to bee or not to bee.'

His companion chuckled, probably not having heard the story before. 'I did hear of a solicitor who had to collect some papers from his house and he was confronted on the doorstep by the sight of your bearded chap sans bee but wearing a very fetching flowery dress with matching accessories. Apparently he greeted him with, 'Never mind this old frock, darling. I was just dressing down for Friday.' Anyway there's no need to be formal. Just call me Gladys.'

'That reminds me of a story that my sister's husband once told me...' I never heard the end because another round was being ordered at our table and if there's one thing that lawyers like doing it's recycling old jokes and then passing them off as their own. I volunteered to help Gavin fetch the drinks so that I could take the opportunity to pick his brains.

'Gavin, what would you do if...'

'If I was Henry? Shoot myself.'

'No, seriously I need your advice about a personal thing because I really don't know what to do.' He looked surprised. 'You see, something once happened in our family, a very long time ago. It was something very bad and nothing was done about it then but now I want to find out all about what really went on and why and...' I trailed off and Gavin looked puzzled.

'Are you talking about the girl, that cousin of yours, the one who was killed and you discovered her body?'

I remembered that I had once, in this very same pub, told him about April and how I had found her body and somehow the fact that he'd remembered made it all less daunting to tell him more. So, as the harassed barman took our orders and as the Guinness flowed creamy-headed from the tap, I gave him a brief resume of Gerald's letter and the contents of the packet.

After I had finished telling him everything I was anxious to add, 'But keep it all to yourself, Gavin, and don't tell anyone, least of all any of our colleagues.' And then I suddenly felt that I didn't want to go any further with the conversation, being suddenly afraid I'd already said too much, or started something I couldn't stop.

'My advice, Chris, for what it's worth, is that you leave everything alone. It's not worth the hassle. It wouldn't do any good to rake over the past – your cousin has been dead for a very long time now and it would probably be a great waste of time and effort to attempt to rake over everything at this late stage. Just think – if the police couldn't solve it then why do you think you could? Don't get me wrong, though, because as you know I've got little enough faith in them, but if they hadn't anything to go on in nineteen seventy whenever it was then you're hardly going to succeed now.'

'I did make a promise to my uncle, though. A sort of promise, anyway...'

'And you now feel that because of that you're in some way duty bound to him to dig up the dirt or whatever that he couldn't or wouldn't himself?'

But before I could reply we were interrupted by Jennifer's unmistakeable war-cry.

'Where the hell are our drinks then, gringos?'

'Hang on!'

He quietly ended with, 'Look, just believe me Chris. Let sleeping dogs lie. Quieter non movere as Henry would say. Don't stir things up now. Just let the past remain the past.'

He studied my face with interest. 'Chris, be honest though, why are you wasting my time asking my opinion? You know that you're going to do it anyway, . whatever I say. Let's face it, I probably would if it were me. Do it if you feel that you must but just remember what I said about keeping the past and the present well clear of each other.'

I could see that he was concerned about me as a friend that he didn't want to see come to any harm.

'Chris, it's really a bit like East and West, never the twain shall meet, that kind of thing. Coming Jen, I've just ordered the drinks so hold your horses.'

And with Gavin's advice going through my head we settled into the serene womb of the Black Friar. Three days later, I was on my way back to the North.

6

CROSBY, a township situated in the former parish of Sefton, in the hundred of West Derby and in the county palatine of Lancaster, stands on the sandy coastline some seven and three-quarter miles north of the great city and port of Liverpool. Although this attractively situated place, with its littoral off-shoot of Blundellsands, is now chiefly known as a suburban resort of the highest calibre, its name, derived from the Scandinavian, suggests that this is a settlement whose very roots go far back into that distant and misunderstood period now known to us as the Dark Ages...

As I watched the train clatter away, I repeated the words which began *A Short History of Great Crosby*, published by the author in 1938 and available from him at the price of three shillings and sixpence (net), postage and packing fourpence extra. It was a slim, largely forgotten book whose only claim to fame, so far as our family were concerned, lay in the fact that it was written by my late grandfather, Septimus J. Kingston, known universally to his friends and foes alike as Sep.

I wondered if my cousin Ben could still outdo me in quoting from what the author described as his 'modest monograph' and smiled, remembering the great rivalry between us when we challenged each other to recall what came next in any randomly picked passage. I pondered on why we had both been so fascinated by it all. Perhaps it was because it had been the only book that any relative of ours had ever written or maybe it was simply a reflection of our fondness and appreciation for the foibles of an affectionate but eccentric grandfather.

I put down my bag and stood and looked at the scene which was at once both so familiar to me and yet so remote now from my everyday life. The phalanx of red-brick houses marched reassuringly westwards. The brave March sun was shining, the well-bred suburban birds were enthusiastically singing and the wind was gusting up from the sea which lay beyond the distant sand dunes at the end of the street.

What, I wondered, would Sep have made of April's death, he who had so doted upon her, his only granddaughter? At least he had been spared the misery and the heartache of it all. By a stroke of both fortune and his failing cardiac system, he had quietly predeceased her by only a matter of months and, in that respect, it could be said that he had been lucky.

I crossed the road and walked up to the solid, imposing and vaguely Jacobean hotel which in my youth I had seldom visited even though it was only a few hundred yards from where we had lived. I booked in, a fresh-faced girl at reception smiled as she handed over the key and I realised on refection that she had not even been born when I had last set foot in the area. Then I went up the broad stairway to my comfortable chintzy bedroom where I lay out on the bed for a few minutes and recovered from the uneventful but tiring journey. Having worked out how to put the kettle on, I began to study the borrowed phone book on the bedside table and soon found the only Twentyman who seemed to fit the picture. Without giving myself time to rethink the matter, I made the call.

While I waited for him to answer, I began to think about what I could expect of him. Twentyman had been in early middle age – in his late forties at least – when I had last seen him so he would be pretty decrepit by now. He must, in any event, have changed a lot for he could hardly still be the pale and rather overweight character with the look of a scrum-half gone to seed that we met in the police station.

I rehearsed again the little speech that I had made up in the hope that when he answered I would seem a little less nervous than I actually was. Quite what it was that was making me nervous I was not sure. The very thought of speaking to him again was like having to having to meet one of your teachers from way back and not knowing whether to defer to the authority which they once had or to treat them like the equal they never were. Perhaps he had even gone a bit gaga with the long passage of time and in any case would he now be able to recall anything useful of the subject that I intended to ask him about?

When the phone was answered, I didn't recognise the voice, for it sounded frail and as though it was coming from a greater distance away than just a handful of miles across the Mersey. Without hesitation I told him who I was and was pleasantly surprised to see how much more on the ball he was than I had expected.

'Ah yes, young Christopher Kingston. It's been a long time you know, indeed a very long time, since we last spoke. Of course, that was in, shall we say, less than happy circumstances. But how are you now lad? Mind, though, you'd hardly be a lad now. I saw that you got your place at Cambridge. It was in the Crosby Herald, so it must have been true, mustn't it? A veritable Pravda of a newspaper they say.'

He chuckled and a fit of coughing ensued so that I never found out who that particular quote was attributed to but I thought that the Herald, like all local papers of old, probably had a lot to answer for.

'I wonder, though, did you ever become a lawyer like you said you were going to be?'

There was clearly nothing wrong with his memory then, although for the life of me I had no recollection of ever having mentioned my career ambitions to him. But he sounded genuinely friendly now and so relaxed that I had an inkling that Gerald must have spoken to him and told him that one day soon he would be hearing from me again. Twentyman warmly invited me to his home the following afternoon and gave me rather convoluted directions as to how to get there, directions which were unnecessary since I had already been studying the street map I'd bought earlier. He then wished me a cheery goodbye, told me that he was looking forward to seeing me and rang off abruptly. I then made a second call.

'Hello, Gateacre Media Services, Lorraine here and how may I help you? Mr Kingston, is it? I'll just put you through – you did say you were Mr Ben's cousin, didn't you?' I confirmed this, so she put me through without delay and a voice answered abruptly.

'It's me – Chris', I said. Ben, having obviously not been told by Lorraine whom to expect, softened his manner and I thought that he sounded pleased to be hearing from me. I told him that I was up in town for a few days on some business, carefully saying nothing about my real reason for being there. 'Any chance of meeting up for a chat? I'm staying at the Blundellsands Hotel.'

'The Blundellsands? Oh, very posh and quite near our old stomping ground as well. Look, it'd be really good to see you again but the thing is that Malcolm and I are off to Scotland chasing up some work and we're going to make a trip of it and visit his folks at the same time. So I'm afraid it would really have to be tonight or... No, no, that's fine, well we'll look forward to seeing you tonight round about seven thirty then and you can see our new home and sample Malcolm's famous cooking.'

It was all a bit sudden and I wondered whether I should have followed my instincts and turned around at Euston before any harm had been done. Let sleeping dogs lie as Gavin had said, so what the hell was I doing back here in the former parish of Sefton, in the hundred of West Derby and the County Palatine of Lancas, many miles away from the world that I now lived in. What indeed? My mother would have said that I was now 'in for a penny, in for a pound'.

I felt that I needed a walk to clear my head and after changing my clothes and taking a quick shower I found myself turning left by the station and heading, as if drawn by a magnet, back towards Serpentine Drive. I had little idea as to why I wanted to see that ill-fated house again and perhaps I half-hoped that it had gone altogether, replaced by one of the flimsy blocks of apartments that had sprung up like unwelcome mushrooms all over the suburbs. I didn't know where it was that Ben had just moved out from but I bet that it hadn't been his former childhood home in Blundellsands where I was now revisiting – not after what had happened there, to be sure.

I turned the corner and, a few minutes and yet all these years later, I was back in that well-remembered stretch of Serpentine Drive. To both my delight and dismay the house was still there, and someone was clearly living there.

I stopped to examine the building. Before me rose a rambling mixture of brick, Carrara and terracotta with barge-boarded gables and, proudly displayed over the rustic front entrance, the date '1898'. From the street a short sweep of gravel passed a neat front lawn on which miniature goalposts and a small football net had been placed. To the right, stood a small building which Gerald had always insisted on calling 'the motorcar house'. I only remembered it being used to store an ancient green Alvis which my uncle had rarely driven but had spent many happy hours taking apart and tinkering with while his rather smart grey Peugeot and Maura's hideous mustard-coloured Volvo estate had been left to sit outside in all weathers.

I found myself pleased to see that the place hadn't been knocked down. Everything about it looked just about the same as I remembered it, and it even seemed to exude the same air of homeliness, respectability and wealth. Yet I knew in myself that things had changed and I could no longer recreate the past. Even if the stage might superficially have been the same the cast of the actors had most definitely changed. I stood beside the freshly painted gate and wondered what the people who now lived at this address were like and whether or not they were aware of its once notorious past.

I held back and then, in a moment of madness, pushed the gate open and walked up the drive. There appeared to be no one in. I waited, cursing my foolhardiness and hoping that the doorbell would remain unanswered since I had no idea of what I was going to say if someone did appear. I could, after all, hardly announce that I had popped round to look at the house in which I had once found a corpse. Fleetingly, it crossed my mind to go straight round to the shrub embowered back.

Several seconds elapsed and I had already turned back towards the road when a voice behind me said, 'Yeah?' It was a boy of about ten wearing shorts and a bright red jersey which gave little doubt as to which of the city's two football teams he supported.

'Er, is your mum in?'

He looked at me with growing suspicion.

'You're not from the bizzes, are you?'

I shook my head, wondering what dark secrets lay on his conscience. He seemed reasonably unsatisfied with this response but went in to get his mother while I tried to work out what to say next. I felt that it was like being in court and realising that you had to say something rather than admit that you hadn't been paying any attention to what the judge had been rabbiting on about. But I was heartened by the fact that I knew, as always, that I would be able to come up with something or other that sounded faintly plausible.

A woman, of about thirty five or so and with an ersatz tan and dressed in an expensive but tacky frock top with a golden dragon design, appeared with a querulous expression on her face.

'Can I help you?'

Not much warmth there, and little curiosity either. The voice was recently refined but still with a slight twang to suggest that this was a family who had come up in the world in the not too distant past.

'Good afternoon, madam! What a lovely house this seems to be, if I may say.'

There was no response so I had to try harder. 'I represent C. A. R. T. – Crosby Architectural Research Trust that is.'

She looked at me as though I had come from another planet. 'We're compiling a record of houses of outstanding merit in the Crosby area. We're particularly interested in beautiful Blundellsands homes such as yours.'

This sounded lame and I paused, hoping that there was no real organisation of that name or, if there was, that she had never heard of it. The woman, however, continued to look blank but less hostile than before.

'I was wondering, er, if it might be possible to have a brief look inside at the principal rooms in the house and possibly take an artistic photograph or two in order to ascertain whether or not the house would be eligible for one of our merit awards. Of course if it does then we would present you with a nice cast plaque which you could put up on the wall so that everyone would know.'

She still looked at me dubiously, possibly misconstruing the term "artistic photograph". 'The plaque would be free of charge of course and might impress your discerning friends who appreciate architectural beauty.' Did she have any discerning friends who were even capable of appreciating architecture? I doubted it, but at least she hadn't thrown me out onto the pavement.

'Oh, by the way, I forgot to introduce myself. My name is, er, Hawksmoor, Nicholas Hawksmoor.'

I wondered if I had made that sound too much like, 'Bond, James Bond', and I could feel her eyes scanning me as though I was an item at the check-out. I was glad that at least I had put on a decent jacket and clean shoes and that I had used my best QC manner of authority and quasi-sincerity. At least, I reassured myself, she didn't seem to think it unlikely that Wren's most promising pupil had been resurrected and had turned up on her doorstep.

She smiled wanly, and invited me in with such little enthusiasm that I doubted if the promise of a plaque had made any real difference either to her imagined importance or even her standing in the area.

I entered the front hall, anxious to see how much the house had changed since I had last been in it and whether the refined taste of Maura was still evident. It appeared that it was was not. Textured wallpaper, Chinese animals, marble topped tables and a plethora of highly decorated wrought iron lamps that had been placed next to soft leather settees were evident throughout. I felt angry that this house, which in its time had meant a lot to me, had now been so thoughtlessly violated by such an obvious display of bad taste. No wonder my daughter accused me of being an aesthetic snob.

I followed the woman along the passage towards the back of the house and as we walked through I realised that there was a further unpleasant surprise in store. I had steeled myself to enter the little conservatory where April's body had lain upon the now vanished tiles but it was there no more. In its stead was a much plainer but considerably larger glass and tasteless aluminium structure containing potted chain-store palms with price-tags still attached, some dubious statues of scantily clad women and some overly expensive bamboo furniture of the kind advertised in those annoying little catalogues of "essential home innovations" that fall out of the Sunday supplements.

A lank-haired girl in a towelled bathrobe was lazily examining her toenails while somewhere in the background an over enthusiastic Radio One voice was aimlessly talking to herself in a flat estuary accent.

'Cheryl love, turn down the sound for the gentleman, will you?' The girl disobligingly ignored her and continued with her pedicure. 'Kids these days! Well now that you're here what do you think of our garden room, then?'

I tried to be non-committal about the abomination of the new structure and its name but found it hard not to say anything that displayed my real thoughts.

'It's really nice this, isn't it? Much better than that dreary old thing that was here before although, mind, we're still having a bit of trouble from that lot on the council. You know those fools from the so-called planning department with their enforcement notices and all that malarkey. What a pain they've been objecting to me getting rid of all that junk and the ugly old flooring.'

I nodded meekly, feeling that the planning department had probably acknowledged defeat in their crusade against the Visigoths, and had resigned themselves to the loss of the Minton tiles. I wondered if the woman was really as bad as she seemed but decided on reflection that she probably was.

We left Cheryl to her wireless delights and I followed the lady of the house into what she described as the lounge and which I had known as the living room, a large and airy place with a full-length window looking out over the generous back garden. Mercifully the room had changed little apart from an invasion of a home cinema and other technological miracles. I was glad that the living room had not been metamorphosed into some tawdry chamber like the 'garden room' for it was in here, at one of Maura's 'at homes' that, perversely, I had first met Ros. I say perversely because at least in my mind the co-existing worlds of Maura and Ros were always kept well apart and I have still never quite worked out what the connection was between my aunt and Ros' family that resulted in her being there on that particular day.

I gazed around the room and imagined the scene again. Maura was, as usual, being intensely irritating and intent on her customary game of forcing introductions upon me while I, sullen from the shyness and adolescent awkwardness which even now I have not quite fully outgrown, was intent upon avoiding all of the people that she might have wanted me to meet. This time even Maura, thick-skinned and persistent as always, could see that I was not even going to pretend to be sociable, particularly if she forced me to be so but she obviously thought that a lack of manners did not excuse me for anything. At last and in near desperation at my truculence, she searched the room for the only other young person present, even though she had clearly forgotten who that person was.

'This, my dear', she gushed, 'is my nephew Topher. He's very clever, you know, very clever indeed and he's going to be a lawyer.'

With this brief and undeniably ludicrous and unfair introduction, Maura was off to forage for a gin and yet more guests to conjoin against their will and I was left in peace, standing next to a nice-looking girl of about my own age and looking equally embarrassed. I smiled at her and explained to her that actually I preferred to be called

Christopher or Chris for short and that I did not necessarily agree with my aunt's view of my intellect. The girl just smiled in an engaging way.

'Never mind, Chris. That's just the kind of thing mad aunties do, isn't it? By the way, my name's Rosamond, but my friends call me Ros.'

I think that I must have made some inane comment to the effect that I too would like to call her Ros. And, in that gauche and awkward way that teenagers often strike up a conversation, we began to talk about what mattered to us most: our friends, family, books, films and even our future plans – the things we liked most and even the things we hated. I remember that we particularly discussed music and after I told her how I was into jazz, folk, Pentangle and Planxty, she told me that she was keen on Steeleye Span, Fairport Convention and, best of all, the, 'He's really great but you won't have heard of him', someone called Nick Drake. We were definitely on the same wavelength there and before long she was humming the tune of 'Bryter Layter'. I think I fell for her right then and there.

We continued to talk to each other for what seemed like several hours and eventually when it was time to go home we had already made arrangements to meet up the next day. I have often looked back on that initial encounter with Ros and tried to analyse my feelings about her. Even though I later on tried to dismiss them as being the product of my youthful hormones or in retrospect the sentimental longings of a dispirited middle-aged man, I think that from then onwards I knew that I was under a spell. Ros, with her flowing green dress and malachite necklace was to me different, spiritual, exciting and, although it sounds pretentious now, I really did believe then that she was the epitome of all the qualities that I could never put a name to but, had I looked up in the old dictionary my father kept for games of Scrabble, would have found the word to fit – 'refulgence.'

Later, when I had got to know Ros better and was accustomed to seeing her still with that string of green beads on but having swapped that dress for something more mundane like her faded grey jeans and a favourite sweater she still somehow managed to retain that same exciting and elusive air that I had found so attractive from the very first. I suppose one could say that by now she had become an almost mythical figure to me but even after all of these years since I had last seen her, I could remember that first meeting.

I was brought back to the present by a discreet and rather too genteel little cough and the woman, looking at me in a disinterested and rather bored way, spoke again.

'Will that be all, Mr, er, Hawker I think you said your name was?'

'Yes, yes, thank you very much for your time. You have a most charming house, most charming and, if you don't mind me saying so, most delightfully furnished.'

As I said it, l wondered why it had been necessary for me to use such pointless and demeaning sarcasm. The woman, however, remained expressionless apart from a slight polite flicker of a smile and, to break the silence, I spoke again.

'I wonder if you wouldn't mind if I took a couple of pictures on my phone?'

'No, go ahead, be my guest.' She obviously trusted me – small wonder, I thought, that I had managed to look as though I liked this house.

I took the pictures and then added, 'Most charming roost, charming indeed.'

She looked pleased so I added, 'As I said before, we'll be in touch about the plaque and everything. Good afternoon to you and thank you very much for kindly giving me your time and letting me see your charming house.'

On the way out I passed the boy and, being unable to resist the temptation, smiled at him to counter the look he was giving me – a leer filled with contempt for the fact that in his eyes I was old and either mad or an Everton fan, or quite possibly both.'

'Goodbye, son.'

Sensing, wrongly, that his mother had retreated into the house, he raised two fingers in the surreptitious but impolite gesture that has formed part of our cultural heritage since the English archers first used it at the battle of Crecy. I ignored the sign and turned my back on the boy only to hear, seconds later, the satisfying sound of a slap and his mother, her thinly applied veneer of good breeding slipping for a moment, shouting at him.

'Do that again an' I'll bloody well murder yer.'

Not, I thought, a very apt thing to say in the setting of that particular house.

7

'Hi! You must be the long-lost cousin. I'm Malcolm, Ben's partner', then turning round to face the hallway, announced, 'Ben! Christopher's here.'

There was a muffled exclamation which sounded like, 'Damn, he's a bit early', and then Ben, unruffled as ever, bounded up.

'Welcome to Bookery Nook, Chris.'

I did not need to ask why. There were books everywhere, piled on the floor, double-banked on shelves, arranged in stacks on a coffee table by the side of the sofa and disarranged in an untidy heap by the window. Instantly I felt at home even if these were all the sort of arty books that I cannot warm to.

'I'll have to do something about them before they engulf us', Malcolm said in the lament of the true bibliophile.

When you could see past the books the house was a real period piece, a Victorian cottage that made me feel as though it was deep in the country rather than in an affluent suburb. Ben, sensing that I liked their house, smiled broadly and seemed to be very much the king of his own castle. He was more relaxed and self-assured than I had seen him in a very long time and I was glad that his relationship with Malcolm obviously seemed to be contributing to this.

There was only a year or so between us with him being the elder, and he had always been quite protective of me as indeed April had been of us both. Looking back on it, I don't suppose that we ever had that much in common since Ben was always much more technically minded than me and also very much into sport, which I was not on either count. But as we walked home together from school every day we would chat and make fun of everyone we could think of, trying hard to outdo each other in mimicry and what we fondly imagined passed for satire.

Half the time we made up absurd dialect words or adopted a variety of ludicrous accents including a particularly useful general-purpose Johnny Foreigner we invented, a special language that we would communicate in to the puzzlement of passers-by. This seemed to add to the over the top nature of our relationship and I suspect that neither of us had really been capable of acting in a mature way, not when we were in each other's company.

As adults we had kept in touch, even if we did limit ourselves to standard English with only the odd 'Lad' thrown in for old times' sake. Now that he had branched out into his video production venture and had a new man in his life we didn't seem to have as much to talk about as we had previously done and in a way I missed our once lengthy phone calls.

'You know Ben, I can't help feeling that this – here, I mean – well, it's all a bit like Crosby of old.'

He poured out some wine.

'Bloody suburbs! Aye, well, once a suburban lad, always a suburban lad, eh our Chris?' I winced at the thought and then began to quote from memory, our favourite publication.

'The village is now the centre of...'

Ben chuckled. 'Much too easy, Chris. Er, the centre of an extensive theatre of motor bus operations.'

'By eck, lad, thees done reet well. Extra pickle point if thee can come out with t'next bit.'

Malcolm, looking puzzled, broke in. 'And what in the name of the wee man, is a pickle point?'

Neither of us felt inclined to enlighten him. It was our own private joke and sensing that it would remain so, he sighed and left the room.

'...which ply the principal roads of the locality at regular intervals.'

'Bravo! You know, Chris, that bit about it being the centre of an extensive theatre of motor bus operations sounds rather military considering that our old grandpappie was a conchie.'

Our family had been Quakers and although grandfather Sep had not been the first to defect to the established church, he had been the one to add an 'e' to our surname. Perhaps his refusal to fight was in some way connected to this but because he had always gone on about how he had really enjoyed driving an ambulance at the front so much, I wondered if he hadn't wanted to follow the colours and fight for King and Country and thus eschew the Friends altogether. On the other hand perhaps, like all of us, he was just a mass of contradictions.

Malcolm reappeared and collected up the glasses which had been placed on an ornate piece of furniture that I thought, but not without any great confidence, might have been described as a chiffonier. 'Dinner is served', he announced gravely.

I noted the striped apron with the disarming slogan 'Sixty Years A Queen' and smiled at his coquettish air. Ben and he were still in the early, uncomplicated stages of their relationship and it showed. The bickering, if it ever came, was something to be left to the future. I thought of how Henry Atterson, an unreconstructed old homophobe, would have reacted to this domestic bliss and restrained myself from laughing out loud.

'Quit the 'Carry On Camping', Malkie and just get the food on the table please.'

And, in general obedience to Ben, he did.

The meal was accompanied by much light-hearted banter. At one point Malcolm said, 'Ben and I want to get married because he'd love to see me in a frilly skirt and flowery hat.' This set off a further bout of repartee between them, leaving me feeling that I couldn't compete with their general hilarity and witticisms.

'I hope we're not venturing beyond your cousin's comfort zone', said Malcolm playfully.

'Nonsense Malkie, Chris is far too much of an unapologetic liberal to be disapproving of even your humour', and broke into a line of Robert Burns delivered in an unbelievable parody of the Scots tongue. 'Twas guilty sinners that he meant, not angels such as you.'

Malcolm announced, after he had brought the coffee in, that he had to go back to the office to finish tweaking some computerised sketches which they would need for their forthcoming business trip, and left us to get himself ready.

I kept to myself the thought that Gerald and Maura would never have been so broad-minded and accommodating as Malcolm's parents in Glasgow appeared to be from what he had hinted during the meal. But then broad-minded or accommodating were not concepts that would ever have readily sprung to mind in connection with my aunt and uncle.

'Have you ever been to Glasgow, Christopher?'

'No, not really. I've been to Edinburgh, though – to the festival and with the kids, and that kind of thing.' I missed out that in the year that I stayed on at school for the extra term to sit the Cambridge entrance papers, I had gone up to Edinburgh and stood outside the university hall of residence where Ros now lived as a first year student. But I hadn't the courage to knock on the door and I hadn't even told her that I was coming up to see her so I never actually managed to see her then. Anyway I wondered whether or not she really wanted nothing more to do with me again after that birthday trip had ended so disastrously. Was it because of April's death or did she feel that I had done something wrong? Perhaps I had failed to do something or had so little courage left in me that I didn't have the guts to face up to her? Maybe I didn't want to acknowledge that times were changing and that she would have made new friends by now and well, I was still so unsure of myself back then, not that I'm that much better now.

On a sudden impulse I turned to Ben.

'Do you still keep up with Graham Allbright, you know that chap you used to play cricket with?' Cricket was one of the constant and abiding passions in Ben's life, as attested to by the heap of old Wisdens which threatened to fall off the bookcase at any moment and bring down the two gleaming bats criss-crossed with the signatures of the Lancashire County Boys' team that he once played for.

'Graham Allbright hmm, let me see...'

For a moment he appeared puzzled and then he smiled.

'Do you, by any chance, mean the Graham Allbright who just happened to be the brother of that little Merchant Taylors' girl you used to hang around with?'

'Little Merchant Taylors' girl, indeed. Isn't that just a wee bittie patronising, Ben?'

Ben grinned broadly at Malcolm, who had just come back into the room and interjected on my behalf.

'Forgive me Chris, but as you're well aware I never was one for the lassies. I do wish, incidentally, that Malcolm wouldn't be so critical of me.'

Malcolm just chuckled and said, 'Och, Ben, I wisnae being critical. Anyway, bye to both of youse as I'm awa to my work', and he disappeared into another room.

'But to continue with our discussion, where was I? Oh, yes, about Graham. Well the answer to your question is both yes and no. Yes, in the sense that I did keep up with him for years and no, in the sense that I haven't seen him for some time. I think that he's working abroad in Singapore or some exotic dump like that.'

'I doubt if Singapore can be properly described as a dump, exotic or otherwise – especially if, as I reckon, you've never even been there.'

'I haven't but I meant 'dump' in a metaphorical rather than figurative sense.'

Not wishing to debate the merits of a place that I'd never been to either I returned the conversation to a more important subject. 'So what does he do there in that metaphorical dump?'

'I believe that he's what you might call a financial high-flyer.'

'Is he still doing that?'

'I think so, assuming that he survived the last round of stock market crashes but really I havenae much of a scoob, as Malcolm would say when he's in one of his "more Scots than the real thing" moods.'

He screwed his eyes up and looked thoughtful. 'But surely, Chris, it's not really Graham that you are bothered about, is it?'

I said nothing and he added, 'No, it's the whereabouts of his sister that you're really interested in, is it not – a question of where's your Rozzie now then?'

I nodded, trying not to seem too anxious.

'Hmm I thought so. Well, I think that Rosamund, to use her proper name, might still be living not a million miles from Crosby if I'm not mistaken. But I don't really know where for sure as I haven't seen her since the seventies. I don't even know what she did after graduating in some science or medical subject. Frightfully clever girl, she was – probably still is, too – but I don't know what she saw in you. Intellectually she was out of your class, though I suspect her degree isn't what interested you about her. Anyway I don't know what has become of her now so I can't answer the question you're really hinting at – whether she's got a man in tow or is attached or has been trapped in unholy matrimony or any of that crap. Who knows, maybe she's ended up in a convent. It does seem though, Chris, that for whatever reason, you might still be interested in her, no?'

I had hoped that I had not displayed any emotions but clearly Ben had seen through my guile.

'I merely asked for the sake of interest but it doesn't really matter.' A lie if I ever heard one. But Ben went on regardless.

'Look, I don't know what ideas you've got but just bear in mind it was a long time ago and she's probably married a doctor, is filthy rich and gone to seed now, overweight with four snivelling kids in tow and horrible screaming grandchildren as well. Do y' know I always found our Rozzie with the green beads and her lack of dress sense, well, a trifle anodyne. You know – colourless, boring and conventional even, if you know what I mean.'

I didn't see what he meant at all, but it was high time to change the subject.

We chatted about some other long-lost friends for a while and then Malcolm returned briefly with a briefcase. Looking straight at me, he could sense that I had been disconcerted by what Ben had said. Acting diplomatically he added, 'Look, I'll leave you two laddies to reminisce about the past. Three's a crowd and it's a bit less than inclusive when I dinnae ken any of them anyway. So cheerio, bye yous twos. Oh, and Christopher, nice to meet you at last.'

'And you, Malcolm.'

And with that he picked up his coat, gave me a totally innocent beam and left the room. A moment later l heard the front door shut.

'How's your mum these days, Ben?'

'OK, all things considered – I mean since Gerald died, that is.'

I thought it strange how he'd always referred to his father by his first name but I let that pass. He shifted his position and then moved his chair closer to me.

'Actually, she's not really OK and I suppose I feel a bit sorry for her as she sort of went to pieces after Gerald's death. Now she's hit the bottle even more had and is showing signs of incipient dementia. The really worrying thing though is that she's threatened to sell up in Chester and come and live here with me. As you can imagine that's about the last thing in the world that I would want to happen.'

Knowing Maura and her ways, I could understand his concern.

'Mother and I haven't exactly been hitting it off lately, you see. She doesn't approve – understatement of the century – of Malcolm. Mind you, it wasn't exactly helped by the fact that the last time they met she caught him standing behind her, putting his fingers up like two horns and mooing, which she took personally. I can't think why.'

I held back any comment on this and he continued. 'That's why I didn't think it was right for Malkie to be at Gerald's funeral, otherwise you two would have met before. The irony was that mum took Malkie's non-appearance as an insult and said as much. Oh, but enough of all this! If you really want to know how Maura is getting on why not give her a visit. There are a lot more interesting things to us to talk about than my mother. How are things with you now, Chris? I was genuinely sorry to hear about you and Francesca splitting up.'

'I thought that you never liked her.'

'To be perfectly honest, I didn't like Fran that much. She never really seemed your type, all la-di-da and stuck up, which you aren't, even if though you are a poxy lawyer. I wouldn't have described you and Francesca as a marriage made in heaven, if you know what I'm getting at. Hmm, by your expression, you obviously don't. Never mind, but tactless as I am, I did think that you of all people would have stuck it out.'

Perhaps I would have, but for the fact that she had run away with the philandering Roland Rat and left me without that option. I smiled bravely.

'You're a survivor, Chris. I can see that. Anyway, new topic time, I think!'

I nodded, not wanting to give him the chance to psychoanalyse me further.

'How's that serious son and sparky little daughter of yours getting on? My nephew and niece, I mean of course.'

I told him that my son Ed was fine, had a degree in – wait for it – law, and that he was taking some time out to travel the world before he became a lawyer himself.

Oh, he isn't? Poor you – or poor him – becoming a lawyer I mean, not travelling the world.'

I then told him that I would be in town for a few days, and as sparky Kirsty would be coming to join me at the weekend, he could judge for himself how she was getting on. He seemed pleased by this and said that Malcolm and he would be back by Saturday and that we'd both be welcome to come and stay over and that they'd make sure that we'd all have a good time. In fact he was so insistent that I swiftly accepted the invitation. Even though by doing so I couldn't help feeling disloyal by not telling him why I was invading his hospitality for undisclosed reasons in the first place. Focusing my thoughts, I decided that I could no longer avoid the subject which had been preying on my mind.

'Ben – do you ever still think of April?'

He looked both a little surprised and a lot hurt.

'Still think of her? Of course I do. All of the time. What a bloody strange question! After all she was my sister and you'd hardly expect me not to. Do you know Chris, it's odd to think that but she'd have been getting to be an old lady by now and probably have had grown up kids and even grandchildren just like Rozzie. Remember how grandfather used to go on about her birthday in April itself falling on the same day as the loss of the Titanic?'

I nodded, and he continued unabated.

'I can't help feeling that April was...'

But he tailed off and I could see by his troubled expression that he was having difficulty in forming the words.

'Actually she was a prize bitch, Chris. There's no escaping from it, that's what she was.'

I must have let the mask slip for he added less than convincingly, 'Look, I didn't really mean it that way.'

I wondered what other way he could mean it but he had stopped talking. After sniffing enigmatically, he took a large slug from the bottle of Beajoulais that had just been uncorked. Pronouncing it, 'rather good actually', he poured me out a glass as well. I hoped that he wasn't going to become maudlin as well as drunk.

'Ben, I didn't mean to upset you by bringing the subject up, but...'

'But what? It doesn't matter. April was basically a good person underneath all of that crap but she wasn't perfect. Who is? I loved her, though, and I do wish that she was still here. You know, Chris, it might seem strange to a wishy-washy C of E like you but I often pray for her.'

He tailed off, obviously too embarrassed to continue. I decided to strike while the iron was still relatively warm.

'Do you ever feel that you'd like to know more about what happened on the day that she died – you know, find out who attacked her and everything?'

He looked at me curiously.

'Why the hell are you asking me that, now?'

'I don't know but it's sort of been on my mind lately and I've always wondered about it all. Maybe it's because I found her there and all that. I never really understood why the police never found out who did it – apart from the fact that they're bloody useless.'

I was embarrassed, muddled up in my thoughts and I wished I'd never brought the subject up. I hated having to keep the bit about Gerald's dying wish and the receiving the packet to myself. I didn't like concealing my motives even if it was a sin of omission rather than a downright fib.

'I am sorry that you and Rozzie had to be the ones that found her like that, I really am. Anyway I'd have thought that you, as a lawyer, would have no illusions about the ineptitude of our friends in blue. Couldn't catch a cold if they tried, as many in this city would have said. I always wondered, though, what part, if any, Barry Leemings played in it all. Remember him?'

I nodded, how could I have forgotten April's hapless boyfriend? He had, after all, had a bloody good attempt at duffing me over at the party. Ben went on. 'I hated him – little toad that he was, and don't know why she ever went out with him. He was a loser from the start. He was horrid, had long dirty hair, a whining voice and that bloody manky Afghan coat that he always wore. He had a right go at you once, didn't he?'

'He did', I confirmed hastily in order to cut him off and then, rather disingenuously added, 'I never really knew him properly but he must have had some good points.'

'There you are, Chris, still the same good-natured fool as usual trying to see the best in everyone. No, just face up to it. Barry was a creep, an unmitigated disaster.

Why the hell did April want to be seen out with such a greaseball as that?'

'Perhaps it was just her way of rebelling against your parents and all that they stood for.'

'Don't be so bloody naive, Chris. She wasn't rebelling against her background, far from it. She was every bit as money-orientated as mum, no different. A chip off the old block, even if she did go in for all of that alternative lifestyle crap like her pal Gillian. But, hey, give me a break! Hanging around with a deadbeat druggie and being bombed out of her mind didn't exactly make her a New Age intellectual, especially when Gerald paid the bills. She liked her luxuries did our April. Yet when all's said and done, she was my sister. I knew her better than anyone else, warts and all, and by God did she have plenty.'

This was not what I was wanting to hear. I thought about the April that I had known, the cousin who had come to my rescue when I had needed her, the person who had patiently taught me all sorts of interesting things that I didn't know. The girl who often made me laugh with her infectious sense of fun, the poet who had often talked about the planets, stars and the afterlife and the clever young woman who was going to get a first and have a brilliant academic career.

My sugary thoughts ground to a halt. I had always looked up to her but maybe I had never really known her, the real April that is. Maybe no-one had, and now nor ever would. She was as fallible as we all are, yet there was something about Ben's concentrated malice that me want to come to her defence now that she could no longer defend herself. But I had no chance as he was already warming to the subject.

'You remember that silly house she lived in when she was at Uni, you knew, that place in Riego Street? Yep, well that house was owned by Gillian, you know, Gillian Ainsdale, daughter of that smarmy architect who lived next to us. You knew that Toby with his damn fool Spanish wife called Elvira or some poxy name like that. Silly tart – Gillian with a G, although for all I knew her mother was as much of a phoney as well. She, Gill I mean, still lives there, I'm sure. Her husband left her, probably not being able to put up with all her horrid pretentiousness, or so I heard. Bloody posers the lot of them.'

He paused and then smiled.

'Remember how we used to take the piss out of people like that and call them pseuds?'

I remembered although I didn't join in his taunts. Ben always seemed to have been perfectly capable of picking on people like the Ainsdales without my help.

'Anyway, Gill with a G and April, goody-two-shoes, the pair of them. They lived there practically rent-free with all those drop out pals of theirs for company. They had a good time on hand-outs from their parents and on the student grant which, even though the hopeless Tories were in power at the time, still meant something. No student loans or tuition fees then and no maintenance grants now! Well all in that house were spongers and April was probably the worst bloody waster and sponger of them all.'

'You're being awfully hard on her.'

'Who, my sister or Gill? Couple of bloody money vultures both of them. Accepting everyone for who they are or who they pretend to be. You know what your trouble is? You're far too sentimental and nice, Chris. And you take everyone at face value. You're unable to see who they really are. Much too sentimental, I've always thought.'

I thought that this was rich, coming from someone much more sentimental than me but I made no comment and he just continued on as he always did.

'You hero-worshipped April but then you seem to do that with all the women who've been in your life. You're not realistic about any of them.'

I protested, but only feebly, as part of me suspected he might be right. Ben ignored me but his temper was visibly subsiding.

'Look Chris, don't take it all as gospel because April wasn't that bad – she wasn't. She was a clever girl and would have achieved her doctorate in literature and some other such studies if she'd lived. But the one thing I can tell you was that when she was bad, she was very bad indeed.' He said this enigmatically and then took another swig from the bottle while I wondered where his ramblings were leading.

'I'll tell you something else...' He hesitated momentarily before continuing in a lower key.

'This is something that I've never told anyone before because I was too ashamed of it. A few days before she died your wonderful April was trying, of all things, to get money off me by threatening to tell mum and Gerald about a certain little incident that I'd been involved in.'

'What sort of little incident?'

'Oh, nothing really, just a miniscule bit of cannabis that I got a police warning for possession of and... well... there was a boy from Wallasey who was a bit younger than me and... Look it doesn't matter, the details aren't important anyway. History now! The point is that she,

April I mean, was going to spill the beans about the Wallasey boy and the hash to my parents if I didn't give her some dosh. Now, to be frank, Gerald wouldn't have been all that bothered about the cannabis. He wouldn't have been bothered by the boy either, but mother – well! "Look what the apple of your eye, Ben the wonder-kid, has done."' He was now cruelly mimicking the slight lisping way in which April had talked and I had decided that enough was enough. It was time to change tack or leave but Ben had still a great deal more to say.

'Anyway, she wanted a hundred quid to keep it quiet and that was a hell of a lot of money in those days. I was used to going to the bank and getting out a fiver to last me the week. So I told her to get lost and do you know the worst of it, Chris? I never spoke to her again so the last words I ever said to her were, "Go to hell, you greedy bitch!" Imagine that – my fond farewell to my sister. How do you think I feel about that now?'

He started to cry and I put my arm around his shoulder.

'God, I never properly grieved for her. I just bottled it all up and became angry with her and with myself and with the bastard who killed her, and I'm still angry.'

He opened another bottle of wine and with a savage gesture threw the cork across the room so that it landed halfway between art and architecture and the reference section of his home library.

'Chris, tell me something. Do you think that they'll ever catch her killer now?'

I said that it was doubtful, that too much time had passed and that it was always the first twenty-four hours or so that were the crucial ones. After that unless there were any new leads or the double helix of DNA came riding to the rescue, then the chances were pretty remote. Another chunk of homespun criminous wisdom that I had garnered in the pub from Gavin along with virtually the whole of my knowledge of the subject of crime and its investigation.

'Chris, you know that I lied to the police, don't you?'

Although I had recently read the copy of his statement that had been in the second white envelope, I had no idea of what he was talking about.

'Who did you lie to, and about what?'

'The two guys in Crosby police station. I lied about where I had been that day. It didn't seem important at the time but maybe I messed up the whole enquiry. You see I told them that I had been away from the house since noon, that I'd gone round to a friend's and stayed there, had a few beers and watched the sport on the telly all day. But I hadn't. I was at home till well after two.'

I remembered that the forensics had established that April had probably died sometime in the early afternoon but I still didn't really see the relevance.

'So why did you tell them all that nonsense about being at Cal's all day?'

'Who said anything about the friend being Cal?'

I managed to get myself out of that one by saying that I had just assumed that it must have been Cal since Ben had always been knocking around with him at that time. I remembered that Cal had been a big sports fan as well, even if he didn't share Ben's liking for watching cricket which he held to be a sublime way of spending a summer afternoon. I held the opposite view, and agreed with those who held that cricket was the closest that the English had ever come to defining eternity.

'But why did that matter anyway?'

'I said that I was at Cal's to avoid pointing the finger at Gerald.'

'I don't understand. What had your father got to do with any of it?'

'I'll tell you what. The day before, Saturday, that was, I was minding my own business in my room when I heard this commotion downstairs and went down to see what the hell was going on. April had been trying to con some dough out of Gerald, some wheedling 'dearest daddy' crap. Mum had burst into the room and said to him that on no account was he to give April a penny. She seemed to be adamant about the money. Well that was it – a right humdinger broke out with April shouting at mum that she was a tight-fisted cow and a failure of a mother. Then mum got the screaming abdabs and said that darling Ben never behaved like that and that April had been trouble from the very beginning and that sometimes she wished that she had never been born.'

He took another drink and sniffed loudly.

'Well of course Gerald then just lost the plot and slapped her – mum I mean, not golden girl April, he'd never ever have hit her. So April, just to rub it in, told them about me smoking and dealing grass, in an amateur way of course, and the Wallasey lad. There was a God-awful hullabaloo and mum said April was a liar, always had been, always would be and that she didn't believe anything that she said. So then our April delivers the final coup de grace by telling Gerald that she'd tell everyone about what he's recently been up to unless he came up with some cash.'

'What had he been up to?'

'I don't know because I didn't hear any more of it, but possibly something about his philandering activities.

But I just skedaddled because by then mum was having her doubts about me and was on the warpath to see if there was any truth in what April had said about me, the drugs and the boy.'

'What did you tell her?'

'I just denied it of course and as usual the stupid woman believed me.'

'But I still don't see what any of this has got to do with pointing the finger at Gerald.'

I'm not surprised because you haven't let me finish yet. The next day, Sunday, they had all gone out early. It was a lovely summer day if you remember. April was back in Riego Street, Gerald had left to do something with his boat activities and mum had left for Southport in that ghastly yellow car of hers. You remember that VW in mustard yellow, I don't know if Gerald told the police where he had gone but mum was at the flower show. You'll remember how important an event locally that was? Still is, I believe.'

I nodded to show that I did remember that unfortunately coloured vehicle and how my parents had once taken me to the Southport Flower Show, an event which had triggered off a bout of severe hayfever in me and put me off flowers, or flower shows, for life.

Ben was still talking. 'I was just in the garage listening to Test-Match Special or something like that on the radio while I was tinkering with my Mini. You remember, that smart red one with the bashed-in door that I bought from Cal's elder brother and tried to pass off as a Mini-Cooper? Some chance – it could no more pass the MoT than fly!

'Anyway I was just checking the brake pads when I saw April pass by going towards the house. I didn't get a good view of her and she didn't see me. Of course I was giving her a wide berth for reasons which were rather obvious. I didn't know what she was up to and why she had left Riego Street but I wasn't waiting around to ask her so I stayed out of her way. All I remember was that she was muttering something about making someone pay for humiliating her. I could see that she was angry, very angry. I didn't want to hang around, not when April was in a mood like that, so I slipped away and went to Cal's. The funny thing was that on the way I saw Gerald's Peugeot parked up the road near the station half-hidden behind some bushes. Anyway Cal and I had some beers and watched sport on television at his house. I'm sure that it was the athletics that was on. We ate almost everything in his house and ended up getting well bevvied, or totally blootered as Malcolm would say. So you see it all now, Chris, don't you?'

I shook my head as none of this made any sense and I began to think that I was perhaps a little drunk too.

'It's the alibi that Gerald gave to the police of course. April had already threatened to expose him for something or other. He told the cops that he'd been in Manchester all day at some pissy show, a boat fair, I think. It was when I was in the police station that I remembered hearing one of the cops saying that they thought that Gerald had lied to them, that he hadn't been seen in Manchester at all that day.'

'Perhaps they just missed him there.'

'Missed him there all right. He was never bloody there at all and they'd done a proper check for both him and the Peugeot.'

'Perhaps he went by train, given that his car was parked near the station.'

'Not likely – he never used trains if he could help it. He used to say that you could get all sorts of ailments from the coughs and sneezes on public transport. He wouldn't have forsaken his car. No, he must have left the car where he did and just gone back to the house for some reason...'

'What house are you talking about?'

'Ours, of course. Whose did you think?'

'Did you see him there?'

'No, because I was at Cal's – didn't you listen to what I said?'

'How do you know that he'd been back to your house?'

'Well I reckon that he'd gone home – he wouldn't have gone for a walk in the park. So he must have returned to our house. Where else would he have gone – he left his car secreted away near Cal's and no-one else was there apart from Cal. Stands to reason doesn't it – our house was the only place he could go.'

'Maybe he did, but you don't really think he killed April do you?'

He waited before answering and when he did his voice sounded far less confident.

'I suppose that he could have done. He had the opportunity. I didn't know what to think then but later on when I'd turned it all over in my mind I tried to convince myself that Gerald wouldn't have had the guts to kill anyone, least of all April. She was the one person above all that he really doted upon. But what was he doing there on that fateful Sunday?'

Ben paused and I could see that he didn't want to say any more.

'Just drop the subject, Chris – they're both dead now, April and Gerald, Oh hell, I don't want to talk about it any longer. It's all in the past now, way in the past and talking about it won't bring them back now. How about another snifter?'

By the time that Malcolm returned Ben and I were sitting on the floor surrounded by a stack of old vinyls and I was having a dispute with no-one in particular on the finer points of the lyrics of Al Stewart's *Swiss Cottage Manouvres*. Ben, being Ben, was standing on a chair and, having done a dreadful karaoke session, was giving a passable imitation of Debbie Harry singing *The Tide is High*. Only, unlike Debbie, he and the tune seemed to have parted company at some point.

'Och, break it up the noo laddies, when the singing starts that's when it's time for bed! Chris, you're no fit to be going home like that. Mind it's late anyway so it's a narrow folding bed for yon, Master C. And dinnae be alarmed – you're a nice boy but you're no my type.'

He sniggered at this remark but Ben was by now at the point of passing out and just met us both with an unfocused smile. For this and for the fact I had mercifully remembered to drink several glasses of water to stave off the inevitable hangover, I was hugely grateful.

8

I was waiting for the mid-day ferry and, as it was still early in the season, there was only a short queue of a handful of Dutch tourists, two bona-fide commuters, a couple of tracksuited girls with brightly painted bikes and the obligatory gaggle of pensioners complaining about the price of everything and the value of nothing.

As I boarded the Woodchurch, I was glad that I had chosen this way of travelling to meet Twentyman. The sun was shining off the wind-furrowed water and as we pulled away from the Pier Head it was impossible not to feel a surge of pride in our town. I noted with interest that I was thinking of it as 'our'. The city was looking at its best and it struck me yet again that its stately setting beats anything London has to offer. I was glad to be able to say that I come from a long line of Liverpudlians, or, as my grandfather always insisted, Liverpolitans.

I remembered that when I was a boy, Sep had taken me on this same trip and over a mug of tea and an iced bun he had said that the Wirral was blessed for one thing and one thing only – its view across the river. He had loved the Mersey and had delighted in recounting tales of the merchants of old who had taken part in the great triangular trading run from Liverpool of cotton cloth to Africa, slaves sold by merchants from rival tribes to work in the sugar plantations of West Indies and rum on the homeward leg. But he had always been careful to add to this account that our family had of course sided with the abolitionists and had refused to trade in anything other than coal, cloth, salt and sugar.

Like many of his stories, I was never sure if it was the truth or mere wishful thinking, but then did it really matter anymore? Perhaps there was no answer to that question, or as Mr Rossiter used to ask us, 'Is history an accurate account of what happened to the common people or merely the embellished folk memory of the privileged few?' We never answered him, not having a clue to the right, or the expected answer.

It had always struck me that Grandfather Seb had lived in the past because he preferred his world before the Luftwaffe had destroyed vast areas of it, including, on the memorable night of the Liverpool blitz, his comfortably shabby Regency house in Waterloo. Gone was his collection of books and prints, his gentle do-gooder wife and his ambitious youngest child – the grandmother and thirty-one year old uncle that I had never even known. I doubt if I would have had the will to go on living after something like that, but then I was not him. And, from what I remembered, Sep was not a bitter man even when age and failing health started to get the better of him.

The taped commentary on the ferry repeated the old joke about the bronze birds on the Royal Liver building and how the female faced out towards the sea to welcome home the returning sailors while the male faced the other way and looked out over the city to see if the pubs were open. I couldn't help but laugh since it had been one of my grandfather's favourites and I could remember how he spluttered every time he told it to Ben and me. To be honest, though, we had preferred Ben's crack about how the Liver Birds only flapped their metal wings when a virgin chanced to walk underneath. But that would have been too vulgar for Septimus J and his rather ponderous sense of humour.

It was a brief and slightly choppy crossing. As I alighted at Seacombe and began to walk up the Egremont shore, I enjoyed taking in the views of the docks and warehouses on the opposite bank, and for a while was distracted from the question of how I was going to play it with Twentyman that afternoon. Then the sight of the beach at Blundellsands brought me back to earth and I tried to make sense of what Ben had told me the night before. April as a would-be blackmailer was bad enough but I could not believe, for one moment, that Gerald had had anything to do with her murder, even if he had a false alibi.

I began to wonder about Ben himself but he would hardly have admitted to seeing April that day, unless he was being very clever indeed. But lingering doubt set in and I began to think what if it actually had been Ben or one of the family who was responsible for her death? What if this was all some wild plot on the part of Gerald to exact his revenge on me but revenge for what? For in my case all I had done was find April's body? But then maybe in his eyes that would have been enough. And, if it came to that, where had Gerald himself been before that?

I had a cheese bap and a half of I.P.A. which brought back memories of the brief lunchtime forays to a small and dingy pub where, in the stained-glass and sanctified seclusion of the snug, Ben, Cal and I discussed life, whilst furtively appearing unconcerned so that no one would doubt that we were eighteen, despite our half-concealed school ties. I wondered if Kirsty found pubs so exciting, now that she was old enough to enter them without

128

contravening the Licensing Acts. That was something that I would have to ask her at the weekend.

By the time that I arrived at New Brighton I was still worn out by the session with Ben yesterday and unprepared for the meeting with Twentyman. So I spent a few minutes looking round the town and trying to calm myself down.

The place seemed a little different and a lot tamer than I had remembered from our family excursions there in the old Morris, my father nervously driving along the congested streets and through the cavernous and echoing tunnel to Birkenhead. In a wave of nostalgia, I could almost smell again the hot leather seats and odour peculiar to British cars of that era. The tram tracks had just been taken tip, the road signs were jaunty little affairs with little red triangular hats and junctions were still guarded with the imperious words 'Halt at Major Road Ahead'. Then I looked at my watch again and decided that I could put Twentyman off no longer.

Aidensbrook Road turned out to be a short terrace of tidy turn-of-the-last-century houses tucked away close to the centre of the town. After knocking loudly, there was a sound of muffled barking and within seconds the door was opened. Twentyman had obviously been awaiting my arrival. Still well built, but now with straggling white hair, a stained pullover and an air of neglect, he greeted me while at the same time trying to fend off the snarling Jack Russell at his feet.

'He won't bite. He's a friendly enough old sod when he gets to know you and likes you.' I wondered if to know me was the same as to like me but after a few half-hearted snarls the dog seemed to lose interest and began to concentrate his attentions on his master's left shoe.

'My study', Twentyman said, pushing the dog away in a fond manner before ushering me into a large room with an uncurtained and dirt-streaked window, through which the afternoon sun was streaming. 'Can't seem to ever get this bloody place tidied up properly, now that Jed and I are on our own. My wife's been gone these three years now.' Jed eyed me with undisguised rancour from under the table. 'Sit down lad, make yourself comfortable, if that's possible. What can I get you – a brew or something?'

While he clattered around in the back of the house and Jed kept a jaundiced eye on me, I had a good look at Twentyman's bookshelves. I'm one of those annoying people who firmly believe that the clue to a man's character is to be found in his book collection but his almost defeated my analytical powers. It was a somewhat eclectic mix of westerns, true crime and fictional, psychology, sociology, local history and various seafarer's reminiscences mixed in with a line of poetry and, in slightly frayed bindings, a magisterial history of the British Empire in thirteen volumes. He caught me dipping into a large work on the principles and practice of prison reform.

'I didn't just try to get them banged away, you know. I cared about what happened to them. Every good policeman does.'

There must have been something in my expression that gave him the feeling that I was mocking him for he added, 'Don't look at me like that.'

'Like what?'

'Like you think that good policemen are about as rare as unicorns in Bootle. We're just like other folk with some good, some bad and some neither one nor t'other.'

'Sorry, I didn't mean to be rude. Tell me, do you miss the job?'

'Aye, well, I enjoyed my days on the force like, but enough's enough and I've been retired a long time now. I'm way over eighty now, lad.'

He paused to allow me to congratulate him on the fact.

'Nearly eighty-nine – don't look or feel a day over seventy, mind.' This was followed by a bout of coughing, followed by a prolonged bronchial wheeze and I wondered whether he had been overplaying the perfect health card. He must have read my thoughts for he added, 'I'm getting on a bit, I suppose, what with my heart and this bloody emphysema...' He lit a cigarette and feebly cleared his throat.

'I went at the reorganisation back in '74. Had me full pension by then and I'd had enough of the job too, if truth be known. Didn't fancy going into the new Merseybloodyside Force.'

He stopped and thought for a few seconds.

'Your cousin's death was just about the last major investigation I ever undertook and I was never happy at the outcome.' He clearly was providing me with a way in and I took it.

'Mr, Twentyman...'

'Call me Robbie, lad, like everyone else does. You're not a youngster anymore and I'm not a detective inspector now neither.'

'Robbie then I suppose you know why I'm here.'

'Aye, I've a fair idea.'

There was an awkward pause and I continued. 'My uncle wanted me to contact you.'

'He were a good man, your uncle.'

On an impulse, I produced the handwritten letter from Gerald and handed it over to him. He sat down, Jed climbed onto his knee in a cat-like way, and he laboriously put on his round glasses. 'Can't see a ruddy thing without them nowadays.'

As he read, slowly and in silence, I watched his lips move with the words and I could almost hear the tick of the Crosby police station clock again. At least the mug of tea that I had now wasn't chipped and the milk wasn't stale. When he had finished reading, he took a long sip then spoke. '"What is truth?" said jesting Pilate, and did not wait for an answer.' He stopped and then added, 'Francis Bacon – learnt it at school at a time when they taught you things, not wasted time pandering to all kinds of stupid notions like they do nowadays. You had to think for yourself in those days, not be namby-pambied by some young whippersnapper with a degree in complete cack and defective common sense.'

He sighed and dipped a digestive biscuit into his tea.

'Truth, justice, retribution, all the things he was on about. They're just words, lad, just bloody words.' He saw that I was looking disconcerted and put the biscuit down. Oh, I dare say that they're noble sentiments right enough but who knows what any of them mean?' And, like jesting Pilate, he did not wait for an answer either.

'But you'll do what he asks, lad. I can see that and your uncle knew that too. I suppose that it's in your make-up or something. You were determined enough that first time that I met you. Couldn't get owt from you in the interview room. You were a stubborn little tyke then and probably still are now. Yes, you'll follow this business through, I've no doubt about that. And I expect that you'll be wanting my help and all.'

132

'Would you be willing to help me?'

'Aye, lad, if you want me to. Your uncle was a good man, one of the old sort. I got to know him well, even went out for a few jars with him. Do you know, I always felt sorry for him and sort of personally guilty because we never got anywhere. We made an arse of the whole case, if you'll pardon my French. You could say that we did and all, although that's not how they put it, officially like. They were too bloody wrapped up in the reorganisation at that time, I reckon.'

'Why, what went wrong with the investigation?'

'Bloody everything', he snorted. 'They were all running about determined to nail that poor bugger Leemings, the only real suspect they ever had. If they'd still had hanging he'd have been strung up just like that poor lad.' He nodded towards a book lying open on the table – *The Cameo Murders*. 'Before your time, lad. Two men killed in a bungled raid on a cinema in the city and someone was fitted up for it. Typical Liverpool, we made an arse of it as well – just like we did with the Wallace case. Still that's only history and your cousin's murder isn't, in a manner of speaking.'

'Tell me more about the hunt for April's killer.'

'You couldn't exactly dignify it by calling it a hunt.' He got up and fetched a small battered box that was lying on the floor beside his chair. 'I looked this out when you phoned. It's what I kept at the time, strictly against regulations, but I thought that it might come in handy one of these days. You can take it with you, read it at your leisure and I don't want it back as it's no bloody use to me any more. Always gutted me, this case has, because I felt we were just pissing around in the dark, if you'll pardon my French. The truth just escaped us or I should say, escaped me since I doubt if anyone else, your family apart, really cared to find out where it lay.'

'Why do you say that?'

He shrugged. 'Just a feeling I got at the time.'

He rummaged around in the box and produced a copy of my statement that looked, apart from its dog-eared edges, identical to the one which my uncle had sent to me. He adjusted his glasses and then began to read it out in a measured and pedantic manner.

'We rang the door bell several times but no-one was in so we went round the side because they usually kept the back door unlocked. I then entered the conservatory, followed by Ros.'

He stopped and looked at me with interest.

'Didn't last, eh? Probably got a family of her own now and forgotten all about you. That's what usually happens. Where was I, yes...' He continued to read my words aloud but now they had little effect on me. It was all so mechanical and unreal. Besides I had read the statement myself so many times in the past few days that it was becoming as familiar to me as Sep's *Short History of Crosby*.

'At least we didn't have any problems identifying the corpse. Aye, you'd be surprised by how many relatives choose the wrong bodies.'

'Why would anyone do that?'

'Lots of reasons – confusion, grief, not wanting to face up to the uncertainty of not being sure. Who knows? But there was no doubt here as to who'd been killed. It was just a matter of who did it and why?'

He went back to the statement and as he droned on I felt increasingly weary.

'I know of no-one who had one reason to kill April. She was friendly to everyone and had no enemies and I cannot understand it. I have nothing to add to this statement.'

It all seemed to be curiously bland and matter-of-fact. The terror and tears shed so long ago now seemed to me like something that had occurred in another century, which, as I ruefully thought, it had. Then I caught sight of Twentyman looking at me, hard-eyed but with a hint of pity, just as he had done on that night in the police station.

'Anything you forgot in the statement, like? I always wondered about that – if you were telling us all that you knew or trying to cover summit up?'

'What do you mean by that?'

'Nowt really but you never told us why you didn't tell the emergency services the whole story – but no time, I suppose and maybe not relevant anyway.'

As he cleared the phlegm from his throat, I considered the matter carefully.

'No, I don't think so. Well maybe a few details were left out but nothing important. But I suppose that I didn't have anything important to say because I didn't know anything.'

'Aye, lad. I know that you only found her and you wish that you hadn't. And in case it's any consolation, you were never in the frame. We checked out your alibi and the garage in Clitheroe confirmed that you bought petrol from them when you said you did. The young lad there remembered your lass and thought that she were right tasty – said he were disappointed to see that there was a boy with her.'

I wondered if the lad still remembered her now but then why should he? After all, I was the one that had a continuing obsession with Ros.

'When did April die? I mean at what time?'

'It's in here', he said, pointing to the box. 'Between two and four. That means that, so far as the family are concerned, you were all in the clear. Ben was at a friend's house all day. I know about your uncle but the less said about that the better. He were up to no good but it's not relevant any longer.'

'What do you mean by any longer.'

'I just mean that it doesn't matter now. Your aunt was at the Southport Flower Show and came back half-pickled on the train at nine thirty. That architect neighbour of yours – Toby something or other – met her at the station. Waited for a couple of hours until the train she was on eventually arrived and she were picked up. Completely bloody pickled. She didn't tell him that she were late. No mobile phones in those days.'

He nodded as if to agree with his own memory.

'You remember Laing? Bless his cotton socks, he were out of the force same time as me – couldn't hack it any longer. He were the one your lass seemed to take such a shine to.'

He chortled and began to cough in an unpleasant hacking way.

'Well he wasn't exactly very sympathetic to her, was he? All that shouting and threats and putting such pressure on her. At least I hope that you'd have handled her differently today, what with post-traumatic stress disorder and the like being recognised nowadays.'

He did not openly disagree with this wisdom but muttered something about preferring the blunt and direct approach and of not mollycoddling witnesses. But seeing that I clearly didn't share his view he clearly changed his mind.

'Perhaps we could and should have treated the lass better.' This was the nearest we would get to an apology.

'Your uncle told us a right porkie that night, though. He said that he was at the Pleasure Craft Trade Fair in Manchester all day but he wasn't. Parked at the station to kid us on that he'd gone by train. Trouble was, he never set foot in bloody Manchester because he was, em, otherwise occupied. If I recall he was more than a bit reluctant to tell us what it was that were occupying him that day.'

'Meaning what?'

'That he was with a woman.'

This seemed unlikely but I couldn't let the suggestion go unchallenged and it seemed to me better than Ben's suggestion that Gerald had returned home and might have murdered April there.'

'Did he tell you that?'

'Gerald you mean? He were a canny bugger. Did he hell! But she did, the woman that is.'

'Was she – well anyone I would have known?'

'Aye, lad, as it happens you would. It was a lady whose son you were friendly with and went to school with, to be more precise.'

I was still in the dark and, I had to admit, slightly shocked. To be told that your uncle was conducting an affair with a married woman might not in itself be all that earth shattering, especially if your uncle had been married to Aunt Maura. But to find out that he had been carrying on with the mother of one of your school friends was, well, distasteful to say the least.

'Who was she, this woman?' I couldn't and didn't want to guess who it had been and yet I had to know.

'A lady who lived in your street right then.'

Was he getting pleasure in drawing it out so? I thought hard. The only school friend who had lived in my street was Cal Moscrop. Surely it could not have been his mother, a buxom and homely woman who baked cakes and was a stalwart of the Townswomen's Guild? I had to know.

'Not Mary Moscrop, was it?'

'Aye, that was her name, though we had to extract it from him like a rotten tooth after we found he'd lied about being in Manchester.'

He paused and then added as an afterthought, 'She and he were together in some fancy empty house out Chorley way that his neighbour – the Toby fellow – was meant to be surveying. To be fair to him, though, when we were questioning your uncle, he was almost out of his mind with grief about April and yet...' He tailed off and looked thoughtful. 'Grief is no excuse for lying, though.'

'My uncle wasn't the only one who lied to you about where he had been that day.'

'Oh, aye? And who else was being less than a hundred per cent?'

He looked surprised when I told him about Ben having seen April at the house that day.

'Know what, lad? You middle classes are the worst bloody fibbers of the lot, leastways so far as us police are concerned. You always have to embellish and farcify everything. Never a straight answer, never the truth, whole truth and not but it.'

I waited until he had finished. 'So, what you're telling me is that Gerald used the Moscrops, Mrs Moscrop that is, for an alibi as well, did he? But how do you know he was telling the truth about Mary?'

'By the way she was carrying on when we spoke to her. Scared witless she was that her husband would find out what she'd been up to and make a right stink.'

The late Morton S. Moscrop had been an insurance rep and, as I had always thought, a veritable mouse among men. But perhaps he had hidden shallows and a highly jealous nature. After all, hadn't a Man from the Pru featured in a murder case in our city once before?

I had to wait until Twentyman had replenished himself with a new brew, explaining that he was now, 'a right bloody tea Jenny', after his doctor had told him to cut down on the beer.

'You said that yon cousin of yours Ben couldn't tell if April arrived alone or was with anyone?'

I confirmed that he had said that he'd only seen a glimpse of April but that it was certainly possible that someone else was present as well.

'It don't really take us any further then. Stands to reason that there's only three possibilities, namely she brought someone with her, that someone arrived while she was already there or else that they were in the house the whole time. Whatever way you look at it, that person must have been the killer. Now, you'll remember that someone had been going through the house looking for valuables. The drawers in your uncle's desk were wide open and papers were scattered about all over the shop. The dining room was a mess like nobody's business and in the bedroom your aunt's jewellery box was upended on the floor.'

He stopped and frowned and I could see that there was something about the situation then that still puzzled him. Then he stood up and began to pace the spiral-patterned carpet.

'I remember once seeing on telly some programme where an American cop was bellyaching about how important it was to just take your time and sit down at a murder scene and slowly take in every little detail. He reckoned that there were lots of clues that you would lose if you didn't just sit tight and absorb the atmosphere, the layout and the feel of the place. He went on about how it was no good trying to reconstruct it all later from photographs and the like because you'd have missed something important by then. Maybe it's just a lot of bloody nonsense but by the time I got there, the plastic bag men were all trampling over everything like clodhoppers and any clue they missed just went west.'

'Where are those scene of crime photos now?'

'Bloody well lost, I shouldn't wonder. Haven't seen them for years but as I remember they weren't much use anyroad.'

He paused, noisily drained his tea and then swilled the dregs around in the bottom of the cup before continuing.

'The most likely theory we ever came up with was that April had come in and surprised a burglar.'

'Who then killed her? Is that very likely?'

'It does happen.'

Though not, I thought, in respectable Blundellsands. Twentyman continued in his line of thought.

'There weren't no signs of a break-in, although as you were at pains to tell us, they always left the back door unlocked so there wouldn't be any need to. To be fair though, no-one used to lock doors in that district then, or so the neighbours claimed. But I reckoned that were just crap, just like how all Canadian folks nowadays claim they still don't lock their doors. I've got a nephew in Edmonton, by the way. He's a policeman too. Says he always locks his bloody doors. But I'm getting diverted, aren't I lad?'

'Do you still think it was a robbery then?'

Well there were no signs of any sexual interference or anything like that. The house had lots of valuables in it like silverware and that kind of fancy stuff though nothing seemed to have been taken. Might have been money taken but no-one could say for sure and Gerald was so bloody vague that I began to wonder if he'd gone barmy. The only thing unaccounted for at the end of the day was the question of the missing money, if it ever existed.'

'What about Barry Leemings?'

'What has that to do with anything? He did a runner afterwards, true and there was a sighting of him that day in Crosby about two thirty or so hanging around the phone box by the station. One of the staff there saw him and reckoned that he was looking right shifty in that grubby sheepskin thing he wore. Oh, don't get me wrong. There were plenty of reasons for thinking that Barry was up to no good, prohibited substances for one. We found an interesting lot in his room, cannabis, cocaine, amphetamines, class A and class bloody everything, well traces of them byroad. We all thought our Barry was a bit of a layabout and the popular theory were that he had done the burglary himself to get cash for whatever he was hoping to be on at the time. Maybe he panicked when April walked in and found him thieving away. He had a good deal of money on him when he were eventually found.'

'Strange thing was also a small iron poker thing missing – they said it were used for planting bulbs and was usually propped up against the pots in that fancy glass lean-to thing at the back. The poker wasn't valuable unless, of course, it was the murder weapon.'

'Did you ever find the poker?'

'Nay, it just disappeared like freshly toasted teacakes in a nunnery.'

'So what part did Barry play in April's murder?'

'Probably none. No evidence whatsover.' He just shrugged and then went on. 'There was, as I said, some money found on him after the accident in which he met his end.'

'How much?'

'Just over a hundred quid, which was a lot of money for them days. It could well have been stolen from your uncle's house. I doubt if it were his own holiday savings or pennies he'd collected for the foreign missions.'

'If Barry was the thief, then might it have been April's idea to get him to steal from her parents? Remember what I told you about Ben saying April wanted someone to pay for humiliating her? But why would Barry have wanted to kill her?'

'Maybe it was a sort of falling out among thieves, but we can't very well ask him unless you've got a Ouija board handy. Mind you there were nowt suspicious about Barry's death. Nowt, that is, unless you call riding an old motorbike at breakneck speeds like a complete headcase and meeting an arctic lorry head-on normal behaviour. Oh, it was his own fault no mistake and the lad in the wagon couldn't have avoided him. Mick Laing, the Super and them others were all for closing the investigation then and there. They thought that it was enough that

142

Barry was a druggie, a student and a gunner but I couldn't be sure which of those counted the most. Thinking on, it was probably being a student because there's summat about an intellectual that we coppers never trust.'

He paused and looked to see what effect this statement was having upon me. I remained inscrutable, wondering if he had been watching too many bluff Northern television detectives lately.

'Mind you, no offence intended – about intellectuals, I mean.' His smile removed any doubt that he had not intended the remark to be personal.

'After he were killed, well, we all started fannying around and realised that your bloody relations all seemed to be going on with each other – your uncle and girlfriend Mary that is, and lying and all, and no-one in the police seemed to take things seriously any more. Then we were told that April's death were possibly an accident occurring during a criminal assault. So the enquiry was scaled down and after taking photographs of likely suspects to your aunt, uncle, Mrs Moscrop and Toby Ainsdale and his wife, and no one recognising any of them at any time that afternoon, our guv' put us on to other more important things like fiddling our expense forms and telling kids not to speak to strangers.'

He laughed at his own wit and began to scratch his nose vigorously while Jed, taking this for his cue, wandered off into the kitchen.

'Leave the dustbin alone, you four-footed booger. As regards yon Barry Leemings, well if you want my opinion, he didn't do it. No real motive and in my book motive is all. Discount the loony element and you've always got to have a motive, however twisted or perverted.'

'Did you discount the loony element?'

'How can you ever? Well there weren't no nutters going about killing the good folk of Blundellsands at that time, if that's what you mean.'

'Wasn't there another murder round about then – a girl found by the canal or something?'

'Aye, a week before. Her name was Sarah Callaghan and she was strangled and the poor lass had her body dumped by the bridge at Pauldings Lane but it were nowt to do with your cousin's death. The lad who did was in custody the whole of that weekend and he'd already confessed to Sarah's murder. Said he couldn't live with the guilt though to be fair we'd given him a little assistance in helping us with our enquiries. Besides April's death was rather different to that other poor lass in that it weren't a sex attack or owt like that.'

'You didn't have offender profiling then either, did you?'

'Bloody right, we didn't – mind you we did have our own knowledge of the area's criminal classes at the time but we drew a blank. We couldn't rely on computers or any of them modern marvels, not like these snazzy American things on the idiot box. All we had to rely on were the brains of our senior officers which is, come to think of it, is why we were jinxed from the start.'

'Well, with virtually nothing to go on, how do I, or how do we, if you really meant that about helping me, go about finding out who killed April, then?'

'Listen lad, it was a long time ago but if you're sure that you want to go on, then if I were you, I'd go about checking the medical side first and find out the proper cause of death. And remember to check the alibis if it's not too late. But remember one thing, lad. There's very little to go on really, very little at all, and you do understand what I'm saying, lad, don't you? If you discount a stranger, a nutter and Barry Leemings (even if those last two may be the same thing) then you've not got much else.'

His eyes narrowed and he looked cautious. 'Except, of course, a friend or your family perhaps. If you start to dig up the past, lad, you might well find things you don't want to. Skeletons might come tumbling out of the closet like choirboys in a vicarage. Just make sure you're strong enough to cope and be careful that no one else gets hurt.'

I took in his advice and, as I sat clutching the battered box of papers that he had given me on the train trundling its dark way back under the Mersey, I wondered if I really did know what I had got myself into.

9

'The professor will see you now, Mr. Kingston.'

With these words I was ushered along a brightly lit passageway and shown into a small room cluttered with books, paraphernalia and a large Kentia palm which seemed to be fighting a losing battle with a heap of green folders all labelled with case names. Robin Drysdale-Scott, as elegant and well-coffuired as ever, rose from behind his desk and held out his hand.

'Hello, Christopher. Good to see you again.'

We exchanged gossip for a few minutes and then, having enquired about Francesca and expressing the view that it was such a shame we'd split up and that he'd always quite fancied her himself but never had the nous to ask her out, he firmly came to the point.

'Now then, you said that you wanted some advice about something to do with a medico-legal matter. Not your corns giving you trouble again, eh?'

He paused to laugh at his own joke and I tried to put to the back of my mind the thought that he still had the capacity to annoy me as much now as when we had first met. We had been at the same college and had a number of friends in common but that was about it. He had been one of the hearty rugger-and-rowing medics and I had been something of a lawyer aesthete and thus beyond the pale, at least so far as the likes of him was concerned. He was the sort of person who would, when passing, ask, 'Hello, how are you?' and not even wait for an answer – a type of would-be doctor that I cannot stand. We had only

146

met on a couple of occasions since our graduation, drinking sessions engineered by the egregious Cal Moscrop who had been his contemporary as a junior house doctor at St. Mary's in Paddington. Still, one had to make allowances, even for Robin Drysdale-Scott, as he was a big wig in residence at the Royal Liverpool University Hospital and from all accounts a pretty good forensic pathologist. The opportunity had been too great to miss and I decided that I would have to control my natural antagonism to him. Although we'd already spoken on the phone, I gave him a brief account of why I had come to see him and then handed him several documents that I had abstracted from Twentyman's file.

'You said that she was your cousin? Then, that's all right then. Mmm give me a few minutes to digest all this and then we'll have a chat.'

He ordered two cups of coffee from his harassed secretary. When they arrived he opened a drawer, produced a bottle of Calvados and, unasked, put a generous splash in each. He settled down to read while I visually explored the nooks and corners of his room. An ageing skull with a careworn expression grinned at me from behind what I took to be an electron microscope but, as my knowledge of such equipment was nil, it could equally well have been a microwave oven. I had to admit that I knew virtually nothing about forensic science. What I did know had been culled from the passages of the Notable British Trials series like most other lawyers who did not dabble with criminal law and whose only knowledge of forensic medicine arose from cases involving medical negligence.

The books on Robin's shelves all had technical and impenetrable titles that were well beyond me so I got up and went to the window. The bleak sixties' architecture outside was not improved by the rain and I found it a bit depressing – 'A vertical filing cabinet for sick human beings', as Cal had once quoted but then added that it was one of the best teaching hospitals in the country and that the particular department I was now in was very highly rated indeed.

After a time Robin scratched his ear thoughtfully and then spoke. 'Now, what is it exactly that you want to know, eh?'

I found the 'eh' quite irritating but not as annoying as the notice on his desk that said, 'If you want a second opinion, come back and see me again later.' I reminded myself that I had to be on my best behaviour.

'Time of death first, please.'

'No problem. Right, where to begin? Well, forget about all that one and a half degrees per hour loss of body temperature nonsense and the stuff you read in detective stories about "between one and one fifteen". It's really more of an art than a science and the trouble here is that we have to rely on the police doctor who attended at the scene and his readings of ambient and body temperature and such, presuming he got it right in the first place. Quite a big thing to be presuming in those days. Now I knew this police medic, not well but more by repute. He was an old chap from Preston way and not the regular but, it being a Sunday, he probably would have been all they could have got. To be quite frank, he wasn't really ever up to much. Bit of a problem with the old oozo boozo, if you get my drift, eh?

'Anyway, assuming that he was sober, he records that he saw the body just after nine fifteen or so and estimated that she'd been dead for between about three

148

to five hours, so that she died between four and six pm. He's noted down her rectal temperature, the ambient temperature, slight onset of rigor, tiled floor, glass walls, door of conservatory partly open, clothing: cotton blouse, light jacket... Mmm I suppose that we'll just have to accept his word for it but in all honesty I doubt if I could really have done any better. Is the precise time of death actually important to you, eh?'

I had to concede that it was not, since none of the family had been present after Ben's departure at two something and there was no prime suspect whose movements had been tracked and whose alibi might have depended on any crucial timetable.

'I'd say the old chap had been right but I would have put it at nearer to four than fix.'

'Cause of death?'

'That's more tricky. I'll need to go into technicalities with you so how hot are you on parts of the body? Mind you, I suppose it depends on which parts and on whose body, eh?'

He laughed and took a sip from the cup of brandy, delicately crooking his finger as he did so.

'Look Robin, I've done a fair bit of civil court work, negligence and that sort of thing but, as we say to expert witnesses before a case, just imagine that I'm a simple-minded judge and explain everything to me in layman's terms.'

'OK, but as long as you don't feel I'm patronising you. One of your colleagues told me about some fancy London QC called Anderson that used to say that if he had to address a jury in the afternoon he'd have a couple of pints at lunchtime so that he could get himself down to their level – good one, eh?'

I groaned inwardly at the thought of Henry Atterson and his ability to pass old chestnuts off as his own.

'Just remember that a dull judge is probably less intelligent than a jury who have been following the case properly. Assuming, of course, that you could find such a jury.'

I didn't want to hear his comments on the jury system but he brought his musing back to my cousin's death.

'Right. Let's start with the Death Certificate, then. Mmm "Subdistrict of Crosby in the County of Lancaster. April Isabella Kingston, fifth August 1973, Student of 19 Riego Street, Liverpool". Here we are: "Cause of death: l(a) Subarachnoid haemorrhage, l(b) Presumed ruptured berry aneurysm." Clear as mud, eh?'

He laughed again and started to sketch something out on the drug company logoed notepad in front of him.

'Let's start with basics, eh? The brain is a pretty delicate thing so, for its own protection, it is covered by a rigid structure, in other words the skull. Now within the skull there's a tough old membrane called the dura mater and within that, in other words between the dura and what you might call the brain itself, you get another much thinner membrane which we call the arachnoid mater. Follow it all so far, eh?'

I nodded and he produced a red felt-tip and began to colour something in on his diagram.

'Right, well, within this second membrane there's quite a large area, called, not surprisingly, the subarachnoid space – that's what I've shown here, see? In this space we get the cerebrospinal fluid, which acts as a sort of cushion or shock absorber to the brain and the main arteries which pass up from the neck to the brain.

I've simplified it all, but you get the picture, eh?

'Now then, if you get a rupture, a break if you like, of any of those blood-carrying vessels, then you get a subarachnoid haemorrhage and you're in trouble. Blood gets out and, depending on how much there is in there, the increase of pressure on your brain does you no good at all and can easily kill you. In the case of your cousin April, it apparently did. That still doesn't take us much further, though, because such haemorrhages can occur either as a result of disease or trauma. In her case the Coroner decided that it was, quote, "natural causes."'

'But what about the injuries, the blood and everything?'

'Right, now here's what they found. "Linear laceration, two and a half inches long on left side of forehead extending to scalp, crushed edges, some bruising, no underlying fracture. The supposition is that she had been struck with a cylindrical object of some weight." So we have a fearful looking cut with lots of blood and that's what you'd have noticed when you found her. The thing is, though, that it was just a cut and it certainly didn't kill her on its own. Now look at the other injuries – "One inch diameter bruise behind left ear, no laceration, no fracture, minor bruises including to back of hand." That's what you call defence wounds, which she might have got while trying to protect herself but at least some of the abrasions would be consistent with falling onto a hard floor surface such as the tiles. Now all of this means that she'd been hit twice, possibly more. I'll bet the second blow, the one towards the side of the face which caused the bruise behind her ear, was a lot more significant than they thought at the time. But let's follow the logic of the postmortem report and see how the

Coroner got to the conclusion that it was death due to natural causes.'

'Back then in the mid-seventies, you'd have thought OK, we've got a young adult here. There'd been some sort of altercation with, I think you said, a burglar. Blows had been struck. Your cousin was excited and with raised blood pressure and an alcohol reading of 60 microgrammes per 100 millilitres of blood. That's a bit lower than the drink-driving limit but she must have had a good couple of measures beforehand by the looks of it.'

He picked up another sheet of paper and studied it with a frown.

'According to this, she'd been complaining of headaches for several weeks and her G.P. had put these down to tension. Right now look at it from the point of view of the pathologist at the time. All the classic factors are there and so you look to the most common cause of death in that age group when you're considering haemorrhages like this. Probably she had something wrong with one of the arteries at the base of the brain, a congenital abnormality. This defect, which it would be reasoned she's always had, leads to a sort of swelling up, what we call a berry aneurysm, and this swelling would have had thin walls a bit like a balloon which are liable to rupture at any time. A sort of walking time-bomb.'

'But wouldn't anyone have noticed that while she was still alive?'

'No reason why, old chap. It could have been asymptomatic or, like the G.P. said, the headaches could be thought to be tension-related. The thing is that given the right circumstances – excitement, alcohol, etc. - the aneurysm could have burst with the result that blood flowed out into the arachnoid space and she died. Maybe not all pathologists at that tine would have concluded that, on a balance of probabilities, it had been a suspected rupture of a berry aneurysm. But in the absence of any better diagnosis, and with no direct correlation between the bruise behind the ear and the site of the bleeding, it would have been a fair bet. Your cousin didn't seem to have permanent raised blood pressure or anything like that but she did have those headaches and the effect of the argument with whoever it was who hit her was enough to blow the safety valve, eh?'

He smiled in a slightly condescending way and I was reminded of one of those oh-so-important consultants portrayed in old comedy films, the kind who always come into conflict with the frosty matrons, horny young doctors and flighty nurses. Robin adjusted his absurd bow tie before continuing.

'Now you might well think that her assailant was still directly responsible for her death. Not because of the actual blows on her head but because he got her into such a state that she went and developed the haemorrhage. You'll know all about "take your victim as you find him or her", eh? Trouble is, whatever the police might have felt, and I can fully sympathise with them, given that there's been a criminal assault on a young woman and then she dies – The coroner has told them that it's natural causes and so far as I know in those circumstances they would never have got a prosecution off the ground, on the basis that the rupture of the aneurysm was the cause of death.

'Now this is the interesting part. Had she died nowadays then things might well have been different. For a start it would all have been investigated by a more highly polished outfit such as the serious crimes squad and it would probably have been the kosher Home Office pathologist who did the P.M. rather than our bibulous old pal and he would well have been looking for different things than our friend had. We'd still have had the subarachnoid haemorrhage as the cause of death but what about the berry aneurysm theory? You see, we've got the bruising to the area behind the ear to explain. That could well have been the result of a heavy blow with little surface evidence as it were. But there could have been underlying damage which would be much more significant. Remember my diagram? Well we're aware now that you can get a subarachnoid haemorrhage through damage to the vertebral artery arising out of trauma. In other words by an injury rather like the one which caused the bruise I've been talking about.'

He rummaged around in his desk drawer for a while and I thought that he was going to produce the Calvados again but this time he brought out a small diamond-shaped bone.

'This chap here is the first cervical vertebra. Nothing to see really but as a diagnostic tool it might have answered the question conclusively. No one seems to have done any radiographs, angiograms or anything like that. I'm not criticising them for not delving around to see if there had been any basilovertebral artery damage, as it wouldn't have been normal procedure then. It wasn't really until the 'eighties that we were aware of the implications of upper cervical trauma in this context. I think it was Harland who wrote an excellent paper on it in about '83 or '84. But you see where I'm getting to with all this, eh?'

'Are you saying that the blow to the neck, the one that caused the bruise behind the ear, was responsible for her death?'

'Yes, in all probability. You see we could never be sure beyond a reasonable doubt without digging her up. And, not being disrespectful to your cousin or yourself but since you're not of the Romanov dynasty or other royal blood, I can't see you getting an exhumation order on your cousin's body so long after her death. Even if you could, we still couldn't be sure what would turn up, as you only find such a fracture in, oh, about half of all such cases anyway. Who's to say what condition her skeletal remains are in now? But if I'd been doing the original autopsy and I'd had the benefit of what we now know, then I could well have gone along the route of the trauma having caused the rupture. The haemorrhage, to be pedantic, would be attributed to a tear in the vertebral artery as it passed from the spinal column to the base of the brain and all this nonsense about tension headaches and alcohol would then be quite irrelevant, eh?'

'So let me see if I understand you correctly. Is what you're saying this, that the blows from her assailant probably caused her death?'

'That's it in a nutshell. Mind you I'm not a lawyer and I don't know whether you'd get a conviction for murder. That would depend upon what your twelve merry punters in the jury room made of it all. One thing's for certain, though, had they caught that burglar, they'd have been able to charge him all right. Although they couldn't necessarily make it stick.'

'If you're right about the traumatic injury, the second blow, he could have been...'

'Ah, but here's the rub. Even if the berry aneurysm was proved, and remember that it was only suspected at the time, and your cousin had died as a result of its rupture, then even though it wasn't as a result of the blow behind the ear, whoever did it might still have been convicted of manslaughter. There was a case in the late seventies from Gibraltar a bit similar to this, where two sailors were in a fight and one of them died and that changed things in law so that since then, as I understand it, some sort of charges arising from the victim's death would probably be brought in this particular set of circumstances. So you see the implication, eh?'

'That April's assailant would almost certainly have been charged with murder or manslaughter if the attack had occurred a few years later than it actually did?'

'You've got it in one.'

'Were there any other clues as to the assailant's identity – fibres, hairs and the like?'

'Not that I can see – the only significant fibres identified were those from her own clothing, blue woollen fibres from yourself and white cotton fibres from the clothes of someone called Miss R. Allbright. No fingerprints, hairs or anything else conclusive.'

Presumably when I had turned her body over I had been wearing my own pullover again, and Ros was carrying her jacket and that would account for fibres from our clothing being transferred on to April's body. But it was curious that no other fibres had been found so perhaps the body had been moved or the area round it cleaned up and all clues removed before we found her.

'Is there nothing to go on in relation to the nature and extent of the wounds?'

'You mean all that about it being a right or left-handed assailant of above average height and weight, etc? Doesn't really happen like that in reality, I'm afraid. Well, not in most cases, anyway. Apart from the obvious, that is that there are no photographs with this report, we don't know the position of the victim or the assailant or what they were doing at the time of the attack. I'd say that they seem to have been facing each other and, ruling out a child or a dwarf, almost anyone could have delivered the blows. They do seem to be deliberate as though whoever did it at least meant to harm her, if not necessarily meaning to kill her. The old poker thing you described as being missing would probably have been substantial enough and you wouldn't need to swing it far or with a great deal of force to deliver the fatal blow. The person could have hit out in a rage, in panic or deliberately to kill. But since we don't know the circumstances there's nothing I can really tell you. I assume that whoever hit her probably thought the first blow had done the damage, what with all the blood that would spurt out. Quite probably they would have got blood on themselves and their clothes but why they had to hit her in the first place and why they hit her again, I don't know.'

I wondered if April had been caught unawares and then I thought back to the time when Barry had assaulted her at the party and she had taken it so submissively. I could still not decide from what I had seen then whether or not she was capable of resisting his or anyone else's violence. The fruity diction continued.

'Not a lot else that I can tell you really. You see things weren't really helped by the fact that you moved her body, turned it over I think you said. There was lots of blood at the scene but any marks of how she fell or if her killer shifted her about a bit afterwards. But that's not really the point, is it Christopher? The finer details don't really matter. The problem here is that, well to put it bluntly, we've got the corpse but, as it were, there's no one else in the frame, eh?'

10

I have always been fascinated by the sea at night and when I was very young I would insist upon being taken by my father to the beach, long after my bedtime, so that I could see and hear the dark waves whose smell and sound would eventually lull me into sleep. My family reckoned that I had salt in my veins inherited from my grandfather who was an ardent enthusiast of anything maritime. He was the son of a man who had run away to sea on the famed tea-clipper Taipei and had been one of the last generations to feel the surging power of wind on canvas.

My mother's people came from Shetland. On our regular family holidays to visit them, I would spend hour after hour leaning over the railings on the old St Clair in the darkness, taking in the exciting emptiness of the black North Sea that stretched far out from the ship's rails towards the dreamworld of beyond. In the morning when we were seated at breakfast and watching the approach to Aberdeen or Lerwick through rain spattered windows, it was all so different, all so disappointing, with the coming of the light and the return to the real and mundane landward world.

This particular evening things were no different. I watched the Belfast packet slip by and thought of grandfather Kingston and his stories of the great ships that had been wrecked upon the sandbanks close by. I remembered that he told me how he had played with his friends around the remains of the Lily Baynes, a wooden schooner that had come to grief long ago at the very spot upon which I was now standing. I began to recite from one of my favourite bits of his book.

From the beach at Blundellsands a commanding view may be had of the shipping inbound from the farthest outposts of the Empire and the Americas staking its way towards the quays and docks of our great port along the congested Crosby Channel. This surprisingly narrow seaway, running as it does between the treacherous Formby and Burbo sand banks on which many a vessel has foundered, is protected by a series of fixed shore and floating lights and by the red and green marker buoys which mark the outer limits for the safe navigation of all the ships that use it.

It was too dark to see the buoys but the lights of the line of ships now leaving port denoted the Channel as clearly as if it were day. On the margin of my vision were the tall windmill generators at Seaforth, looming like staggering giants with their arms outstretched to greet whatever gods these gaunt structures believed in. I wondered what Sep would have thought about having these intruders standing guard on his home beach let alone the metal men of Anthony Gormley's *Another Place*.

My attention drifted back to the glittering lamps of the Wirral peninsula, faintly discernible in the distance, and I thought about the untidy house in which Twentyman and Jed lived, surrounded by a clutter of tea mugs, past crimes and fading memories. I would have to contact him, tell him that he had been right all along that April had indeed been murdered and that justice had once again been weighed up and found to be wanting.

Then I tried to think objectively about April. Who had she really been? I wondered if maybe she was a mere cipher, a person who I had never properly known and who had now entered the land of the dead where I could not join her? The key to her death must in some way have been connected with her character for, as Twentyman had pointed out by elimination, she had been killed by someone that she had known, however briefly. But who? And why?

'Do not ask for whom the bell tolls...'

Hell, it must have been a family trait, for April, Ben and I were always quoting from books, poems and songs and using other people's words, other people's thoughts and never our own. Gavin had once said that he could sum up my entire character as being 'merely derivative', I was standing behind a mirror and reflecting not my own personality but that of anyone who chanced to look in. Even though he had been very angry with me at the time (although I can't for the life of me remember why), the image of the mirror stuck in my mind and I wondered if it were true. Perhaps, like Dylan Thomas, I was in love with words or perhaps, according to Francesca in one of her waspish moods, I was just full of crap.

Not long before my fight with Barry, April and I had met up in town and had gone for a coffee in a greasy spoon café close to the university. There April, looking quite out of place in the seediness of ketchup bottles, peeling notices and bentwood chairs, had started to recite verses of a minor Tudor poet whose name I can never remember but whose lines have stuck in my head.

'My glass is full, and now my glass is run, And now I live, and now my life is done.'

160

She had sounded prophetic enough then and even more so now, considering that within weeks, her own glass was run and her life was done.

My thoughts turned to her funeral, the second one that I had attended that year; for that matter, the second one that I had been to in my whole life. Almost all of the same people had been at both and virtually the same hymns had been sung, despite the different denominations of the corpses. One thing was different though. None of those present had been surprised by Sep's death, but no one had expected April to die so young and so soon after. I remembered the only words uttered by Gerald at her funeral. 'She was my only daughter and I thought that she would live forever.'

Although this made little sense, I, for one, knew exactly what he had meant, for the greatest human tragedy is to outlive your own children. Somewhat inconsequentially I thought of how Gerald had been cheating on his wife. What a frightful old hypocrite he was, given his great play on morals and the truth. And then I thought who am I to cast the first stone? I realised that what actually went on in his and Maura's life was probably not as simple as I had thought it was.

April had been buried in the rain a few days after the coroner had released her body. I remembered the occasion as having marked the very beginning of the end of summer's short lease. The chilling early winds of autumn were already entering into the mourners' bones and making them, somewhat ashamedly, look forward to the post-funeral buffet and tea in the hotel close to the bleak golf course which had all but formed a second home to Gerald.

Maura, dressed over-dramatically in black, had been all too obviously drunk and was sobbing sherry-stained tears while Gerald had stoically looked into the distance, alone and unsupported, taking nothing in. As I recalled, Ben had been the strong one although he had probably been in such a deep state of shock that the whole proceedings had passed him by.

That Friday, the day of April's interment, had also been the last time I had seen Ros, for although she had not been present, I had caught a glimpse of her later that day as she passed by in a taxi with her parents on the way to the airport to spend a couple of weeks in Greece – a holiday to compensate her for all she had been through and, in all probability, to distance her from me and my ill-omened family. By the time that she had returned I had already left for a fortnight's holiday with Meg and my parents in Cornwall. I felt that by now our lives were drifting apart and that Ros and I were definitely no longer an item. Perhaps she no longer cared for me or perhaps it was her parents' doing but I was almost glad that our paths never again crossed, whether by accident on my part or design on hers.

Suddenly I decided that I wanted to go back to the hotel. A northerly wind was blowing in from the sea and the past was beginning to flood back and overwhelm me. April and Ros were dominating my thoughts and I was in danger of becoming confused and unable to untangle one from the other. Where were they both, under what April called 'this clouded canopy of stars?' And, for that matter, from whom was I now quoting or had I made up the clouded canopy myself? Fact or fantasy, trick or treat – it was all getting too much for me. All that I knew for certain was that I desperately needed a drink.

'Is anything the matter... can I help?'

A calm voice – April or Ros? No, a kindly woman, who reminded me of a slightly older version of Jennifer Collman, was standing beside me, her two Labradors chasing after each other and barking with glee.

'Yes, No, I mean I'm fine. Just a bit upset, thinking about a family bereavement actually. But thank you, all the same. I'll be all right now.'

I managed to blurt the words out as I headed back to the dunes and the woman, sympathetic but at the same time highly embarrassed in a very British way, turned her attention back to her gambolling mutts.

I walked back the long way round, passing the small church dedicated to the Star of the Sea, in which April's funeral had taken place. I turned the handle but the door was locked. I was relieved for I had not really wanted to intrude into this private place of a religion which was not mine and which I did not understand. The curving streets were quiet now and apart from the occasional cawing of late crows in the pollarded elms, nothing seemed to be moving. The old houses, survivors from a more confident age, were bathed in pale moonlight. The intermittent glow of the street lamps made a picture which reminded me of one of those atmospheric scenes by Atkinson Grimshaw which had caught and held my attention on the unruly school trips that we had made to the Walker Gallery.

School trips made me think of the past again and I remembered back to a time when Ben and I had been children and April had come to our rescue. We were about eight or nine at the time and we were playing out in the street on our bikes when a number of older boys had started to chase us and throw stones in order to make us fall off. We were both in great fear until suddenly, as if from nowhere, April had appeared brandishing a large stick and letting out such blood-curdling yells that our persecutors took to their heels, pursued by a latter day enraged Boudica of Blundellsands. Ever since that day I had come to think of April as my protector and whenever in morning assembly we had sung the words, 'Our shield and defender, the Ancient of Days', I had always thought of her as a sort of warrior ready to defy the odds and act heroically on my behalf. And then I became sad again because I knew that I still missed her and that led me to feeling that I needed a stiff drink, and something to eat in order to avoid a complete descent into an all engulfing mire of sentimentality.

When I got back to the hotel I accessed my laptop and found that there were a number of emails awaiting me. One was from John, reminding me that I had a continued arbitration next Wednesday, a difficult case conference the next day about a proposed settlement in an action and the pre-trial review in the Glenbreen case on Friday. I had not forgotten any of these but wondered if John had been worried by the fact that my absence was almost certainly due to something unconnected with my business life which he took so seriously. Perhaps Gavin had said something to him about what I was doing up here and he was worried that I had had some sort of a mid-life crisis.

The second was a short communication from Robin Drysdale-Scott saying that I had inadvertently gone away with his copy of Knight's Forensic Pathology, but that he did not need it back in a hurry and that 'anytime will do, old chap, no problem.'

Last, but in her view hardly least, there was an irate message from Francesca asking me to call her. I resisted the temptation to phone her back immediately as demanded. I had no desire to enter into an argument with her which would have begun with, 'What the hell were you thinking of, leaving Kirsty all alone in the flat?' and no doubt ending with a withering account of my various failings as a father, husband and general representative of male humanity. I was in no mood for Fearless Fran on this evening and, following my instincts, I headed straight for the warm and inviting fug of the bar.

*****

The next morning it was raining – a depressing drizzle that could not be bothered to be proper rain and which made everything feel damp and whatever the opposite of exhilarated is. I took my hat and hopefully non-leaking shoes and headed out to the ancestral homelands which lay across the railway line. For the next few minutes, I trudged the increasingly familiar pavements. St. Roman's Terrace was looking much as it had always looked when my parents and I had lived at number eight, Silverdale. The terrace was a short dead-end road of tall Edwardian terraced houses, each with neat bay windows and decorative features. On either side of the solid front doors there were panels of stained glass through which a gentle haze of colours would permeate the halls. They were the sort of houses put up in their thousands before the First War and could still be found in the brick-built suburbs of almost every large English town. Hardly worth a visit for their architecture but then few people ever consider their own houses with the detachment of a

Murray or a Pevsner. More importantly though, once upon a time, St Roman's Terrace had been home to me and that was all that mattered.

I stopped by number two, Bellevue, where the Willoughbys, solemn stalwarts of the Local Liberal Association and thus a target for our unsubtle juvenile humour, had lived with their three pretty daughters, whom I had always admired from afar. Was it my imagination or had the street come up a bit since the rather run down 'fifties when, according to Maura in one of her put-downs to my father, it had been, 'not really a very fashionable or even nice place to live.' My father, his indignation exacerbated by the begrudged regular payments that he had made over the years to the Woolwich Permanent Building Society, had come close to throwing her out of the house for this unguarded comment. Relationships had been very strained for a couple of months until, cap in hand, Maura had come back and apologised for her tactlessness, but only because Gerald had made her do so.

I looked up at the blank windows with their Neighbourhood Watch stickers but they yielded few clues. Who lived in the street now? The question of whether or not number eight, Sandilands, had changed hands since my time was answered when a rather old Vauxhall Astra stopped almost directly outside it and a much older Mary Moscrop, got out of the car. She was wearing a rather bedraggled grey woollen coat and holding a clutch of striped Tesco shopping bags in hand. Catching sight of me, she frowned.

'Christopher?! It is Christopher, isn't it?'

I was invited into the kitchen where, with schoolbags and books weighing us down, Cal, Ben and I had been ushered in to savour the delights of Vimto and a prodigious selection of home baking. Even now I felt hungry for those lemon meringue slices, bakewell tarts and macaroons of childhood. I still remembered her cheese scones whose crumbs took forever to pick up off the floor when it was time to go home.

'What brings you back to these parts, then?'

I muttered something about combining a sentimental journey with having legal business in town and, seemingly satisfied, she asked after my parents and how I was getting on.

'Your parents well and enjoying their retirement in the country?'

I told her that my father had died a number of years ago and that my mother was now in sheltered accommodation in Grange but her eyes were glazed over. I realised that she was just being polite and that she had fallen out with my parents years ago though I had never known why.

'I saw something about you having taken silk some years ago. That is the term for when you become a Q.C., isn't it?' I said it was.

'I saw you at Gerald's funeral but you were talking to someone else the whole time so didn't get to chat.'

I nodded and listened while she told me about Cal's latest achievement as a paediatric consultant. I thought that the only interest that you have in me was that I was Cal's friend at school and the only interest you had in my family was that you were screwing my uncle although God knows what he saw in you. I tried to resist the urge to ask her if the amazing Cal had become as self-important and obsessed as most consultants that I had ever met had, but I already I knew the answer from Mary would be,

'Yes, just like you barristers are!' It was curious but at school the now staid Cal had been something of a radical socialist, inspired by a feisty red haired girl called Annie Shipman who he had met at a fringe meeting in Fazakerley. Her favourite chant about the monied classes had been, 'The only thing you can do with them is squeeze them till the pips come out', before breaking into a deep and fruity chuckle. Cal's conversion to her cause was adoring and complete and such was his own zeal on the metaphoric soapbox that even in the staff room at school he was known, in that pre-Hattonista era, as Cal 'wharrabout the wairkers' Moscrop. I wondered what had happened to Annie and whether he had ever introduced her to his mother.

I dearly wanted to ask Mary about what she and Gerald had been up to on the day that April had died and whether Cal and Ben knew about their affair but I could not bring myself to do so. Mary was by now well into her eighties. Still rather prim and upstanding as she had always seemed to have been, although I doubt if that was how Gerald had seen her. How curious life is when you no longer view everything through the prism of childhood eyes.

I coughed discretely and felt that it would be improper for me to harass her now, whatever indiscretions the past might have held. Let sleeping dogs lie, indeed Gavin? And yet I raised the subject of my late uncle and she asked me how Maura was coping. There was no hint of any past relationship here, no tender feelings revealed towards either Gerald or Maura and, in fact, no suggestion of Gerald having been anything other than a fairly distant acquaintance. I wondered if Twentyman had got it all wrong and then I saw that he had not. For to my embarrassment Mary began to sob while telling me that Gerald had been a good man, a kind man, that nobody had really appreciated him and that the poor soul had never got over April's death. I surmised that her relationship, like mine, had been another casualty of that August day.

Mary's conversation drifted into reminiscences of the things that Cal and I had got up to as children and she chuckled over some story concerning a football and a back window. I dutifully laughed but this, like many early memories we are bombarded with, only formed part of the prehistory that one's relatives come out with at family gatherings. For all it meant to me now, it could have been a tale of any two little boys and the sound of breaking glass.

I wondered if Cal had ever told his mother about what he and Annie from Fazakerley had got up to on rainy afternoons when school games had been cancelled but it hadn't been my business to tell her, then or now. Come to think of it, I never actually knew myself how much Cal had been exaggerating but his tales of his salacious exploits with the fiery maiden had always been amusing and shocking to one such as myself, untutored in the subtleties of Red Annie or, for that matter, any other girl from Fazakerley or anywhere else.

I consulted my watch. The thought of an urgent opinion on an agricultural tenancy which I had promised to email on my phone when I returned to my hotel room, was starting to prey upon my mind. It was already three months late and John had phoned up again that morning to tell me that the solicitors were losing patience with me and that he had almost run out of excuses that they would accept. I was feeling moderately guilty about that and, at the same time, I felt the same about being an intruder in Mary's house.

For whatever reason, I needed out of St. Roman's Terrace now. I shut my eyes as Mary continued to prattle on about the past. I momentarily recalled the scene as Ben, Cal and I walked home from school, discussing life, girls, football, the charts and what was on telly that night. Then, as I approached my house, the soul of black-and-white Meg was in my mind and I thought of her barking hysterically and bounding along the pavement to meet me. When I got to the front gate of No.8, mum and dad would be standing waiting for me and looking much younger and more animated than I could ever remember them to have been in reality. I knew that it was only a vision, but a comforting one at that. If I tried really hard then I could even see Ros in her striped school blouse and smart blazer waving to me from the end of the street and beckoning me to join her.

'Are you sure that you're not feeling ill?'

I returned to the present.

'No, just a bit tired from doing too much work recently!'

I gulped down the rest of the tea, gathered up the crumbs and again denied that I was suffering from any physical ailment.

'Oh, one thing Christopher, before you go. You'll find this interesting. I was talking to the woman who bought your uncle's house. She's a bit, well, vulgar you might say. They're from Kirkby, I believe.'

She paused here, so that the full enormity of 'from Kirkby' might sink in and underline the fact that Mary had always been so terribly socially aware. If she could have got away with it, she would have had made the lower orders use the tradesman's entrance if she had been lucky enough to have afforded such a thing. Momentarily I thought of one of Cal's tales about a wedding he had attended in the parish church in Kirkby. A wedding that was particularly memorable because it had ended in the best fight that he had ever seen at a wedding, and only ended when the groom and best man fell out just after the knot had been tied and were eventually arrested when the police had to be called.

'They came into money, I believe, and moved out here.' She made the 'out here' sound as though she lived in the deepest boondocks, far away from the suburbs of what she regarded as common old Liverpool.

'Yes, well anyway she told me that a couple of days ago a man came round, and was snooping about. She said he was full of some sort of cock and bull story about historic buildings plaques or some such nonsense. He claimed he was from the Crosby Architectural Society or something or other. Never heard of it, I must say, and nor had she. Anyway, she was very suspicious and wasn't going to let him in but apparently her son took a liking to the man and insisted. Anyway the strange thing was...'

She paused again and looked at me shrewdly.

'She described this man and do you know what, Christopher? He sounded rather like you, with a bit of a posh accent and a fancy jacket just like the one you're wearing today. I don't suppose it was you, was it?'

'No, I only arrived yesterday', I lied, 'and anyway I've got no interest in historic buildings or stuff like that.'

Reluctantly I realised that Mary Moscrop was not quite as naive as I had I taken her for.

11

Riego Street forms part of the maze of small thoroughfares lying between the southern ends of Hope Street and Rodney Street, almost in the shadow of the older of the two great cathedrals which dominate the Liverpool skyline. The houses, four-storey Georgian with pilasters, window boxes and front railings, looked a lot more prosperous and respectable than they did in the days when Gill and April had lived there, now that rising house prices and gentrification had reached the area.

I knocked on the blue painted door of number nineteen and it was opened with alacrity, as if my visit had been anticipated. A young man dressed in a neat and prohibitively expensive suit stood in front of me.

'Yeah?'

'I wonder if you could help me. I'm looking for a lady...'

'Ain't we all, mate?' he chuckled.

I ignored that and continued. 'Gillian Harmer.'

'Ah, that's a bit difficult innit.'

'Why is that?'

'Because she's not here.'

I looked surprised and said, 'But she does live here?'

'She does, mate, but like I said before, she ain't in right now.'

There was something about his manner and in particular his outrageously bogus cockney accent that made me want to be really rude but not being quite sure of what to make of him, I decided that I would try one more time. As usual, I embellished the truth.

'Look, I don't really know what your problem is but I'm an old friend of hers, back on a short visit and I'd like to know when you're expecting her back, if you are expecting her back, that is... Mr, er...'

'What the hell do want with her if you don't mind me asking?'

'I need to speak to her on a purely personal matter.' I stopped short of adding that it was none of his bloody business. But he didn't rise to the bait and after looking at me in a deliberately vacant way he shrugged his shoulders.

'Whatever', was his only comment.

'Whatever what?' I replied, irritated by his play acting.

'Just whatever, nuffink else mate.' Then seeing that a further comment was called for he added by way of explanation, 'Fought you was one of her students, didn't I? I was about to tell you to piss off back to the uni an' make a bleedin' appointment but it's just as well that I didn't. Anyway, she'll be back at half two but you can't wait here, know what I'm saying?' And with that he slammed the door in my face.

I stood there for a moment and, resisting the temptation to shout something inappropriate through the letterbox, I turned on my heels and retraced my steps back up the street. Who was this strange person who seemed to enjoy being so gratuitously rude to complete strangers? But then being gratuitously rude to complete strangers is a trick which I do not wholly disapprove of myself!

173

On an impulse I walked towards the cathedral. A building of superlatives, it never failed to impress me and I inwardly genuflected in homage before walking in and standing underneath the vast soaring arches. It was an edifice built on a scale that the mediaeval masons would have marvelled at and, truly, a monument fit for my city. I smiled. 'My city' – I liked that. I was home. I sat down and shut my eyes and thought that when I had left Liverpool for good, this proud but enormous building had not even been finished.

'Rather a lot of wasted space in here – it's much too empty, don't you think?'

I was tempted to say 'No speaka da English' to an old bore in a Barbour jacket who, for reasons best known to himself, was trying to engage me in conversation. But instead I mumbled something vague about Scott's great vision and the spirit of the age and then pretended to pray in an ostentatious manner. Obviously having little staying power when it came to downright aloofness and put-on piety he strode away to annoy someone else. For a moment I was tempted to shout after him that, 'No, it bloody well isn't a waste of space', even if Gerald had dismissed it as being Gimcrack Gothic unlike its glitzy rival down the road. Give me this one any day for at least it looks like a church unlike the Mersey Funnel. My passion subsided and I lit a candle for April and another for Gerald. Then, I walked out into the blustery temporal world.

A couple of pints later I was feeling at ease again and as I sat amongst the mahogany and copper calm of the Philharmonic Bar taking in its atmosphere, I thought about music and how it could evoke people and places from the past. Gavin and I would often attend live performances of a surprising variety and, even though our tastes were poles apart (mine being generally eclectic and good and his being generally conventional and bad), we never seemed to lose our desire to travel to outlandish venues in the dingiest parts of London and relive our youth with monotonous regularity. One high point had been a Siberian rock band we had seen at a venue in deepest darkest Fulham where every raucous number had been introduced by, 'The next song is about women and horses and mountains', interspersed with, 'And now a song about horses, mountains and women.' After a while we began to wish they would sing about something different, and by the end we wished that they would just stop singing at all.

I thought about everything I had seen with Gavin and then inconsequentially remembered going with Fran to the Hammersmith Odeon to see Steeleye Span play on their Rocket Cottage tour. As I sat next to her in the stalls, I wished that I had been there on my own for I was still hankering after Ros and it was all too much listening to one of her favourite bands without having her there at my side. Why had I never communicated with Ros after hearing of Nick Drake's untimely demise? Why, for that matter, had I never communicated with her in the last forty years? Time for a sharp exit.

I finished my drink and, as I was leaving, a man in a shabby mackintosh approached me.

'Excuse me sir, but are you a Christian, like?'

I wondered if I really looked like one. 'How much?'

He was obviously thrown by not having to relate a tale of not having enough money for the bus to Wigan or wherever it was that he would claim his 'sick auld mudder' was living, he did a quick mental calculation as to the price of a can of whatever his special brew was and was suitably grateful when I dropped a handful of pound coins into his outstretched hand. Then, feeling better for having distributed alms to the deserving but unwashed, I went in search of lunch.

Just after two thirty I was back in Riego Street and this time the door was opened by a tall, slender and pretty woman in a cotton print dress.

'Ah, you must be the person who called earlier, the one Rajiv told me about.'

'Rajiv, is that his name? He didn't seem to be very welcoming.'

'Oh, that's just Raj for you. He never is. He's my lodger, by the way. He's a bit eccentric. I suppose he put on his East End accent. He does that sometimes. It's pure invention on his part as he's doing a doctorate in applied linguistics and comes from a very superior part of Cheshire – Alderley Edge I think.'

She was looking rather puzzled as if she was trying to remember how she knew me. 'Raj told me that he thought that you were a "stuck-up git", if you'll pardon the expression, so he laid it on thick. He's a great one for taking instant dislikes.'

My opinion of Rajiv was going up. Then I noticed her looking intently at me and I felt a little uncomfortable.

'I do know you don't I? You're, er...'

'Christopher Kingston. April's cousin.'

'Of course you are! I remember now but I haven't seen you for what must be ages. Well, come in, come in, what a surprise.' It was odd but she seemed to have changed little since the days when she was Gillian Ainsdale and lived in Serpentine Drive, next door to April and Ben. Granted, she was a bit older but somehow she looked much better than in the days when she wore Kaftans and Indian dresses and had her hair permed in that loathsome way which, mercifully, died with the end of that most style-conscious and visually challenging decade. Whether she was still such an objectionable phoney who I had so resolutely disliked when I had first met all those years ago, was another matter that was yet for me to find out.

'You've been here before, haven't you?'

I told her that I had been, twice, but long ago, and she replied that of course she remembered that now and we went down the stairs and in to the kitchen. At her bidding I sat down at a long limed oak table and she placed a large glass of red wine before me.

'A bit early in the day, perhaps. So what on earth brings you again to Riego Street on this beautiful spring afternoon, Christopher?'

'Oh, I was just curious to know how you were getting on. I live in London now, you see, been there for years. I thought I'd just drop in and say hello.'

'Well that's nice isn't it? Rather unexpected and, oh, Rajiv said you asked at the door for Gillian Harmer. How on earth did you know my married name?'

'I cheated by looking up this address in the electoral roll in the Crosby library to see who lived in the house now. Ben said that he thought you might have moved back here but he wasn't sure.'

'Well he was right, I did move back a few years ago. You'll notice that the area's changed for the better now.'

'I sort of gathered that but to be honest most of the middle of Liverpool has.' I was stuck for something else to say and the whole situation seemed so false.

'Hmm, well, flattered as I and my home city are by this sudden attention, I don't suppose that you want to discuss property prices in the district, do you, or even want to talk about one of my parties which, correct me if I'm wrong, you came to with your Rosamund once? Nice girl she was but you're not in touch with her any more – so far as I know anyway.'

'No, I'm not', I said hesitantly, wondering how she could possibly have known that.

'And this isn't just a social call on me, is it?'

'Well, not really, - you don't mind if I call you Gill?'

'Not at all, most people do.' She smiled disarmingly and I felt that, in some way, I was beginning to open up the past again.

'Maybe it sounds a bit odd but I wanted to have a chat with you about something important.'

I paused and Gill made no effort to help me out of my impasse. Instead she just looked puzzled.

'The thing is well, I wanted to know more about April, what sort of person she was. I feel that I never got to know her as an adult, not properly anyway and I've been wondering...' I tailed off. Once again it all sounded so completely unbelievable, to me to be talking about April to another person whom I had never really known.

'Christopher, I can't think why after so many years away you should now want to know more about what April was like. I would have thought that Ben or almost any other members of your family could have told you much more than I can.'

'But that's why I'm asking you. She was my cousin and I don't want to be rude but it's because you're not family, and therefore sort of detached from us all, that I thought that you might be able to give me a less involved view.' I could see a tear forming in her eye.

'I mean that even though you were undoubtedly her best friend.'

She regained her composure. 'I'm not sure how well I really knew her myself – *really* knew her, I mean.'

'What do you mean?' I asked.

'Well, you're asking me about someone that I haven't seen...' She broke off and added softly, 'It's been such a long time since she died.'

'I know that.' I lent over and gave her a hug, realising that this was just as difficult for her as me.

'Gill, tell me something about her – the real her as you remember her. Tell me anything or everything.'

'If you really want me to...' She sounded doubtful but I nodded and hoped that my smile was suitably disarming.

'I don't really know where to start.' She paused and after rolling up her sleeves in a very workmanlike way took a delicate sip of wine before settling down in a wicker chair.

'Well, the first thing you should know is that April was quite a complex person – aren't we all? And although I was certainly her best friend when we were both little, at primary school and as teenagers and even at university...' She trailed off. 'What I mean to say is that I don't think I ever really knew all the sides to her character. I doubt if anyone did really.'

Having got over the awkwardness of the beginning, she went on to tell me that April was witty, had style, was clever, could be good fun but would wallow in sulkiness, that she was incredibly clever and hard working at school and after that. She was sometimes incredibly generous and on other occasions miserably mean, that she was

179

open hearted and yet often spiteful. That she could be guileless or scheming to order, in fact nothing that I hadn't already known myself or heard from Ben. Sensing that she seemed to want some input from me, I told her that I had never really got over April's death and that I often thought about all the things that had led up to that fateful Sunday when I and Ros had discovered her body. Now I was trying to make sense of everything so many years later.

'Gill, tell one something. Was April any different in the week before her death? Did she do anything unusual or act out of character?'

'Out of character? One thing that you could always confidently say about April was that she was completely unpredictable – loopy if you like, in a nice way. But in that particular week I did notice that she was definitely preoccupied about something. I don't know what it was that was worrying her but she did hint to me that she needed some money but she didn't say what it was for. Mind you, that wasn't strange in itself because she always seemed to have more than enough money than she let on and yet was always talking about needing more.'

I found that odd coming from one who, despite her political pretensions, had been so positively spoiled herself. I tried to forget my earlier dislike of Gill. Maybe dislike was too strong a word. I just found her intensely annoying. I returned to cross-examination mode.

'Did she mention anything about trying to get a hundred pounds from Ben?'

'A hundred pounds? From Ben? I don't think so. He never seemed to have very much himself. As April used to say, what little he had he spent on his dirty little pleasures. But even if he had a hundred pounds I can't see that he would have given it to April, can you?'

'Not really. But was she getting money from anyone else at the time?'

'You mean not from Ben or her dad? Well, I wouldn't have mentioned it only you seem to want to know everything and you are family. She had another man, a lover she claimed he was, who gave her money regularly.'

'Who are you talking about, Barry Leemings?'

'Of course not! That poor sod didn't have a penny to his name although that wasn't the only reason why I didn't care for him.' At least she hadn't dissociated herself from not liking him because of his lack of class or of money. Gill didn't seem to have changed, at least where lifestyle was concerned. She wrinkled her brow as if in deep thought. 'I got the impression that her lover was quite a bit older than Barry.'

'But did she have a lover, other than Barry?'

'Well I don't really know but she let on that she did.'

'What was his name?'

'I don't know. She never said anything about him other than this one time when we'd had a drink. She didn't tell me much other than this bloke was regularly giving her money. Ten or twelve pounds a week I think, but I can't remember the exact figure. She seemed friendly enough with him because I once heard her on the phone to him, laughing and joking and being all April-like and coy.'

'When was that?'

'Oh, about a month or so before she died.'

'But you must know who that man was?'

'Must I? Why must I? She didn't tell me and, believe me, I was desperate to know all the gossip in the way that genuine old friends do. But she said was that it was none of my business and I just had to leave it at that.'

'What do you think that the money was for?'

'Who knows? She never told me but I was pretty sure that Barry knew about it.'

'What, that she was being bankrolled by a lover – a sort of sugar daddy?'

She laughed at my use of the term.

'I don't think so or if he was she never let on.'

'Didn't he mind?' I added as she smiled.

'Who, Barry? I wouldn't have thought so. He was happy enough to spend her cash wherever it came from. In fact, he was always happy to spend anyone's money. Although I'm not sure that I'd call getting a tenner a week being bankrolled exactly. But don't get me wrong, Christopher – Barry wasn't a bad sort, really. I always felt that he was much maligned, especially by me. He had a brilliant mind and I know it sounds corny, but it was something I admired and envied him for. Truth was I always had a bit of an inferiority complex when it came to academic matters and I always felt a bit sort of second-rate compared to April and Barry. You do know that Barry had already started on his doctorate, don't you?'

She rummaged around in one of the drawers of the large dresser and produced a folder containing a wad of close-typed foolscap sheets held together with a rusty bulldog clip.

'This is the unfinished manuscript of his thesis although in truth he had barely started it.'

'Why on earth do you have it? And why have you kept it all these years?'

'What else could I do with it? I didn't want to throw it away and his brother didn't want it.'

'He had a brother?'

'He had, but he was a bit peculiar too. His name was Guy and he was a bit of a waster – into his drugs in a big way. Dropped out of university and went round always in the same black clothes and cowboy hat on, talking to himself in lines out of a Pinter play – "Jenkins, is your name Jenkins?" was one of his favourites. God knows what became of him, poor sod. I don't think that he had anything to do with April's death because he was always much too spaced out to do anything.'

'I remember meeting him at that party in this house and thinking he looked ridiculous like a Lone Ranger or something. But go on with telling me about people that April knew.'

She stopped and gave me a sly look.

'It is April's death, rather than her life or her friends, that you're interested in, isn't it?' I didn't answer but decided to take advantage of her direct approach.

'Gill, where was Barry on the day that April died?'

'I've no idea because I never saw him after the party. That awful Sunday began so ordinarily. April and I had breakfast together. Weetabix, honey and yoghurt and, because it was Sunday, a bacon butty as well. It's strange how you remember banal things like that after a traumatic event, isn't it. Anyway April left the house at twelve or so to meet Barry. According to her, they had something important to do. She never said where they were going and I had no idea. Then I went out in Daisy to meet some pals – you remember Daisy, my little green 2CV with the yellow mudguards? And well that's it and I never saw April, or Barry for that matter, again. The next thing I knew was that Dad phoned me in the evening and said that was April was dead and you and Ros were the ones who had found her.'

'Do you think it was Barry that killed her?'

'I suppose that's what I assumed at the time but then I didn't know what to think. Then after Barry got killed himself in that horrible accident the next day, I felt guilty because I'd never liked him and hated it when he took April out on the back of that nasty bike. Maybe I didn't want to think the worst of Barry after April died but I'm not sure I could seriously have branded him a killer. He was never that bad to her.'

'What about your party when he attacked both April and me?'

'Oh, God, will I ever forget it! After you left without warning he went kind of berserk and started smashing up things in April's room and shouting blue murder. We nearly called the police to have him thrown out. We would have done too, if only they're hadn't been so much funny stuff in the house that they might have taken an interest in. But listen, Christopher, that kind of behaviour wasn't typical of Barry. He wasn't a violent person and if he had been then April was strong-minded enough to have dumped him.' I was far from convinced about that and told her so.

'Oh, April and Barry had their ups and downs but they were good together. They used to talk about literature, art, history and the lot. True soulmates I would have said, made for each other despite the rather obvious social differences.'

I was amused by this observation from one who had always prided herself in being the great leveller and claimed to have recognised no class system or divisions.

Interesting how a handy chunk of parental wealth helps to iron out one's own internal inconsistencies.

'He was very pleased that April was expecting a baby.'

'What do you mean?'

This was news to me and certainly not something that had shown up on the post-mortem report or been hinted at by anyone before now.

'Don't sound so angry, Christopher! I don't know if she really was pregnant but that's what April told me and she said she was really pleased.'

'Whose child was it going to be?' She looked surprised and was about to say, 'Barry's of course', but I could see that I had planted the seeds of doubt in her mind. She just shrugged and did not hazard a guess.

'When was the baby supposed to be due?'

'Well it must have been quite early in the pregnancy and she never mentioned any dates to me.'

'Was she was going to keep it or was the money for an abortion...'

She cut in angrily. 'Just remember that she was a good Catholic girl and that she really believed in the gift of life as she called it. Oh, I know it's really easy for us to mock her and her beliefs but she and Barry very positively wanted that child.'

'I wasn't mocking her, Gill.'

'I should hope not. She was sincere and they were both very interested in the spirit world too.'

I didn't quite follow the logic of this but as Gill waved the fragments of the thesis at me, I read the title: 'Sir William Crookes and Nineteenth Century Psychokinesis - A study of the Scientific Approach to Parapsychology in later Victorian literature.'

'Here, look at that', she said, pointing to a shelf on which sat a thing like a large light bulb containing a revolving metal vane. 'It's a Crookes' radiometer. Sir William Crookes was their hero – an eminent scientist as well as an experimenter into spirit mediums, levitation, electro-psychic fields and all that sort of thing. Once of his inventions was this fellow but I can't for the life of me remember what principle it's supposed to be demonstrating. Science never was my strong point. Anyway it belonged to Barry and I remember him buying it in a little shop near here. The sort of place that sold almost anything useless that you could imagine. Like everything else of interest in this city, sadly it's been swept away for road improvements and such. This was a present from him to April and I hadn't the heart to chuck it out.'

I handed it back to her and she said, 'He had a favourite medium, you know. She was called Florence something or other.'

'Who had a favourite medium? Barry?'

'No, Sir William of course. She was a young woman who lived in Hackney or somewhere like that. Anyway Crooks was eminent in his field, just like Sir Oliver Lodge and Charles Richet, other famous scientists who dabbled in the sprit world around the time of the Great War. Many of them did because so many of their young relatives had died.'

She smiled and then added, 'One thing I do remember though, was April quoting Richet in defence of spiritualism when he was asked whether there was any proof of its existence. He just said, "I never said it was possible. I only said it was true."'

She handed the thesis to me.

'Well it is a sort of touching memento to both of them, April and Barry. I've got two copies of it so you can have one to keep yourself since you're so interested in April and what made her tick.'

As she refilled the glasses I glanced at one of the pages of the thesis. It was neatly typed out but its contents were way beyond me. 'Reductionist formulae', 'recurrent spontaneous phenomena' and 'the undisputed link between poltergeist and the sexual frustrations of adolescence' meant little to the uninitiated or uninterested.

'Did she believe in all this phooey?'

'I think she did.'

I wondered what all of this had to do with April and her perception of life up to then. Then I noticed Gillian studying me with an air of amused detachment and as I put the sheets down she laughed.

'All this is a bit of a blast from the past, isn't it, Christopher? You're very inquisitive about everything. Dad did say that you'd gone to London and become a lawyer – a Q.C. no less. That's why you're always asking questions I suppose.'

'I like asking questions. It's my job.' I thought about it and it was true. I did like asking questions and hearing the answers too. I enjoyed the fact that my job gave me an insight into other people's lives, even if it was unfortunately usually only at a time of crisis.

Gill was still studying me intently and I felt that I had to say something to break the silences. I had the feeling that she was beginning to take more than a passing interest in me.

'So tell me then Gill, how has your life turned out since we last met? What have you been up to?'

'Oh, just the usual things. I met a bloke named Harmer, lived with him and got married. Not a great success, in fact a bloody disaster, so I divorced him, returned here and now I'm free and easy again. I'm teaching up the road. End of story and quite boring really. That's my son, by the way.'

She produced a framed graduation photograph of a handsome youth standing next to a weedy looking female.

'B.A. (Hons.), Warwick, with the lovely Wendy in tow, also BA. (Hons.), Warwick. I think that you'll agree with me, she's pretty awful, isn't she? But then you can't choose for them, even if you waste time trying to.'

I wondered what would happen if I ever dared to express any views to Kirsty as to her choice of boyfriends.

'And you, Christopher?'

'I'm in the throws of... well I'm about to be divorced and I have two children, boy and a girl, both grown up but the girl is still living with me in London and about to apply to Cambridge if she gets the grades. But tell me Gill how do you occupy your time now – apart from the University teaching, I mean?'

She smiled. 'Oh, a bit of this and a bit of that. I suppose Rajiv would call it doing a bit of ducking and diving. Actually I do a bit of writing for literary academic journals and the like, although I'm being rather modest. I've flowered rather late in life with my own literary career, I mean.'

I looked blank but suitably impressed that I was in the company of a writer.

'I remember you always quoting from poets and books all the time when you were a teenager – I suppose that came from doing English at school. But Christopher

188

I guess my works aren't erudite enough for your tastes now. They're modern novels, not exactly post-structuralist but quite popular in their own way. They're in the genre known to the sceptical non-highbrow reader as Aga Sagas, although I hate that expression.'

I noticed the cream-coloured Aga in the corner and the penny dropped.

'Of course – Gill Harmer, The Raven's Nest, etc.' I couldn't have named any more of them so the 'etc.' was a bit of a cheek. But I did remember Francesca had once read The Raven's Nest and described it as 'a load of pretentious, badly written feminist nonsense where all men are bastards and quite rightly so.' I decided not to pass on my estranged wife's views on Gill's novels which I would probably have agreed with. I had already decided they wouldn't have been my cup of tea, even if I had never bothered to read them.

Gill went on unabashed. 'At the moment I'm writing a novel set in the early seventies, dealing with student life then. It's loosely based on this house and the people who visited it then.'

'Tell me more, Gill. I am genuinely interested in all of that. I was just but a boy back then...'

'Rather a coy way to describe a surly teenager who thought he knew it all.'

'Ros might have put it that way I suppose. Well I prefer the phrase "a failed Bohemian" according to others. But I do remember that the goings on here were, to coin a phrase, a bit way out.'

'Two cliches at once, Christopher! You'd never make it now in the publishing world with such corny words. But, anyway, the "goings on" were very much of their time in the seventies – an unromantic era if there ever was one. All sorts of weirdos who hadn't been invited used to turn up and that was half the fun. The other half was trying to get rid of them again afterwards. Oh God, you remember the clothes we wore?'

She shrieked with laughter. 'Flower patterned shirts and frilly gypsy skirts, Indian prints and crushed velvet, jackets with wide lapels and browns in all shades – brown, I ask you! Horrible Cheesecloth shirts, ludicrous loons with gold stars on them, tie-dye tee-shirts, flares...'

She collapsed in hysterics at the very thought of it all and then added, 'I can understand why gear like that went out of fashion. But why does no one ever have parties like that nowadays?'

'Because', I ventured, 'perhaps Party Sevens, joints on the stairs and rock music at full blast in rooms where someone's taken out the lightbulbs would all be a bit passé now, just like spider-plants in macramé potholders.'

She chuckled, refilled our glasses and moved her chair closer to mine. 'And what about the people themselves? They always seemed to be making up their own life stories and pretending to be someone that they weren't. I remember one chap went around telling everyone that he was something high up in Her Majesty's Diplomatic Service when he was actually one of the lab technicians at the vet school. He was a friend of that Zoe, the small blonde lass who came from Darwen and always wanted to marry a farmer. Remember her?'

I nodded, wondering if Zoe had achieved her ambition and settled into an agricultural existence and if she still said 'Bloody Hell Fire' in such a distinctive way. Maybe she was still worrying about the indigenous people and still wore the same purple tee shirt.

'What happened to Zoe?' I asked.

'I think she became an organic market gardener up Garstang way – not a farmer's wife mucking out the cowsheds or anything like that. You sound as though you liked her.'

'She did make an impression', I said, trying not to sound so pompous and disapproving.

'Hmm – then there was Amber Darks – that wasn't her real name by the way, it was Louisa Crumpshawe. Oh and we can't forget Cady, short for Cadenza – that was her real name believe it or not. Her parents were musicians and were clearly improvising when it came to naming her. Then there was good old Shez who married Pete Dwyer and that Susie Clayton person who you probably didn't meet and, oh yes, there was Nano. We called him that because he had an attention span of a nano-second and...'

I let her ramble about people I had never met or had mercifully forgotten while I drank the wine until I realised that she had paused and was reflecting on something. 'But I suppose that you didn't really know them all because I forget that you were a couple of years or so younger than us. Still are, of course', she laughed. 'Anyone else you remember?'

'Zac Wildfire. Whatever happened to him?'

'Oh, you mean that weird bloke Zac? His real name was Roger Bulmerton by the way.'

'I didn't know his name, but I remember being really annoyed by him because he was trying to chat up Ros at one of your parties.' This was a bit disingenuous because 'one of your parties' implied that I had been to more than one of them. But Gill ignored this and went on.

'No idea where he is now and I don't care either. Probably even more well off than he was then but I thought he was a right plonker, all those half-truths that he told. Mind you, Christopher, I've always rather enjoyed telling fibs myself so perhaps that's why I write novels nowadays. They're a good chance to tell a string of lies from beginning to end. I always maintain that some of my best friends are the ones that I've put into books. But who cares about the truth anyway? Long live the seventies, though! Eee, them were t'days and there's nowt like nostalgia, eh?'

I remembered Gavin's point that, when it came to remembering the past, reality was unimportant but detail was everything. And so we continued in the same vein, with the wine being consumed until she suggested that we must have something to eat and produced an already prepared vegetable risotto and popped it to heat up in the very Aga of the sagas.

I enjoyed telling tales of things and people that I remembered, or thought I did, and had not talked about since my Liverpool days. Gill seemed pleased to be able to supply the details along with interesting footnotes until the meal was ready. I began to think that maybe I had misjudged Gill when we first met and perhaps she was no more a phoney than I had been when we first met. The wine and the subjects discussed ebbed and flowed: Pinot Noir, Chardonnay and Vinho Verde (which contrary to my views about that delicacy from Portugal I surprisingly enjoyed) mixed with marriage and its intrinsically unsatisfactory nature, children and their intrinsically unsatisfactory nature, politics (also unsatisfactory in current times), education, tuition fees, life in general and an awful lot of little consequence. The mellow evening merged imperceptibly into the mellow night.

I was feeling extraordinarily relaxed and the alcohol and the company had made me so forget about April that when Gill said, 'Raj is out tonight and we've got the place to ourselves', I misread all the signs, as I usually did when women are concerned and, wondering what she was on about, I innocently said, 'It's getting rather late now and I better be off to catch the train back to Crosby if I haven't already missed it.'

'Don't go, Christopher. The evening's young and it would be very nice if you could stay longer – in fact stay the night if you like.'

Flattered that she was making a pass at me and being too shy to demur, I looked into her face and merely grinned foolishly. Then she took my hand.

'She sleeps up in the attic there alone, poor maid', said Gill. 'And 'tis but a stair betwixt us.'

'Too derivative – some sentimental Victorian guff', I heard myself say.

'Ah, Christopher, sentimental and Victorian and guff no doubt but be careful as you may be treading on my dreams as well as my stairs.'

And gently we trod up her stairs as she led me up to a bedroom at the top of the house next to the room where April had once lived. All I could do when I flopped down on the bed was to address the wallpaper with, 'Sweetbriar or is it the Strawberry Thief? Some more sentimental Victorian William Morris rubbish.'

She laughed and began to remove my clothes. I felt like a teenager being with a woman for the very first time. I shivered with excitement and exhilaration as I watched her slipping off her dress and merely said, 'Her rich attire creeps rustling to her knees.'

'It's hardly the Eve of St. Agnes, Christopher, and I'm certainly not Madeline', she laughed, 'even though I may indeed sleep in blanched linen, smooth and lavender'd.'

Fast forward to 'the wee sma' hours', as Malkie would have put it, and I lay in the darkness listening to Gill's gentle breathing at my side. I thought of the mess that I had made of my life already and of how Francesca and I could have been really happy. Perhaps it could have worked out if we had given it another chance and then a new thought occurred to me. What on earth was I doing here in bed with a woman who had been April's best friend? Keats came back into my head and as Gill slept in an azure-lidded sleep beside me I needlessly wondered why had I enjoyed this encounter so much? The answer to the latter question was obvious even to me but the first question, if it had any answer, eluded me. And then, being me, I was feeling full of remorse and guilt and self-pity. The worst thing was that I knew it was all absurd, completely absurd and that both of us might regret it in the morning.

I heard a bell in the distance ring the quarter hour. 'The chime of the city clock...' – another line from a half-forgotten Nick Drake song and I was firmly back in the past. I lay still and thought of April and of Ros and of all the other things I regretted. And as the waxing moon rose high over the cold Lenten city of the present, my mind drifted back away from the lost domain of my childhood.

12

Shortly before eleven I was standing at Lime Street listening to the announcer telling a scarcely believing public that Virgin Trains regretted the late arrival of the service from London Euston. Twenty minutes delay was just about enough time for a coffee, a Kit-Kat and a chance to observe the human condition. When we were in London supposedly attending lectures for our Bar finals, Gavin and I had often spent hours sitting at a window table in a teashop at Holborn Viaduct casting a critical eye over those whose paths were unfortunate enough to cross our line of vision.

Neither of us had never quite grown out of this pleasure. We would invent names, occupations and even vices for the more interesting passers-by and decided where they were going and why. On rare occasions Gavin would actually follow them into the street and accost complete strangers with, 'Ah, it's Mr er...', and invariably they would then give him their name and he would add knowingly, 'Oh, yes, I thought it was you. How's...' trying then to guess their names of their husband or wife and offspring. Childish pleasures, no doubt, but certainly a good way of passing the time. Much better than sitting through dull hours of lectures on the drafting of pleadings, petition procedure and the art of advocacy taught by those who we thought had not mastered it themselves.

I settled down and looked around to see if there was anyone interesting enough to describe to Gavin the next time we met. I studied a man with a sort of Mr Potato Head set of disparate features, including an amazing pair of jug-handle ears when someone spoke to me.

'Do you ever wonder who they all are and what they're up to?'

'Who do you mean, the people here?'

A man sitting nearby must have noticed my obvious interest in the passing scene and I was taken aback to find that my stares had been quite so obvious. Just as I was about to reply a straggly-haired teenage girl in a long fawn coat came up to him and, judging by their social interaction (one of Gavin's phrases) I could see that they were father and daughter. My thoughts turned to my own straggly-haired daughter. It must have been, what, eight or nine years since Kirsty had last been here. I felt a little unsure as to how she would react to it, now that she was no longer the little pig-tailed child who had held my hand so tightly and cried because her feet were sore from walking so much on the hard streets. I wanted her to like Liverpool, for in the last few days I had come to realise how much this place meant to me. More so, I guessed, because I was a self-imposed exile who had no intention of ever returning here to live. I enjoyed reminiscing about Liverpool – lost domain, indeed!

I laughed mirthlessly at my pretentious thoughts the night before and wondered what Gill had made of it all – enjoyed it, I hoped, without having had my ridiculous moral or emotional qualms. Then, in response to the muffled announcements echoing under the glass and iron sky, I gathered up my non-existent belongings and hurried to the platform as the London train slid in.

My worries about Kirsty not liking my hometown were as unfounded as most of my worries. Within minutes she was enthusing about the atmosphere, the buildings, the vibrancy and the accent which she had always thought was great. She relayed a verbal vignette which she had overheard on the train consisting of 'What's the matter witchew?' with the reply 'Our Perry's whipped me Crunchie, mam and I hadn't done nuffin at all to her', followed by their mother's retort of 'Will yer just shurrup Ryan, before I get a cob on and bloody belt yer one.'

I relaxed a little and we set off, myself anxious to avoid the shops and Kirsty anxious to see them, before arriving in due course with two laden carrier bags at the Pier Head. For the second time that week I took the ferry, although this time it was just for the round cruise.

As we approached Woodside Pier a large herring gull perched itself on the seat next to us and Kirsty, a sentimentalist at heart like myself, began to feed it with some crisps. A man in a turquoise top pointed to the gull and remarked, 'Bloody hell, is that yer pet, love? Put a saddle on it an' it'd win the frigging cup at Aintree!'

My daughter, more of a social realist than myself, laughed and began a spirited conversation with him on the recent improvements made to the city. She told him that she worked for a P.R. firm intent on attracting inward investment to Merseyside. I made no comment as she was carrying it off superbly and I was glad that, if nothing else, I had taught my daughter to dissemble unflinchingly. Maybe, on second thoughts, that had been Francesca's doing, for she could out-lie more convincingly than me any time.

Over lunch (strictly vegetarian, for Kirsty would brook no animal products and was toying with the idea of going the whole way and becoming a vegan), she produced a postcard from her bag and waved it in front of me. The card depicted an Alpine scene of chalets with window boxes full of flowers, cows with bells and an impressive backdrop of jagged peaks covered in snow. I knew, even though I had never been there, that it must be Murren. I tried to grab the card but Kirsty was too quick for me.

'Who's this Jessica then?' she said in a tormenting voice. 'Nice name – do you call her Jess?'

'You've no right to read my postcard but, since you ask, no one special. Only a friend.'

'Tee-hee, only a friend, eh? Then why does she look forward to meeting up with you again on her return? Mmm, I think that she's your...'

She tailed off and smiled at me. At least she hadn't used the multipurpose and apparently non-derogatory Liverpool word which could mean either a girlfriend or a wife but, not usually, a woman of ill repute.

'Will I have to call her mummy then?'

I aimed a swipe at her head with the Tate guidebook and suggested, forcibly that she change the subject.

We returned back to the Pier Head and the afternoon passed in a round of sightseeing, shopping and intense questioning about the Liverpool dialect. The latter subject, I kept reminding her, was hardly my forte as middle-class Crosby was not exactly a bastion of undiluted scouse. This time as we talked and walked the hard streets I felt that it was my feet which were getting sore and I was reminded of my own advancing years. By five we were both exhausted and ready to leave for Ben's.

Kirsty was suitably impressed with where Ben and Malcolm lived, as indeed I had been earlier in the week. From Cressington railway station onwards, the feel of a sleepy Victorian suburb was almost overwhelming and I said that, 'We must come back here on a warm evening and take in the balmy scents of all the flowering bushes arid exotic trees which must be growing in these sequestered gardens.' Kirsty looked at me as though I was as mad as a box of frogs. She had already decided to annex the phrase 'sequestered gardens' for her own use even though neither of us were quite sure what sequestered meant.

When we reached Bookery Nook our welcome was warm and spontaneous. Within minutes my daughter and Malcolm seemed to have hit it off.

'But why, when you have such a bonnie name as Kirsty, are you evidently so English?'

'My dad's grannie was fae Shetland, Stromness ye ken, so I'm a fellow countrywoman of yours wi' only a wee bit of Sassenach in me.'

He gave a mock grimace, possibly because her attempt to sound so Scots was merely comical rather than convincing.

'Och, is that right? But I cannie understand why ye don't speak as yer Grannie taught ye – and by speak it I mean all of the time', Malcolm replied and, as Kirsty graciously draped her jacket over his arm, she answered in her best Sarf-Lunnon accent.

'Pwobably, Malkie me old cock, cause I an English, Geddit?'

Dinner was a success both from the social and the culinary point of view. I was relieved to see that Malcolm had carefully scoured the kitchen and removed all traces of any meat, fish or animal by-products so that the Gelatine Finder General had no cause for concern when she did her customary inspection of the facilities. By nine o'clock Ben and I were tired but Kirsty seemed to have found a second wind and Malcolm was proposing to take her out on the town. I assented, although my agreement was merely cosmetic given the strong-willed nature of my daughter, and a lively discussion as to clubbing possibilities ensued. Kirsty mentioned a club that she had read about but Malkie replied with, 'Och, lassie, dinnae be daft. I ken mair exciting places than ye've ever heard of.'

'For God's sake stop being so bloody Scots all the time, Malcolm', said Ben. 'Just be careful, young Kirsty, as he's determined to make you a fag hag. So make sure that you both look after each other and don't come to any harm.'

A few minutes later they departed, Malcolm looking very suave and respectable and my daughter dressed in the kind of clothes that I pretended she never wore. Then Ben and I settled down with some eighties rock and just as I was tempted to tell him that his musical tastes were absolutely dreadful, he produced a very good bottle of dessert wine. After reading the label, I decided to drop my role as a wine critic.

'Ben, you remember our discussion the other night about April?'

He grunted but seemed moderately interested.

'Well I wasn't exactly entirely honest about the reason why I was asking you about her.'

'Em, you've lost me there, Chris.'

So I told him about the last meeting that I'd had with Gerald and about the solicitors' packet that had followed and about what I had been up to the last few days, including the meeting with Gillian Harmer, though I purposefully missed out how that evening had panned out. I remembered his old crack about 'She was only an architect's daughter, but she let the borough surveyor' and resisted the temptation to smile.

Then he said quietly, 'Why did you tell her something that was none of her business especially when you obviously slept with her last night. Don't deny it – I can see it in your face, you smug creep.'

Perhaps if Ben hadn't been so hospitable to me and perhaps if I hadn't been so desperate to discuss April with someone else, I would have respected Gerald's request to keep it all to myself. But it was all becoming too difficult for me to cope with on my own. The strange thing was that he didn't seem to be all that disconcerted as if trying to discover who had killed your sister was the most natural thing in the world. Perhaps it was. I moved the discussion on.

'Did you know about your dad and Mary Moscrop?'

Why, I wondered, was I poking at an open wound?

'Yes, Cal and I knew all along. We actually thought that it was a bit of a laugh, as if it made us like step-brothers. You know you're still as naive now as you were back then, Chris. I know Cal was your friend as well but it was all quite open if you saw the signs and, well, mum didn't exactly mind about Mary.'

'What do you mean, didn't mind?'

'Jesus! Look I suppose that when you're a kid you don't exactly think about your parents, or your uncles or aunts or any of your relations for that matter, as being real people. You only see them as two-dimensional cardboard cut-outs not as grown ups with adult motivations, sexual desires and all that kind of thing.' He paused and I wondered what revelation would come next.

'The Gerald and Mary thing had been going on for several months at least but she wasn't the first one by any means, or the last either. My father was a serial adulterer and he'd had lots of women, strings of affairs. Mum wasn't really hurt since I think she'd fallen out of love with him years before, that is if she ever had been in love with Gerald in the first place. He was the sort who couldn't pass a woman without making eyes at her. The great irony of it all was that apart from you it was only April, the great nosey parker who was always sticking her neb into everyone else's business, who didn't know anything about it either.'

'Did anyone eventually tell her, then?'

'Yes. Surprise Surprise, it was Cal, Mr. Super-cool-never-blab-about-anything. He told her when he and she were both under the influence of the pernicious plant, as indeed they, actually we all, often were. Incidentally Chris, how come you and that prissy little girlfriend of yours never smoked pot?'

'Not everyone in the seventies did, Ben, especially if they were in touch with the real world.'

'Ha! That category could hardly encompass you, Chris. You still haven't a bloody clue about how the real world works even now.'

I was about to protest when he cut me short with an even more withering line.

'Actually Chris, I always thought that you never got high because you were a bit of a control freak who never liked to let your guard down which is probably why you became a lawyer.'

Things were getting a little heated and the good-natured argument seemed to be developing into an undignified squabble. He might, I conceded, have a good point about me and the real world but I wasn't going to let him have the satisfaction of knowing that. I demanded a coffee and he went off to play with Malcolm's espresso machine. On his return I continued on the subject of Gerald's affair with Mary.

'You're quite sure that April knew about your dad and Cal's mum?'

'That's what I said already. Cal told her, if you remember.'

'And Aunt Maura knew about it as well?'

'Certainly, she knew. As you might imagine it caused a bit of friction between her and the Moscrops as a result.'

'So April's threat about exposing Gerald for whatever he had done couldn't have been about him and Mary?'

'That's right. Everyone knew and nobody bloody cared.'

'Did April ever say anything to you about having an older man – her boyfriend, or her protector or whatever he was?'

I had avoided any reference to a possible pregnancy since that perhaps had been an invention of April's, if the medical side of things was to be believed and I didn't want Ben going off on the huff with me.

'Not a word. I'd no idea that she was two-timing Barry but, if she was, good on her. He was such a low-life pond specimen. Maybe though that's the motive – one or other of the boyfriends was jealous of the other. It does happen, you know, that eternal triangle thing.'

'Eternal triangle's a bit corny, Ben. Tell me, why do you think that April came back to the house that afternoon?'

'Probably to try and get more money out of Gerald or maybe just to collect something that she'd forgotten. Does it really matter? When she did come in she probably found whoever it was that was ransacking the house and that person killed her.'

'Have you ever thought that it might have been the other way round and that she was the one who was ransacking the house. Maybe stealing things from your parents with the intent of "making someone pay", as she put it and that someone else might have appeared on the scene and confronted her?'

'Wouldn't that be a bit of an unlikely coincidence Chris? Two tealeaves in the house at the same time would be rather stretching it. Suppose though that it could have been one of the two boyfriends who had come across her in the act of thieving things?'

'And what would the motive have been then – jealousy, protection of property or their own moral outrage?'

'In the case of Barry Leemings, morals didn't enter into it. He didn't have any. But outrage is another matter.'

He saw my indignant expression and added, 'I won't hear a good word spoken about him.'

He poured the milky froth on the coffee and sniffed it in appreciation while I declined. Hot milk always reminded me of being sent to bed early when I had misbehaved.

'Ben, don't forget that Barry Leemings was sighted at the phone box by the station. It doesn't supply the motive but it might narrow it down to being Barry who was in the house with April, rather than that elusive second boyfriend.'

Ben yawned, got up and noisily stretched his legs.

'Fancy a walk?' I think that things are getting a bit heated at the moment.'

As we walked along the Grassington Promenade in the evening twilight and I took in the sea air, Ben wasted little time in returning the conversation to April.

'If I ever found out who did it I'd kill the bastard. I'm not joking, Chris, I really would. You don't know how much all of this has been eating into me ever since April died. I tell you that if I ever found out who it was, I'd kill him with my own bare hands. I don't want justice, I just want vengeance, pure and simple.'

He hurled a stone into the water with great vehemence and as he watched the widening rings, his wrath seemed to subside.

'Well at least it wasn't one of the family', he said.

'That's true enough. But one thing that puzzles me. Where was your dad that afternoon?'

'With Mary, in an empty house in College Road of all places. I may be wrong about where, but they were certainly together humping. Sordid or what?'

'So whose place in college Road were they in then?'

'I don't know. One that had something to do with Toby Ainsdale.' He snorted and said, 'Good old Toby Ainsdale, the great facilitator of course. He and Gerald were great pals from years back. They met just after the war, I think, but I've no idea where. Anyway they bought houses next to each other in Blundellsands and remained bosom buddies and you probably don't know it but Toby put some of the cash up when Gerald started his own business. Later on Gerald lent Toby money when one of his little speculations went wrong. So, when Gerald wanted the loan of a venue for his sordid little activities with Madame Moscrop, Toby was only too happy to oblige by giving him the keys to a property that he was doing up. Just another favour, naturally.'

At least he hadn't shortened it to the 'natch' that Kirsty liked to infuriate me with.

'Did Toby do a lot of properties up for people?'

'Not likely, he owned them all himself. Oh he was a right one for doing all sorts of things. I don't think that, as an architect, he was really supposed to go in for property speculation but he did. If I'm right, he did one or two joint ventures with Gerald. I did hear that the two of them bribed a lot of people – planning officers, councillors and the like. Oh, nothing big I think, but they must have ruined a few big old houses round Crosby, buying out the tenants and then dividing them into rabbit-hutch flats on the cheap and flogging them off. In time Toby smartened his act up because he was desperate to get onto some architects' committee but I'm really not sure. He was a right social climber, actually more of a bloody social mountaineer really. But you'd have to ask someone who knew both Toby and Gerald back then to know what they were really up to. I suppose that Toby was harmless enough though, a good friend to Gerald. He put up that five hundred reward after April died. Not that anyone was ever in a position to claim it. His wife was a silly woman, all over-acting and flirtatious although not to Gerald in public which made me think that they'd probably been up to something in the past. But why are we talking about the Ainsdales? They're boring and provincial and got nothing to do with it, even if you did bonk their daughter yesterday.'

'You brought the subject up didn't you, not me. Seriously Ben, one other question. Did April ever mention that she might be pregnant?'

I surprised myself by dropping this clanger when I hadn't intended to.

'What? I think you've got the wrong end of the stick there, Chris. She definitely wasn't and if she had been then I'd have known. What made you say that she was expecting?'

'Gillian told me.'

He snorted.

'As if that daft cow Gill would know anything. She was too busy prancing about or writing her crappy novels. Anyway if April had been pregnant it'd have shown up in the post-mortem and been mentioned by the Coroner. You know, don't you, that there was a great fuss about an autopsy? Gerald tried to stop it because he said it was against our religious beliefs. Take my word for it, Chris. Gillian's got it all mixed up as usual. I'm sure if April had thought that she was pregnant then she'd certainly have told Gerald. She'd have known that he'd stand by her and come to her assistance, financially or otherwise. He always did. I can see by the way that you're looking at me that you might think I'm being a bit nasty here, Chris, but I'm not. All of my life I always felt that I was playing second fiddle to April, so far as my father was concerned anyway. He was always so blinkered about her. Perhaps that's why I always thought of him as Gerald rather than Dad.'

Malcolm and Kirsty returned long after I'd gone to sleep and I did not see my daughter again until well after noon on the Sunday. She looked disgustingly healthy and full of cheer. In a quite unconcerned manner she wolfed down half a dozen pieces of toast and Marmite before demanding that Malcolm make her some more. I gathered that the night out had been a great success. My daughter had apparently held court in a gay club much to the chagrin of a person referred to by Malcolm as, 'you know the one, Ben, the lezzie with the funny hat and that hideous leopardskin thingy.'

*****

The next afternoon, Sunday, was going to be a quiet one, so far as I was concerned. Ben was off to work to catch up on some paperwork and Kirsty and Malcolm were taking the Magical Mystery Tour bus-trip. She tried to persuade me to come with them but I affected the slightly detached and deprecatory attitude to the Beatles which many from our city adopt as a cover when tourists mention them. I did point out to them that I had already been round Penny Lane and Strawberry Fields many times as a teenager myself but omitted to mention that I had made a pilgrimage to Paul's house in Forthlin Road earlier that very week and had the postcards and brochure to prove it.

At tea-time I returned to the hotel to collect my things for Ben had invited us to stay till Tuesday when we were due to return to London. Kirsty was returning to her exam revision and busy social life and myself to the sober delights of work and perhaps Jessica too, who would be back from her holiday in Murren any time now. But I was feeling dissatisfied as things had not really progressed in Liverpool very much and I was little nearer to finding out the truth about April's death than when I had started. On an impulse I phoned Twentyman and we talked for a few minutes about how I might take things further.

'Try a new angle, lad. See if you can find someone who knew the family then, who might have an outsider's view, so to speak.'

Easier said than done. I ran through the possibilities and drew up a short list. The list, however, which became even shorter when I had crossed off my one remaining parent who was in indifferent health and whom I didn't want to bother with such clumsy questions. I was paying the hotel bill when a leaflet left on the desk caught my attention. 'Take the Fast Ferry from Liverpool to Dublin.'

That inspired me to look out the number I had written down for Patrick Tierney in Ireland and soon I had translated it into the proper form with the international dialling code.

When I call a new number I always try to envisage the scene at the other end of the line. I remembered Sep telling me that when you called a Liverpool number during the war, you would always wonder if the building at the other end still existed or if it had been bombed to oblivion, an observation made all the more poignant by his own personal tragedy. This bright Sunday afternoon, however, I envisaged an old-fashioned black phone ringing out on a polished table in one of those foursquare elegant rectories that are the enduring monument to the protestant ascendancy in our sister island.

'I'm sorry but the number you have dialled has not been recognised.'

I was about to vent my spleen on the automatic voice but sanity prevailed and I contacted the operator instead. After demanding to know in a querulous voice what the problem was, I was told abruptly to 'miss out the 00353 and put back the 0. Love, it's an Isle of Man number you've been trying to obtain.' Still not quite believing her, I re-dialled and a minute later I was being passed from Madelaine Tierney to her husband.

'Hello Mr Kingston and it's grand to hear from you.'

He dealt with the call in a phlegmatic way and within a minute had issued a cordial invitation to both myself and Kirsty to 'come over to Mona's isle', where they had been living now for several years, and visit them for the day. I accepted and, using my debit card swiftly bought two day returns to the island, to be picked up at the ferry office the next morning before eight.

13

As I watched the great buildings of the Pier Head disappearing in the fine mist that lay over the city, Kirsty came to join me on the aft deck.

'Pretty cool, this old Sea-Cat is.'

She laughed and, after informing me that the word 'cool' was a bit, well, uncool when used by fogies of my age, asked me about the people we were going to visit. It didn't take long to tell her everything I knew about Tierney. Being somewhat economical with the truth, I said that I had certain business matters to discuss with him. As I had banked on, it didn't occur to her that barristers do not normally approach their clients directly on business matters and that the business was certainly personal.

We watched as the Blundellsands shore passed by and soon the fast moving craft was coming to the end of the Crosby Channel. I showed Kirsty the spot close to the Mersey Bar where, in a hurricane a hundred years ago, the Ellen Vannin on a night sailing from Ramsey to Liverpool had gone down with all her passengers and crew. This had been one of my grandfather's most dramatic tales and I told Kirsty of how, in the days before ships had radio, nobody had realised that she had been lost until the bodies of the sheep which had been in the pens were washed ashore together with a couple of mailbags. Hope had only finally been abandoned when her lifeboats were seen drifting aimlessly with all of their equipment intact and unused. The story had always fascinated me and, I described with gusto how the little ship batted against the waves on a cold December morning and was last seen by the crew of the nearby lightship in the midst of a storm the like of which had never been seen before. As I recounted the story in Sep's own words Kirsty's eyes were wide open with anticipation.

'God, I wish I'd met my great grandfather. He must have been a fascinating guy to have known. Is that why you're so interested in great disasters, ships sinking, train crashes, the war and things like that.'

I said, 'Probably – I could listen to his stories for hours. He loved stories of the sea and when he'd had a nip or two he would recite from one of the psalms. "They that go down to the sea in ships and occupy their business in great waters; These men see the works of the Lord and his wonders in the deep." I'm sure that it's because of him that I like the sea and ships and things about voyages of discovery so much.'

'You've got a bit of a romantic streak for a lawyer, haven't you Dad? You know, sometimes I think of you as being a bit of a romantic rationalist. But then I just think of you as my father and, well, I can't take you seriously however hard I try.'

I did not doubt this but I told her that I was probably not the only lawyer who was a romantic rationalist nor for that matter the only one whose daughter could not take them seriously. But then the more I thought about it, the more convinced I was that there were few romantic colleagues of mine and even fewer rational ones at that.

We settled down to do the crossword in the paper and, 'ere long (as grandfather would have put it), I had fallen asleep. Kirsty woke me as we were approaching

Douglas. Entering the harbour, the sun lit up the gaily painted houses along the front.

As we disembarked at the curious concrete terminal Tierney was waiting to meet us and I was a bit surprised to see that he was dressed like a country gent, with a tweed jacket and one of those checked shirts that gentlemen farmers affect. He was effusive in his greeting and kissing Kirsty's hand very gravely, told her that he was pleased to make her acquaintance. Outside the building was a green Land Rover with authentic mud and grass markings and as we climbed aboard a brindled cross-collie creature strained forward to lick us in welcome.

As we left the streets of the town behind, I noticed how Tierney was far more relaxed and natural than when I had last seen him at the conference in chambers. He smiled absent-mindedly and then started to tell us how much he liked the Island and how it reminded him of Donegal when he was a boy.

The road narrowed and the bends were becoming more tortuous as we climbed past the reservoir and plantations at Injebreck. From my seat in the back I was aware that we had left the sea and farmland behind us and were now in a country of bleak moorland, relieved by splashes of purple heather and outcrops of brown grey rock. We passed a finger post for the intriguingly named Druidale and soon we swung through a pillared gateway and pulled up outside Ballaweague, a stone-built farmhouse dating back to at least the 1880s, or so Tierney told us with great authority. Whatever other changes had taken place since then the prospect itself must have altered little from the time that the house had been built. It stood on a slight eminence commanding a view over a sweep of open moorland and a small group of Rowan trees which were bent over in the direction of the prevailing wind.

Madeleine Tierney, a tall and rather determined person, was there to meet us and was equally welcoming. She might well have wondered who the hell we were and why we had suddenly decided to come over and visit them for the day. If she did wonder, she was polite enough not to show it.

'Sadie my dear, Mr and Miss Kingston – Christopher and Kirsty.'

It was my turn to feel puzzled for who was Sadie? Then Tierney saw my expression and explained.

'Just a pet name for my wife. Madeleine's so formal sounding, don't you know and I wouldn't ever have a Maddie in the house, so it's Sadie, you see and...'

He didn't finish the sentence because the brindled one reappeared with a saliva-covered tennis ball which he dropped at my daughter's feet on the clear understanding that she would play with him forthwith. She obliged and a happy interlude was had by both.

Lunch was a pleasant affair. Despite the minimalist interior (for Madeleine/Sadie had been a lecturer at the art school in Dublin), the table was set very traditionally with a white linen cloth, fine tableware and elegant but plain antique glasses. After a red pepper soup, bowls of goats cheese, mixed salads and a tofu pasta appeared and Tierney explained that he hoped we didn't mind the lack of carnivorous fare but that Sadie was a 'damned veggie, so she is.'

'Meat's filthy stuff!' she barked and I could see Kirsty warming to her instantly.

'Ever been to the island before, Christopher?'

I told him about how I had been as a child to stay for a week with my parents in the youth hostel at Laxey. He became lyrical about how grand the Isle of Man was and how it's much more rural and pretty than people gave it credit for.

'We've been here for, what is it nearly ten years now is it Sadie? Sure I'd never go back over except for business.'

'Which you do at least once a week, despite being officially retired', his wife chipped in. Any anyway you said that we're only here because the tax is sixteen pence in the pound, there's no death duties and you can't stand Ireland nowadays.'

'Do you know what the trouble is with my home land, Christopher? God help us, Ireland is becoming a parody of itself. When I was young things were hard but we seemed to believe in the future, in science and in progress. Now we've sold out to ourselves and to the tourists. It's all a theme park of holiday houses dotted willy-nilly round the coast, soda bread and potatoes, turf fires and porter galore. "Visit our friendly pubs and enjoy the craic. Travel our beautiful roads where time stands still." All complete baloney, the lot of it. Why, Father Ted and the like isn't the half of it. Do you know it's that bad that I can't even take myself seriously now.'

'Well I never could take you seriously', chipped in his wife. He ignored her and helped himself to some pudding while he developed his argument.

'Only two profitable things in my country. The church and the law but now we've lost the faith, thanks to the scandals and everything, it's a good job that we're still so litigious. And still remaining in the European Union unlike yourselves!'

'Try some of that Manx cream, it's delicious', Sadie offered.

Tierney's wrath seemed to have subsided and returned to his usual geniality and he distributed the wine.

Kirsty and Sadie were discussing fox-hunting in heated tones and I could hear our hostess, with my daughter's encouragement, dismissing it as 'only fit for jackasses and what harm did Mr. Fox do to anyone?'

'Plenty, you ridiculous woman', added Tierney good naturedly, 'especially to chickens. But I don't really hold with hunting either and the sooner we get rid of that whole damn show the better.' I imagined that 'we' referred to his adopted home country but I didn't know if the Manx ever went in for hunting.

'Mind we'll be keeping it in Ireland, no doubt because it's the kind of picturesque nonsense that we like and 'twould be profitable as well.'

'Filthy so-called sport, even so.'

'Ach Sadie, don't get so worked up! I'll have some more of that excellent apple pie and cream, girl.'

After coffee the females went outside to see the stables where two hacks and a cob (whatever a hack and a cob might be) were kept. A few minutes later, to my great surprise, I saw my daughter passing by on a neat looking mount, looking serene and fully in control, followed by Sadie on a rascally looking horse with a large swishing tail. What is it about women and horses and where did Kirsty learn to ride like that? Francesca had a thing about the ghastliness of little girls and horses, born out of her much-hated pony club days as a child in the chalky Chilterns. I could only guess that Kirsty was a natural when it came to riding, apparently displaying yet another of her hidden talents.

'Now then, Christopher, You said that there was something you wanted to ask me about?'

'You said to Miss Goodchild...'

'Ah yes, the delightful Jessica. I'd say she was a wee tad keen on you, Christopher.'

I went slightly red and he guffawed into his Armagnac.

'You said to her that you'd known my uncle, Gerald Kingston.'

'Ah, I did indeed and I was very sorry to hear of his demise. By the by, I saw your name in the Times law reports just after he died. You were in some case or other dealing with easements and burdens and well your family name has an unusual spelling. I put two and two together as he'd said that his nephew was an eminent lawyer – an honest one too. Well, after checking out your reputation which, I hasten to add, is a good one, here we are.'

'I'm not sure about the eminent lawyer bit but thanks all the same. What I did want to know was, well, how well did you actually know Gerald? I'm interested because I was always quite close to him but you never know your relatives as real people, not when you're a child anyway. Then when you've grown up, either you don't have time to get to know them or else they've gone and died on you.'

I was conscious that I was paraphrasing Ben's words of the night before but Tierney wouldn't have recognised them as being crudely recycled.

'Let me see, now. I met your uncle in what would it be, the mid sixties? Maybe it was 1965 but I'm not sure. Anyway, I had a small boat then, a twenty something foot ketch, and I wanted some work done on it. I was a bit short of the old green-folding department, to put it bluntly. I was short of cash from having just started business on my own account and at that time I was doing a bit of development work in the Liverpool area. Someone recommended your uncle's yard for my boat and I have to say that I liked Gerald from the start. He was very helpful, very obliging and, best of all, his prices were very cheap, too cheap I told him. After that we had several pints together and went on a few social outings, that sort of thing. Did a bit of business, too, in the property field but I'd have to say we didn't exactly see eye to eye on that.'

'What was the problem?'

'Well, sure there he had this business partner called Ainsdale. He was a long-standing friend of Gerald's so I believe. But I thought him a bit of an upstart and, well, a gobshite. He was obsessed with being something in society but I didn't really care for his ways. To be brutally honest, I thought he was a blackguard and a conman!'

'In what way?'

'If you want to know I'll tell you, but you might not like it. He and Gerald were as thick as thieves, if you'll forgive that expression. Gerald, who was quite well off by that time, had invested a wad of money in some joint venture with this Ainsdale devil. Property development might have been the name but getting up to no good was definitely the game.'

He swirled the last of the amber liquor round in the glass and looked rather apologetic.

'Your uncle Gerald didn't seem to know, or care, that Ainsdale was a crook. To him the fact that they were making money was enough in itself.'

This seemed to have unfortunate echoes of April and her attitude to cash.

'They wanted me to come in on a joint venture to build on what we would now call a brownfield site. I wasn't so keen and remember this was long before that Hesletine fellow and the regeneration of your city, so I had my doubts on purely commercial grounds. Ainsdale had the bright idea of using connections and, as he put it, greasing palms. He had this great scheme for building a leisure centre on some heavily contaminated land and he wasn't going to pay the cost of a proper environmental assessment or pay for the cleaning up of the toxic substances there, both of which would have been necessary before the site clearance could begin. So he fixed up the officials but, sadly for him, one of the workers on the project died of some sort of alkaloid poisoning. It had been a foundry or something like that in former times, and was covered in industrial waste. There was a great hoo-hah to be sure and Ainsdale was quick to distance himself from that particular problem. But people began to mutter things and put two and two together. I think that he had to buy off a hell of a lot more people than he thought. Need I go on? With him there was always money changing hands for favours done by officials, councillors, contractors and the like. You remember that scandal about Paulson, Pottinger and T. Dan Smith? Well maybe not, since I suppose that you'd still have been at school back then.'

I didn't correct him. I was still at school but I had followed it all in the papers. It was about the time that I was first becoming interested in the reality rather than the rhetoric of British politics.

'To put it bluntly Christopher, even if I had been on the make like them I would have thought twice before going in with their harebrained schemes. Ainsdale was forever trying to get planning permission in exchange for bribes and Gerald was the one in whose name the plans were usually submitted. I didn't know which was the one who was going to pay the money out and I didn't care. Not a very subtle scenario, in fact a viper's nest. You know I almost went to the police myself when that worker died. But, well, I liked your uncle and then that dreadful business about his daughter dying came up and well, I just didn't have the heart. We've no children of our own, more's the pity for Sadie would have made a grand mother to any child, but I can imagine what it would have been like for the poor man when his daughter died. Had I not been so soft, the pair of them would have ended up going to jail and deservedly so.'

'Did my Aunt Maura know anything about this?'

'About all the wheeling and dealing and crookery? Probably not as I got the impression that she and Gerald were, how to put it, not very close. I don't really think that she gave a damn about what he was up to, as long as it brought the money in. Look, perhaps I shouldn't really be telling you this but I did hear an ugly rumour that Ainsdale and your Aunt Maura had once been lovers although I think that it was a long, long time ago, before she met Gerald. The trouble with your uncle, and I'm not intending any disrespect of the dead, God rest his soul, but the trouble with your uncle was that he was a bit weak, easily led and influenced by others, especially if they were women. It was the same in his own business – he was often cheated by unscrupulous boat owners and suppliers. But Gerald was basically a good man. It's just that I would have had a good deal more respect for him had he not allowed himself to stray from the path, business-wise, of course, with that Ainsdale man. I'm not one to make personal judgements about more personal matters such as, ah, the sexual life.'

He gave me a knowing wink and I quickly steered the conversation away from what might go on with or without his good wife's knowledge.

'What about Toby Ainsdale? Tell me about him as a businessman.'

'Well I've told you what I think of him. He was a spineless charlatan, an unprincipled fly-boy who was rotten to the core. I've known some talented architects in my time and some crooked ones but I've never known an architect who was both talented and crooked at the same time – I'd say that there's no such beast. Sure, the man had no design skill at all but he still went far because of his corruption. He was obsessed with his own image and he dreamt of getting on to the area committee of the R.I.B.A. He maybe he even thought of becoming President in time but I'll fancy not too many presidents of that august body have been in prison, for that was where he was heading.'

By the time Sadie and Kirsty returned we were discussing the Euro and its effect on our respective economies, 'Old fart's talk', as my daughter afterwards described it. Following on from a cup of tea and a slice of Sadie's toffee and walnut cake, it was time to be heading back for the Sea-Cat. Kirsty was now so enthusiastic about horses that Sadie, in all sincerity, said that my daughter must come back and stay for a week in the summer holidays so that they could go riding every day. Kirsty, looking pleased and very much at home with her new-found friends, accepted with alacrity and Tierney smiled in an avuncular way.

As we alighted from the Land Rover he asked me about the Glenbreen hearing on Friday and suggested that he would take Jessica and I out to lunch afterwards. I was tempted to ask him what she thought of me but he foreshadowed this.

'To say that she likes you would be a bit of an understatement as I've already said, Christopher. Rather like old Noah looking up at the sky and saying that he thought it might be about to rain. But please be careful with her. I believe that Jessica's been hurt by a man once already and she's a nice girl. Take care of her, won't you?'

Kirsty overheard this but for once in her life acted sensitively and kept silent.

A short time afterwards we were heading across the dark sea back to Liverpool.

14

'Good afternoon, Mr. K. Nice to have you back with us.'

Gary gave me a flash of his snake-like eyes and I felt an almost uncontrollable desire to produce my fountain pen and methodically poke them out. His insolence was getting too subtle for his own good and the sooner that I spoke to John about him the better.

As if on cue our head clerk, looking as unperturbed and in control as usual, put his head round the door and handed me three sets of instructions – briefs for the Thursday conferences. One of these was a medical negligence action involving the damaged sinuses of a lady from East Finchley, one was a union-backed industrial accident accompanied by lurid photographs of a man, a crane and a fearful head injury and the last was something about oppression of minority shareholders. This was a company law matter which had come from a new partner in Freshfields whom I was sure that I had once met at a party at Gavin's and had presumably impressed in some way, probably by telling him as usual something well beyond my understanding. I sorted the papers out and then opened up the bundle relating to tomorrow's arbitration.

For a few moments I listened to the snippets of conversation coming out of the clerks' room.

'...and you want someone to advise about the effect on the case of the Sienkewicz judgement in the Supremes? Well, I can say that we've got just the right counsel for you in our Miss Watkins...'

'...so I said to him leave it alone, can't you? It's only a naffing junior league game and you're right out of order there, Sunshine...'

'...if I'd meant bleeding Chigwell, Gary, I'd have said bleeding Chigwell. Oh, Good Morning, Mr Ferlinghetti, I'm afraid that he's just on a call at the moment, but he shouldn't be long...'

Evidently business as usual. I shut my door and got down to work on my papers. Several hours later I was only too glad to accept Jennifer's invitation to attend to her at The Rising Sun, a small pub tucked away in a back street near St. Paul's. When we had settled in I told her, in the most cursory way, that I had been to Liverpool to meet some old friends but she steered the conversation round to the topic that I was least interested in.

'I think you should know that Gavin's been putting your name forward for Head of Chambers'

'I've told him that I'm not interested in it so why in God's name does he refuse to listen?'

'Haven't you even...?'

'No! Look, Jennie, I'm not sure what being Head of Chambers actually entails because I've never even seen a job description, but I don't want it anyway.'

She laughed and told me that, apart from being a figurehead, having to make decisions about important matters such as the colour of the bog-paper and organising the way the chambers was run, she didn't have much of a clue either.'

'You know there's been great comings and goings all last week and all manner of Machiavellian schemes put forward. There's two clear front runners so far – Tom Keady and Jack Tappman. Keady reckons that he's the man for the job. He thinks that unless we all specialise in financial regulation and capital reconstructions and all that bollocks then there's no future for our chambers, or for the Bar in general. Talk about being single minded, why the man's a half-wit!'

A phrase regularly used by Jennifer to denote anyone who did not share her point of view.

'Does Tom actually command any support?'

'Only the usual sad lackeys, I'm sure. And as for Tappman, well at least he isn't such a complete idiot as Keady, even if he does seem to be night-foundered most of the time.'

Her opinions, as usual, were strongly expressed and allowed for little in the way of compromise.

'When do they have to declare their hand and announce that they're standing for election, if an election is what we're going to have?'

'A week on Thursday and we'll have a ballot right after.'

'So why don't you stand yourself, Jennifer? It would be refreshing to have a woman as Head of Chambers, especially one who had a bit of life in her, unlike those other two boring lawyer clones.'

'Boring lawyer clones? I like that. Maybe we're all boring lawyer clones. But I ask you, Chris, do I look mad? I'm hoping to serve my days out at the Bar in a profitable and peaceful way and retire back to God's Own County before I'm completely buggered, that is if my pension plan's still worth anything by then. Believe it or not, I actually like my existence here as it is and I don't want to change it. I know that George agrees with me and he's all one for the quiet life as well.'

I couldn't help thinking that if George Collman was really one for the quiet life then he would have thought twice before marrying Jennifer. But then I could imagine them both pottering around the Dales in green wellies and waxed jackets in perfect, if somewhat noisy, harmony.

'How's the voting likely to divide up?'

'Well no one's exactly canvassing anyone but you'd have to ask Gavin. He seems to be the man working behind the scenes. Ah, here's the lad now.'

Gavin was looking flustered after some great pyrrhic victory in the appeal court. While he downed a Guinness, he blasted away at the unbelievable stupidity of certain members of the judiciary, particularly those who disagreed with him. A remarkable similarity in outlook to Jennifer, I thought.

We got round to discussing the shenanigans in chambers but Gavin just laughed and told Jennifer that she was wasting her time with me, and that I would probably vote for whoever asked me in the nicest way, being a bit soft in the head. Then they talked a bit more about the non-existent hustings before we all went to our respective homes merrier and better informed but no wiser.

*****

The next day was hell. My client, a rascally Armenian entrepreneur by the name of Eddie Kopalians, had reached an impasse with a Czech builder named Ludjic whom he had employed to carry out extensive works at a half-timbered road house near Fisher which had formerly been known as the Hillside Inn and was now to be dubbed Eddie K's. Aesthetically Eddie had done his best to wreck the place while Ludjic contrived to do the same in a more practical sense. The dispute over money promised but never paid at one point threatened to escalate into the sort of conflict that would put the lamps out all over Europe and after much cajoling had finally gone to arbitration. We had by now battled through seventeen days of evidence and comments on evidence and glosses upon comments on evidence and it was time to present our submissions. The arbiter, a dozy quantity surveyor who seemed to have even less of an attention span than the average juror on a hot afternoon, was clearly bored and it showed.

My opponent, a cheeky solicitor who looked down on a mere Q.C. now that he had his own rights of audience, was droning on interminably. I felt much as I had done when presenting a less than successful appeal in the Supreme Court – I wanted out of the room as soon as possible. I thought of Gavin's saying that the self importance of a lawyer is measured by the width of the pinstripes on his suit. A maxim which if applied to my opponent today, whose jacket bore veritable motorways, would very much have proved the point.

As he droned on, Eddie gripped my arm and in a stage whisper demanded to know 'why dis solicitor fellow tell dis blooming lies about me.' I had to tell him to shut up as Mr Stripey was in fact reading out a transcript of Eddie's own evidence. He still didn't get the point and continued to mutter that 'should not be allow, dis blumming devil to speak dis perking lies.' Perking lies or not, I tried, largely successfully, to completely ignore both my client and my opponent.

Eventually we ground to a finish. Eddie, who was so well-disposed to me that I began to be suspicious about whether or not he would ever pay my fees, thanked me profusely. 'Dis devil will never succeed in lying about case', he assured me while I tried to get over to him the point that the arbitration would need to be decided at a later stage while he pushed into my hand a strange coloured bottle of something which he assured me was, 'ver gut, old speciality of my country.' It looked foul and has remained unopened in the cupboard next to the washing machine ever since.

That evening I went for a swift half with Gavin in The Black Friar, catching him for once on his own.

'What have you been up to, Chris?'

I was so non-committal that he took umbrage. 'You never let on what you're doing and I reckon that you only ever reveal yourself to others what you want them to see on a needs-to-know basis.'

'How does that make me different from any other lawyer, then?'

'Point taken. How's your detecting lark going, Chris?'

I told him the bare outlines, leaving out the embarrassing facts that I didn't want him to know and he seemed quite impressed. We agreed that despite my efforts I was hardly any further forward and I asked him what he thought I should do next.

'If I were you, I'd find out a bit more about what April was up to at the time and exactly what she needed the money for. That is, of course, if I hadn't already come to my senses and chucked the whole thing in as being none of my business. Just be careful and remember that you might being stirring up more trouble than you can handle.'

I ignored him and made a great show of opening a bag of salted peanuts, such a great show in fact that I showered the table with them and almost upset Gavin's glass.

'Could April have been blackmailing the older man?'

'Possibly. It's a pity that Barry Leemings isn't still around since he seemed to be April's partner in crime. I tell you what, Chris, cherchez l'homme – find him and you're half way there. Your cousin Ben was probably right about it being the old eternal triangle. I'll bet that the money's only a red herring and that there's a deeper motive you've yet to find.'

The talk then drifted around to what we had been doing that day and when I told him about Mr Kopalians he laughed and said that the other day he had been defending a lady who insisted on adding 'May Jesus be my Witness' at the end of every one of her answers to his examination-in-chief. So much so that the judge was heard to mutter, 'Is Christ on the list of witnesses then?' Then we then went on to trade lawyers jokes and I mused on how we all liked to pass them off as though they had actually happened in one of our own cases. Until we ran out of jokes. Gavin smiled mischievously before asking me whether or not I had thought any more about 'that girl from the past' again. What was her name, anyway, Ros as in "Rosalind, whom no jewel is like"?'

'No, actually, Ros as in "Fair Rosamond of Woodstock" or rather "Fair Rosamond of Crosby". Why do you ask?'

He puckered his lips and made a kissing noise.

'Do you think that I should contact her again?'

'Certainly not! It would be a great mistake to do that. You're not eighteen any more Chris, and neither is she.'

'But I wondered maybe...'

'Maybe nothing! Look, I'm not denying that if you liked someone at that age and you met them again you'd probably see something to remind you of how they used to be, but it's not really the same, is it? You're not comparing like to like and we both know that you can never go back to the land of lost content. People change with time.'

He paused for a moment to gather his thoughts. 'The real question Chris is this. Are you essentially the same person that you were at eighteen, and is she?'

'I don't know but wouldn't it be worth running the risk, just to find out?'

'Find out what – that your Ros still has the capacity to enchant you? Suppose she doesn't. Suppose that you now find her as boring and middle-aged as you are now and not interested in any of the things that you were then. Wouldn't that destroy all your illusions?'

'Maybe it's time I did destroy a few illusions.'

'You're opening too much of the past up as it is and I'm not just talking about Fair Rosamond. Think about it, Chris. You're probably still feeling rejected by Francesca and you're unsure of your wooing of Jessica. With that and the business about the death of your cousin, it's hardly surprising you're all mixed up and becoming obsessed with the first girl that you went out with.'

'Rubbish!' But of course I knew that it wasn't.

'Don't deny it, Chris. Just look to the future, can't you? Go somewhere nice at Easter with Kirsty and forget about everything. Relax, have a good time and come back refreshed. Remember that you've got the comely Jessica in the picture now. But don't hurry things, just let everything develop at its own pace. Enjoy life for once and stop being anxious.'

He must have seen that I was looking a bit crestfallen because he continued in a gentler tone.

'You're really a strange one, Chris. Sometimes I think that I understand you and then by the way you act I realise that after all the time I've known you half my life now but I still don't know what makes you tick. But cheer up! Maybe you and your Ros will meet again some time. But if that's going to happen just let it be by complete chance, not by design. Then you can put it all down to serendipity, or is it synchronicity? I never can remember the difference. Anyway, it's time to stop this alarming slide into middle-age pathos and have another drink.'

'Perhaps you're right, Gav. Let sleeping dogs lie, as you keep saying. I will have another, thanks. One for the road.'

Much to my embarrassment he then broke into song.

'Let the toast pass, Drink to the lass, I warrant she'll prove an excuse for the glass!'

'I'll warrant that too, if Gavin's drinking to her. By the way, is the lass anyone I know?' Jennifer sat down and the swift half passed into yet another convivial evening.

*****

Thursday was hectic, but somehow much less trying. For one thing Eddie Kopalians was not breathing garlic sausage all over me and for another, my clients were a lot more honest, if not quite so exotic. By the time the man from Freshfields was through, and I decided incidentally that I had never seen him before in my life and certainly not at any party at Gavin's, I was feeling exhausted. Then Michael Shalday poked his head round the door. I refrained from telling him that I was not in the mood for a chat, particularly with him, and tried to look busy. As usual he did not take the hint but sat down, coffee mug in hand, and began to tell me about who was backing who in our amusing little display of chambers' democracy.

'Tom Keady is certainly the one with the best game plan. He sees our chambers as a sort of specialist high-class chancery and posh commercial lot.'

'Not much good to a common-law hack like me then, is it? Anyway, I thought he wanted to specialise in tax to the exclusion of all else?'

'You've been listening to Jennifer. She's got a fixation about that, which is a shame since Tom's never said anything of the sort. But on the other hand Jack's the one with all the bright ideas. He says we're fine as we are and that one of the strengths of our chambers is that we do have such a mix of talents. His real contribution would be to completely reorganise the business side of things.

'John's been on at Henry for ages about a new computer system and a radical overhaul of our admin including fee collection and Jack's very enthusiastic. So enthusiastic, in fact, that he wants to retitle John as the "Practice Manager". He's even talking about opening a branch set in some God-forsaken town in the Midlands, which would be a complete anathema to Tom who thinks that such places are full of "frightful oiks" and that's just the solicitors rather than the clients!'

I laughed and thought that I could warm a little to Michael.

'Talking about this chambers thing, who's going to volunteer to get rid of Gary? That'd be a real vote winner.'

'I would imagine that the dumping of Gary will have to be in both manifestos because I think there's near unanimity on that one. Poor old Gary but who in their right mind would employ him?'

'Well we did, for a start – or rather Henry, man of decision and judge to-be did.'

*****

Friday morning was sunny and inviting, so inviting in fact that I almost overslept, missed my Fruit and Fibre and arrived in chambers hungry and with very little time to spare before going on to the review hearing. Gary leered at me and pointedly stated that Mrs Kingston, your wife if you remember, was on the phone and that she urgently wanted a word with me. Then he added the sting in the tail and mentioned that she was apparently rather annoyed because I hadn't answered any of her calls.

While he was busy telling me this, Jessica arrived with Tierney and, shunting Gary into a siding, I asked John to tell my ex Francesca that I'd gone straight to court and that I'd phone her back later when I had the time. I had no desire, right then or at any time, to enter into a discussion of how she would keep the house in Wickham Road and how I would get nothing at all or, by the way, why was I poisoning Kirsty's mind against her mother as she hardly ever saw her these days? Francesca, unlike life, was at least highly predictable.

On the way down the Strand, Jessica told us about the beauty of Switzerland and the grandeur of the Alps and how Murren was especially pleasing at this time of year, a little snow-capped village perched high above cliffs. I pictured her all wrapped up against the cold and flying down the piste like a snow encrusted angel. Then I returned to reality, narrowly avoiding a Boris bus that was bearing down on us as we shunned the nearby zebra crossing, and said to her that I was glad that she had enjoyed her annual sojourn amidst the wonders of the Bernese Oberland. I wondered if I had sounded sincere but Tierney said nothing and as we entered the Law Courts he was smiling like a veritable Kilkenny Cat. But he kept to his word and no mention was made of our meeting at Ballaweague or of what we had discussed there.

The pre-trial review in the Glenbreen case was not the complete disaster I had foreseen. The defendants' counsel was an unfortunate junior who had obviously been a last-minute substitution for a more highly-paid chap who no doubt had better fish to fry and he put up a cringe-making performance. When maliciously pushed as to exactly what preparations had been done and why certain documents and reports had not been disclosed before now, he seemed to have no convincing answers.

The outcome was that Martin Teals, the insurance man who had insisted on attending the meeting and who I knew from old as a doughty fighter and tough negotiator, took Jessica and I aside in one of the gothic nooks of the main hall and had a discussion. Our talks culminated in him saying that they would be producing settlement terms which they thought might well be viewed by all as being favourable. Everyone wanted to get shot of the action as soon as they could and Jessica would be contacted shortly about an informal meeting at which these terms could be discussed. She went off to phone her office whilst Martin Teals continued talking.

'You were lucky there. Our defence is a shambles to put it mildly and the way your case was pled was, unfortunately, bloody good. I always think that's important when it's a commercial action like this. Your Mr Tierney's a right bloody nuisance who never gives up, which is always an additional incentive to settle. Anyway, how are you getting on? I was sorry to hear about you and Francesca, Christopher. Cal Moscop told one.' It turned out that Cal was married to his sister-in-law Renata and I wondered if there was anyone in the world who didn't know or wasn't related to Cal. His spy network was remarkably effective. After agreeing that it was a small world, that it was a pity that Easter was still a good week away and that perhaps the weather might improve, he finally took his leave after throwing in, 'Oh, by the way, your instructing solicitor is rather nice, isn't she?' Did everyone have to know my damn business? It seemed so.

Then Tierney tapped me on the shoulder. 'Give me a ring on my mobile soon. Here's the number. I think I might have turned something up for you about your uncle. By the way, Jessica keeps giving you fond looks. A good sign, I'd say. She's a pleasing little thing as I've already said. Ah, Miss Goodchild, you're back with us, so. I'd love to tarry but I'm sorry for I have an important engagement elsewhere, so I'll wish you both well.'

I reckoned that he was just being tactful but at the same time I was pleased that Jessica and I would now have a little time with just the two of us.

'It's a bit early but do you fancy a spot of lunch?'

She laughed. 'A spot of lunch? What a very "sort of you" expression, Christopher! Well as long as you don't take me back to that horrid little Italian place we went to last time.'

I chose a place called the Deli in the Park, a sort of up-market tent thing in Lincoln's Inn Fields and one of the few decent outdoor eateries in London. Gavin and I had frequented it often in its previous incarnation as a wooden hut that sold bacon-and-egg rolls. It was a perfect place to drink coffee and feed the pigeons while our respective pupil masters were wondering where the hell we had got to and we were wondering what unlikely explanations to give them. Now the place had come up in the world.

As we were eating I looked up to see Henry waving his furled umbrella to us as he strode past. I reckoned that we must have spoilt his day for if it hadn't been for us I was sure that he would have stopped and ogled 'those most charming young women' playing netball nearby. Poor old fellow! Then the thought of Dilwys dressed for netball caused me to choke and I had to gulp down a large glass of iced water to regain my usual equanimity.

We ended up in the strange setting of Sir John Soane's house, a particular favourite of mine. The cluttered eccentricity of the great architect's home with its very personal and totally lunatic collection of just about anything and everything has always caught my imagination. Jessica listened politely as I bored her with the details of what was on view and what was not. I resisted the temptation to play to the gallery, for a number of tourists had somehow got in tow and the official guides were eyeing me unfavourably. Eventually we beat a retreat and I casually asked Jessica what she was doing tomorrow. The hoped-for reply was given and I made arrangements to meet her at eleven-thirty outside what I have always thought was Sir John's finest building, the Dulwich Picture Gallery. As we parted, I began to think that it was now definitely a case of Aslan being on the move.

By the time I arrived back at my desk all hell seemed to have broken loose in the clerk's room. Henry was standing shouting at Gary that if he was going to intercept his personal mail then at least he could do so in a way that didn't make it so obvious. I beat a retreat into my paper-strewn room. As I sat down to a coffee and a mental re-run of lunch with Jessica, I could not help but feeling that like Henry, Gary's days in our chambers were mercifully numbered.

15

As I watched the rapidly changing scene flashing past the train windows I was apprehensive and yet expectant, wondering what was awaiting me in my home town. I was feeling much as I had imagined Michael Caine's character felt in the opening scene of *Get Carter*. I had a sheaf of papers spread across the table and was glad that I had gone first class, even more so because my client was paying. I hummed the opening bars of a Benny Goodman number in my head and felt satisfied. No damn children, in fact no damn other passengers at all and time to drink my muddy complimentary coffee in peace. And time to think.

Not, of course, that I needed time to think. It was the last thing I needed that Monday morning as I was heading back to Liverpool via Runcorn, where I was stopping off to meet with a solicitor who was an old friend from my early days at the bar. He had unaccountably jumped ship and become a member of what Henry always referred to as 'the junior branch of the profession'. Curiously Henry never seemed to refer to female solicitors in such a patronising way, particularly if they were good-looking. Thinking of solicitrixes, to use Gavin's name for them, and especially good-looking ones at that, my mind drifted back to the weekend which had just passed.

I had arrived late at the Dulwich Picture Gallery although it wasn't completely my fault this time. I had been trying to avoid Francesca's phone calls while at the same time arranging for the car to be taken in on Monday to have the automatic transmission looked at yet again. I was inclined to blame Kirsty for the failure of the latter, not solely from an instinct to attribute such mechanical malfunctioning to the fact that she was a young woman, but more due to the fact that she had been mainly driving the bloody thing.

Jessica was not waiting at the entrance to the Gallery and I began to think that she had stood me up. Being stood up was the nightmare of my adolescence even though in reality it had only happened once. That was when I myself had stood up a sturdy farmhand of a girl called Lizzie Parkinson who had come all the way from Thornton on the bus to see Love Story with me. On our first date she had insisted on giving me sloppy kisses in public and had been given the unflattering nickname of Ponko by Cal, for no immediately apparent reason. However guilt being what it is, I still only had to think of the Plaza cinema in Crosby to feel remorse about that particular evening or, rather, non-evening.

As we passed over the junctions at Crewe, I tried to divert my focus onto the business in hand. The meeting was to be about the interpretation of a will, all dry stuff revolving around Clause Twelve and a codicil. Quite frankly the sort of thing that would not normally merit someone of my seniority but Sam Linacre had said that it was important and that he did not want anyone he had never met before to deal with it. John had had surprisingly little trouble in getting me to go up. Everything had gone quiet for the week before Easter and no one else fancied the journey up north. No one, that is, except me, as I was going there anyway. I was still not quite sure what my plans would be for the next few days but I was certain that the weekend would feature chocolate eggs, Kirsty and, although I had not quite worked the logistics of it out, hopefully Jessica. My thoughts returned to the Dulwich Picture Gallery.

Jessica had never been there before and was suitably impressed. She seemed to be quite knowledgeable about Rubens, Rembrandt and Ruskin so I did not try to compete. Gavin is wont to remark, one of the things that a legal training fails to teach you is when to recognise that you don't know what you're talking about and to shut up. As I listened to her discourse on *A Woman Playing a Clavichord*, a Dutch painting that had particularly caught her fancy, I liked the way she talked about the colours and textures used and was taken by her knowledge of technique and detail. Jessica, unlike me, knew what she was talking about when it came to art. I don't suppose that it would really have mattered what she was talking about as I merely wanted to look at her, listen to her voice and wonder what she saw in me.

An hour later, our cultural appetites having been satisfied, I suggested lunch.

'What about the Dog?'

This was interesting. A North Londoner, born and bred, is not supposed to know anything about those dark and mysterious places south of the river, and therefore the soubriquet of The Crown & Greyhound should not have tripped off the tongue of a West Hampstead girl quite so easily.

'Well you know, I once went out with a boy from Dulwich', she explained over the salmon and courgette tart. I smiled indulgently, while thinking how pretty Jess was. She looked more like a real woman in her dark blue jeans and fetching long jacket than when she was wearing the smart but sombre outfits of a court practitioner. Maybe all women did and I just hadn't noticed before. Perhaps I was just smitten.

In the afternoon we explored the park, the tollgate and the woods on Sydenham Hill before it threatened to rain and we decided to catch the bus back into town. Alighting at Trafalgar Square, we innocently fed the birds for a while and narrowly avoided having our picture taken by a babel tower of seed-laden tourists. Then we went down to the river and sat on a bench next to Cleopatra's Needle, where we shared a Bounty and discussed the relevant merits of Miles Davis and Wynton Marsalis, but came to no conclusion other than that we would have to catch Garbarek the next time he was in London.

When talking about jazz palled we paid a visit to a small French restaurant in Covent Garden and then decided that it had been such a good day that we would try to catch the first set at Ronnie Scott's. I was impressed by the fact that Jessica was a member and decided that there was a lot about her that I didn't know but would enjoy finding out.

We stayed out into the cold hour before the dawn was going to break. After I had worked up enough courage to put my arm around her she told me that she had had a great time and that we should have lots more days together like this. Combined with the jazz, this was music in my ears.

Having despatched Jessica back to West Hampstead in the tender hands of a jolly Turkish taxi driver called Ermret, I got home to find Kirsty was still up.

Over a nightcap of hot chocolate liberally sprayed with that curiously unsatisfying aerosol cream that she liked, she demanded a blow-by-blow account of my first real date since her mother had abandoned me. When she was sated with the details her only comment was, 'Go for it, Dad! Jess sounds nice' – advice which in the circumstances I was only too happy to follow.

*****

'The buffet car is now closing...'

And with that my thoughts returned to the present and I concentrated hard on the brief before me, so hard in fact that within minutes the wheelbeats of the train made me fall fast asleep. That evening, having had a quick drink with Sam Linacre in a soulless chain establishment in downtown Runcorn, I was back again at the Blundellsands Hotel. I supposed that I could have invited myself back to Ben and Malcolm's but felt that I needed to think and to have some space to myself. I was at a reality checkpoint and had to think carefully which path to take. Was I going to go on, irrespective of who might get hurt or would I call it a day and abandon the chase? I ruminated on this and then repeated to myself the words of Kipling – 'Was it to be Tilbury and a tender or Gallions and the docks?' Then the tune of 'Hazey Jane' came flooding back into my mind. Once again, I felt alone.

I leaned over from the bed, picked up the phone and dialled Gill's number. A cultured northern voice answered and, for a moment, I was quite thrown.

'Hullo, yes, who is it that you would like to speak to?'

'Er, is that Mr. Rajiv?

I couldn't use his surname for the simple reason that I didn't know it.

'Ah, you're the geezer what was at the door the other day, innit?'

A clear case of confused identity, but the confusion was on his part rather than mine. I wondered if he could help slipping into his cockney persona and thought that his cultural crisis was all the more interesting for being so blatantly self-induced. Then Gill came on the line, sounding as though she was pleased to hear from me again, even though I hadn't contacted her during the last ten days.

'Christopher! How are you?'

'Oh, fine thanks, and you? Listen, sorry about the lack of communication but I've been really busy in London and er...'

Why couldn't I tell the truth and admit that I had now regretted our brief dalliance? She saved me the trouble as I was becoming increasingly lost for words.

'Don't worry about it Christopher. Look I enjoyed our night last week but you'll understand me when I say that it was a one-off. A case of ships that pass. Let's just say that if we meet again, it'll be as friends and nothing more. I can almost sense your embarrassment but don't worry. I've got a significant other in my life as well. So let's leave it at that, OK. Now that we've got that sorted out, what were you wanting to ask me?'

I could have sworn that she sounded ever-so-slightly disappointed but I was greatly relieved. My life was complicated enough without adding an entanglement with a slinky lady novelist who just so happened to have been April's best friend.

'I just wanted to clarify one or two of the things that we were talking about last time, Gill.'

'Fire away then.'

'You did say that April told you that she was pregnant, didn't you?'

'I said that she thought she was pregnant, yes. Not necessarily the same thing as actually being pregnant.'

'Well if she was, could the baby have been that older man's, the boyfriend who was giving her the money?'

'I suppose it could've been but the money seemed to have been coming in for some time before she told me that she was expecting.'

'Was she the mistress of the older man?'

'That's a quaint expression. Do you mean, were they having a fling as in a sexual relationship? I would imagine so. Although if you're suggesting that she was a kept woman, it doesn't seem very likely, even for then. I can't really see April charging for sex even if she was so concerned about a lack of dough. The money she was getting from whoever was only on a sort of generous pocket money level. You couldn't exactly have lived in style on that amount.'

'Then what were the payments for?'

'I've no idea but I'm sure that Barry knew all about them. But since Barry isn't around you can't very well ask him, can you?'

'What about that brother of his – Guy, wasn't it?'

'God knows if Guy even survived the seventies. If snorting and injecting everything in sight didn't land him in an early grave then you might be able to find him.'

'Any idea where?'

'Honestly I have no idea of what happened to him or where he might be. I think his family came from somewhere near the city but I couldn't be sure. But mind you Leemings isn't exactly a very common name and there can't be very many of them floating about so why don't you try to look him up. Hmm, anything else you want to know, Mr. Holmes?'

'No, not really, Gill. Thanks anyway and perhaps we could meet for a drink some time.' Even I was conscious of the fact that I didn't really mean it.

'That would be great. Give me a call when you want to. Take care.'

And we both knew that there would never be another meeting. The ships had well and truly passed in the night.

*****

The next call was to Gavin. As I waited and waited, I counted the rings at the other end. I was about to put the receiver down on the assumption that all of the inhabitants of that splendid spa town were out when there was a sudden clatter and Julia's voice answered.

'Christopher, how absolutely lovely to hear from you.' How she managed to seem so husky and yet smooth at the same time I have never worked out. I always felt that her voice was like one of those screen sirens of the forties, a sort of Lauren Bacall crossed with Veronica Lake or Barbara Stanwyck.

'Una, go and get your father, it's Uncle Chris! I suppose that you're returning Gavin's call. He was back early today from a plea in mitigation at Lewes, I think he said. I hear that you're up in Liverpool at the moment.'

She managed to make the city sound as though it was on the other side of the globe and I had no doubt that to her, it probably was.

'Gavin's all so excited about this damn chambers election thing but I can't think why. It all sounds such a bore playing politics like a load of silly little boys and girls. Oh, just before he speaks to you, there's one thing I need to say. Do you think that, possibly, you could refrain from leading Gavin astray quite so much by dragging him off to hostelries for a "quick one after work"? The children and I hardly ever see him these days and if I didn't know your reputation for public house socialising then I might have thought that Gavin had another woman.

I ruminated on the cheek of the man. 'The children' indeed – the youngest, Una, was now twenty one and as it was Gavin who was the initiator of the swift one drink scenario, it was a bit rich of him to blame me. Still, I suppose that is what real friends are for, someone convenient to shift your own shortcomings on to. Even so, I reckoned that he must have been up to something to be using me as an alibi.

Then Gavin himself spoke.

'Huh! Some chance of me having a bit on the side! I can hardly cope with dear Julia here, who stands at my side both in a figurative and literal sense, don't you dear? All right then, see you soon and could you pick up an evening paper for me while you're out? Bye!

'Sorry about that, Chris. So how are you getting on then? Good. Listen, one reason I need to speak to you is that we've reached a bit of a deadlock in this chambers election pantomime. The result's likely to be a draw: seven of us – seven, an equal split between Tom and Jack. But things have moved on. In terms of our chambers constitution, Henry has the casting vote. The old fool says he'll refuse to use it. His reason, would you believe, is that he doesn't want to be seen as divisive. He says that it would be far better if we choose his successor by reaching a consensus. So much for Henry the Kingmaker. You know the real reason, don't you Chris? He's afraid that he'll get so many complaints when he's on the bench that he's trying to avoid at least seven from here. Seven disgruntled people who supported whoever he didn't come down in favour of.' It was just like Gavin to attribute base motives to Henry, and just like Henry to have those base motives in the first place.

'Anyway, the upshot is that both Tom and Jack have threatened to withdraw their nominations. I don't suppose that either wants to be seen as the loser or, in the circumstances, as the winner.'

I didn't follow this logic but knew that there was more to come. 'Chris, I don't suppose that you would consider?'

'How many times do I have to tell you, Gavin? No definitely means No. Which part of the word don't you understand? End of discussion. I don't want to stand, I don't want the job and I refuse the nomination. But thanks for asking. Be serious, please.'

'Are you sure?'

'Do I sound sure? Look, a client of mine once was being plagued by his local council and he wrote a letter to them saying, "I am not rich, I am not famous, I do not have friends in high places. But I do have this pencil and if you do not stop harassing me I will attend at your offices personally and stick it as far as it will go up your nostrils. An early reply will not oblige. Yours faithfully..." Get the message?'

I felt quite proud of this reminiscence, particularly as I had just made it up on the spur of the moment.

'Message received and understood, over and out. But the women in our chambers will be disappointed – they all think you're a very nice man and Sabrina sings your praises, especially after you stopped her from being bored to death – or worse – by Henry.'

'Oh, be quiet for a moment Gav and talk about some thing else for a change?'

'OK, something much more exciting. I've got those tickets for the gig in Brixton next week.'

I was amused by his use of 'gig', but then Gavin was a great one for believing that a good word or expression can never have its day. I wondered what he would make of the lyrics of the lead singer of the group that we were going to hear. Perhaps Oysterband would be too radical for his tastes.

'Oh, by the way I haven't forgotten about the tickets for the Kate Rusby thing or that jazz festival in Welwyn although that's a bit of a trek but I'm sure they'll both be worthwhile.'

'And the other thing that you wanted to tell me, Gavin, is what?'

He dropped his voice to a conspiratorial whisper. 'Chris, sorry to land you in it with Julia but you remember that woman I was telling you about?'

'The mysterious Vi, the dame you were sweet on?'

He laughed and said that was not quite how he would have put it.

'Yes, well you see Vi and I have, well, sort of seeing each other a bit in the evenings and...'

'You want me to say that you and I were in the pub together on a particular evening? You know I don't approve of that. Anyway what does seeing her actually entail?'

'Can't you guess – she's gorgeous.'

'Do I know her?'

'Shouldn't think so. Her name's actually Veronica, Veronica Dangerfield. I mean, what a name!'

'Five six, medium length brown hair, sometimes wears it in a ponytail and likes dark red scarves?'

'What the hell, are you a mind-reader or what?'

'Definitely "or what". Your Vee just happens to be the mother of Imogen, one of Kirsty's school pals. Not one of your better ideas, Gavin, she's a formidable lady is our Veronica if you cross her and I'm not convinced that there still isn't a husband somewhere in the background who might just break your balls, to use a crude expression, if he finds out. Just be careful how you play it, if you must play it at all.'

'I will, Chris, I always am with... Oh, Julia, you startled me! Back so soon? I was just telling Chris about the election. But before I go, a bit of news, Chris. Michael caught Gary going through your desk. Said that he was looking for a registered packet that arrived a couple of weeks ago and that you might have forgotten to open.'

'What did Michael do?'

'Said he'd tell Henry. Not that that it would do a lot of good, Can't stand him. He's always so bloody pompous!' I assumed it was Gary that Gavin was talking about, rather than Henry or Michael but I wasn't really sure because all three of them would fit the description adequately.

'The first time I ever met Gary I asked him the time and he produced a fob watch, looked at it as if it was a complicated chronometer and then said, "Well sir, I'd say it was er, just coming up for ten minutes to three, give or take a minute." Why couldn't he have contented himself with "two fifty", like anyone else?'

Gavin had no answer to this conundrum.

*****

My last call was to Twentyman, who sounded a bit heartier than when I had last spoken to him.

'Doesn't really add up, does it lad? All this about April being expecting and getting money from an older man and Barry not objecting. Hmm, you'd better see if that brother of his is still around. Guy Leemings, his name was, I think you said.'

'But how can I trace him when I don't know where he lives or anything?'

'Easy, lad, through the wonders of technology. Thing called the internet and its got some useful "apps" which, I believe, is the correct term.'

I must have sounded surprised by his interaction with technology because he scoffed at my thinking that he, 'were antediluvian or summat', and went on to say that he would try and find him on his own machine.

'If he's still alive and in the British Isles then I'll find him, lad, never fear.

'Now about that incident concerning that man who worked for him that died – just leave it to me, I'll dig around a bit and see what I can find. I've a few old pals in and out the Force and I've already spoken to Mick Laing about the whole business. You don't mind that I told him about those papers from Gerald and the file I gave you?'

I did but it was too late for recriminations now and I realised that he was only trying to help. But then, since I was getting nowhere anyway, did it matter?

'Another thing, lad. I've been thinking a bit and trying to come up with some answers. Why, for instance, was the murder committed at such a high-risk time of day? What was it that April knew and why did he need to shut her up by killing her? Lots of bloody questions and not a lot to go on but I'll do my best.'

We arranged to meet up later the following evening in a pub that I vaguely remembered the name of and, after saying that he would invite Mick along too, he explained that, 'Our Jed's desperate for a pee so cheerio, lad', and rang off.

I switched on the television and although desperately tired, I started to watch an old Robert Mitchell film – the one in which he played a mad preacher chasing two children. At least it was a change from the Gideon Bible in the bedside drawer.

16

The journey back into town from the hotel was uneventful and as I watched the familiar litany of names passing by, I thought how reassuring they sounded. Where else would you get Blundellsands & Crosby followed by Waterloo, Seaforth & Litherland and Bootle Oriel Road? Sometimes, I feel, there is more romance in a series of local station names than in the wildest entries picked out of a world atlas although I haven't tried that theory out on Gavin. Not yet, anyway.

I got off at the tamely-titled Liverpool Central and walked up Brownlow Hill towards the university. Robin was expecting me and was affable enough, although I suspected that he was more pleased to see his errant book than me. I thought that he had probably been the sort of sad spotty schoolboy who would have written 'If this book should chance to roam, box its ears and send it home' in every Eagle annual and Biggles book that he had ever owned. He took the book with grace and bade me sit down.

'Sorry but I've only a few minutes to spare so I won't offer you a snifter, but if there's anything else that you'd like to ask me about your cousin's death, then fire away.'

'Were there any signs of a struggle at the scene? Any marks on her body which might have suggested that she put up a struggle?'

'Nothing very obvious, I'm afraid. But if what you're asking me is did she know her killer? I'd have to say that all I could rule out is that they were brawling before she was hit as there's no sign that she might have injured her assailant. Anything else would be just surmising and I know that you legal chappies are all against people like us surmising things.'

'There's nothing in the P.M. about April being pregnant, is there?'

'No signs of any indication whatsoever – she wasn't even in the first trimester.'

'Could they have missed the fact that she might have been expecting?'

'It's theoretically possible but highly unlikely. But what bought that notion on, eh?'

'Because apparently she thought she was pregnant or at least that's what she was going round telling people at the time.'

'I wonder why she thought that. Was it a missed period, feelings of nausea, a woman's intuition, that kind of thing? The P.M. was in some ways quite thorough and in others not so but it would have been mentioned if they'd found any signs of pregnancy. I couldn't absolutely rule it out but I couldn't be absolutely certain that she wasn't pregnant either, if you catch my drift, eh?'

I thanked him and, just as I was leaving, remembered to hand back his book.

'Oh, before you go – I bumped into Cal Moscrop the other day and he thought that we should all go out for a noggin or two some time soon.' I mumbled a half-hearted concord. 'He also wanted you to know that apparently his mother greatly enjoyed the little chat you had with her and wonders how your architectural researches are getting on. You do seem to have rather a lot to occupy you at the moment, Christopher. Keep in touch though.'

An hour or two later I was sitting in a small pub on a corner close to the Bluecoat Arts Centre, waiting tor Twentyman to show up. The bar was near empty and, as I listened in on a far from fascinating conversation about the new line up of Tranmere Rovers, I wondered why this city was so obsessed with football. Does nobody talk of anything else?

There was a muffled jingle in the corner as an amusement machine chuntered out its meagre prize winnings. Then the doors swung open and Twentyman came in.

'What'll you have, Robbie?'

I had still not got used to what I regarded as an over-familiarity with someone whom we would have been told at primary school was one of our elders and betters. He sat down with a bottle of Bass and stopped puffing.

'Nice place this.'

He looked around approvingly at the red and gold walls and the gilt light fittings. Not my kind of pub, but he evidently felt at home here.

'I had quite a chat with Mick Laing this morning. By the way he's sorry not to be here tonight but he had a prior engagement. Probably a bit o' fluff, knowing him and his missus. She's a right hard one, is Mick's wife – a pernickety, bad tempered lass who's put on a bit of beef, so much so that I reckon she could probably sing a duet on her own.' He chuckled at his own witticism.

'And what did Mick say about April's death?'

'As it happens he didn't know much about it at all. Said that he was surprised by the post-mortem being so bloody unhelpful about how April had been killed and thought the coroner had probably got it wrong. He told me, though, that Toby had nowt to do with it as he'd investigated him at the time, checked out his statement and that, even though I hadn't asked him to. Bloody officious type, was our Mick. He always liked to go the extra mile especially if it involved sticking his nose into other people's business. He came out with summat about "every saint has a past, every sinner has a future", referring I reckon to Toby but he didn't explain further. I really do think that our Mick's gone a bit peculiar over the years.'

'Did he know anything about Gerald and Toby's business dealings?'

'Swore that he'd never heard a thing and knew newt about bribes to councillors or death of any workers, all of which I took with a large pinch of salt. But then to be fair to Mick it mayn't be that surprising because we were both in the county force. It'd be the city fraud squad lot who would have had them two in their sights. I had a word with a few of the city lads I'd known in the past. They're all long retired now just like me and Mick, though he went and became a security consultant or some such shite.' He chuckled and wiped his mouth off on his none-too-clean sleeve.

'Director of Security Operations, that's what he were. Poxy title, poxy little job. He was in charge of a handful of security men – jumped up bouncers if you ask me – for some company called Berkeley, Barclay – no SerCley, that's the name. What was it that your lass called Mick in the station – "nout but a big lanky bastard?" I congratulate her for that. He still is, in my book. But anyroad it's what the city lot told me that'll really interest you. I wrote it all down for you'

He cleared his throat and pulled out a much folded piece of paper.

'Quendoline Investments – that was the name of the firm that Toby Ainsdale was involved with. Its owner turned out to be a Mrs Elvira Ainsdale of Serpentine Drive, Crosby, L23, a nominee for you know who, and the company secretary is listed as Gerald Kingston, also of Serpentine Drive, Crosby, holding one share out of the hundred issued. Nowt unusual about that but there was a rumour to the effect that by the early seventies your uncle's boat business was near bust and that your chum Toby Ainsdale had been putting a great deal of money into Gerald's business to shore it up as it were, if you'll forgive the pun.'

He laughed, wheezed and took an enormous draught of his Bass, apparently without ill effect.

'Now here's the interesting part about Quendoline. By the way I bet it were one of them silly names you buy as a ready-made company for ninety quid that sounds like summat you'd clean the windows with. Quendoline was involved in various projects all over the city and surrounding areas. Newt big, but a lot that added up to big and some of what they were up to involved demolishing buildings that were about to be listed and putting right ugly things up in areas zoned for other things, if you catch my drift. What it all comes down to, lad, is skulduggery.'

He stopped and dwelt on the word.

'Skulduggery – lovely word, lad, isn't it? Goes well with its partners in rhyme, thuggery and buggery. Been one of my favourites for years and seems particularly appropriate for this sordid affair. To be more precise it was a case of corruptly influencing planning applications in return for financial gain, seeking to influence and aiding and abetting corruption. In other words, lad, plain bloody bribery, pure and simple. They were on to him all right but yon Toby was much too clever for them, in his own eyes at least. Come reorganisation we had new councils, new councillors and nobody would say owt about nowt. So Mr squeaky-clean Ainsdale seems to have got away with it or maybe he cashed in when he could. I've asked Mick to look at it all again – I told him that you'd be interested in everything about your uncle and Ainsdale's business affairs.'

'What would have happened if they'd been caught?'

'Your guess is as good as mine, lad, but I reckon Toby would've gone to prison for certain, and your uncle, as company secretary, would have gone down with him, along with half the bloody council, and all.'

I expected him to add a, 'Think on, lad', as Cal, Ben and I had often done in the exaggerated Lancashire argot that we had spoken on the way home from school. But Twentyman merely chuckled and ordered another round while I asked him what he thought that April was meaning when she threatened to tell Maura what Gerald had been up to.

'I suppose it must have been the skulduggery like that. Unless they were any other dark secrets, any more Mrs Moscrops, if you get me meaning.'

'Have you changed your mind about Gerald not being the killer?'

'Never said he were, never said he weren't. You all claimed to have been out of the house that afternoon and all got perfect alibis that could well have been made-up. How were we supposed to check them? Turns out Gerald was knocking off Mary at the time, down the road his son was watching the telly with her son. Only Ben wasn't there all of the time, was he? Then your aunt Maura was at the Southport Flower Show all day and had a day ticket to prove it but how long was a day? According to Toby, Mr. Straight-as-a-die Archibloodytect she phoned him from the show some time after three to ask about some damn fool seed catalogue or summat. Which would tend to suggest that she was there at that time. She'd had a fair bit to drink when Toby met her off the train later that evening so it's not surprising that she stayed on at the end of the show to have a few. We did hear that she was fond of a drink and she was certainly right refreshed out of her mind by the time we spoke to her.'

'Did you ever trace the phone call about the seed catalogue and check that it really had been made?'

'Hang about, lad! We're talking about thirty or more years ago and you didn't have none of that System X doo-dah in place back then.'

'What? You've lost me there.'

'We're talking Strowger exchanges then and not your electronic marvels of today. The Strowgers were named after the Kansas City undertaker who, oh a hundred years or more ago, was worried that the girls on the manual exchange might divert business calls away to his rivals. Remember back then those lasses could listen in to any call that they wanted to. So old man Strowger invented the automatic exchange so there'd be no human intervention, as it were. Now think of those old films and all that "keep 'em talking while we trace the call" stuff. Trouble was that once the connection were broken and the switches and sliding bars and all that gubbins had gone back to their original positions, there would be no record of where the call had come from and no way of finding out neither.

'So, to put it shortly, she might have made that call just after three thirty from Southport and she might not have, but in the absence of anything better we have to accept that she said she'd made the call and Ainsdale said he'd received it. We took a statement from him about half an hour before he met your aunt up off the Southport train. Since there weren't no mobiles in them days and triangulation and the like, their statements would have been enough corroboration of the phone call having been made and received. Remember that we spoke to her after we had spoken to Ainsdale so that she didn't know what he had said. But she backed up his account of the call before we'd mentioned it, so that suggests that neither of them could have have made it up before we spoke to them. And another thing was that her admission ticket to the show was issued before noon that day. We checked its number.'

'How about Toby's involvements?'

'Fancy him as the mystery man, do you lad?'

'It doesn't seem very likely, does it? I can't really see him being April's boyfriend – too old and too boring I'd have thought.'

'You're probably right there but when it comes to affairs of the heart you never can tell, lad. Love moves in mysterious ways as they say. As for his movements he told us that his wife was out all day shopping and that he was in his house up until about 3.30 or so, listening to a radio performance of The Faery Queen. By Purcell, that is. No need to look so surprised, lad. I may be an old fool in your eyes but I'm not so ignorant that I don't know the difference between a great composer and something that "washes even whiter".'

He chuckled again and it reminded me of my grandfather's old joke about preferring Bach often to Offenbach rarely, which was marginally better than the one about the tone-deaf hound's bite being better than his Bach.'

'He said that thing had finished on the radio – we checked with the BBC and it did actually finish at 3.35. He said that he enjoyed it and if its at all relevant he quoted something about, "by your gentle mind and deeds shall you be known" or something like that – buggered if I understood what he was on about. The important thing is that your aunt called him as soon as he turned the set off. We got that confirmed by both of them. Then he finished a cup of tea and went out for a drive down to the beach to take the dog for a walk.'

'That'd have been Rufus. He was a wolfhound I remember, a really nice animal.'

'With respect lad, I don't think it matters a tinker's arse if he was a cross between a poodle and a police constable – he was only a sodding dog being taken for a walk. Anyway, on the way there, Toby decided that he'd better fill up the car with petrol.'

'How convenient – an instant alibi!'

Twentyman ignored this unhelpful remark.

'If I may be allowed to continue without further interruption...' He gave me the same pained look that he had given me at the police station on that night. 'He went to a petrol station on the main road and bought eight gallons of four star at about 3.45.'

'How was he so precise?'

'He wasn't but the girl in the garage was off for a week before and when she came back she confirmed that she had issued the handwritten receipt and that they had run out of four star that day at about four o' clock so that it must have been bought before then. As Ainsdale had said that it was just before four then he was probably right. He was the one who gave us the receipt but they didn't print the date on the receipts in those days. Anyhow, after that, when he was out with the dog he met an old acquaintance of his on the beach, Terry Battersby by name, and they stopped for quite a while having a natter about this and that. Finally the dog – Master Rufus to you – got fed up and decided that there were no more piddles that he wanted to sniff so he and Ainsdale set off for home. And when he returned home his wife Elvira had come back and heard the sound of his return. They were there when you arrived on the scene. And before you ask me, yes Mick checked up on all of their alibis and apart from Battersby, who was a bit vague about when he'd spoken to Toby – poor old soul couldn't remember what day of the week it was today but he did remember a long conversation on the beach. So you see all of the accounts check out.'

'Suppose April was blackmailing Toby about the corruption and things?'

'Fanciful maybe, but there were quite a few blackmailers who got away over the years with blackmail and then get caught by their victims who kill them. But don't worry, lad. I'll rootle around a bit more and see what I can pick up.'

I thanked him and put another Bass down on the table which he downed with relish.

'Maybe our April was pregnant, maybe the elusive boyfriend does exist. But it seems all the prime suspects so far have an alibi for between 3 and well after 6. This might help, though.' He rummaged in his pocket and produced a bus ticket which I looked at with confused expression. 'Other side, you clown. I've written on it the address you wanted. Mr Guy Leemings no less. He's living close by in Warrington. The lad might not want to talk to you though. Opening up old wounds, that kind of thing. On the other hand.'

I bid him farewell and was moving towards the door when he grabbed my arm.

'One more thing, lad. About Warrington. They say that salmon have returned to the Mersey and that you can find them as far upstream as there but why any self-respecting fish would want to go anywhere near sodding Warrington beats me! Ta-ra!'

*****

Outside it was warm and surprisingly clammy for the time of year and I went down to the Pier head to see what the tide was doing and if any ships might be passing. I stayed for a time until I noticed that it was beginning to get dark and I decided to have a bit of a walk before I returned to the station. I set off in the general direction of Hanover Street and then took a left turning beside a bar whose garish neon lighting made it look like a dive that Philip Marlow himself might have frequented. It was unfamiliar territory and I looked up at the street name. The cast iron plate informed me in its heavy serifs that this was Adam & Eve Street, L1.

I have to say that I was more impressed by the name than by the street itself. It was a narrow canyon fronted by tall brick warehouses mostly awaiting their metamorphosis into whatever trend of fate awaited them and I was surprised that they hadn't already fallen to the developers. Here and there were signs of life like a dubious basement club that shunned passers-by and a neon-lit bar which sought to attract the bright young things from the new dockland flats.

I realised, quite soon, that I had made a big mistake. The street was longer, narrower and more menacing at night than I had thought. The dying street lights gave out a dim glow like the sweet juice of a blood orange. Rubbish blew along in the gutter as though it were a long abandoned ghost town somewhere in the Old Wild West. The graffiti was menacing and stark – 'Norrie Killers Rule', 'Give us some noise, the noise that destroys', and the obvious pun of 'Pay no more than twenty a score'. I was already uneasy and becoming increasingly so as something was telling me that I was being followed. Quite how I knew this I couldn't say, but with a heightened sense of danger I knew that somewhere beyond the dark pools, someone or something was definitely watching me. Two workmen walked past wearing donkey jackets that read "SCSC" but they seemed to be in earnest conversation with each other and disappeared up a turning in the distance.

Perhaps I had become too taken with my own image as a private investigator or perhaps I was suffering from an excess of bravado as a result of a couple of pints of flat warm beer but I decided, against all caution, to see who was keeping me under surveillance.

I was standing near to an open doorway belonging to a gaunt and probably quite unsafe tenement building which still bore in fading gilt letters on a peeling black background the legend 'Cranmoore, Tuttis & Coy. Scientific Instrument Makers, First Floor'. A painted hand pointed up a broad sweep of stairs which had been boarded off though some of the boards had been wrenched off. I hesitated and then climbed through the gap, taking the first flight cautiously and at the half landing I found myself in complete darkness.

I waited, concealed by a bird-stained pillar, but there was no sign of life apart from a scuffling sound of unseen rodents making the roost of their tenancy before the renovations began. There was a faint smell of urine and my initial impression that this was a wino's hang out was confirmed by the faint glint of discarded bottles and lager cans heaped untidily in the corner. An old syringe told me of darker dangers. I switched off the light in my phone and put it away in my coat.

Perhaps I had been wrong and my imagination had run away with me. There was no sign of anyone following me. I picked my way slowly down the stairway, taking care to avoid tripping on the broken treads. The last thing I wanted at that particular time was a sprained ankle, given that as part of my post-Francesca rehabilitation I had set my sights on training for the London Marathon next year, perhaps watched proudly by Jessica. I stopped and waited but there was no sound apart from the faint hum of traffic in the distance and so with increasing confidence I strode down the last couple of steps and emerged in the street.

I bent down to check the time on my watch and, almost simultaneously, felt a sharp blow on the top of my skull. I fell backwards onto the damp stairs and, stunned momentarily, passed out.

It must have been only a matter of seconds before I came round again. I blinked my eyes in pain and thought that I could hear the sound of footsteps running away towards the end of the street. As I struggled into an upright position, the street was uncannily quiet. Then an unshaven, sour smell reached my nose.

'You all right there, son?'

'I think so. Did you see who did it?'

A rough but kind face peered into mine. 'No chance, like. I were at the top o' the stairs and came down when I heard you fall. I think two scallies were running away. Was it a mugging, like? There's a lot of radio rental types around here, like. Huh, Care in the community they call it. Fat chance!'

'I don't know. Maybe it was an accident. I must have banged my head. Had a bit too much to drink and stumbled on that.' I pointed to part of a wooden box, the kind that apples come in, which was lying on the pavement close to the doorway. He nodded in an understanding way and kicked it to the side.

'I'll 'ave a bit of the same trouble oneself, with drink, like. Times enough I've been paralytic and promised meself I'd give it up. Fancy some?' He offered me some fortified wine but I declined, as politely as possible.

'Are you sure you're not hurt, a bit woozy or such? Maybe you should go to the hozzie if you've hurt yer head and gerrit seen to. Here don't forget yer bewk.'

He handed me something that had fallen from my pocket – the spare copy of grandfather Kingston's *Short Account* which I had forgotten to give to Twentyman. After I thanked him and assured him that I would be fine he shuffled back to his gloomy perch at the top of the building and I checked my pockets. My wallet had gone. Just as well that I had left my credit cards and everything personal and of any value in the hotel. But there had been a small selection of banknotes in it. So I had been mugged had I, the victim of a common robber who had

265

selected me as a target and followed me into this quiet street?

I felt my head and it was bruised, and probably with a bump but no broken skin and no blood. Just one of these things, I thought fatalistically, and not much point in reporting it to the police. Besides what about the publicity? I could do without something like 'Top QC Attacked in Alcoholic's Drinking Den Shock'. Why, I wondered, were we always 'top QCs' and never just ordinary or not particularly good ones?

Put it down to experience, Chris, I told myself, and better avoid the sleazier parts of the city at night. At least the bastards had left me with enough loose change to get back to my chintzy hotel room in Blundellsands. Thank God for small mercies! That this attack might be a warning to me from someone connected with April's death never even crossed my mind at the time. But then why should it have done?

17

I was now on the verge of giving up altogether. Returning to London, now that Jessica and I were more or less officially 'seeing each other' (an expression that Gavin thought was hilariously genteel), was presenting a more attractive prospect than Liverpool in the rain. Actually, come to think of it, almost anywhere else at this particular moment seemed to present a more attractive prospect than Liverpool in the rain.

I rubbed the lump on my head, still feeling sorry for myself. I was disillusioned with my progress so far and felt like I had drawn a blank. Perhaps I might get some answers out of Guy Leemings.

After a sleepless night I had made a number of calls to the Warrington number which Twentyman had given me but I failed to get a reply. Perhaps Guy had moved away, was on holiday or perhaps he was at work. Perhaps Twentyman's faith in the internet was misplaced and Guy didn't live there at all. I tried his number one last time, and then in desperation I decided to visit Warrington myself and try to find him even though my head was still throbbing.

A couple of hours later, I was walking down a snaking road of identical pinkish bricked executive homes all placed at slightly different angles. The whole effect was if a child had tipped out a box of toy houses and arranged them haphazardly before his mother called him in for tea. The colour of the bricks reminded me of

Twentyman's jest about salmon in the Mersey and I could see that maybe he had a point there.

I stopped outside the third house on the left, the one with a carved wooden sign announcing that it was incongruously called 'Green Acres'. The driveway was empty, the curtains were drawn and there was no sign of life. I waited as the bell rang before deciding what to do next and wondered if I should leave a note. Not being sure if this was the right house or not, I tried to see through the frosted glass of the door and read the writing on the upturned letter that I could see lying on the floor. But it was hopeless, the glass was too thick and my eyesight was too poor to see through it.

I was thinking about leaving when I noticed a skinny woman with a humourless mouth and a selection of gold bracelets straight out of a TV shopping channel standing at the porch of the next house. Cigarette in hand, she eyed me suspiciously.

'They're not in', she said in a mechanical way.

I shivered as the rain renewed its attempts to soak me through to the skin.

'So I see.'

I pushed the wet hair away from my eyes and attempted to smile.

'Do you know how I can get hold of them? It's Guy that I want to speak to. He's an old friend, you see.'

She tried to assess what I wanted from Guy but I was giving nothing away. Then she returned my smile, shifted her stance from one leg to the other and decided to be more helpful.

'He's at work, she's at her mothers, like and she's not well, is the mother. Shingles this time, poor thing, although there's always something up with the old duck.

Don't know why they bother though, she's a bit of a crank. Always going on at them for never bothering about her, though they're up there all the bloody time. No pleasing some folk, is there?'

'Well, you know what old people are like.'

She nodded as though she and I were some sort of experts in geriatric care.

'Do you want Guy urgently?'

I made up some tale about an impending school re-union and she went back in, re-emerging with a scrap of paper torn off the bottom of a sheet of kitchen roll. She wrote something on it and handed it over to me saying, 'Here's her number. You can get hold of him through her. Her mother lives in Widnes, not far really.'

I thanked her and started to walk back to the town centre, cursing the fact that the soles of my shoes seemed to be doing their best to detach themselves from the uppers and that my socks were getting wet. They don't make shoes like they used to. Hell, I realised that I sounded just like Henry who was always on about the poor quality of everything except, of course, the legal advice that he gave to his clients. Bloody rain! Doesn't it ever stop? We could do with some bloody global warming around here.

My curmudgeonly mood was lifted by the enticing smell of chips coming from a shop with an Italian name displayed in extravagantly painted curls and swirls. The window display promised in whitewash 'Pizza's, Chip's and The Best Damn Cod in Town!' I sighed at the misuse of apostrophes and searched for my mobile, then remembered I had left it still plugged in to the charger in the hotel bedroom. Never mind, for next to the cafe was a phone box and I slipped inside. The rain was running down the glass door in spiralling rivulets over the prancing figure of Mercury and the box smelt of stale mustiness or something worse. I frowned at the grinning BT girl on the poster who was telling me how easy it was to make a call to a friend anywhere in the world. Dismissing her facile message, I dropped the required coins into the slot.

'Hello?' The voice didn't sound too sure and I was initially thrown as well.

'Is Mr Guy Leemings there, please?'

'I'm afraid he's not.'

I couldn't place the accent but it had the flat tones of someone who came from somewhere near Birmingham. If Ben was there he'd have said, 'Dudley or possibly Wednesbury', quite confidently. But like most things Ben said, it would have been a bluff. I settled for the less contentious bet of somewhere around the Black Country, give or take twenty miles.

'Is that, er, Mrs Leemings?'

There was a slight intake of breath and I sensed that I was speaking to a common-law rather than a statutory wife.

'I am her. It's Shula', she said by way of unhelpful explanation. 'I'm just coming back from visiting my mum.'

'Can you tell me how I can get hold of Guy, please. It's urgent.' Quite what the urgency was, I didn't know unless it was something to do with the fact that I was cold, depressed and in need of some of Mr Ianelli's chips, hot from the fryer, liberally sprinkled with salt and vinegar and dipped in ketchup. Even better with a pickled onion or two on the side. Clearly my mind was set on my next port of call.

'You could get him through the Department. You do know the number, don't you?'

What Department? Did he work in a shop, was he a civil servant, a lecturer or what? The woman's disinterest was beginning to annoy me. I couldn't help feeling that Francesca had been right when she used to upbraid me for taking instant dislike to people like this.

'I'm sorry but I don't seem to have it at hand. You couldn't give it to me again, could you?''

She muttered something ungraciously and then went to get the number for me. I was glad that she hadn't suggested that I look it up myself in the phone book.

Ten minutes later, and fortified by a bag of chips but sadly no onions, I was back in the phone box.

'Hello, Child Welfare Team 2P, how may I help you?'

I could have sworn that it was Lorraine at Gateacre Media and Film Services and wondered if Ben was playing a trick on me. Perhaps every girl who answered the phone in Lancashire used the same voice. Maybe Shula was a relation of Lorraine even if she came from the Midlands rather than West Allerton.

'Is Mr Guy Leemings there please?'

'Who shall I say is calling?'

I was stumped at that one and told her just to say that it was a friend and that I was calling on important personal business. She sounded doubtful and I was put onto hold. After a few rounds of the Blue Danube, a man answered and although I had never spoken to him before, I could have sworn that he sounded bored. Perhaps the Belle of Wednesbury or wherever it was had worn him down, perhaps his job in Child Welfare Team 2P was not all that interesting, or maybe he just couldn't be bothered with interruptions at his work for personal business, important or otherwise.

I told him that I had known his brother Barry and he suddenly sounded interested.

'He's been gone a long time now. You knew Barry?'

'I did – back in the seventies. You see, I knew him and his girlfriend April.'

His surprise seemed to intensify.

'But I still don't see why you are interested in both of them now.'

'Well, actually I am or rather was, April Kingston's cousin and I was close to both of them.'

I half expected that he would start berating me for wasting his time, telling me to get lost and to mind my own business but he did not. Barely an hour later, I was sipping a tepid pint of Tetleys and waiting for him in a warm saloon bar close to the Town Hall. I was at a loss as to how I was going to recognise him and doubted if Gill's description of him would be very helpful now. I reckoned that he probably didn't look like the Lone Ranger any more. All I had to go on was that he was some kind of a social worker now and probably a senior one at that. Among the small crowd tucking in to the 'real pub fayre', I was looking for a middle-aged male of medium height and half the customers here were that.

'Mr. Kingston? I thought it was. Easy to pick you out since you're not one of the regulars here and I am. Have we ever met before?'

'I think we have – once, but it was a very long time ago. I think it was about a week or so before they died – at a party at April's. By the way my first name is Christopher.'

He was thin and confident and was dressed quite soberly in a rather good dark suit and a tie which I thought was quite tasteful. The latter observation, however, might have been suspect as both Kirsty and Francesca seemed to have doubts as to my sartorial skills. They had always insisted on choosing my ties for me despite my protestations.

'Well nice to meet you again, Christopher.' But I could see from his questioning look that he didn't know me from Adam.

'I can't stay too long', he said apologetically. 'I've got a protection hearing at two fifteen and I've got to get from here to the Magistrates.'

We sat down and ordered lunch although I was still feeling a little bloated from the chips earlier. As my mixed salad was placed before me, I decided to start the ball rolling.

'Do you mind if I ask you some things about Barry and April?'

He looked up from his ham and mushroom pie. I told him that I had always thought that Barry had a raw deal in life, losing April and then his own life in the same week. An understatement if ever there was one. But it only seemed right now that when I was proposing to delve into the past at least I should be honest with him as to my motives. So I told him about Gerald's letter and what I had been up to and he looked interested. Then he started to open up and as we talked about the house in Riego Street he became distinctly animated.

'That Gill was a horrid, nasty, patronising person! She used to laugh at me in a really malicious way, tease me for having ridiculous clothes and go round telling everyone that I was a junkie and a no hoper. Yes, perhaps at one time all of that was true. I did, like my amphetamines back then and perhaps an occasional bit of coke too but I was hardly a junkie or an addict. And I was only trying to mask all the other things that were wrong with me at the time. You see it was all very well being judged by the likes of goody-goody little Gill with her wealth and position in society. You have to remember that Barry and I were from a very different background to her. We grew up in Ashton not petty bourgeoisie bloody Blundellsands.'

He stopped for a moment and then ate some more of his pie.

'We came from a poor working class area, you know. It was the sort of place where everyone was either on drugs, on the dole or a house-breaker, or a mixture of all three. We joked that even the local Co-op had "steal by" dates on the food, it was that bad. But then I don't suppose that we knew that we'd been deprived because we'd never had any money or known the freedom it buys. When we went to university it was a sort of mind-blowing experience. Literally so, in my case. I couldn't cope with all the pressure. Unlike Barry, who was a natural academic, I found it all much too much.'

He stopped, emotionally exhausted from this outburst and I could tell that it still hurt, even now. I didn't know what to say, but I reckoned that I should just leave him to say whatever he wanted to and not interrupt him. He finished his lime and lemonade and dropped its lump of ice back in the glass.

'The truth is, Christopher, that I was ill, very ill. I thought I was having delusions, paranoia, that sort of thing. When I was finally diagnosed they said that I had a form of bi-polar disorder, a sort of manic depression

274

exacerbated by drug use and that led on to a nervous breakdown. So you see I wasn't just the hopeless piece of dung that Gillian thought I was.

'Anyway for months I'd been virtually secluded, hiding away in my digs, getting madder and madder by the day and in fear of being sectioned. Then Barry stepped in. He was great! He took me under his wing and brought me food and things and told me he'd help me to get it all sorted out. He was my twin by the way, not identical or anything like that but my twin nevertheless and older than me by twenty six minutes. He always liked to remind me of that and said I was his kid brother and that he'd always take care of me. April was really kind too. I liked your cousin. I suppose she was really the sister that I never had. Anyway Barry helped me get treatment, proper treatment with lithium, anti-depressants, that kind of thing and I kicked the drugs and got myself back on my feet. In fact giving up the drugs was the easy part. Maybe that was because I was taking my prescribed medication or maybe it was because Barry and April were giving me the moral support I needed. They were so good to me.'

'Do you think that they would have stayed together?'

'Do you mean April and Barry?'

'Yes.'

'In the long term? They were very close and I think that they cared very much for each other. So I think they probably would have done.' He began to look sad.

'When did you last see either of them?'

'Oh, on the Saturday before he... before they both died. As I said, I felt that I was getting over the worst of my illness by then. That was mainly April's doing – I reckon that she had the willpower that I probably didn't have. Anyway, she'd encouraged me to try and be more outward looking and positive. By that time I was beginning to emerge from my cocoon of madness into some sort of reality. I really did think that I was beginning to turn the corner. So I decided to tell Barry that I was going to travel, see the world, that kind of thing. I felt that I could now do anything, everything, if I put my mind to it. So I took some lived-in old black Levi's, a couple of shirts, a jacket and a large bag with not much in it and I set out to hitch my way across the world. Naive maybe, but that's what I wanted to do and felt that I could now that I was getting better.'

'How far did you actually get – around the world, I mean?'

'Certainly not bloody Kathmandu, which is where I'd intended to go. How I would have got that far without any money I'm not sure. Actually I only got as far as the Newport Pagnell service area. And it was there that I met a girl called Jan and we spent four very happy weeks together in a sort of commune over Olney way. I only found out exactly where we were much later on because it was in an old cottage in the middle of nowhere and a mile or so from the nearest road. It was her brother Will who ran it and they were a weird lot but very welcoming in a sort of tail-end hippie way. So we lived in bliss, cut off from the world. I only later found out that April and Barry had died. You see we had no phone or access to papers of any sort – in fact no real contact with the outside world at all. Will would take his old VW campervan into the village to get supplies like food and beer and we'd all chip in with our money or, in my case with April's because she'd given me something to tide me over. She was generous that way.'

'What about the publicity following April's death and the bike crash, didn't any of that ever get to you?'

'No, because none of us ever went with Will to the shop and even if he had seen or heard anything it wouldn't have meant anything to him as he didn't even know my second name. Or my first name, come to think of it, because I just called myself Marcus T – Pretentious, or what? It was all very seventies really and a bit of an anachronism even then. So I knew nothing about what had happened to Barry and April until I returned to Liverpool in mid-September to start the new term and it was only then that I found out that April had been killed and that Barry had written himself off along with my beautiful bike. All three of them gone!'

'What did you do when you found out?'

'What could I have done? I thought that I had fully recovered in myself and was going to get things straight again. But I just couldn't handle it when I found out that my brother and his girl were both dead. I hadn't even been at their funerals and my parents held that against me too – the fact that I hadn't got in touch, I just went to pieces again and lost the plot and it all imploded. I ended up in hospital again and it was months before I really sorted myself out properly. But I did come through it all in the end, as you can see and now I'm sufficiently sane enough to be a social worker. Even though there are plenty who would argue that sanity and social workers don't necessarily go together.'

'But you knew then that the police thought that Barry might have killed April?'

'I do now, but look, why would they have ever thought that someone like Barry would have done that?'

'Maybe because there was evidence that they had been quarrelling about something on that day.'

'They often quarrelled about things. But the important thing to bear in mind was that Barry really loved April – really and utterly I mean. There was no way that he would have ever harmed her.'

I didn't think that it would be helpful to point out that I had myself seen Barry threaten April a week before she died so I waited to see if he would justify his faith in his brother's gentle character. I added, 'How do you know that Barry didn't do anything to hurt April?'

'I can't really explain it but I just know that he didn't do it. Kill her, I mean.'

'Then who did?'

'I've no idea although I've wondered about it all these years. One thing I do know, though, is what Barry and April were doing on the day she died. Barry told me himself, in writing just after April died.'

'But I thought that you were away with Jan and the hippies at the time and that you never saw Barry and April again.'

'I was away, but what happened later was strange, really strange. When I got back to Liverpool there was a letter waiting for me. My landlady had kept it for me which was very good of her because I'd done the dirty on her and owed her quite a lot of rent money. But the letter was from Barry and he'd written it to me on the day April had died. I think that he was frightened that if anything happened to him then the truth would never come out. I don't suppose, that he ever thought he'd be dead by the time I read it, mind.'

'He wanted the truth to come out? The truth about what?'

'The truth about how it hadn't been him who had killed April. Why he didn't just stick around and tell the police I don't know but he took my old bike, my old Triumph Bonneville it was, a lovely machine that I'd spent hours and money I didn't have restoring, and then he went and got himself killed on it.'

He pulled out a handkerchief and noisily blew into it and I could see that he needed a moment to pull himself together. I didn't want to be unkind to him but I had to know what was in the letter.

'Did you show that letter to the police?'

'What was the point? They'd decided that April hadn't been murdered anyway because the Coroner had told them that there wasn't enough evidence of that and I was told that if had anything relevant that I should speak to a policeman called Leng or something like that. I did, but that smarmy bastard wasn't interested. The ponce told me to keep it to myself and that it wasn't worth stirring everything up again and that I should be careful not to make myself ill again. So I just left it at that. Barry's death was an accident, a complete accident and there's no doubt about that. Poor Barry had about as much road sense as a... I don't know what.'

While he struggled to find a comparison I added, 'But April's death wasn't an accident.'

'I know that now. But I believe Barry when he said he had nothing to do with it.'

'So you say but they knew about the letter didn't they?'

'No, because I never showed it to them because Leng wasn't interested.'

'Do you still have that letter now?'

'Oh, its around somewhere or other. I didn't throw it out if that's what you're thinking as it was the last thing that I had from my twin. If you really want to see it then I'll make a copy at work and send it to you. It might take a few days or so.'

'This is a bit of a cheek, Guy, but I don't suppose that I could come round and collect it this evening? It's just that time's a bit short and...'

'Well, I don't know why you're so interested but if you really want it that urgently you could borrow the original, I suppose.

I told him that I was interested to see anything that might give me a clue as to why April died and to exonerate Barry. This seemed to satisfy Guy.

'Look, I've got to visit my sister-in-law later tonight and tell her the latest about her mum. She lives near Magill, not far from Blundellsands so provided I can find it, I could probably deliver it to you at your hotel on my way. But I want it back as it's the only thing in Barry's handwriting that I still have.'

He left me to settle up his bill. When Guy returned from the toilet, he began to anxiously glance at the clock on the wall.

'Did you ever see that Jan girl again?'

He looked wistful and blew his nose, possibly to play for more time.

'No, more's the pity. I would have liked to see her again. I can still remember what she was like, what she wore and even the sound of her voice and...'

I waited for him to continue and I already had a good idea of what he was going to finish up saying.

280

'It would have been nice, really nice if we'd stayed in touch and remained good friends – that's what you wanted to say, wasn't it?'

He nodded. 'But then that sort of thing doesn't happen in real life, does it? After all, you never really meet anyone who has kept up with a girlfriend or boyfriend years and years after they'd parted, do you?'

Wisely and perhaps philosophically, I was inclined to agree with him.

18

I had just settled down to listen to a programme on the radio about communication between whales when there was a call from reception and I found Guy waiting for me with an envelope in his hand. He said that he was in a hurry and was somewhat flustered but I noticed that he had obviously spent some time on his appearance. As I watched his green hatchback pull away I got a glimpse of a well-upholstered lady in the passenger seat and considered whether or not she was Shula's sister in Maghull, a possible romantic liaison or maybe both at the same time. However that was his business and what was in the envelope was mine.

I sat down on the bed and studied the letter. It had apparently been written on feint lined paper of the sort that comes in those spiral bound reporter's notebooks. The whole document was only three pages long and I felt slightly disappointed. After all, what could anybody really say in such a short note? I read the date: Sunday 9/8 and then began on the text which was written in leaky blue ball pen ink by a shaky hand.

Dear Guy,

I'm in deep shit and I want you to know the truth, whatever they're going to say about me. April is dead and I don't know if I can now go on living. It was like this – she'd fallen out with her folks because they wouldn't give her any money and she needed it bad. So she lay awake all night thinking this one up and basically it involved her *going to their house in Blundellsands and nicking whatever she could lay her hands on. She was going to keep the cash and she reckoned they had quite a stash hidden away. Then she was going to pawn or sell the rest. I was to meet her later but on no account go to the house. She said it was personal, nothing that I was to be involved in and that I was only to help her spend it afterwards. Anyway something went wrong, badly wrong.*

'I waited around at a phone box for April to call me back and she never phoned. I was there for ages and started getting worried, real worried. I sat on a bench by the phone for a couple of hours then rang her house but no-one answered and by 4 o' clock I decided I'd had enough waiting for her and went round to the house. Her mum's car was outside so I reckoned that she must have come back but I didn't see her and it looked like no one was around. I was about to go away but I went round to the back just to check things out and that's when I found April. She was on the floor and she was dead. I knelt down beside her and cried. I couldn't bear it because her eyes were wide open and she was looking at me and I swear that I had nothing to do with it. I didn't kill her and I don't know who did. I loved her, Guy, you know that I did and I can't believe she's dead but I had nothing to do with it. I never told you about the baby but you must know that I would never do anything bad to her or to our child.

That's it, Guy. She's dead and they'll think it's me. Someone killed her and I don't know who. I just feel that I can't go on now. The police will be on to me and they'll try and nail me for it. I don't know what to do, Guy! I'll never find anyone else like April, however long I live. I've got to get some money somehow, enough to live on for a bit while I lie low and sort my head out. I reckon I know who I can get it from. I'm going to borrow your bike for a week or so. I hope that's OK. I'll look after it properly, don't worry. When they get on to you just tell them what happened, what I've told you here and I'll be back to sort things out. I loved her and I always will. Help me, Guy! Help Me!

His signature was scrawled at the foot and the ink was smudged as though he had been crying. I put the letter aside and felt empty inside. What did it all mean? Had Barry been telling the truth or was it an elaborate scheme on his part? God, I had no reason to like him after he'd tried to give me a battering but somehow his direct appeal to Guy seemed to be both moving and yet rather pathetic. What was I going to do next, seeing that I was still that interfering kid cousin?

Twentyman had given me a press cutting about the accident and I now looked it out. It was from a local paper, a Penrith rag only I couldn't see its full name because part of the top of the page was missing.

The investigation into the death of Liverpool student Barry Arthur Leemings (22), who was killed in a collision between his motorbike and an Albion lorry on the 26th of last month, was held last Tuesday in Kendal. The lorry driver, James Peter Watson (33), of Possilpark Mains, Glasgow, stated that he was travelling south on the A6 when the deceased had crossed into his path on the double bend south of the Shap Wells turning and that he had no time or opportunity of avoiding him. A farm worker Jack Lofthouse (60), of Snowfell Farm Cottages, confirmed that he had seen the bike pass 'like a bat out of

hell' seconds before and had estimated that he was doing,
'at least sixty or more probably something above
seventy'. A police witness was called to testify that road
conditions were good, the surface was dry and that the
site of the accident was not a notorious one.

The coroner, who described the accident as an
unfortunate waste of a young life, recorded a verdict of
accidental death. He added that it was important for
motor bike riders to keep their machines under control
at all times, to obey all speed limits assiduously and to
always ride their bikes having regard to the "3 C's" that is,
showing care, courtesy and consideration towards all
other road users and sadly the deceased showed none of
these. Fortunately the road will shortly be replaced by
the new motorway under construction.'

Nothing, I noted, about the late Barry Leemings having
been the boyfriend of the late April, and nothing about
him having been a murder suspect either. By dying
inconveniently he was no longer a suspect, let alone the
principal one. Perhaps the police didn't really have any
real clue as to why April had been killed as Twentyman
had already hinted. Then I remembered the inquest into
the death of my cousin a couple of weeks later. It had
been my first time in a court of any sort and my last in a
coroner's.

I had been called to give a formal account of how I
had discovered the body, whom I formally identified as
being that of April Isabella Kingston, whom I had known
all of my life. I said that I had last seen her on the
previous Saturday night at the party in Riego Street and
that she appeared to have been in good health – how this
was remotely relevant to how she had died I had no idea.

I was however, happy that I was asked nothing further and told to stand down. The coroner said that the inquest was adjourned while the police were making further enquiries. That, so far as I remember, was it and nothing appears to have arisen out of those enquiries. Unlike the proceedings into Barry's death, the Coroner in Crosby had delivered no little homilies, no handy hints for motorists.

I started to let my mind wander and pictured Barry's family sitting red-eyed on the public benches in Kendal and having to endure the treacly sympathy of the court. They must have been in despair and doubly so because Barry's twin was absent, masquerading as Marcus T in deepest Buckinghamshire with Jan and Will and their merry band of pranksters. How his parents must have hated it all and, given the blameworthiness of the lorry driver, how they must have despaired of finding a suitable target for their hatred.

I saw that Guy had put down on the envelope his home phone number and another number which seemed to be a mobile, and the message, '*If you want to know anything else, try me on either of these numbers. GL*'

I rang the mobile number but it was switched off so I turned the radio on again and listened to The Archers while I thought more about Barry and the letter. Then I dialled Twentyman's number and was surprised when a woman answered. She sounded tense, as if she was under great strain and when I asked to speak to Robbie she told me that she was his daughter and that he was in bed and unwell. She added that he was to get his rest and that she did not want to worry him. At least she didn't come out with any of that "doctor's orders" nonsense. There was a pause and she must have relented for then I heard laboured breathing and Twentyman answered in a trait and unsteady voice.

'I thought it were you, lad. Nowt to fuss about, Lia. That lass of mine isn't half a worrier. I'm fine, just fine and away you go while I speak to my friend.'

I was quite touched to be addressed as his friend. I told him about what I had learnt since we had last met and read over to him the letter from Barry that I had just been given.

'Well that's all very interesting but if our Barry was in the house after four o'clock or whenever it was then he would have been the last person to see April's body before you did. But he wasn't, was he?'

He paused for dramatic emphasis and the chance to gather his strength. He really did sound ill and I wondered if Lia would let him continue with the conversation. But she did and he went on unperturbed while I tried to work out what he was getting at.

'Don't you see it, lad? It doesn't really make sense.'

'What doesn't?'

'You're a slow one on the uptake, even for one of Her Majesty's bloody counsel. It's cracking obvious, it is. Either Barry were lying or he were telling the truth – it's one or t'other.'

I still didn't get it and he made his displeasure clear by stopping to cough.

'Listen, lad. You told me that you turned April's body over because when you found her she was face down. Well, if Barry was right and her eyes were looking at him, then she must have been face up when he saw her, mustn't she? So if he was telling the truth it looks as if someone had moved her between the time Barry saw her and the time you did. Stands to reason as she certainly didn't move herself. And there's another thing, too. We only found the fingerprints of you and your lass at the scene so it looks as though someone had cleaned up between times and wiped away any prints there might have been there since there weren't even any of April's when we examined the scene. Well I bet that young Barry weren't too fastidious about cleanliness being next to godliness, so where were his prints? That, no pun intended, is the rub. Someone either came back to the house to wipe them or he was there all of the time.'

'But wouldn't it have been the perfect way of pinning the blame on Barry to have left his prints there? Why wipe them off?'

'Maybe he was wiping his own prints off or maybe he went out for a bit after killing her and came back later on. If that were so then he'd not know that Barry had been there but why the killer would have come back beats me.'

'One other thing though, before I forget.'

'What's that, lad?'

'Well you kind of implied when I was at your house that I didn't tell you everything I knew at the Police station?'

'No, I just meant that you didn't give a report to the operator when you made the emergency call. You never told them anything about what happened or where your cousin's body actually was. You just said you found her dead and we had to find out from Toby Ainsdale the address and where the body was in that glass room thing.'

'I suppose that I was too upset then, given that we had only just found April dead. But hang on, how did he know where the body was unless he saw it himself? I'm pretty sure I hadn't told him anything at that point, I just burst in and demanded to use the phone, and I think that Ros was too upset to say much.'

'Maybe you did tell him – he couldn't have guessed where the body was unless you had told him or perhaps he saw which part of the house you were coming out from.'

'But the conservatory was hidden from the hedge and he couldn't have guessed unless...'

'Unless he already knew – is that what you're saying lad? He seemed sure enough on the phone. But you may have something there lad – how would he have known unless he had already seen her?'

'Perhaps he saw the body because it was he who had actually killed her.'

'Maybe but I don't really think that your theory holds much water. He had known the family for years and the motive doesn't appear to have anything to do with sex as she hadn't been touched. Burglary is unlikely as all of them buggers weren't short of cash. We still don't know what motive he might have had. Remember that we didn't know how it all happened or why, and probably never will unless someone confesses and nobody has done so far – even if we did try and put the pressure on at the time.'

'But put the pressure on whom? My money would be on Toby Ainsdale.'

'Lad, I don't like the cut of his jib. Didn't like it when I first met him and even after so many years still don't. So, Christopher, why don't you go back and see him and try to get him confess to April's murder if you think that he actually did it. You might get him to confess even though we were unsuccessful.'

This suggestion seemed to me to be beside the point.

'But why would he confess if he didn't actually do it.'

'It never stopped any of my colleagues framing someone like him if they could get away with it.'

A voice broke in. It was Lia and she was exasperated both with him and with me.

'I know Dad's enjoying this game of Cluedo or whatever it is but I must insist you stop now. He's tired as anything and not at all a well man, If you don't mind, please let him get some rest.'

I apologised and said goodnight to him and he wished me well, adding with a cough that, 'My lass Lia will be the death of me. Just you wait and see.'

Then I gave Ben a call but he was out and as I listened to the answering machine I wondered whether I should arrange to see him at this stage but then, being unsure of what to do next, I just rang off. In any event I have an irrational fear of such machines and leaving a message on them, a fear that is only replaced by dislike if the recorded message is supposedly witty or a poor impersonation of a second-rate celebrity.

I returned to the machinations of everyday farming folk in Ambridge and was just following the unspeakable Brian's latest exploits when the phone rang. It was Kirsty.

'Mum says you're to get in touch as soon as possible, it's urgent!'

I groaned inwardly. I couldn't go on ignoring Francesca's calls indefinitely but I could probably put off replying to them for another few days. 'A problem shelved is a problem solved', as Gavin would say.

'How are things at home, Kirsty?'

'Oh, fine, fine – well not really fine. Someone tried to break in to the flat today while I was out at the shops.'

'How do you mean?'

'There were signs that the lock had been tampered with but whoever it was didn't get in.'

'Did you call the police?'

'Yes, they came round but they said it was probably just a yob who had got past the entry system and was just trying his luck and that our impressive lock had probably thwarted him. But don't worry, Pops. Old Mrs Abronovitch next door said she'd keep an eye on me which is a bit rich considering that she's about two hundred, walks with a Zimmer and is practically blind.'

'Don't exaggerate! She's about the same age as me, doesn't have a zimmer and can see as well as I can. But look, you've obviously had a fright – do you want me to come back to London right now?'

I was in two minds and was dithering between the options of staying here or returning home.

'No, I really am fine. Stop worrying – If I get scared I'll go and stay with Sophie or Imogen. Their parents would be fine to put me up. But honestly, Dad, I'm quite alright – whatever mum might think. Just don't fret so!'

'If I can't worry about the wellbeing of my own daughter, who else can I worry about?'

'Keep your cool Daddio! Oh, one thing – are you still planning to come home this weekend as you promised? Sweet! Anyway, I've got something much more interesting to tell you.'

'Not about crimes that you didn't witness or have committed?'

'No, no, I mean something much more interesting.'

She did not say anything further, clearly wanting me to lead her on.

'What is it, oh most delightful and clever daughter of mine?'

She laughed and I wondered what bombshell she was about to land on me.

'Well I've been a bit naughty in your absence.'

I wondered if she had managed to wreck the flat or been prosecuted for something like a breach of the peace or a contravention of the Licensing or Road Traffic Acts.

'What is it?' I enquired sheepishly.

'Oh don't worry, nothing really terrible. I just had a little dinner party a couple of nights ago. Just an alfresco affair with a few of the girls from school.' This sounded unlikely and I groaned inwardly again, thinking of the D.B.I. brigade (Kirsty's own term for her pals, the initials standing for "Daddy Bought It"). Their girlish glee would, no doubt, have been fuelled by Bacardi and my best white wine. Kirsty's friends are all high spirited enough by themselves to enliven any alfresco dinner party. For a moment I had visions of the flat being comprehensively trashed by that well-spoken rabble.

'I hope you don't mind but I might have accidentally broken that folding table you had propped up behind the door. But in fairness it was an ugly thing anyway so you could say I did you a favour cause now you can replace it with something more tasteful.'

What cheek! I blamed Francesca for having made Kirsty so wilful, headstrong and lacking in constraint. But then Fran always said that our daughter was just like me – stubborn, one-tracked and never willing to change her mind. Attributes that I continue to deny of course.

'Oh Dad, I nearly forgot to tell you that Paddy called and left a message for you, something about Glen Brian having settled for some vast sum that I can't remember and with full costs. He is apparently very pleased and sends his thanks. He did say that he wants to take us to dinner and he was so jolly about it all that I reckon that I really will go back in the summer and get to ride the horses at Ballaweague. Perhaps we should think about buying me a horse of my own. It'd be a super investment now you're apparently in the money.'

'An investment, really?'

'I'm only joshing you. I know that you're really a hard-up QC with a huge overdraft because solicitors never pay you. But I wouldn't mind a horse. Anyway, must go now Old Bean, so take care! Byeee!'

It took me a few moments to recover from the indignity of being called Old Bean by my overly forward daughter and then I remembered that I had not given Tierney the call that he had requested.

'Christopher, how grand! Glad you phoned. An absolutely splendid result, absolutely splendid! They didn't have the backbone to stand up to the strength of our case and it ended up costing them plenty. Not of course that plenty wasn't what was due to me for all my losses, inconvenience and the like. Well done! If you're interested I was going to be sending you a planning matter that was all supposed to be a bit hush-hush but somehow things went a bit awry and well, never mind now, Jessica will have all the papers next week and I'll tell her to send them on. How are you two getting on, by the way? Grand, pleased to hear it, she's a fine girl – actually both of them are, Miss Goodchild and your daughter Kirsty, I mean. Enough of that Christopher, look I'm a bit tied up with a business matter at the moment so I'll have to be brief. It's about Toby Ainsdale and the worker who got poisoned. The health and safety people, or rather the factory inspectors as I think they were back then, did an investigation and handed over their findings to the police. There was no prosecution, though and I heard that vital papers and photographs had been mislaid, deliberately or otherwise. The worker's family never sued because they were bought off and seemed to have been happy enough. What you may find interesting is that one particular police officer, it is claimed, deliberately lost the paperwork and covered up his trail so well that by the time they found out they couldn't prove anything but the stink remained. After a decent time, he resigned. His name, if you're interested, was Laing, Michael Laing. Does that ring any bells with you?'

It took me some time to digest this information and while I was doing so the phone rang again. This time it was Guy Leemings.

'Hang on a minute while I go outside', he said. 'There's a bit of interference in here.'

I could hear quite distinctly the sounds of a crowded pub in the background with a lot of noisy people laughing and shouting. There was a slight delay before Guy, presumably having abandoned his sister-in-law temporarily by going outside, was now free to speak. I could have sworn that he was relieved that it was me he talking to and not the dour Shula.

'What did you make of the letter, then?'

'I've read it and I'm very sure Barry was telling the truth.'

This was a gut reaction and it sounded like the right thing to say in the circumstances. It was what I genuinely felt. Guy said he was glad that I was prepared to see things from Barry's point of view and he asked me if I had known that April was pregnant.

'Only in the last few days or so – it wasn't mentioned at the P.M. though.'

'Was Barry the father?'

'I haven't any reason to think otherwise, Guy. Why do you ask?'

'It's only that, well, I would have really liked so much to have been an uncle. It would have been fun. Maybe that sounds strange but my two are almost grown-up now and live with their mum so I don't see as much of them as I'd like...'

I commiserated with him, not knowing the details and not wanting to know them either. Then I asked him if he'd had any idea from whom Barry had got the hundred pounds that was found on him after the crash.

'Didn't I mention it? Oh, it was one of April's friends.'

'How do you know that? Barry didn't mention it in the letter, did he?'

'No, she told me herself. She came and saw me when I was out of hospital and staying with my aunt Betty in Skelmersdale. I think Gillian must have told her where I was.'

'I think that the girl felt guilty because she'd helped Barry to flee after April died. Maybe she thought that if she hadn't given him the money that he'd have ended up in jail rather than killed in the crash. I reassured her that nothing was her fault. I'm sure she only meant well even if that is a damning indictment of anyone.'

'Do you know the name of that girl?'

'Her name? I don't recall that now, I barely knew her though I recall seeing her with April a few times. I can remember what she looked like though. Quite a good looker, I thought. She had long reddish brown hair but the thing I remember most of all was that she always seemed to be wearing the same green bead things,

295

leastways whenever I saw her she had them on. Is that of any help?'

I groaned. Now all I needed was for Gavin to phone me up and harass me again about the election at work and, as fate would have it, he did.

19

I had never visited Ben at his work before and I was a bit surprised by the collection of huts and old buildings that comprised the business premises of Gateacre Media and Film Services Limited. The name was smartly displayed on a large mauve and white enamel sign but I was disappointed in what I found when I passed the sign. I had expected a "high-tech large plants in indigo glazed pots" sort of scenario and this almost run-down clutter of what looked like an overgrown wartime factory detracted a bit from my faith in Ben and his commercial acumen. But perhaps I was being a bit unfair since Malcolm said he had only begun their venture a few months before and was probably still moving from the start-up to the profitable stage. They were keen and anxious to get things going and maybe one day they would be able to afford the kind of offices that a business like theirs deserved.

I opened the door marked "Enquiries" and walked in. A girl with bleached hair done up in a strange sort of beehive style reminiscent of the sixties was sitting by a desk, idly picking her nails with a straightened-out paper clip. She jumped when she saw me enter and then smiled in an engaging and perfectly natural way.

'Are you our Mr. Kingston's cousin, the one who called earlier on?'

Her voice was unmistakeable and I knew that this must be Lorraine, the demi-goddess of the switchboard. I confirmed my identity and she said that she thought I must be related to Ben because of our family resemblance. This threw me as she was the first person ever to have commented on it. I resisted the temptation to add that Ben was the fatter one. She pushed the open paperback aside and I noticed with some surprise that it was an old green Penguin. Then she adjusted her toppling hair style and buzzed through to Ben.

He came out to meet me and bundled me in to his office.

'Remember to get those shots out by courier as soon as possible, Lorraine. Winslets must have them by lunchtime.'

He shut the door and by way of unnecessary explanation told me that these were some stills that were to be incorporated into a promotional video. Malcolm, apparently, was out supervising some outdoor takes for the same project. He sighed as he told me he had always wanted to be a director of real films, not the crappy super-advert rubbish that now occupied his time but never mind because that was where the real money was.

'Creativity? Not likely, but then where there's muck...' he added, until Lorraine put her head round the door and took orders for two coffees, milk and no sugar, but since these never appeared I think she must have completely forgotten. Either that or the Maxwell House had run out.

'You said you had some more information for me.'

'I told him about my conversations with Tierney and Guy and I produced Barry's letter. He took and read it two or three times in silence while I watched a boy climbing off a yellow motorbike and coming in to collect the package for Winslets.'

'Wotcher, Chicken, how's tricks?' Lorraine asked.

'Not bad, Quiche my love, not bad at all.'

Then the front door closed and the boy started to rev up his engine before he and the bike disappeared up the road. In the silence that followed I tried to identify the birdsong coming from a tree in the yard outside and had narrowed it down to a choice of two. Eventually Ben waved Barry's letter at me and spoke.

'Do you believe all of what was in this?'

'I guess so. Barry didn't have to write it and I don't expect he thought anyone else was ever going to read it, apart from Guy.'

'I'm not sure that I could ever trust anything that came from Barry', said Ben. 'You notice how he was quick to deny ever having been in the house itself with April.'

'Yes, but on the other hand he could have just said he hadn't seen April that day and had never even been in the area at all.'

'But what about him being seen in the phone box by the station?' Ben asked.

'Well I doubt if he realised that held been seen there by anyone. After all he probably thought that everyone went around dressed like him as a grubby Afghan peasant and looking completely spaced-out. Possibly everyone did look like that then.'

'Even so he was... maybe you're right. Well, look, just suppose, that because I never trusted him anyway, he was telling the truth and that it all happened like he says. Then...'

He paused and I could see him trying to work something out in his mind. He frowned and re-read part of the letter.

'Chris, if April had come back to steal things from the house then it would tie up with what I heard her saying that she was going to make someone pay. But who was she talking about? Who was going to make her pay, and why?'

'Your parents, I suppose, were the people who would pay and I think that she meant that they would pay for the way she had been treated.'

'Unless...'

As I waited for him to go on, I saw as the digital clock on the wall flipping over from 11.59 to 12.00 and thought that the slight clunk was most satisfactory.

'No, that doesn't make sense either, Chris. If what Barry says is true then we know why April was going to the house alone and that she wasn't intending to meet anyone there. She knew that Gerald and Mum would all be out because they'd talked about their plans on the Saturday.'

'What about you, then? Did you say where you were going to be on the Sunday?'

'I don't remember saying what my plans were but I suppose that I might well have said that I was going over to Cal's to watch the cricket on their telly. Anyway she came back at two o' clock-ish, faked the signs of a burglary, and started taking things from the house. Maybe someone surprised her while she was doing that.'

'Why do you say that she had been surprised?'

'Well, he hit her from behind didn't he?'

'I don't think so. Robin told me that she tried to defend herself at the last minute. There were bruises on her hand where she presumably held it up to protect her head and I think that the position of the wounds on her head meant that she was hit from the front but I'm not sure if I ever checked that out properly with Robin. I can't see that it's all that significant as to the identity of her assailant, though. Anyway if a thief had already been there then how come I hadn't seen him. Remember that I had been in fiddling with my car until April arrived and no-one would have broken into or even entered, the house when at least one of the family had been obviously present. And for that matter they would have made a rapid departure when April had entered herself. They wouldn't have wanted to confront a member of the family when they could have easily avoided them. I'm sure the conservatory door was unlocked so the burglar could have avoided confronting April and just slipped out into the garden when she was still in the house.'

'Was it always locked when no-one was at home?'

'Yes – and remember that there were no signs of a forced entry so even if had been left unlocked and the burglar went in that way, he could certainly have got out from that door as well.'

The phone rang, its shrill tones creating an unwelcome break.

'Not now Lorraine, tell them to call back and where's our coffee you promised?'

The beehive-haired one produced a couple of steaming mugs before Ben continued in outlining his theories.

'So was April confronted by someone she knew already rather than someone unknown who clandestinely crept up on her?'

I said that I thought this was likely and that since we had already discounted the second burglar theory that left either an intruder who had just happened to notice her going in to the house and had followed her in or someone who was already in the house all along.

'This Mr. X thing, the man she was blackmailing – do you think that it could it have been him? I mean if she was having an affair with Mr. X then he might have turned nasty if she'd tried to up the stakes by demanding more money or by threatening to tell his wife or partner.'

'Ben, you're mixing two different things up. The older man she was having the relationship with was probably not being blackmailed by her at all, not for the sake of a measly ten quid a week. Anyway what would the motive for murdering her have been? Just think about it Ben, if you were blackmailing someone you'd hardly be laughing and joking with them on the phone in the way that Gill said she was. Anyway how would Mr X, as you call him, have known that April was going to be in her parent's house on her own at that time – surely he would have assumed that she would have been in Riego Street where she usually lived?'

'Perhaps he followed her in to our parents' house.'

'Well he must have been tailing her all day then as he wouldn't have been going past the house just by chance and seen her there. Serpentine Drive isn't exactly a busy through route to anywhere plus all the houses were occupied and it's the sort of place that people up to no good would be challenged.'

'Fair enough, Chris, you may be right.'

Ben looked as though he had exhausted all of our conjecturing but then added, 'But I tell you who I don't trust at all, that Toby Ainsdale. From what you've said he was even more of a wrong 'un than I thought. Mind you, even if Gerald had been in league with him on that council scam, how would April have known enough about it to be blackmailing him?'

I refrained from mentioning that she had probably read through her father's letters since from what I had heard from other people that would have been entirely in character for my beautiful cousin April. Ben paused for a few seconds presumably having come to the same conclusion himself.

'Perhaps she found out enough to make Toby worried and turned the screw on him so he got nasty. But maybe I'm letting my imagination run away a bit. I think you should go and have a word with the man himself. I've known him all my life and I still don't trust him.'

I laughed nervously.

'Where does he live and how on earth do you suggest that I go about it? I'm hardly going to ask him outright if he murdered April.'

'First part's easy enough as he lives at Cley Moss Farm up Cley Moss Lane. It's not a real working farm in that there's no land to speak of now but it's still a nice old farmhouse. I went there once, years ago, just after he moved in. I think his wife Elvira had died by then – breast cancer, it was, and she was only fifty something. But as to what you do when you get there, I don't know. You're the supposed expert in asking probing questions, elucidating answers and all that. You'll just have to think that one out for yourself. Keep me informed, though, and let me know what you turn up. You can always leave a message on the answering machine. If you've got enough then I can deal with him in my own way.'

I remembered his previous threats along these lines and felt a shiver pass.

'Nae, lad, we'll go back to yon Twentyman and get 'im to do summat to nail t'booger instead.'

I had slipped into mimic again in an attempt to defuse the situation but his mood seemed to have improved spontaneously and a smile appeared on his face.

'Don't worry, Chris, I won't really do anything foolish. Listen, before you go, here's another pickle point quote from grandpa's book. The fine sandstone Parish Church of St. Luke...'

I thought about it momentarily and then continued, '...is a handsome modern structure dating from the middle of the last century and boasting a tower with a commanding spire. Here's one for you, Ben. See if you can tell me who was the principal local benefactor in the field of education having been imbued from an early age with the spirit of learning and having a thirst for knowledge?'

He laughed and without hesitation replied, 'John Harrison, a Crosby man who had made his fortune in trade in the city of London and whose original grammar school building is still in use for the girls of his foundation. Much too easy, Chris and for you to have brought up that girls grammar school, you must have been thinking of your Albright girl again.'

I realised that I hadn't mentioned the fact that Ros was now somehow entangled in the plot but this was something I didn't feel like disclosing to him. I needed some space and an opportunity to think things over. Fortunately he had changed tack again.

'Did you realise that the Short History wasn't the only book that Sep wrote?'

'Really? I never heard of anything else he'd written.'

'He wrote a work of fiction, a novel no less. It never got published but April said that she'd read the manuscript that had been neatly typed out on that ancient typewriter that we used to play with. Apparently it was a bit racy, a sort of salacious bodice ripper set in a large Victorian city and seaport in the North of England. I can't guess where he meant but according to April, the story was based on his own exploits when he was young.'

'I didn't know he had any exploits when he was young. I always thought of him as a bit tame.'

'Oh, then there's a lot you don't know about our family. Sep was a bit of a lad in his time and it's rumoured that we might even have some distaff relatives in the States. Well howdy there, partner, Are you dudes members of the Kingston clan of Liverpool in old Engerland? But seriously Chris, I wish that I knew what had happened to the manuscript as I'd have loved to have read it. I bet you that someone will have thrown it out and that someone was probably mum. She never could stand what she called smut and filth. What a prude to produce a son like me.'

We were interrupted by Lorraine who wanted Ben's immediate answer to an email from a dissatisfied supplier who, not unreasonably, was fed up with not having been paid.

'Give him the usual bull.'

'I'm afraid that the usual bull won't do. He's threatening to raise a county court action against us.'

'I'll deal with it later. Maybe I can get some free legal advice from my learned cousin, here. He's a barrister.'

'Sure', I said. I'm more than happy to give you my legal opinion. It's simple, really. My advice is that if you owe him the money, just pay up.'

Lorraine sniggered and left the room and as she shut the door his mood darkened again.

'Chris, something's just occurred to me. You said that Twentyman was still in contact with Laing, didn't you?'

'He said that he'd told him about Gerald's letter and everything I was doing, yes. Wait a minute...'

It was beginning to dawn on me. Laing was the one that Guy had said he had shown Barry's letter to, Laing was the one who had covered things up for Toby in the past and Laing had been employed as head of security by a company called SerCley. It didn't take much imagination to see where that name had come from – an amalgam of Serpentine Drive and Cley Moss. I hadn't the time or the inclination to check it out but I was fairly sure that at some point or other there would have been a member's resolution to have changed the barely pronounceable Quendoline into the at least more appropriate SerCley, maybe when the share capital had been transferred into the name of another possible nominee, perhaps the literary Ms. Gill Harmer, author of The Raven's Nest and the seductress of Riego Street. I told Ben of my suspicions and he said that I was probably correct.

'You don't think that he was trying to warn me off by getting me mugged, do you?'

'Who? Laing? Quite likely but then there are quite a few people who knew that you were stirring up the past, Gill, for one, myself for another, Twentyman and, of course, Laing. But I doubt very much if our bent copper had anything to do with covering up a murder. He'd have drawn the line at that, surely? No, Chris, I'll tell you what I think. It's my belief that Laing told Toby that you were enquiring into the events of that time and that Toby told him to put the frighteners on you to keep you away from unearthing his skulduggery, that was the word you said that Twentyman used, wasn't it?'

'That's all very well, Ben, but why would he bother? Surely he's way past caring about his reputation now. Even if Quendoline/SerCley is still trading there's not much I could drag up which would affect him now.'

Ben frowned and began to audibly run over his thoughts.

'If he didn't kill her for the blackmail reason then is it possible that he was actually the older man, the one having the affair with April? I know it doesn't seem very likely but...'

'So where was the motive to kill her?'

'You're right. Even if he was her lover, there's still no motive there.'

He clearly was unconvinced and added as an afterthought, 'I wonder did they quarrel about something? Maybe they fell out about the baby or about her two-timing him with Barry?'

I shook my head. Even Ben seemed to have little faith in that one. We both agreed that unless we knew for sure the identity of April's lover then we weren't going to get very far with what we called the non-blackmail theory.

Looking puzzled, Ben added, 'And how did the girl that Barry's brother said gave him the money to flee fit into it the picture? Who the hell was she and what was her motive for doing that?' I shrugged, pleased that I hadn't given him Guy's description of the girl. That was something I'd have to follow up for myself.

As Ben showed me out he told me to be sure to contact him as soon as I knew any more. Lorraine smiled again and went back to *The Case of the Wayward Wife*.

I trudged back to the bus-stop and as my shoes finally disintegrated I wished, not for the first time, that I had brought the car with me from London. I would have to stop in town and buy another pair. I hated buying shoes. What a bloody waste of money! Perhaps I could find time to visit a bookshop or two while I was looking. I was definitely not looking forward to the meeting that I was going to have to have with Toby Ainsdale and I began to wonder about trying to trace the girl with the green beads and therefore having to speak to Ros again was the lesser of two evils. I was soon to find out.

20

It took me a long time to get to Cley Moss, not least because I had to walk the last mile or so down the muddy lane that led its way in a winding course from the main road. I was tired and disinterested or maybe I just knew I didn't want to go there.

The house was set back from the lane behind a stand of wind-stunted trees and was invisible until I had turned the last corner. Beyond it stretched the flat and featureless valley of the meandering River Alt and it was a strange and rather bleak place, even in the late afternoon sun of this breezy spring day.

When I got nearer I was pleasantly surprised. Cley Moss Farm turned out not to be the Victorian brick box that I had expected or even the modern replacement whose gaping picture windows would have disfigured the slumbering Lancashire countryside. It was something much more unusual – a long, low building fashioned from the hard Perrine grit-stone of its native county.

I was still fearful of what I was going to say when I got to speak to Toby. So playing for time, I studied the tidy, small coursed stonework and neat mullioned windows of the seventeenth century farmhouse. I imagined the yeoman farmer who had first lived here being proud that his home had survived for so long and endured the ravages of time so well. I envied Ainsdale and that house.

I stepped under the sturdy stone porch and pulled the old-fashioned handle. From somewhere within the house I heard a melodious jingle of brass. Once there would have been servants, perhaps fresh faced country girls with rosy cheeks and clean white aprons, to open the door. This being the beginning of the twenty-first century, I doubted if there were any such servants now, rosy checked or otherwise.

Toby Ainsdale came to the door and I admit that I was a little surprised. I had last remembered him in the 1970s when he was in early middle age, always standing upright and straight backed. A figure who if not commanding respect or affection, at least held one's attention. I could still picture him as a dapper and meticulous man wearing his bespoke suits, Jermyn Street shirts and ties of the finest Italian silk, all set off by the most highly-polished shoes I had ever seen. He had often affected large silver cufflinks of a size so monstrous that I had sometimes wondered if he had taken some of Elvira's earrings and refashioned them for his own use. When he spoke he had always sounded so urbane and sure of himself.

The contrast with the present was telling. He had shrunk in both stature and presence. He stood the door wearing old corduroy trousers, a faded tartan shirt and a cardigan that by rights should have been binned years ago. He had shabby slippers on and, by his general appearance, I wondered if he had been drinking, or had suffered a stroke or perhaps both.

Toby eyed me for some time while saying nothing and I wondered where the dogs were. The sign on the gate had warned me to beware of them and a second more strident notice had born a faded picture of an Alsatian with the slogan, 'It only takes six seconds for me to get to the gate. How long does it take you?' I decided that I could do it in a lot less than the dogs could. Judging by the state of the notice by they had probably been long deceased.

'Young Christopher Kingston. I was expecting you.'

There was no warmth in his voice and he dispensed with the customary pleasantries such as, 'How lovely to see you', or, 'It must be ages since we last met.' He ushered me in to his study and I followed his shuffles towards a small room that seemed to be a cross between a workroom and a midden judging by the heap of papers strewn everywhere.

He then produced a bottle of Laphroaig from within a small lacquer chest of exquisite design overlaid with dust. I remembered how his wife Elvira had been a great one for auction sales and antique shops, in the days when such places still sold items of real antiquity and not tawdry reproductions mass-manufactured in the far east. I watched as he poured himself a generous glassful of malt but he offered me none.

'I heard that you were back in town. I understand that you've been asking a lot of questions, haven't you? Questions about April and her family. My daughter Gillian told me that.'

I wondered what else she might have told him and I was unnerved by his coldness and sense of purpose. I decided to avoid generalities and move straight to the chase but he continued on with a firm resolve.

'You have also been asking about what sort of things I may have done in connection with my former business activities although I am damned if I can see what business that is of yours as I had virtually retired when you were still at school so I repeat that all of my business activities were long over and in the past. Dead and buried.'

'Presumably Mick Laing told you that, and that's why you set those goons of yours on to me.'

He looked puzzled and politely affected never to have heard of Laing nor of the exploits of any so-called "goons".

'Who was Laing? Well, you should know! You employed him at SerCley and it was you who got him to attack me in Adam and Eve Street the other night, wasn't it? Oh, don't waste my time by denying it. I know that it was either him or a couple of his minions acting on your behalf!' It had taken me some time to work out what the SCSC embroidered on the jackets of the two workmen I had seen before I was mugged had stood for.

Toby's expression softened. He became more relaxed and, without asking me, poured me a small tot of the whisky.

'I think there's been some kind of misunderstanding here, Christopher my lad. I don't know anything about an incident in that delightfully-named thoroughfare or anything involving the SerCley company or any of its employees, whose services I don't deny that I used to use. If you are referring to someone called Laing, I presume that you mean ex-Detective Constable Laing – a person that I once had business dealings with. With respect Christopher, all I can say is that you're barking up the wrong tree.

'You're an extremely abrupt young fellow and I imagine that when you were asking about me you did so using the manner that you adopt when you are in court. I did employ Laing once upon a time but it was in the time when he left the police in, what was it, the mid-seventies and I haven't had anything to do with him, or with SerCley Properties since then. As for the alleged physical attack on you but why would I have anything to do with something like that? I retired from business after Elvira's death, which was many years ago now. And Christopher, just to set the record straight, Gillian only phoned me last night to say that you were in town and that you'd been talking to her about April, although I can't think why after all these years.'

'I apologised for my accusation about Laing, while not believing him for an instant. He waited, expectantly, for my next move. So I decided that I should show my hand. I told him about Gerald's letter and the packet I had received in London. To my astonishment, he just smiled.'

'I already know about that letter. Gerald told me all about it himself and said that he was going to send you the damn thing. I tried to talk him out of it and said things should be left as they are. I said that April is long dead and nothing will ever bring her back. Just leave the past alone. But he was insistent. In fact, very insistent for a dying man. But he evidently did send it and that's why you're here now, I presume?'

I nodded and, feeling that I could dispense with the preliminaries, I told him that I knew all about his shady business activities and about the fixing of consents and the bribing of councillors for obtaining planning permission. I made it clear that if he didn't cooperate I was going to do my best to reveal these and all other murky scams and goings-ons and make them public. I didn't add that even though I knew it all, in reality I knew only what I had been told by others and that, I would have to concede, amounted to almost nothing at all. Ainsdale was unperturbed and his face displayed little emotion so I decided to reveal what I thought was my trump card.

'I also know about how Mick Laing covered up evidence at your insistence to stop you from getting prosecuted for negligently killing one of your workers. You could have been fined a great deal and even jailed for perverting the course of justice.'

'Hmm, there was never sufficient evidence for any criminal charge to be brought and anyway it was the deceased worker's own fault. He went ahead when I told him not to. But let me congratulate you on your industry and your perspicacity up to now but why would any of my supposed activities in the past be of interest to anyone at the present time?'

'The fatal accident was his own fault! That's rich coming from the managing director!'

His sneer grew in response to my horrified reaction. 'But it was all a very long time ago, though and, as I said, no charges were brought. Christopher, I'm not really prepared to discuss my past business dealings, such as they might have been, with you – old acquaintance though you might be. It all happened when you were nothing more than a child. It's no business of yours and I'm not prepared to talk about it with you or anyone else, for that matter.'

'Not even if you were being blackmailed because of those business dealings?'

There was an intake of breath and for a moment I thought that he was going to deny it. He poured another whisky and proffered me the bottle. I declined.

'Your uncle never liked spirits, either, if I recall. Who on earth, Christopher, told you that nonsense about blackmail?'

He seemed to be spinning things out until I would get fed up and leave. I became aware of a clock somewhere in the background striking the hour and waited until the chime stopped, while desperately thinking of what I could say next.

'April herself told me at Gill's party.'

Knowing that she hadn't told me anything of the sort wasn't going to stop me – Toby hadn't been there so he couldn't contradict me on that score. He continued to look at me with disdain, as though I was something unpleasant that I had picked up on his shoe.

'Don't jump to the wrong conclusions, Christopher. It's not becoming of a barrister. Unfortunately you have to remember that April did not always tell the truth. Blackmailing me – absolute poppycock! Do you really think that the poor girl would have blackmailed me over a paltry set of innuendoes and false conclusions? She wouldn't have even cared, let alone known about, even five per cent of what was allegedly going on at that time.'

He looked at me slyly and continued. 'But, for the limited purposes of this conversation, yes, maybe at times there were certain, um, irregularities in my conduct in business matters. And yes, it would have been rather unfortunate if certain alleged activities had become public, particularly because persons in my position – responsible architects, that is – were not supposed to be involved in property dealing.'

'But there was the corruption aspect as well – bribing of officials and so on.'

'Corruption? I never liked the term. Come on Christopher, you know how the world of business works. Maybe from time to time, the gears of industry were oiled by donations to certain well placed individuals within the councils and corporations of this fair county of the red rose. It was certainly nothing that wasn't happening in Yorkshire or the north or anywhere else for that matter.'

'Call it what you like it's still corruption, wherever it took place, and always was. April was a smart young woman and recognised it as so.'

'She was without doubt a smart young woman. But you're wrong in your general surmise because by the 1970s, the writing was rather on the wall with local council work and the payment of "honoraria".'

'You mean bribes.'

'I wouldn't use that term – merely payments for facilitating good will. By then I had, how to put it, seen the light. I'm not talking of a Pauline conversion on the road to Damascus. What I'm saying is that the whole ethos, the culture of corruption, was changing in the post-Poulson era and, to be perfectly frank, I could make enough money, more than enough, from my legitimate work and from my wife's income from our property company. You'll no doubt be pleased to know that my transactions with that company were very much at arm's length. Honoraria were a thing of the past. So there wasn't very much that April could have been interested in by that time and nothing she could have translated into money, if you see what I mean. Nothing that she could have blackmailed me for, to use that unfortunate expression. Does that answer your question?'

'No, it does not – on two grounds. First – you could still have been ruined by the evidence of your past misdemeanours coming out...'

'The ever-useful Mr Laing and his contacts might well have prevented what you so euphemistically call my past misdemeanours from coming out. You could say I was always one step ahead thanks to inside information

316

and of course the redoubtable Michael was also very useful as a human paper-shredder, so to speak. You do remember, I hope, that I was never charged and never prosecuted, with anything. And I would of course have threatened to sue if anything had been suggested in public. As a lawyer, you are well aware of what protection the law of libel would have afforded an innocent person such as myself against whom nothing could be proved. A case based on smearing tactics and innuendoes would never have been successful. And your second ground?'

'The money. You've never denied that you gave money to April, have you?'

'Didn't I? How careless.' He was now sneering and confident that he had got the better of me.

'I know all about that, too. It was you who was paying April every week, regular as clockwork, wasn't in? I've done a little work behind the scenes and I have managed to go through your entire bank records.'

He was shaken by this and I wondered if I'd hit home. It was a lie about the bank records. What did that matter since half of what I was dealing with these days were lies anyway.

'My bank records – how did you?' He relaxed. 'Oh, that's nonsense because I never even used...'

He stopped and saw he had gone too far. As he considered matters, I studied his face. I remembered Gavin once describing someone he knew as having a face which was 'more partied in than lived in.' Looking at his ruined features, this would have been a good way of summing up Toby's face. His supercilious manner seemed to be fading fast.

'All right, damn you Christopher, you've caught me out there. I admit it then. Yes I was giving April regularly a little money, but it was nothing to do with any business matters. It was straight question of what I felt was my duty, that I could help her with her expenses for her studies. If Gerald couldn't help her...'

'But he did – uncle Gerald was always very generous to her.'

'Hmm, too generous, some said. But my motivation was simply love.'

'Love?'

He was now looking distressed and for a moment I hesitated and he began to speak.

'I wish to terminate this meeting now. When you and that girl found April dead, I was very upset. To see poor April lying there dead... I couldn't bear the look in her sad eyes.'

To my horror, he started to cry. But I was totally without pity now and I decided to press home the advantage. His remark about 'if Gerald could not help her' and Lorraine's comments about Ben and I looking alike were reverberating around my brain and, in a wild shot, I realised that had him. Bull's eye!

'I'll ask again – you talked about love, the pure love that you had for her. So you were jealous, weren't you?'

'You still don't get it, do you, Christopher?'

'You were jealous of April – because she preferred Barry to you.'

'Don't be ridiculous - that was never anything to do with it. She couldn't have been jealous of Barry because I wasn't fit to be her lover. Who told you about what I thought about April in the first place?'

'No need for anyone to tell me. You yourself did, talking about your pure love for April. Tell me were you jealous of Barry because he was making love to her?'

'No – not at all. Do I need to tell you that again? If it was anyone I was jealous of it was your uncle Gerald – just ask Maura.'

'Why her?'

'Just ask Maura about April and me – although I haven't seen Maura since Gerald's funeral.'

This seemed hardly relevant and certainly wasn't an answer to my question at all. Then it just came to me. Someone had told me how Maura and Toby had been lovers before she married Gerald. No wonder Toby was attracted to April because she would have been a younger and prettier version of his old love Maura. The more I thought about I could see how similar she must have been to her mother and why Toby had lusted after April.

'Tell me, though, did Gerald know about you and April?'

'Know what?'

'What do you think?'

'Gerald wasn't a fool so of course he knew but it didn't seem to make any difference to the way he treated April.'

'And Ben – did he know you loved April?'

'I'm certain he didn't have an inkling in that way.'

'But you two were lovers?'

'We had been in the past.'

'So when did it end?'

'That was all over before April was born. When Maura married Gerald, it was her who ended it. But I still loved Maura so very much. It got even worse when I saw April growing up into a pretty young woman just like her mother and I couldn't help but love her as well. Love is such a very strange thing, sometimes it is so powerful that there comes a time when you can no longer hold it back.'

He trailed off and began to cry again and I watched his distress in an ironic detachment. He seemed to be a vain and supercilious men who was only capable of thinking of himself and his own needs and desires, and lacking the imagination to see things from anyone else's position. I could have been touched by his hankering after Maura long after their affair was over. But to prey on April instead?

He looked closely into my face as though he was trying to work out what I was thinking and then, failing to find what he was looking for, continued.

'With time, I just transferred my affections on to April as she got older. She grew up to be the double of her mother and turned into a very beautiful young woman, just like Maura had been in her time, but even more so. A sort of, well, highly sexual young woman, too. Oh, I loved April very much and I just wanted to have her be acknowledged as my own, to look after her, to have a proper loving relationship with her. Yes, I wanted her. Was that so wrong, so perverse? Why couldn't I have what other men had, what was natural to them? Love isn't such a bad thing, such a destructive emotion as people sometimes paint it.' He paused and I wondered if the colour that love was painted depended on the palette that the artist was using.

'Anyway on that dreadful day when April told me she was pregnant, I couldn't cope with the thought of that no-good Barry Leemings impregnating her.'

He stopped and the life seemed to have gone out of him as he slumped back on his chair. I looked at him and was now unable to hide my disgust. Everything seemed to have fallen into place. But not neatly, and I felt sick.

'When I asked you about you two being lovers, I meant you and April, not you and Maura. Now you've made the answer clear. What was it that made you kill her? Was jealousy the motive, that you were unable to stomach the fact that another man had made April pregnant? Was that why you couldn't bear looking in her eyes after you'd killed her and went back to turn her body over after Barry found her?'

'I would never have killed her – I loved her, don't you see that, as stupid as you self-evidently are?'

Everything was beginning to unravel – the motive, the timing and even the fact that it was he and not me who told the police where to find the body. But why did he have to kill her – they could have just eloped together and taken the baby with them but clearly Toby didn't have the guts. He may have loved her but I felt it was certain that, knowing April, she didn't love him. I was confused and once again I was in a situation that was past my understanding.

'People like you disgust me! You think you are strong by preying on the vulnerable but you're nothing but weak and jealous!'

His face became animated and began to twitch violently before he sprang up like a whisky-enraged Lazarus and with great force hurled the contents of his glass over me. Then, as I stood there before him, he began to shout at me, wildly and incoherently.

'Fuck you! How dare you! You meddling little fool! You stupid, bloody little idiot. You'll never understand, people like you don't, never never! Get the fuck out of my home!'

I hoped he would have an apoplectic fit and keel over then and there but he did not. By the time I was through the door and running down the lane he was still shouting at me. I was conscious of the sound of his threats reverberating after me until the wind carried them away across the low-lying meadows and I could no longer hear anything but the panting of my own breath.

I stopped and hurled a stone towards him. But he was by now too far away, too small in the distance, for it to be anything other than a feeble gesture of my hatred towards him for killing April.

21

As soon as the woman opened the door I knew what had happened. Her red-rimmed eyes and streaked make-up announced it as boldly as if I'd read it in the *Echo*. She stood, uncomprehending in her obvious grief, and I could think of little to say.

'I'm Lia, his daughter.'

'I'm really sorry. When did Robbie, your dad, I mean...'

'Yesterday morning at eight o'clock. We all knew he was living on borrowed time ever since he'd been taken in to hospital last year.'

'Was it...?'

'Myocardial infarction, they called it. A heart attack. Although I'd call it a broken heart. You see he never really got over the death of mum.'

She sniffed and the colour of her eyes reminded me of the bottled Bass that had been her father's favourite tipple and there was something about her that made me think of places more exotic than the Wirral. She blew noisily into a white handkerchief and tried to pull herself together.

'I hope you don't mind me asking but you are Mr Kingston, the man who phoned my dad the other day, aren't you? We've never met but I know that he thought highly of you. I think he felt that he understood you.'

Did the fact that I had spoken to him over the phone and actually met him a couple of times single me out as someone unusual? Perhaps few folk had ever contacted him in the last few years other than retired colleagues or people trying to sell him something that he didn't need. Maybe that was one of the things that happened when you got older and began to outlive your lifelong friends, sinking into a loneliness that only a knock on the door or the ring of the phone can alleviate.

She smiled, looked at me nervously and held her hand out.

'You'd best come in.'

She led me through to the back kitchen and gestured towards the small table. I sat down but could think of little to say and I felt numb. I had hardly known her father but somehow that didn't seem to matter. I had grown to trust him, to like him and now the old man was gone. What did he mean by saying that he understood me? I thought that he got on with me when we recently met again and possibly even liked me – I hoped so anyway. Lia poured me out a cup of tea and then put her hand into the pocket of her apron.

'He told me about the time he first met you after you and your girlfriend found the body of your cousin. He said that she had been murdered but that they never found out who had done it.'

Perhaps feeling that she needed to defend his honour in some way, she continued, 'I'm sure that dad didn't mean to let you down. I think he was a little out of his depth. Let's face it murders in Crosby weren't all that common then. I think house breakings and bicycle thefts were his usual line of work. He told me about your uncle's request to help discover who actually did it and dad said that he was more than pleased to be able to assist you, even though such a long time had passed since the murder. To be honest I think that he'd been quite bored since his retirement and I got the impression it was a case he'd dwelt upon quite a bit over the years. He'd have been too proud to say it but I think he was pissed off with the fact that his pals in the CID had failed so badly and got your cousin's killer "banged to rights" as he put it.'

'Well if I'm being honest, many members of my family are also pretty resentful against the police for that but it wasn't a grudge against any particular officer but rather the whole system that had let them down. But your dad has been more than helpful after I contacted him recently and it's been an exciting ride – a sort of who-dun-it long after most of the clues have gone cold.'

'Dad said that you were a lawyer, a QC in fact. Maybe you're the sort of wig and gown guy that he sometimes battled with in the criminal courts.'

'I'm afraid not. I only do civil work these days. I have to admit I have barely tread the boards before a criminal jury – I've seen more of that in the cinema or on television dramas than in real life.'

'That's a shame.'

'Not for me – I don't think that I would enjoyed that kind of life.'

She smiled and then pulled something out of her apron pocket.

'My dad said that he wanted you to have this.'

I looked suitably surprised.

'He told me that he really enjoyed his chats with you and he certainly spoke a lot about you in the last few weeks. It seemed to have given him, well, a purpose, something to get his teeth into. You see, it was sad really, but Dad was never the same after my mum died. When he retired they had a great life as two of the old buffers who go round museums and art galleries and have numerous cups of tea and cheese scones while they puzzle out what they were going to do tomorrow. They travelled throughout Europe and visited all the places they'd ever heard of and wanted to see. But when mum went, he just sort of retreated into his shell and never came out of it again, He just seemed to be biding his time and waiting to rejoin her. Anyway as I said he was glad of your friendship recently, so go on, take it please.'

She handed me an object. It was a wristwatch, a rather unusual one, with a white face and handsome Roman numerals edged in gold. I turned it over and on the back of the case, well worn where the base metal was beginning to show through the gilt, was an inscription. 'To Robbie, from all your friends in the Lancashire C.I.D.' I could not read the date as it had been almost rubbed away but it must have been a gift given to him on his retirement. I was about to say something in gratitude but this wasn't the time for an oration and instead I just put the watch into my pocket and thanked her, touched by Robbie Twentyman's last gesture towards someone he had hardly known but felt deserved his friendship, if that's indeed what it was, and his watch.

I wanted to ask her if he had left anything else for me – any notes, memory sticks, letters? I guess I was hoping for one last communication that would have given me the final pieces of the puzzle and answers to the questions that I was still burning to ask him. And then it hit me. There would be no more meetings, no long phone calls, no further chance to get things right and, in Gerald's words, bring this whole thing to a close. I was on my own now.

I drained the tea while Lia looked on like a mournful spaniel and searched my face as if it would help her to make sense of her father's death. I felt that I had to say something.

'Lia – that's an unusual name.'

A smile broke through.

'Its Romanian actually – that's where my mother came from. My grandfather was the captain of a small tramp steamer the Aggelos, which I think means "angel" or "messenger" in Greek. He made regular runs from Constanta on the Black Sea out to the Mediterranean ports and beyond. Once, when she was a child, my mother came on board with him, just to see what the world really looked like, she said. On that particular trip they travelled out as far as Liverpool with a cargo of goods including Romanian wine – which was evidently well thought of back then. The voyage was in the summer of 1939 – I don't suppose it was really such a good time to see the wonders of the world then, was it?'

I shook my head and agreed and then gave her time to gather her thoughts.

'Both my granddad and my mum really loved the experience – they thought Liverpool was the finest city they'd ever seen but I don't suppose they had much to compare it with. They never forgot that trip, and six years later, two after the war had just ended – they returned to Liverpool on the Aggelos. My mother was eighteen then and granddad wanted her to stay in Britain because he thought that our King Michael would stand down and the communists were about to take over and that they would have a better life in the "free" west. He talked about going to America but they didn't have money for enough fuel for such a journey. So he got in touch with a man who was an official in the Liverpool dockers union who he'd been friendly with before the war and he asked for his help in getting permission to allow them to stay. He did and to cut a long story short it was through him that my mother met his son – my father, Robbie.'

She stopped and dabbed her eyes.

'My dad said that first time he met her that he thought she was the most beautiful girl he had ever seen, with flowing, dark silky hair and eyes which he said reflected the strength of her soul. He said that it was her, not the ship, that was the angel sent to him.'

She smiled at me, happy to have found someone to share the past with.

'Well, things sort of developed and my father and mother started courting, and dad joined the county police force and became a constable. Then they married and the result was my brother and me. We had a lovely council house and a garden where he grew lilies for her. She loved lilies. My father was a passionate man, even to the end, and he just adored her, always. As he used to say to me, he just wanted to spend the rest of his life with her. And he did until she died.'

She paused and I had a vision of Twentyman looking down on us and saying, 'Bloody Nora! Listen, lass, don't tell him me whole bloody life history. It's nowt to do with the lad and you're just embarrassing him.' Lia, oblivious, wiped away a tear and went on.

'It was because you can see the ships from here that they came to live in New Brighton. After he'd retired from the force that was. I suppose it was a reminder to them of how they had first met and they were both happy here, really happy. Then when mum died, what other way is there of putting it? He just went to pieces. He didn't know how he could go on without her and if it wasn't for Jed, and the grandchildren...'

I stayed and talked with her for a while but it was a rather one-sided conversation. Her curiosity about me had already been sated and she asked no further questions for the rest of my visit, giving me no polite opportunities to punctuate her family history with any comments of my own aside from occasional mumbles of agreement. She spoke as if her father and I had been the greatest of pals and I saw no need to tell her otherwise. I listened to her story but there was little that I could contribute and I found myself glancing at her father's watch and trying to work out the least impolite way to extricate myself from her company. My mind returned to the present to hear her say, 'Dad said that my name means "the bringer of good news" and I was – the daughter he had always dreamed of!'

She offered me another cup of tea and was just about to pour it when I seized the moment to make a departure on the pretence of an important business matter. I got up, thanked her for the tea and said that I would have to be going now.

'You will come to the funeral, won't you? It'll be sometime next week. I'm sure my brother Brian would want to meet you too, what with you being a friend of Dad's and everything. Please come, please.'

I assured her that I would be happy to do so and gave her the phone number for the flat in London, telling her to leave a message with the details. I felt that I owed it to her and to Twentyman's memory to attend. I asked where the mischievous Jed was and was told that he was fine, and was being taken out for a walk by one of the neighbours. He would be going home to live in Hoylake with Lia and her husband and another Jack Russell called Bingo. As I left, I gave her a kiss on the cheek and told her that I had respected her father and, subconsciously echoing his view of my uncle, said that he was one of the old sort, a true gentleman. I didn't know what any of that actually meant but it seemed to be the right thing to say in the circumstances.

As I walked away from Aidensbook Road I felt thoroughly demoralised and without consciously directing myself, ventured towards the sea and found myself sitting down on a low wall overlooking the flat sands. I breathed in the ozone and watched the wheeling seagulls and thought about the Aggelos and its epic journey through the shadows of a Europe spoiling for war. I wondered how Lia would get through the next few days. Then, as I looked out towards the mouth of the river, past the Perch Rock Battery and lighthouse, my thoughts returned to her father.

I turned over in my mind all the questions that I had wanted to ask him, all the loose ends that I wanted to tie up before I had Toby Ainsdale well and truly snared in a web of lies of his own making. His protestations of innocence were clearly untrue. He had been both April's lover and her killer. That, at least, was certain. There was no other explanation that fitted and nothing else that I wanted to hear. Nothing could let him off the hook now. I was determined that he was going to pay the price for what he did to her.

I looked up and saw a man and woman whom I imagined to be Twentyman's neighbours, pass by with Jed, who seemed rather dejected and careworn as he trotted along on the end of his bright red lead. I felt a great sympathy for the little creature for he and I were both missing his master and uncertain about facing the future without him.

I began to list in my mind all of the lies that Toby had told, and all the involuntary truths that he had come out with. Neither list was long and I was still not sure if I had enough to nail him yet. He had the motive – he'd as much as confessed that to me himself. The green-eyed god of jealousy had devoured him. He had been denied his first love Maura when he lost her to Gerald, and had then seduced and fallen for her daughter April, who looked just like Maura had when they'd first met. Then, when it seemed as if he was about to lose April to Barry, he flew into a jealous rage. How he must have hated Barry when he had learnt that April was pregnant, and refused to share her with that no-good boy whom he despised so bitterly. Just as the birth of April had meant that Maura was lost to him forever, so the birth of April's child would have meant the same for April.

What were the dark thoughts that must have seeped through his brain to make him cross the barrier that few lovers would ever dream of crossing – to murder the one you loved. But what does it matter? I couldn't care less for him – I had no sympathy for him whatsoever, no desire to try to understand him. I hated him for what he had done to April, and what he had done to Gerald and Maura and Ben. Most of all, I hated him for what he had done to Ros and I, for making us the ones who had to suffer by finding April's body.

And then I began to think more practically. I could ensure that justice would be done by breaking his alibi and, with some help, I would break it. He had never been to any filling station that afternoon, I was sure of that for, having checked with Ben, the receipt could not have been his. What was it that Twentyman had said? Eight gallons of four star as I recall. The car that the Ainsdales had driven back then was one of those big diesel Peugeots, not unusual for the time but since when did diesels run on four star? Not then, not now. He must have picked up someone else's carelessly discarded receipt and passed it off as his own. And the strange thing was, he had got away with it. Why had the police been so lackadaisical in checking the receipt out or had Toby got Laing to put a spanner in the works just as he had done a hundred times before in his business affairs?

I visualised Toby at home, listening to the Faery Queen when he had seen April enter the house next door. He must have gone after her to see what she was up to. Then she had told him that it was all over, that she was going to have Barry's child and that she had no further use for his money. So he picked up the poker and killed her to silence all the voices in his mind, all the envy, all the hatred. No wonder he couldn't bear looking into her open eyes.

What then? Barry's unexpected arrival must have caught him in the middle of wiping the fingerprints away. I could picture Toby hiding somewhere in the house, desperate for Barry to leave and all the time in a panic that he would be discovered. And yet why hadn't he killed Barry for he was the one who had put April beyond his reach? Maybe he didn't have the opportunity to smash him over the head with that mundane little poker. Perhaps his blood lust had been satisfied when he realised that he had already killed the only person that he had really cared about.

Then when Barry had left the house, I supposed that Toby, fearful that he would alert the police, must have got into his own car and driven somewhere to seek out an acquaintance so that he could cobble together an alibi and land the blame on Barry in a final act of revenge. God knows where he had found the receipt but luck was surely with him that day. And yet if he'd only thought about it he could have just sat tight at home, watched the television on a Sunday like millions of others, and he could have told the police that he had fallen asleep and had seen and heard nothing that whole afternoon. Who, after all, would have suspected him of being April's lover, the one who had been paying her money regularly and the one who had killed her?

A man like that deserved to be caught and to die. But I never have had the stomach for capital punishment. A banal wish, maybe, but why not lock him up for life and throw away the key. Who would care? Perhaps I would for I felt so angry that I wanted to kill him myself. "An eye for an eye" and my thoughts were running wild.

Another thought came into my mind – the emergency call. I may not have given the operator the details of where the Police could find the body but Ainsdale had. He knew where April had been killed because he was the one who had killed her. But how had Twentyman even remembered that? Surely he couldn't have recalled that small detail from all those years ago? He must have seen a transcript of the call! But it wasn't amongst the papers he'd given me – maybe Laing had already shredded it. If by some miracle it has survived then it could be the crucial piece of evidence I need to nail that bastard.

I was trying to work it all out when I became aware of the time. I had to get moving for I had an appointment to keep and I did not want to keep Ros waiting.

22

I arrived early, a state of affairs that was rare for me considering that my idea of perfect timing was, as I used to explain to my pupils at the bar, that there was a great deal of difference between arriving at court five minutes before the court was due rather than five minutes after. Today, however, was different and I felt that I would have the advantage that I needed, or at least the courage to stay, if I could familiarise myself again with the surroundings and try to look not quite so anxious.

What would I now say to Ros and how would she react? I remembered what Gavin had said about neither of us being eighteen again. I wondered how I had even been brave enough to turn up to meet her again after all this time. Perhaps I was not quite such an emotional coward as my wife had always claimed. Oh, Christ Almighty? Bloody Francesca was the last person in the world that I wanted to think about right now.

I sat down on a green painted bench and read the carved 'WB LVS KG 4VR'. Probably the same message on the same bench had been here the last time I was in this park. When had that been? Not since those days when after school I had sat and waited for Ros to appear with a satchel of books carelessly slung over her shoulder and her long hair blowing in the wind. Was she the same Ros that I was now waiting for? What if she had changed and we didn't recognise each other?

I looked at my watch. It was just after the allotted time of quarter past four so she was already late. Was she going to come at all or was she, too, afraid of this unscheduled reunion? Perhaps, like me, she had mixed feelings. And yet how easy it had been to find her. The phone book had revealed that her (by now I imagined quite elderly) parents were living in the same house that they had been in when I had been going out with her and after I had tapped in the number, and was waiting for the phone to connect, I wondered what I would say. I spoke to her mother who seemed neither particularly surprised nor particularly pleased to be hearing from me again, so long after Ros and I had finally parted. She sounded frail but promised to let her daughter know on her mobile as soon as possible.

After I had been waiting for what seemed like eternity but what was in reality less than twenty minutes, my phone rang. It was Ros and I instantly recognised her, a voice that had been once so familiar to me and had not changed in my memory. Hearing her disembodied voice was almost too surreal to register. I could form no clear picture of her to displace the snapshot image that I had in my mind of the girl in the malachite beads and the white rugby shirt standing against the backdrop of Pendle Hill in the hazy heat of a long vanished August afternoon.

'Chris, is that really you? It's strange and, well, so bizarre and unexpected to be hearing from you again after such a long time? How are you anyway?'

I thought the same as her but I pulled myself together and explained that I had to discuss something important with her about a family matter, my family and not hers. She sounded rather surprised and somewhat apprehensive and asked me why now after so many years. So I told her that it was something that had just come up and assured her that the matter was too important to discuss on the phone and that it would be preferable if we could meet. She seemed to accept this so we arranged to meet in a local park rather than in a café – or at her house – the same park, and at almost the exact same time of day as we used to regularly meet after school but I can't remember whose idea it been to choose that place or time.

The day and time had arrived and so I had prepared myself for the event. I had kept repeating that it would be just like seeing any old friend again, but I knew that it would not for Ros was not just any old friend whom I had temporarily lost touch with. She was, after all, the Ros Allbright that had once meant so much to me.

I took a deep breath to calm myself down and studied the Great Boulder Stone of Crosby.

This impressive reminder of the last great ice age of antiquity, is a massive erratic transported from the wilds of Cumbria and deposited in the locality by the slowly creeping glacial sheet that once covered the Lancashire Plain. Composed mainly of hydrated sulphate of lime, mostly in the semi-crystalline form of alabaster, the boulder stone weighs close on 25 tons and was formerly displayed in a railed enclosure in the village close to the junction of Liverpool Road and Islington before its recent removal to a new home in the flower-decked oasis of the Coronation Park.

Now that I had been told that there had been a rather different side of my grandfather from that which I had known, I started to wonder if Sep had ever met a woman in this flower-decked park and, if so, what his purpose had been. His Short History does not relate whether any surreptitious encounters by municipal bandstands or in shady dells adorned with great boulder stones had ever taken place. My grandfather was the sort of man whom women always recognised as having a gleam in his eye, and he had enjoyed female company – almost as much as he had enjoyed spending time on his own, engrossed in solitary literary pursuits. I respected him for both of these and was sorry that I had never had the chance to read the manuscript of his novel.

'Hello, Christopher.'

Standing before me was a woman of about my own age, five foot eight, slim and with a strained smile on her face. She was not now wearing the green necklace and shirt that she had once been so fond of and her hair seemed to be shorter, tamer than I had remembered it and in a more subdued shade of that reddish brown colour that imprinted itself in my mind. She must have noticed me looking at her hair.

'I use henna now you see.'

I must have looked puzzled.

'You probably think that I've changed a lot since you last saw me. I'm just trying to try to hide the grey in it now. Don't look at me like that!'

And this time the background was not the sun on Pendle Hill but the homely suburban terraces of Crosby on a dull day.

'You've not changed a bit', I mumbled.

'I very much doubt it. But I would have recognised you anywhere – a bit older and greyer but still the same Chris even though it's been, what, how many years...?'

I could have told her exactly how long for I had already worked it out to the half day. I remained silent. There were so many things that I wanted to say to her and yet, barrister or not, I was at a complete loss for words. She seemed to be cool towards me but then what did I expect, in the circumstances – some flicker of the feelings which we had once had for each other?

She sat down next to me and I noticed her long legs. I remembered that I had always liked those long legs.

'You said on the phone yesterday that you had to see me again, to speak to me and something personal and that it was very urgent.'

I nodded and she added rather waspishly, 'I hope that you're not going to tell me that you want to go out with me again or anything like that, are you, Chris?'

This seemed so cruel, so unlike the Ros of old, that I flinched. She seemed to be so aggressive and negative towards me that I thought she must surely dislike me. Perhaps she did. After all, as I had had to admit to Gavin, the way I had seen it was that she was the one who had dumped me and not the other way round. Gavin had replied that in that case I was the one with the unfinished business, not her. But was there any unfinished business between us? What did I expect now – for her to hug me and give me a kiss like she did when we were teenage lovers? I tried to explain.

'No, it's not that, although I might once have asked you that.' I didn't add that part of me wished that that was exactly what I was going to ask her.

I trailed off into an embarrassed silence. I could feel her gaze taking everything in and assessing how I had weathered since those far off days when I had been her boyfriend. I studied her face in return, taking in the fine lines that spoke of half a lifetime's experiences in which I had played no part. Then, all of a sudden, she seemed to relent and smiled, allowing me to see something of the girl that I had once known. I remembered that smile, but how could I have forgotten it?

'Sorry, Chris. I didn't mean it like that but it's been a very long time since we teenagers and went our separate ways. I suppose you could say we weren't really that grown up at the time and were forced to grow up after that, only separately.'

'Ros...'

It seemed so strange to be saying her name again, to hear myself saying it. A name which once I used as a mantra and doodled in the margins of my school books. Possibly, even carved it with the point of my penknife on a seat like this. She gave me that same quizzical look that I had once found so attractive.

'I want to talk to you about something important but it's nothing to do with us going out with each other.'

Did she look slightly disappointed or was that only my racing imagination? It was now or never I had to broach the subject.

'It's something about my cousin April.'

'I thought it might be. Finding her like that was definitely the end of us, wasn't it?'

I thought I saw a tear forming in her eye. As I agreed with her I too felt overwhelmed and had to remind myself of the many decades that separated our current and former selves.

And so I began to tell her everything – about Gerald, the Liverpool packet and all the reasons why I was revisiting the past and all that had happened. I could tell by her expression that she was both appalled and yet fascinated by what I had to say. As the tale progressed and I mentioned my visits to Twentyman and Ben, I watched her reaction. As the darkness of the past opened itself up before us, I felt this familiar bond as if a part of us was still shackled together as those two young people who long ago had been in love and had played a part in a drama that was all but forgotten. And I knew, as I had always known, that it was that bond of common experience and grief that had driven us apart for good. When I had almost finished I told her about my meeting with Gill and what we had discussed.

She smiled in the way that I had always found hard to resist.

'I know all about your meeting with Gill.'

She grinned and although I tried to cover up my embarrassment, it was plain that she was already aware of what manner of a meeting it had been.

'She spoke to me about it yesterday.'

I reddened and wondered if my careless fling had already made the headlines in the Crosby Herald as it seemed now to be virtually public knowledge. I said nothing while she continued to display the same Gioconda smile. All I could think of saying was, 'I didn't know that you and Gill were still in touch with each other.'

'She was never really what you might call a close friend of mine but we did keep in contact after April's death. So you see, Chris, it wasn't actually so amazing – your getting in touch with me. Gill told me that you were in town and asking questions about April, and she had her suspicions that you might try to contact me again.'

She grinned again and then added unnecessarily, 'She thought that you might have been going through some sort of mid-life crisis or something.'

Undoubtedly I was in the middle years of life but was I having a crisis? Not that I would admit to anyway.

'Ros, forgive me but...'

'Is there ever anything that I had to forgive you for, Chris?'

'Only you can answer that, Ros.'

It was her turn to blush.

'There is something that I have to ask you about and it involves April and the past...'

'I still have nightmares about her death and about us finding her, Chris.'

'If I could have just stopped you coming into the house and seeing her. I truly regret that I didn't have the sense to stop you. But I can't turn the clock back, however much I want to.'

Ros produced a handkerchief and began to ineffectually mop her eyes.

'It's OK, Chris. It wasn't your fault – you didn't know what either of would see but why stir up the half-forgotten rags of time now? What good will it do anyone?'

'I don't know but I did promise Uncle Gerald...'

Was that really my motivation for continuing with all this?

'Ros, if only I'd had the chance to speak to you in the police station or later at April's funeral. You must have been...'

She wasn't going to fill any of the gaps in.

'Twentyman, you remember the older one, the inspector. He told me that he realised that you were suffering from obvious grief. The anger and all that, well, that wasn't really you, I knew that myself.'

'Was he the fat one? I told the other one, the skinny one with the mean mouth, where he could go. I swore at him in the most filthy language I knew. He bloody well deserved it.'

She laughed and I saw the old Ros, my Ros, breaking through the barrier. Except, of course, that she wasn't my Ros any more. Maybe she never had been. We started to talk about the day on which April had died, the trip to the witch country and how neither of us had ever been back there since. She asked me the fate of The Beast and was sorry to hear of its demise not long afterwards in a scrap yard in St Helens and I couldn't help asking her if she still liked Nick Drake's songs.

'Nick who?'

Then she giggled. 'Some things will never change.' I wanted the conversation to continue like this but I could feel that time was running out.

'Why did you never tell me that you had spoken to Barry Leemings after April's death?'

'Well, I never told you afterwards because when you didn't come round to see me again after April's funeral, I thought that you were distancing yourself from me. We were about to be going our different ways – me to Edinburgh and you to Cambridge. We'd be meeting new friends and yours would be sophisticated people, out of my league. So that's why I didn't chase it and we lost contact and I said to myself that I didn't want to see you ever again.'

'But that's nonsense! Did you really think I had outgrown you? If you'd only known what I...'

She broke in and I could see the tears forming again.

'But you were sort of different after that, Chris, pre-occupied at the funeral and then, well, you didn't seem to care about me any more.'

She stopped speaking and I was lost for words.

'I'm sorry. I don't suppose that you meant it that way, Chris, and you must have been shocked and grieving for April as I was. I guess neither of us ever faced up to the reality of what had happened. I liked April and I liked Barry, too. He wasn't the person that you had always judged him to be.'

She was right, I had written him off as a ne'er-do-well who hadn't been good enough for April. Jesus, I must have sounded just like Gerald or worse, just like Maura in one of her less pleasant moods. It pained me to think that I had been like that when Ros had first known me.

'Barry was interested in lots of things and he was quite a nice guy beneath it all even though I remember that time when he tried to beat you up at the party. I can't really explain it but I felt sorry for him after April's death, even though, rationally, there was a chance that he might have killed her. But I'm pretty sure he didn't.'

'How can you possibly know that?!'

'Because he told me so, that's how.'

'Of course he would say that.'

'I know but it's how he came across. He phoned me on the Monday morning and told me that he had to get away from everything until the hue and cry died down. He said that he just had to get his head together and think things out.'

'It was you that gave him the money to do that, wasn't it?'

'And was that such a bad thing in the circumstances? He needed cash for food and a tent and fuel tor his bike. He said that he was going to get everything together in his head and that once he had, he'd go to the police and tell them everything and even his suspicions as to who killed April. So yes, I did gave it to him. No one else would have and he did promise to pay me back.'

'Where did you get it from?'

343

'I'd already taken all the money that I'd had in the Post Office Savings Bank out, just over £98 or so which I'd been saving up for ages from my Saturday job in Boots. I had something that the money was earmarked for. Don't laugh, Chris, but I had been going to give it to you, as a present.'

'A present? Whatever for?'

'I wanted you to have a new car, one that didn't keep threatening to break down all the time like The Beast. Oh, don't look at me like that! It would have been overgenerous but it didn't seem so at the time because of the way I felt about you. Anyway a hundred quid wouldn't have bought that good a second-hand car even then. I couldn't turn Barry away when he needed my help so I went to meet him at the place we'd agreed, just beside the barrier at Exchange station – you remember the place the trains to Crosby used to go from?'

I nodded and said that had she asked me to be there too I would have come with her. I added unnecessarily that she had taken a great risk, carrying all that money to someone whom the police were looking for. She ignored my strictures and went on with the story.

'He told me that when he got to the house he found April lying there, her body still warm. Then he started going on about how she'd brought it on herself – no, I don't follow that either, Chris, but his words just stuck in my mind. He started to cry and said that he was sorry for all that he had ever done to her and that he loved her.'

'You went to see his brother, Guy later on, after Barry had been killed.'

'Yes I did and I gave him some money as well – not much because I'd given most of it to Barry. He was down on his luck and missing Barry terribly.'

She paused while I wondered about what she had said but I did not doubt her conviction about Barry's innocence. Then she added softly, 'Chris – how did you know about Guy?'

'He told me a couple of days ago. He didn't name you but I guessed from his description of you.'

She smiled. 'Chris – did you ever try to find me again, after the funeral?'

This threw me. All I could say was, 'I did go up to Edinburgh once but you weren't there at the place where you were living. And again, when I heard that Nick Drake had died, I...'

A tall man with a little girl in a red dress and carrying a large yellow ball walked past us and the child gave us a wave, which Ros returned.

'I didn't ever intend to lose contact with you for ever – I really didn't.'

She said nothing and I changed the subject to avoid recriminations.

'You know all about what Toby did, don't you?'

She looked puzzled and I went on.

'I mean about him being her lover, the one who was paying her the money and...'

I paused before going on. 'He was the one who killed her because he was jealous of her and Barry and her pregnancy and all that?'

'Don't be so completely bloody daft, Chris, you haven't thought it all through, have you? You jumped to the wrong conclusion, just as you often used to do. Yes, Toby was paying her money all right, but that was nothing to do with him being her lover. He wasn't anything of the sort. I don't know how you worked that one out but you are totally wrong.'

I was dumbfounded and Ros, seeing the expression on my face, put her hand gently on mine.

'He was giving her cash because he was her father – her biological father. You've worked that one out, surely? It wasn't really that much of a secret. April told me before I even met you and thought it was a bit of a laugh. She didn't tell Gill because she might have been rather upset to discover that her best friend was also her half-sister and that they shared a dad.'

The final redactio ad absurdum came into my mind.

'But if that's true it means that April wasn't even my cousin, in the true sense of it although I suppose she was by marriage or lack of it...'

'Stop talking nonsense, Chris. She was, and always will be your cousin and Gerald will always be her father – the one who brought her up and loved her as his daughter. But that's not the point. Whatever gave you the idea that Toby and April had ever jumped into bed together? Had a sexual relationship? That's just a ghastly thing to say let alone think.'

'But he told me that he was in love with her.'

The thought was dawning on me that perhaps that was not quite what he had said and it was just possible that I had wildly jumped to the wrong conclusion.

'Wasn't it April who told Gill that there was an older man, her lover, who was paying her money?'

'If she did say that, then it was probably just to put Gill off the scent. I don't suppose she or Toby wanted to complicate matters any further. As for the money, well I suppose he felt guilty that he couldn't openly acknowledge her as his daughter or even provide support for her. I expect that he thought that his wife would have divorced him and taken half his dough if she'd known about it. April, being April, was just happy to take the money. She always was happy to take anyone's money.'

'But the baby she was expecting, wasn't she, only...'

'Oh, that! That was pure invention on her part. April wasn't really pregnant at all. She told everyone that as a wind-up just to see what the result would be. She loved stirring up trouble. When I challenged her about it she admitted that it was a lie, and made me swear that I'd never tell anyone, not even you. She told me that it was mostly to get Barry to stay with her. She was convinced that he was going to go off with another woman. She was wrong about that. Barry was and always would have been faithful to her – it was only her own insecurity that made her think otherwise. She never told you her baby story because she thought you were a sort of puritan who would have disapproved since you had such a high opinion of her. She liked that, by the way, you having a high opinion of her.'

'So all that about having to burgle the house because her parents would cut her off when they knew she was pregnant was a lot of nonsense?'

'Yes but Barry didn't know that, of course. He'd have been worried sick and thought that once the baby came then they'd get no money from Gerald or Maura. She'd probably lose the postgraduate grant that she'd been promised and he could hardly have supported the three of them. He couldn't even support himself, come to think of it. He was hopeless with money.'

'But Uncle Gerald and Maura were Catholics and they'd wouldn't have allowed her to get rid of the baby. They'd have supported April and her child, surely?'

'You're forgetting the human angle. They both hated Barry and one of the only things they could ever agree about was that he was an insignificant member of the lower orders. They would never have given him the chance to marry their daughter, let alone allow him to be acknowledged as the lawful father of her child. Snobbery was almost like a second religion to them although God knows they had enough of the first. Anyway, April was determined to marry Barry and live with him but she wanted enough cash to be able to do. That was probably why she ransacked her own house, pretending it was burglars. Barry would have sold the valuables to dealers. Once married she'd have told Barry that she'd had a miscarriage or something. They would have to try again for a baby and no harm would have been done. They'd have held on to the money and Gerald and Maura would have claimed off their insurers for the things that the unknown burglar or burglars would have taken and no one would have known because they weren't even there that day!'

'You make it sound so easy – but she wasn't the only burglar in the house that day which accounts for us finding April dead.'

'It was easy– so far as April and Barry were concerned.'

'But who killed her then? And what about Toby? How does he fit into the picture?'

'I don't know but April told me he was really looking forward to being a grandfather, even if he was going to have to be one on the quiet. I think that he was upset that he couldn't be a proper father to April and an acknowledged grandparent of her child. He was frustrated and terribly jealous of Gerald. Come to think of it, Gerald would have been just as jealous, if not more so, of Toby. Chris, can you even begin to imagine what kind of hornet's nest April was stirring up when she told everyone that she thought she was pregnant?'

'But I still don't get it – why then did he kill her?'

'Why makes you think that Toby did kill her? Surely it was the real burglar who did. Chris, being jealous because she was expecting his grandchild doesn't seem much of a motive for a father killing his own daughter, does it?'

And why, I wondered, was I so sure that Toby had been the killer? And why was I now so intent on stirring up another hornet's nest now? What if it was the wrong hornet's nest?

'What were Barry and April arguing about that time at the party when he hit me?'

'I've no idea – drugs maybe. That's what they usually argued about. April told me that Barry wanted her to cut them all out when she was pregnant but she just told him to mind his own business. She told me that she had already decided to give the drugs up but I suppose that she didn't like him telling her what to do. She could be very strong-willed at times. I think that she wanted herself and Barry to face up to things now that they were going to become parents.'

'But she wasn't strong-willed enough to stop him hitting her, though.'

Her eyes opened wide. 'You know Chris, I was quite proud of you that time when you stood up to him.'

I blushed and rapidly moved matters on.

'Did Barry say anything else to you about the day that April died – about seeing anyone in the house for instance?'

'No, he said that he was too busy hiding away in a phone box, terrified that he'd be recognised by someone.'

She paused and gave me a direct look which made any possibility of my blush fading most unlikely.

'Look, Chris, are you sure this is doing any good? Why bother with the past when it's over now? Barry's not around to clear his name and it probably was a tramp or burglar or someone like that who killed her.'

She saw that I didn't agree so she added, 'Or maybe it was Toby or Gerald or Ben or even Barry, But why didn't the police find the burglar? What makes you think the truth will come out after so long, and why the hell does any of it matter now? I mean does anyone care now that Barry and April have been dead for so long and probably the burglar is too? He probably stole to buy drugs. April was just in the wrong place at the wrong time, and as it turned out, you and I were too. But I never forgot you, Chris. You were, after all, my first real boyfriend.'

'I know it's pointless to say it now but I always regret that we lost touch though perhaps that where all such relationships like ours finish – first love, I mean.'

'I kept everything you ever gave me, you know.'

'What did I ever give you?' I asked, hoping that she would sentimentally have cherished all of my gifts.

'Oh, the book, Mist over Pendle, the birthday presents and the card that you drew yourself. But listen, Chris, the one thing that I still cherish and keep most of all is the memory of is our trip to Pendle Hill on that day. It was really great, even if it did end up as it did.'

I, not too obviously, wiped a tear from my eye. Then we talked a little more about that day but I could see that she seemed to have both tired of the subject and the past. Perhaps I was beginning to bore her. Perhaps I always had done. She looked at her watch pointedly.

'Nearly five thirty, I think that I'd better be off.'

'At least you didn't say "is that the time?" before leaving.'

This had been one of our favourite catch-phrases and one which had always reduced us to a helpless state of laughter for no apparent reason, especially when said in Scouse. She smiled and I hoped that she was remembering this too.

'Ros, I'll be in town for a couple of days more and I don't suppose that you'd like to meet up again for, a drink or something.'

The thought suddenly occurred to me that we hadn't discussed the progress of our own separate lives since that late summer day on which we had last been together. I didn't know anything about what she was doing now, whether she was married, living with anyone or divorced, had children or indeed anything else and she had never asked me anything of a personal nature either other than to enquire as to how my father was keeping. In answer to my invitation she just sadly shook her head.

'No Chris, thank you but it wouldn't work, would it? You and I well, we belong to the past, not to the present and let's just say that it's a bit late to be just friends again. Let's just leave it as it now.'

My polite smile betrayed what was going on inside my head. I just wanted to shake her and say 'Ros, you can't just leave things unsaid and undone!' But she did.

'So goodbye now, Chris. Take care of yourself.'

As she put on her scarf she added, 'It was lovely to see you again and, well, to see you are well and everything and...'

Then she seemed to check her thoughts and merely finished with, 'Look after yourself Chris. Goodbye.'

She bent over and kissed me and then she was gone. I wished momentarily that I was still eighteen, at school, and in love with this woman who had once been the girl who had fascinated me so, the one whom I had dreamed about a future which we were going to have together.

Then, being a lot older yet not much wiser, and feeling my mood lower in the cold dampness of the chilly spring evening air, I shivered. The sun had gone in and the afternoon was wearing on and the sight of the damp leaves left on the wet grass in the empty park was beginning to depress me more than I cared to admit.

23

It was just after eleven, on the morning of Good Friday, and I was on an almost empty train rattling its way across a half-deserted Wirral towards the lovely city of Chester. As I saw Rock Ferry, Port Sunlight, Bromborough Rake and the homely sounding Hooton pass by, I thought that I had spent an awful lot of the last week travelling on trains to places that I didn't really want to go to. It was some sort of allegorical reference to my life that I was wasting my time by going nowhere, moderately fast. But as the spring-struck fields slipped by and the hedgerows seemed to be ready to burst with new colour, a tune by Art Blakely ran through my head and although I tried hard to forget it, I was still humming the number when we unceremoniously arrived at the gloomy terminus four and a half minutes late.

Both the sun and the visitors were conspicuously absent and the tourist-board image of the place was rather lost under the grey clouds that were threatening to liberate themselves of vast reserves of water upon my head at any minute and wash away the last vestiges of my good mood. As I walked out towards the suburban fringes of the city past banks of jasmine and witch hazel I noticed that daffodils were growing in swathes on the verges and I thought of Gerald. Daffodils had been his favourite flowers and April's too. He had once told me that their name came from old Dutch and meant something like "that which comes early". The "Easter Lily" was certainly out in force now. If my uncle had been passing he would have stooped to gather up a large bunch of them up to lay upon April's grave.

Far away in Crosby, but not on a green hill, April lay beside a stone which bore the legend 'But where shall wisdom be found? Where is the place of understanding?' and, below in smaller lettering, 'Until the shadows flee, R.I.P.' Now Gerald too had exchanged time for eternity and was lying alongside his much mourned April and I was on my own and looking neither for wisdom nor understanding. I was merely trying to ensure that April's killer, whoever he might be, would be brought to justice, at least the only kind of flawed justice that our legal system could deliver.

I stopped at a Shell garage and considered buying a bouquet of those peculiarly anaemic Dutch flowers done up in coloured cellophane. Only garages are crass enough to sell them and only married men with guilty secrets are crass enough to buy them before thinking better of it. Beware of Greeks bearing gifts and beware of lawyers bearing no gifts at all. No flowers, no chocolates, nothing, for I was not in a particularly generous frame of mind.

In time I reached the widely spaced line of bungalows, each set back far from the road in trees and grass, unkempt grass in the case of my aunt's. I opened the gate, listening as my feet scrunched on the deep gravelled path leading up to the sunrise-pattern front door. I knocked loudly and wondered why I was visiting my aunt on this of all days, Good Friday.

A large and red-faced young man came to the door and I was surprised to see that he was dressed as a priest, albeit a priest who seemed to be literally bursting out of his clerical suit. I told him I was there to see Maura Kingston and he pushed me out a little distance from the still open door before adopting a confidential pose and whispering into my ear so that the inhabitant of the house would not overhear.

'And you are?'

I told him and he replied, 'I'm afraid your aunt is a little, how shall I put it, under the weather and not quite compos mentis today. In fact I would have to say that she is not really in a state to receive visitors. Or to go to Mass either, for that matter.'

He grinned conspiratorially and made a tipping gesture with his hand to signify that Maura had been imbibing. Unfortunately the news did not shock me for from what I had heard Maura and her beloved sherry were becoming better and better acquainted these days. He told me that he was Father O'Connor from St. Something-or-others and that he visited my aunt regularly. He sighed and his already not insubstantial girth seemed to increase.

'I regret to say that your aunt is, how to put it, not the most popular of our parishioners when it comes to pastoral visits. I have no issue with her myself but for some of my fellow priests they are, in short, a duty rather than a pleasure.'

'Is that because of her drinking?' I asked.

'Good Lord, no! That's but a minor transgression that's not exactly unknown amongst us clergy.' Judging by his complexion, I guessed that he might have had some empathy with Maura over that one.

'Then what is the problem? Perhaps I could have a word with her son Ben about it?'

'I doubt it I'm afraid. To be candid, it's all rather delicate you see, but your aunt has, for a number of years I am sorry to say, been a thorn in the side of our parish.

To put it bluntly she has been in the habit of developing what you might call crushes on our young priests and has been known to make, er, advances towards them. She has sent them letters, harangued them at church and, well, made certain comments which are, for want of a better turn of phrase, rather intimate and, I'm afraid, explicit in their nature.'

This did not seem at all to be like the Maura that I had known. I had always regarded her as being something of a prude, particularly where anything even vaguely touching on procreation was concerned. Perhaps she had been rather wild in her past. But before I could comment the priest now seemed, by his embarrassed expression, to regret having been quite so frank with me and I let it pass.

'I'm glad that you do visit her though, Father. She must be rather lonely now that my uncle has passed away so I do thank you for doing your Christian duty and I will speak to her son, Ben.' I knew, however, that I would not.

He did not pick up my sarcastic tone but beamed at the compliment then told me that he must be off on his way before wishing me a 'Happy Easter when it comes and God Bless' and waddling away down the path like an over-fed duckling.

There was something about Father O'Conner that made me think back to a time when I had been a child of seven and an elderly priest, a Monsignor, I think, had walked past our primary school. A boy called Billy Evans had shouted through the railings to the black cassocked cleric, 'Farder Bunloaf, Farder Bunloaf, gi' us a tenner'. We had all thought that so hilarious that we had repeated it even more loudly. I laughed so much that I fell backwards into one of the scrappy flowerbeds in which our normally placid teacher Miss Griffiths had been growing nasturtiums and ended up in a heap of crushed flowers. As a result she had rapped my knuckles sharply with a wooden ruler and told me to remember that I was a young gentleman from Crosby and that I was not to behave myself like some disrespectful little ruffian boy who knew no better.

I pushed the front door of the bungalow open and walked in, halting by an antique vase of wilting freesias. I looked up and read the barometer which, prophetically, was hovering towards "Stormy".

'Come in then, if you are coming in that is.'

I went straight through to the sitting room. There was an untidy array of cups, glasses and magazines on the floor. Yesterday's Daily Mail had been deconstructed and strewn carelessly across the sofa. I pushed the smudged sheets aside and sat down.

'And how are you Aunt Maura?'

She blinked in surprise and, turning towards me, smiled vacantly.

'Topher, how nice! I haven't seen you in a long time. Ages, in fact. Sit down and have a drink, perhaps a little sherry before lunch?'

The sun was barely over the yardarm but this was clearly not the first of the day for her. I thought that it was rather sad that both she and Toby had ended up in such a similar and, to be honest, rather pathetic state.

'The cleaning lady, Cindy, my little treasure I call her, has not been in today so I'm sorry but everything is just a bit disorganised and...'

Through the open kitchen door I could see the overflowing dustbin and the several-day old pile of dirty dishes-in the sink and wondered how long it had been since Cindy had last paid a visit. Maybe she had given up altogether. Who could have blamed her?

'So what have you been up to lately then, Topher?'

I wondered if I should emulate Rajiv and tell her that I'd been, 'Here and there doing a little ducking and diving', but I decided to settle on a non-committal 'not much' instead. Correctly I had guessed that she wasn't really very interested in the answer and I was anxious to get to the heart of the matter as soon as possible. I was certainly not in the mood to indulge in any verbal fencing with her.

'Aunt Maura, I want to ask you about something. Something that happened a long time ago.'

She looked puzzled so I continued, 'I need to know the truth about what happened to April.'

She didn't seem to be concentrating on what I was saying and was vaguely absorbed in something on the television which involved two women in dungarees, a step-ladder and a room which they were repainting in a particularly hateful colour. I guessed that Father O'Connor had already turned the sound down before he left and had given up the battle of trying to focus her attention away from the crapulous home-improvement show.

I walked over and switched the box off. She looked disorientated as the picture disappeared and blinked sadly at me through her spectacles.

'I was enjoying that. You know, Topher, the telly's the only real friend I've got nowadays. You see apart from my dear Ben and that lodger of his, no one ever visits me now. Well no one unless you count Friar Tuck there. It should be a comfort to have a visit from the church, especially on a Holy Day like this. But I'm afraid that priest is a bit of a boor. No offence to the cloth but he's neither cultured nor, I fear, very intelligent.'

I laughed at this. At least Maura had still got some of her wits about her. She smiled at the thought of the man in black and his shortcomings...

'I hope that he doesn't start coming back more regularly. He's quite dreadful and I'm sure his motives are suspect. Why if I were any younger I certainly wouldn't trust him to be left alone with me. He looks like a philanderer and, to be quite frank, I think he drinks – the levels on some of my medicinal sherry bottles seem to be lower after he'd paid a visit. But don't get me wrong Topher, I am grateful that at least he makes the effort to come and see me. Sometimes I think all I ever do now is to sit here in this house and reminisce about the better times in my life. If I gaze at these walls I can see it all going by, everything passing like a constant stream of all the people I've known and...'

As she began drifting from the present into the past I seized the opportunity.

'Tell me about Toby Ainsdale and you, Aunt Maura. You two had a strong friendship didn't you.'

She looked coy at first then, realising the futility of keeping up a pretence, smiled knowingly and began telling me, with apparent relish, of how she had first met Toby.

'We were both students at the Art College here and Toby was so very talented, the most handsome and gifted boy that I had ever seen. He worshipped me, you know. He said I was like Leo the lioness, proud and beautiful with a defiant attitude and a mane of golden hair which made me stand out from all the other students there. Silly boy, but he made me feel invincible, proud and strong, as he put it, the queen of all I surveyed. He took me everywhere, showed me off, paraded me, wrote poetry for me and it was beautiful poetry – not the kind of slush you read on Valentine's cards. Above all else he loved me. He loved me like no other man ever has, before or since. Do you know that until I met him I didn't know the meaning of the word but he showed me what love was in a way that I will never forget.'

She took another sip of sherry and I could see that by now she was miles away.

'And then the inevitable happened. He put me in the family way. That's what we used to say then, Topher, we called it being in the family way rather than pregnant. It sounds tame now, but it was anything but tame.'

'So what did you do after that?'

'What could we do? We had nothing at that time. No job. No money. No place to live. Toby didn't want to ask his people. We couldn't, you see. I don't suppose you can really know what the shame of it would have been then. An unmarried mother was something reprehensible, an outcast, not like it is now what with every filthy little guttersnipe having a child here, there and everywhere on the social security with a free council house thrown into the bargain. Oh no, being a single parent back then wasn't something to be proud of. You were, what's the word for it? A pariah.' She paused to take a long drink.

'But I really wanted to have that baby, Topher don't get me wrong. I really wanted to have his baby and I'm quite sure Toby would have married me if he could. He wanted to, you understand, but he just couldn't marry me. His parents would have stopped his allowance and he'd have nothing to live on at all. He couldn't have gone on to complete his studies and become the great architect that he'd always dreamed of being ever since he was a boy. He had wanted to design fine buildings that everyone would admire – he called them public sculptures that would adorn the streets and represent the spirit of the age we then lived in.'

That sounded so undeniably grandiose from someone who had only got as far as third-rate concrete shopping centres and hideous bungalows that were an embarrassing blight upon any true artist's record of achievements. I could almost hear the words of Maura coming straight out of Toby's mouth and I was sure that they had. But I wanted to keep Maura on the subject of Toby himself and not his dreams that had turned to ashes when confronted by his lack of vision and his venial greed.

'Why would his parents have done that – surely they'd have still helped you when you were carrying their grandchild?'

She laughed hollowly.

'Oh, no, they would have helped him but not me. You see my folk were working class, poor Catholic folk from Manchester. Irish stock who didn't have two ha'pennies to rub together. We were looked down upon by snobs like the Ainsdales in their big house in Aigburth, their fancy car, private schooling for their son, all of that sort of thing. My mother always said that, 'people like us were nothings and that people like the Ainsdales thought that no one from our part of Manchester ever came to anything worthwhile'. But by getting into college and doing well there I had been determined to prove her wrong. But it didn't work out like that. Their superior son got me pregnant. They suggested that I got an abortion but I would not even think of so doing. I was a Catholic and that was not something that any true Catholic would even dream of.'

I thought that the way she described it all was rich coming from one who had aspired to the very same things for her own children that the Ainsdales had wanted for Toby, she who had looked down on a poor boy like Barry Leemings because he had come from the same underclass as she had. It was strange to envisage Maura as the poor pregnant waif, the potentially unacceptable poor daughter-in-law. She downed the remains in her glass and I discretely but firmly took the empty bottle out of her hand and placed it on top of a tea-stained copy of Vogue.

'Good old days? Do you know I read some nonsense about the 'forties and 'fifties being a golden era. Rubbish! My mother used to say that when she as a girl her mother talked about the good old days, too. She got a cuff off her for saying that if she wanted to return to the good old days she could always give up her pension and send her grandchildren down the mine instead. No-one wanted to return to poverty like it was in the time of the good old days of Queen Victoria.'

I tried to get her back on track her for I had no intention of spending a day on the outskirts of Chester discussing the good old days with an increasingly intoxicated wayward old aunt.

'The baby you were carrying – that was April, right?'

She nodded and became suddenly more animated as though mention of her daughter was stirring long pent-up currents in her life.

'I was determined to have her, but what could I do? His parents said that I should go to the Magdalene Sisters or some such godforsaken institution of our church and have the baby adopted. I knew that Toby wouldn't give up his dreams of going up in the world as a brilliant architect just to marry me, not then anyway. I wanted to keep her but I didn't want the child to be illegitimate. It was still a terrible stigma in having a bastard then even if the Yanks had left Britain full of them after the war. I was weak and you can think what you like but I did the only thing I could, I married your uncle Gerald, who asked me to marry him with no doubts and conditions of any sort.'

'How did you know Gerald?'

'He was a friend of Toby's who went sailing with him and I'd known him well for a couple of years by then. We used to go out as a foursome then, Toby and me and Gerald and his girlfriend, Elvira de Sausmaurez, the daughter of a refugee businessman of some sort. They came over in the Spanish Civil War. He was a nice man was Gerald, truly kind, right from the very start. He said that he'd help me and the child that I was expecting out and make an honest woman out of me and he would bring up the child as his own. He kept his side of the bargain and he was a good man, Topher, a really good man. Never think ill of him, whatever you might think of me. He loved April just as if she'd been his own flesh-and-blood, he really did. Sometimes, I couldn't help thinking that he loved her more than he loved our own son Ben!

'How did Toby react when he knew you were going to marry my uncle?'

'What could he say? He wouldn't have me himself so I had to do the best I could. Don't judge me wrongly, Topher. I didn't have any real choice at all. Your uncle, and indeed your whole family, treated me wonderfully. They welcomed me in to the fold. Your grandfather, old

Seb, he just said that I was the daughter he'd always wanted and never had. He was a grand old man, a bit of a flirt in his own time, but you couldn't have imagined a kinder grandfather to April. But everything didn't end happily ever after – it never does, I suppose. Gerald didn't really love me, not in the way that Toby had, but he tried to. But I don't think it was all his fault. I wasn't always all that easy to live with either. I know I have my faults, no one's perfect.'

This, coming from Maura, was a surprising admission, if somewhat of an understatement.

'Then things between us were fair to middling and I could put up with his approaches to me by turning myself off and thinking of other things. When I was carrying Ben, our marital relations ceased altogether. Gerald just drifted away from me after that and had a string of other women. He never made much of an effort to hide them from me, or from anyone else for that matter. You don't know how insulting that was – it really was. But none of them were ever of any consequence to him and he didn't even pretend to love them. It was just sex, that's all. He said that they were just barren bitches from the boring suburbs. God help me, but I'd gone beyond caring by that time, wouldn't anyone? Can you believe that he even had that stupid Elvira again, who by that time was Toby's wife, and I could hardly credit that he would sink so low as to have that Sausmaurez slut again.'

'What did Toby have to say about that?' I asked, while at the same time thinking of how Elvira, the unloved girlfriend and later wife who had died before her time, seemed to have drawn the short straw in life, whatever Maura's opinion of her was.

'He just said that it was fair enough, because by then he didn't really care either. He said that he'd always regretted marrying Elvira because she was rich but that I had been the true love of his life had he wished that he could have lived with April and I. I really thought that was a terrible thing to say of his wife but he explained that once he'd lost me and his daughter, nothing else in life really mattered. All other women were, well, just women to him, including Elvira whom he'd just taken off Gerald's hands so that Gerald would be free to marry me because I deserved to be a wife and April deserved a father.'

'If he felt like that about you then why didn't you leave Gerald and go back to Toby?'

She gave me a withering look and then leaned over and poured herself another drink.

'My religion for one thing – you know, the sanctity of marriage, all that sort of cant. And of course by then he had a daughter by Elvira – Gillian. She turned out to grow into as much as a bitch and money-grabber as her mother. Never liked her one bit. And besides I didn't trust Toby. I didn't really think he was the faithful sort, whatever promises he made to anyone. Oh, I wished I could have believed him when we made love. Topher, he was such a liar, such a flatterer. He could charm the birds off the trees, could that one. If he'd been with me I know that he would have cheated on me if we'd been married. He told me all sorts of little lies and half-truths. It was in his nature and he just couldn't help it. Anyway Toby's daughter Gillian was born just a few months after he and Elvira were married and there's no doubt that Toby is her father. I should know and just look at how alike they were, especially their bone structure and colouring and you can even see a bit of April in her as well. So I realised that he must have been carrying on with that Spanish bitch at the same time as he was making love to me and promising me the earth and the stars and that didn't exactly make me feel that I was the true love of his life, whatever he said.

'And then, of course, there was April. She thought that Gerald was her real father and that nice kind Uncle Toby, who had moved in to the house next door so that he could see her as she grew up, was just a family friend.'

'When did she find out that Toby was her father?'

'She was sixteen. Toby had just done some big property deal and he effectively bailed out Gerald's boatyard yet again. Gerald never had a head for figures, he was a hopeless business man, hopeless with money but very generous and kind to his clients and brilliant with all of the practical aspects of boatbuilding. Toby, of course, wanted something in return for the money, he always did. A quid quo pro was what he grandly called it. So Toby told April, just like he had promised to do when she was sixteen, that he was her biological father.'

'How did she take being told that her dad wasn't her real father?'

'Surpringly calmly. Said it made no real difference to her, that Gerald was still her real dad – he was the one who had always loved her and brought her up and that Toby was and always would be just Uncle Toby to her. I was really proud of her putting it the way she did. Anyway a few months later Toby started giving her money, not a lot, a few pounds a week or something like that. Just a bit of extra pocket money to tide her over and then when she got into the University and her needs were greater he gave her an allowance, a bit more than what you might call pocket money. He told April that it was because he was impressed by her academic efforts, which to be fair, so were we. But he went on giving her money and told her that it was important that she got a good education and that she was a very special person and that she should never forget that.'

'What did Gerald think of that?'

'He was absurdly jealous at first, which was hardly surprising in the circumstances. He tried to match Toby's money and it ended up with April getting two lots of cash. He felt it was undermining him in his role as her father. As usual, she got the best of both worlds. She was a very greedy person, you know, a very greedy person indeed.'

She slowly got up from the chair and drifted in to the kitchen. I followed her just in time to see her reach up to one of the cupboards and bring out another bottle of sherry. I declined her offer and watched as she filled her own glass almost to overflowing. We resumed our places in the sitting room. I felt impatient and wanted to move the conversation on. I had a long way to go yet.

'Maura...'

The doorbell rang.

'Who is it, Topher? Go and see, will you? I don't want to see anyone else.'

She seemed peeved by this unwelcome interruption and so was I. Getting up reluctantly I slipped in to the front door from where, behind the net curtains and in the best nosy housewife manner, I took a peek to see who our unexpected visitor might be. And when I saw who it was, my heart missed a beat.

There on the doorstep stood Toby Ainsdale, his face as anxious and strained as puce as the paint on the television show that Maura had been watching. The purpose of his call was clear and I knew that I was going to have to follow my instincts and act immediately.

24

I resisted the urge to panic and decided that the only course left open to me was one which I had of late become rather too readily inclined to follow – that of lying through my teeth. Taking care not to dislodge the curtains, I walked softly back into the living-room and put my finger to my lips and motioned for Maura to be silent..

'Who is it...'

'Shhh, I think it's that Father O'Connor again. You don't want him here now, do you?'

'Who will rid me of that pestilent priest?' she whispered and then coughed into her sherry. 'That rebarbative Jesuit puts himself on a par with God, or even slightly above Him. No sense of timing, either.'

I took her hand and lead her into the large walk-in broom cupboard next to the kitchen, taking care that we would end up in the only part of the house that could not be seen into from outside.

'Keep quite still, Aunt Maura and don't drop your glass. We'll just pretend that nobody's here.'

The doorbell rang again and was this time accompanied by a fist hammering so loudly that it would have wakened the dead, let alone the whole district.

'Stay where you are and don't come out, whatever you do. I'm going to have a reccie on our plump pal out there.'

She giggled like a recalcitrant schoolgirl.

'This is fun, Topher, great fun. It's just like when we used to hide as children from the tally man then mother would clip our ears if we dared to move or make a sound.'

I ventured back into the hall and hid behind the outsize grandfather clock. Then, cautiously, I tiptoed up to the door and listened carefully.

'Can I help you, old boy?'

This was presumably one of the neighbours who had been alarmed by the assault on the door. I heard Toby muttering something in reply. Then the neighbour said something about having seen a priest who had called earlier and that perhaps he had taken Maura to Mass, adding that, 'It is Good Friday today, don't you know.'

Evidently Toby did not, but the theory must have seemed plausible enough. A short while later there was a scrabbling noise and a piece of paper was pushed through the letterbox. I listened as Toby stumped off down the path, slamming the gate shut behind him. Moments later I heard him savagely start up his car and drive off in the wrong gear, full of road and every other kind of rage.

I retrieved the note from the wire letter basket. It was a page torn out of the end of a diary and the ink was barely dry.

Maura, I called today but you weren't in and the phone seems not to be working. You've left it off the hook or forgotten to pay the bill again. Something very important has come up. Your nephew Christopher is up here asking a lot of awkward questions and determined to cause trouble, big trouble. On no account say anything to him. In fact don't even let him try to visit you. Get in touch with me as soon as you're back from church. T.

I scrunched up the paper and put it in my pocket. No need to bring the message to Maura's attention now, I thought.

'Topher, has the priest gone now?'

'Yes. I don't think he'll be back today.'

'Good', she said simply. 'Bloody interfering cleric! Now how about some lunch?'

Surprisingly, the fridge in the kitchen was stocked with fresh food. I reckoned that Maura might be expecting guests for Easter. Using the resources sparingly, I busied myself and soon had prepared a passable meal of salad, cheese and crusty bread. Maura looked appreciatively at my efforts and evidently approved of the fresh tablecloth and properly set table.

'Very civilised', she said approvingly.

I smiled and placed the jar of mayonnaise on the table, having carefully checked the "best before" date to see if Maura was inadvertently trying to poison us both.

'You always were a favourite nephew of mine, Topher'.

She gobbled down the food hungrily and I wondered when she had last had a good meal. Maybe she was not eating properly these days like so many old people. Within minutes she had finished and looked happy when I suggested a cup of tea. We went back into the sitting-room and I helped her into her armchair and then I returned to the kitchen to search for the teabags.'

Through the glass door I saw her surreptitiously reach behind her chair and fish out another bottle, fill her glass and empty it almost immediately. When I came in, she meekly accepted the tea but did not touch it and her mood seemed to change. She began to slip back into melancholia.

'I get so bored these days Topher, so bored and lonely since Gerald died, poor soul. You visited him not long before he passed, didn't you? You remember the state he got into then, don't you? It so depressed me and I just couldn't bear to see him wasting away. I just wished that they would have eased his passing. Oh, I know what you're thinking – a good Catholic like me doesn't believe in euthanasia. But if I were a doctor I know that I wouldn't want to stand by and see him go on and on in pain that had become unbearable. You won't know what I'm talking about but it was like that announcement about "the King's life drawing peacefully to a close" and all that nonsense. Why even God himself...'

I cut into her ramblings. I could not allow her to lose the way now. She was beginning to slur her words and I feared for the worst.

'Maura, tell me about the day that April died.'

Having obviously forgotten what we had been talking about and enjoying sailing away on a new tack, she seemed displeased to be re-directed back to this subject.

'What a dreadful thing it was. My heart died that day you know. What more is there to tell you, Topher?'

'Well for a start, where were you on that day?'

'Where was I? Why I...'

She paused to think.

'I was at the Flower Show in Southport all day and it was lovely. Such beautiful displays they have. I've always liked flowers ever since I was little. Do you know that they named me after one. Marguerite, that's what Maura comes from. A pretty name I think.'

'When did you come home?'

'I came home from Southport that evening, and

Toby was waiting there at the station for me and then the police came and...'

She began to cry and I went over and put my arm on her shoulder as a kindly gesture but without any real affection. I knew that I now had her in my confidence. Either that or the flood of sherry was loosening her tongue. I refilled her already empty glass and handed it back to her.

'You left the house just after breakfast and went to Southport in your car, the yellow Volvo, didn't you?'

She nodded, ignoring all the danger signals and seemingly unconcerned by the fact that I appeared to already know the answers.

'And yet you came back on the train.'

Her eyes were glazing over and she was pouring yet another sherry and so I raised my voice.

'Ben saw you drive off after breakfast and yet Barry Leemings saw your car outside the house about four o'clock. Toby told the police that he had been out all afternoon and even had a receipt for petrol to prove it. But it couldn't have been his receipt because his car was a big Peugeot – a diesel car, wasn't it. So it must have been a receipt for your car but it was stamped August 5th at 3.45 p.m.' I had made up the time on the receipt as it did not even have a date on it.

'Yes you're right, that was my receipt– I may have come home a little early from the Flower Show. What does it matter now? I'd been feeling poorly – a headache. I do suffer from stress and migraines, you understand.'

'But Toby said you returned by train from the show and he went to meet you at the station in the evening. But you had already been home before that. Whether you went back to the flower show later that afternoon or not doesn't really matter. You were home at the house that day. Ben and Barry both saw your car parked there.'

She nodded and sniffed then slumped her head forward in her chair.

'So just tell me what really happened that day.'

Gradually the final pieces of the jigsaw were all fitting into place. I was beginning to see how I had been wrong all along, misled by my ever-present readiness to attribute the wrong motive to the wrong person. Maura was sprawled in her chair and I shook her to try and prevent her from falling into a drunken stupor. I didn't care about her feelings any more, I just wanted one thing now, one thing only, plain and simple. I needed to find out the truth. Maura stirred and began to speak like an automaton.

'What really happened to April that day?'

She looked distraught.

'I did go back, Topher, you're right. God knows I wish I hadn't gone back but I wasn't feeling well, a bit poorly and dizzy. It was a hot day, I remember that, and it had been much too hot at the show. Perhaps I'd had a bit to drink – the odd glass of wine. But I wasn't that bad because felt I could still drive safely. And, yes, I think I did stop for petrol on the way because I'd almost run out but I couldn't be sure about that now.'

The narrative ceased and she began to cry again in that unfocused way which drunks do. I got up and went over to her and shook her again and she asked me for a cup of tea. I gave her the tea I had already made and she drank it up while all the time staring at the ceiling, oblivious of everything.

'Go on, Aunt Maura. You bought the petrol and...'

'I think that I bought it but I'm not really sure any more. But yes I did return home. Well, when I got back to the house, I just couldn't believe what I was seeing. April was there and I couldn't understand what she was up to. Everything of mine had been thrown higgledy-piggledy everywhere – clothes, books, papers, ornaments, the lot. I thought that there had been a burglary until I saw her there, going through my jewellery box, tipping it up and taking anything of value, even things that Gerald had given to me.'

She began to fiddle nervously with her cup and it fell and rolled away across the carpet, spilling the remains of her tea. She motioned to go and clean it up but I stopped her and implored her to continue.

'I told April to stop it immediately and put everything back in its place. You've no right to touch any of my things and leave Gerald's papers alone, too. She only turned to me and laughed in my face. She said that she was going to get all the money she needed from Gerald and me by stealing it from us because she was damned sure that we wouldn't give her any and that I couldn't do a thing to stop her because I was such a weak person. It was true. I never really could stop her from doing anything, she was so headstrong, even as a little girl and quite beyond my control. So I...'

She stopped talking and I needed to prompt her to continue before she collapsed finally.

'And what happened next, Aunt Maura?'

April went downstairs and in to the conservatory. She picked up a bag, a holdall sort of thing that Ben used as a sports bag. She had tipped his kit out and...'

'And then...'

'I saw that she had filled it with silverware, antiques that we had collected over the years and were worth quite a bit by that time. I was shocked, really shocked, and I grabbed her arm and asked her what she was doing. She just laughed and I said that she was a wicked girl, a very wicked girl. Topher, do you know what she did? She just laughed again and said that she'd always been much wickeder that I could ever have imagined and that she thought that she was going to have a baby. It was Barry's baby. When I asked her if that was true and what she was going to do, she just said that she was going to get married to Barry anyway and that there was nothing that Gerald or I could do about it, nothing at all.'

She paused and seemed to be biting her lip. I signalled to her to go on.

'Then, then I got a bit carried away and I called her bad things. A little whore. She just replied that if she was then it was a case of like mother like daughter and that we were both whores. She'd been drinking you see, and she had a terrible tongue in her when she'd been drinking.'

I poured Maura another sherry to loosen her up and thought that drink and terrible tongues were both things that April and Maura had in common.

Apparently refreshed, I pressed her for more and she continued. 'Well, she said that she was going to have the child, and that at least Barry had wanted her and that he wasn't going to dump her like Toby had dumped me when I was pregnant with her. She said that her father had been led a merry dance by me. She meant Gerald of course, because she never thought of Toby as her father, and certainly never referred to him as that. She said it wasn't surprising that he'd had to get off with other woman like Elvira or that silly little Moscrop bitch and

376

that was all because I was probably rotten in bed anyway. A Frigid Bridget from the bogs was what she called me. Then she said that I was jealous of her, that I'd always been jealous of her, and even more so now that I had lost my looks. That no man in their right mind would want me ever again and that no man had probably ever wanted me because I was cold and incapable of love. And I saw her expression and it was the same contemptuous look that Toby had given me when I had begged him to marry me. He had told me to find someone else to bail me out because he had a future that he was going to go off and chase and he didn't want his life spoiled because of me.'

I could see that she was now beginning to get worked up but I didn't want to stop her at that point.

'And then well then something in me sort of snapped.' She stopped and tears began to flow down her old raddled face.

'Aunt Maura, what happened next?'

She screwed her eyes up as if in pain and then continued – speaking in a low and resigned manner.

'I hit her. I'd had enough and I couldn't stand it any more and so I picked up...'

She hesitated.

'Picked up what?'

'You know – that poker thing from the old boiler – you remember I used it to pull up weeds in the garden. It was the only thing I could lay my hands on. I didn't mean to injure her or do anything other than bring her to her senses. Well I only hit her once and she staggered about in shock and started yelling. So I hit her again. It was to stop her saying all those cruel and wicked things to me. She just fell onto the floor and lay there on the tiles without moving. She was moaning and held her hand to her head and then...'

'And then what, Maura?'

'And then, well. Then she was quiet and I knew that she was dead and I that I had killed her and I didn't know for the life of me what to do.'

She started wailing with tears and the sound of her crying made me feel sorry for her until I thought about what she had done and then I just felt sickened.

'I didn't mean it, any of it. She was my daughter, my only daughter and oh, believe me I didn't mean it, you have to believe me Topher because it was all an accident, a horrible accident.'

She continued to weep uncontrollably but I no longer cared about consoling her. Frankly I thought she deserved to be old and alone.

'What did you do then, after she was dead?' I asked as gently as I could manage.

'I went round to get Toby to help me. I didn't know what else to do. I was shocked and I started to cry as well. I realised that Toby hadn't heard any of the argument with April because I'm sure that if he had, he would have tried to stop it and calm both of us down. When I told him what had happened he said that he would come back with me to see if we could do anything to help April. When he did go next door he just said that April really was dead. He was crying and out of his mind with grief and shock. But he knew I hadn't meant to kill her, Topher. He said that I'd never have harmed a hair on her head and that I had always been a good mother. He knew what April was like and how spiteful she was. You know just a few days before she had even threatened to blackmail Gerald by telling Mary Moscrop's husband all about their affair. She had no scruples, none at all. She was amoral, completely amoral...'

I presumed that she was referring to April rather than Mary Moscrop though conceivably it could have been them both but I didn't want to interrupt Maura now. She was looking very tired but she was still anxious to justify what she had done. I felt no pity for her as nothing could undo that moment of violence and bring April back. With as much insincere compassion as I could muster, I urged her to finish the tale.

'After the shock of finding April's body, Toby was wonderfully calm and he just arranged everything. He took me back to Southport in my car and then he bought the petrol – I remember now – and he told me to stay at the Flower Show and then to come back later on the train at the time we had agreed. He said he'd tell the police that I had been there all day and had never left the show and that I had phoned him from there in the afternoon. Then he tidied up, got rid of the fingerprints and then he put the things in the bag as they had been before. He did everything he could to make it look as though April had been killed by a burglar. The police never suspected that we had anything to do with April's death. And they still don't.'

She wiped her eyes and then looked at me straight in the face. 'You see that Toby helped me with everything, Topher. He helped me when I needed help the most. He said that everything would turn out OK. He was true to me in the end and he did really did love me and he still does. And what else could he have done after all? He understood that I didn't mean to harm her and that I loved her and that it was all an accident, a pure accident.'

'But why didn't you tell the police about it being an accident?'

'They wouldn't have believed me. I was going to say that April had threatened me with the poker after I caught her stealing but Toby said don't do that. He explained that when he had had a bit of trouble himself in his business the police were very unhelpful to him and called him a liar and that they would do the same to me if I told them about April. He said that he didn't want the truth to come out as to who her father was – it was all a dirty scandal that those bitches would love.'

It was unclear as to which particular bitches these were but I let it pass.

'Gerald would have turned nasty and said it was all my fault and that I was never a good mother to April. That wasn't true because I loved her more than anything else in the world.'

She slumped back into her chair but was determined not to let her go.

'Did you know that Barry Leemings found April's body before we did?'

'No he didn't, that's not right! You were first to find her, believe me Topher, or else why didn't he tell the police that? Barry was never there. I was careful not to mention his his name to the police anyway. But they, the fat one at any event, was convinced that her death was something to do with Barry. Just let them think the worst and I wasn't going to put them right on that score...'

I was no longer sure about anything now but I let her continue.

'Topher, I am really, really, sorry that you and that little Rosa of yours found her – I didn't mean to put either of you through that because it wasn't supposed to have been you.'

'Well who was supposed to find her, then?'

'Toby was. He said he'd go round to the house on a pretext when Elvira was back from wherever she had been that day, and then he'd discover the body and phone the police. I never understood how but you beat him to it. You and that dreary little Rosa. God she was awful.'

I was in no mood to rise to the bait and I could see that Maura was only just managing to keep awake now that the sherry had worked its way through her system and was numbing her from the pain of the last forty years of her own guilt.

'You see, Topher, Toby told me that you two just appeared and went into the house and found April.'

I remembered what Ros had said to me yesterday about us being in the wrong place at the wrong time.

'Have you ever told anyone, other than Toby, the truth about what happened that day?'

'Who else was there to tell? I wasn't going to make a statement and admit everything to those unpleasant policeman. You see I would never have let him take the blame.'

'Who, Barry?'

'No, I mean Toby. God knows, I might have tried to hint that Barry had been involved if I thought that I could get away with it. And then, well, he was killed in that crash, poor soul. The police expert told me that April's death wasn't murder anyway but some sort of an accident. And so it was Topher, it was just an accident. I never meant any of it to happen. How do you think I've lived with the guilt ever since? I've committed a sin, a terrible sin and can there be a worse sin than a mother killing her own child? Oh, I've been to confession. Oh yes, I've been there all right but they never took me seriously. How could they when I was drunk every time with Dutch courage because I couldn't face up to what I'd done. I used to go so often to the church that they must have thought I was sweet on the priests there. Maybe I was, Christ half the time I was out of my mind. But believe me, Topher, I've never told anyone else about how April died. How could I? Toby would have been sent to prison for helping me, for making up those lies, that alibi and things. What would Ben have thought if he knew that I had killed his sister? What was I going to say to him? He'd have never have spoken to me again. Oh, sweet Jesus I didn't mean it. God believe me, I didn't mean it.'

The alcohol had taken its effect and I could see that she was on the point of passing out completely. I shook her roughly in one last attempt to try to keep her awake.

'Did Gerald know that it was you who killed April?'

'Of course not. Gerald would've... Oh, Gerald...'

But it was too late, she had passed out and was snoring like an animal through her open mouth. I left the lifeless house behind. It was three o'clock, exactly.

25

When I got back to the hotel that evening the last person that I expected to see standing there at the reception desk was Francesca, resplendent in a Liberty print dress with a silk scarf dramatically draped like a victor's garland around her slender neck. As usual, I heard her before I saw her.

'When do you expect him back then? He is staying here, isn't he?'

I half thought that she would add something along the lines of, 'What kind of hotel is this anyway, where your guests refuse to answer their phones when their wives are trying to get hold of them at all hours of the day?', but she didn't. Francesca always liked an argument, especially with me, and I always thought that my persistent failure to answer her back was one of the factors that had eventually led her to take up with another man.

I attempted to sneak up the green-carpeted stairway without being seen but Roland Rat, the little sneak that he was, saw me from his vantage point in the corner of the bar and he called out in a loud but nervous voice to Francesca.

'Christopher's just come in.'

She spun round, giving the receptionist a well-deserved break.

'And where the hell have you been, then? I've been trying to get hold of you for ages.'

'I'm sorry I've been, um... How did you track me down? What's wrong? Has anything happened to Kirsty?'

'No, don't be silly. She's fine. I've just spoken to her on the phone.'

I realised that Kirsty must have actually listened to me for once when I'd requested her not to tell Francesca of the attempted break-in at the flat.

'But Chris, you look absolutely terrible. You look as though you've seen a ghost or something.'

I had – her. But her tone had softened and she looked almost genuinely concerned.

You sure that you're not ill or something? I've heard that there's some sort of bug going around and...'

'No, it's nothing like that. Just went out for a walk in the rain and I got a bit wet. I think that I might get a chill if I don't change my clothes. I'll only be a minute.'

On the way up to my room I thought about doing a bolt down the fire escape but the fire seemed to have gone out of me completely and I no longer wanted to escape. As I came back downstairs the receptionist, who was going off duty and was about to leave by the front door, gave me a wink and pointed into the bar. Roland was sitting there looking glum while Francesca was studying some sort of document.

'Chris - I need to talk to you about the house in Wickham Road.'

That was all I needed. I knew what this was about. It was the chance for me to sign over the former matrimonial home to her on the understanding that she, very generously, would make no claims on me in the divorce. I had already got my defence ready on that one thanks to some research that Michael Shalway had done for me. I hoped that he hadn't figured out yet that the mythical client was me.

'Send the monkey out, then. I'm not discussing anything in front of him.'

I said it just loud enough for Roland to hear and he left in a surly but humbled way to 'check the road atlas in the car outside'.

I almost felt sorry for the Rat for he seemed to lack any substance and was the kind of person who, left to his own resources, would have found them wanting. Then, dismissing him completely from my thoughts, I went over and fetched a pint for myself and a gin and lime for Francesca.

'Stop being so unpleasant to him. It's not his fault.'

I grunted, 'I'm sure that it never is.'

'Christopher just try to act like a civilised adult human being for once.'

I retorted with something unpleasant and she looked at me as though I was a tiresome child.

'Oh, shut up. You can be so absolutely puerile at times.'

This didn't even deserve a comment being as it was completely true.

'Your clerk told me where I would find you and the hotel confirmed that you were staying here. I had to see you in person since you keep giving me the slip.'

I chose not to plead innocent to that particular charge – I had been avoiding her for days because she was driving me mad.

'So just pay attention, Chris. I want you to sign this deed. It's very urgent.'

I frowned as she produced a document from the depths of the handbag that I had bought for her from a very expensive shop in the Via Condotti on our last but ill-fated wedding anniversary visit to Rome.

'Don't worry, I'll give you the chance to read it first. I know what you lawyers are supposed to be like with the small print. Bloody fools that you all are when it comes to your personal lives.'

'That's hardly fair, Fran.'

She ignored this half-hearted attempt at defending myself.

'Just read it. It's all perfectly above board, I can assure you.'

I put on my glasses and scanned the document in record time.

'But it's an agreement that you and I will share the net free proceeds of sale of Wickham Road equally, fifty-fifty.'

'Well spotted.'

'But I thought that you were going to claim...'

'I've had a change of heart. That solicitor of mine was far too pushy for his own good. I feel that I would like what I am entitled to now. Nothing more or nothing less without resorting to any silliness in court.'

I was glad. At least her solicitor knew the law.

'But why the change in heart, Fran? Have you won the lottery or has Roland Rat decided to do the decent thing?'

She ignored this.

'Actually Chris, I've been given a two-year sabbatical at UCLA and Roland has agreed that he will come with me. He's been offered a good job by his cousin Walter and we've been given the loan of an apartment near Santa Barbara. So I'm all set to do that research project I've always talked about.'

I had no idea of what the research project that she had always talked about actually was and I realised that, for years now, I had never really properly listened to her anyway. But this was not the time to be picking an argument, particularly in the light of the sudden promised amelioration of my finances.

'Have you finally sold our house, then Fran?'

She nodded but added that it was, 'subject to contract and that there was some urgency because the buyers wanted in by the beginning of next week and there was no chain involved to hold things up. Then she handed me the paper to sign and Roland had to be recalled to witness my signature.'

'Have you got any plans for the future then, Christopher?'

I was vague, having no particular plans that I could think of, or at least plans that I wanted to tell her of. So I assured her that I would do my best to look after Kirsty and that she could stay with me for as long as she wanted to. And we began to talk a bit about how the future might look for our son and daughter. I thought that, whatever the differences that Fran and I had, we still had a lot in common. I laughed at Fran's caustic comments about one of our former neighbours who had taken up the trumpet late in life and was tone deaf but had taken a particular shine to her. Then, fleetingly, I remembered Fran at the time when we had first gone out with each other in Cambridge after the Trinity May Ball that we had both gatecrashed. As we had walked back hand-in-hand across the empty Market Square and the bells of Great St Mary's had rung out to greet the laid-back Cambridge morning, I had never wanted to be out of her company again. How things have changed! For many years we were never out of each other's company. I shut my eyes and turned my mind back to what she was saying now, while at the same time thinking ruefully that being besotted with women was practically my epitaph.

'I hear that you've get a new lady in your life, Christopher. Kirsty tells me she hasn't met her yet but from what you've told her she seems to approve. Well I'm happy for you and you deserve a break. We both do.'

Bloody hell, Kirsty, why can't you ever keep your mouth shut for a change?

I made some sheepish reply to her magnanimous gesture and we idly chatted for some time while Roland read the stale news in yesterday's Echo. As I listened to her voice I wondered where things between Fran and I had gone wrong. Her infectious laugh, her mischievous but malevolent sense of humour and her innate generosity were still there. But somehow we no longer could, or indeed wanted to, live together again. Had things been different then we would have grown old together and have become a touching old Darby and Joan couple like the Twentymans had. Maybe that was what I missed most, the fact that we were not going to share anything with each other any more. I began to feel quite morose until my suppressed aggression towards Roland took over. He bleated out that unless they set off soon they would not be back in London before midnight. What an utterly contemptible little toad he was.

But before I could summon up the energy to insult him, Fran gave me a kiss and said, 'Well I suppose this is goodbye then, Chris. We haven't made any definite plans yet but it's possible that we might be able to stay on in the States on a more or less permanent basis. Don't say anything to Kirsty yet as you know how she frets. I'll be in touch soon and maybe she and Ed can come out and see us both in the summer.'

I said that I would help with the fares and Fran smiled at me in the old way.

'It's hard for me to say this and I know that Ed's a boy who knows his own way in life but I think that Kirsty's sort of outgrown me. But she still seems to need you and it's a comfort to me to know that you'll always be there for the children and for her in particular. You always were there for them and I mean that.

She stopped and I could see a tear forming. I, too, felt overcome. I sniffed loudly and felt that I just wanted to hold her hand tightly to reassure her that everything would be fine. But then Roland returned from tinkering with the lights on the Audi and the moment passed.

'I hope it all works out with you and your Jess. You've been awfully good about everything. In a funny way I think that I'll miss you, Chris. You're a good man and, well, no hard feelings?'

'No hard feelings, Fran.' I immediately regretted having said that as I didn't mean it, though I knew there was no point in admitting that.

She kissed me on the cheek and for what I fatalistically thought would probably be the last time. I turned and went back up to my room feeling chastened and hungry. It had already been a traumatic day and the long walk back to Chester station had used up what little of Maura's food I had eaten. As I awaited room service, I hummed the opening bars from Freddy Redd's San Francisco Suite. Once upon a time, there might have been the realistic prospect of a reconciliation with Fran. But, as life teaches us, second chances are rare things and, on reflection, maybe I didn't want a second chance with

Fran. Then in a mood of cynicism, I recalled Gavin's words when one night in the pub he confided in me that the older he became, the more convinced he was that life was merely a series of crossed wires and missed opportunities, a haphazard journey along one-way streets with no direction signs. Now I wasn't so sure that he was wrong.

Room service came promptly and went, the egg and cress sandwiches and dried-out fruit cake were all hastily eaten while I tried to avoid spreading crumbs on the railway timetable that I was consulting to plan out my journey the next day. Having done that, I was listening to the weather reports from coastal stations when the phone rang.

'Christopher, is that you?'

'Malcolm?'

'Aye. Look, it's about Ben. I think something terrible is about to happen. I've been trying to get you for ages, but you weren't answering.' He sounded almost hysterical.

'What do you mean, terrible? What's going to happen?'

'Ben and I were away and it was only when we got back that he read your last message.'

I was just about to say, 'What message?' when I remembered. I had sent him an email before I had set out yesterday morning to see Twentyman and learned of his death from his daughter Lia. I tried to call Ben after that but he didn't reply and I didn't leave an answerphone message because surely nobody ever uses their answerphone nowadays, even on their mobiles. I opened up my laptop and scrolled down to the "sent" folder to remind myself what I'd written.

Ben, your suspicions are correct. I have been to see Ainsdale today and I'm sure that he was April's lover and I think that he probably killed her as he gave me answers that show that he knew more than he should have. But leave it for the moment. I'm not completely sure yet but I'm going to try to prove it. I just need to check a couple of things with Twentyman before we've got enough evidence to go to the police and get him jailed right and proper. Don't do anything until I speak to you again. We need to make this watertight. Ainsdale won't get away with it again, if we can help it. Chris.

Re-reading it I had the alarming realisation that, having not spoken to him since, I had never followed it up with what Ros had told me, and what I had just found out in my meeting with Maura. The visit from Fran had distracted me completely. Things had simply overtaken me, as they frequently seem to do.

'Malcolm, what's Ben done?'

'It's not what's he done, it's what I think he's going to do. He says he's going to sort out someone called Toby Ainsdale. He's been brooding about it for days and whatever it was that you said to him in that email triggered off some terrible force in him. I've never seen him in such a blind rage. He's out of his mind.'

'Did he say how he was going to sort him out?'

'No but I think he wants to beat the hell out of him – or maybe even worse.'

'Hang on a minute there, Malcolm...'

'No need! I've found out where Ainsdale lives and I'm already on my way there in the work van – I've got to get to him before he hurts someone. Honestly, Chris, I've never seen him like this. I'm worried he's going to do something dreadful.'

'Bloody hell, okay well you'd better keep going. I'm coming as fast as I can. I'll meet you there.'

26

The taxi seemed to take forever to arrive and, as I paced up and down the pavement in front of the hotel, I was cursing the delay. I hoped that I would get to Toby's before Ben had the chance to do something that he might always regret.

'Are you the one for the cab?'

I had failed to notice the rather nondescript saloon car which had pulled up. I jumped into the back, a habit born of the fact that the only taxis I habitually used were ones in which you didn't have the option of sitting next to the driver – 'proper hackney cabs with taximeters', as Henry had once described them.

'Do you know the way to Clay Moss Lane?'

He nodded gloomily and as we set off he began to deliver a monologue on some 'bloody nonsense at Goodison Park' which was somehow related to the doings or lack of them of the management at Anfield. I let him drone on, for football, never my greatest interest at any time, was of even less concern to me this evening. My mind was desperately trying to block out any thoughts about what Ben might have done or be about to do. I went over Malcolm's words again.

Why could Ben not have waited for me to confirm my suspicions instead of pouncing at the first moment's notice? We had both got it all wrong. April might well have been a scheming little blackmailer and quite probably the sort to have two-timed her lover, but in the end neither of these had led to her death. She had died simply because of pride, spite, hormones and the purest form of jealousy than can exist, a jealousy so strong, so beyond any reason that it could transcend the normal bounds of human behaviour and end with a mother killing her own child. A child that she had both loved and yet hated beyond endurance.

By the time we had cleared the built-up area, the traffic snarled up, the result of a minor fracas between a blue car and a white van. As we sat waiting to get past I began to wonder if Malcolm had misinterpreted the situation. But I knew that I was only hoping against hope and that the message had been simple enough. When Ben meant business, he meant business.

As we came round the bends by the church at Little Crosby I pictured my grandfather again. I remembered something which he had often said to me about how sometimes a man needs to be by himself with only his thoughts for company, far away from the city and its people. 'A man can't contemplate with all that going on about him.' He had then quoted from the Book of the Prophet Isiah: 'Woe unto them that join house to house, that lay field to field, till there be no place that they may be placed alone in the midst of the earth.'

Well I certainly felt alone now, isolated in this metal box which was carrying me through the half forgotten lands of my youth. I thought of Sep saying 'King James version, Christopher. I don't hold with any of the fancy modern translations.' I wondered what he would have done if he had been in my shoes now. I was only glad that he was long dead and out of it.

As we approached, the rain, which had been an intermittent drizzle until then, intensified and the view became obscured as large globules of water splattered and spread across the windows.

'Nasty night for anyone unfortunate to be out in it', the driver remarked above the incessant crack of the windscreen wipers.

'Is the turning far down here?'

'See that tree over there? That's the entrance lane on the right. Just drop me right here and I'll walk the rest of the way.'

'It's cats and dogs out there! Are you sure? You'll get soaked on a night like this.'

'Yes this is fine – I've got an umbrella. I want to wait for someone who will be here soon.'

'Suit yourself then but make sure your 'brella doesn't get blown inside out by the wind.'

The driver looked at me as I paid the fare and then shrugged before turning the car round and proceeding back towards the distant orange glow of the suburbs.

As I fought through the driving rain I remembered this lane, not just from my visit two days ago but from when I was a child. It was the same lane which led to the flat marshland around the River Alt, a place where my father had taken me bird-watching when I was young. What were the birds that we had waited so patiently to see? It seemed important now to remember their names – the grebes, sandpipers, swallows, red-breasted mergansers and blackwing gulls that circled round the land close to the sea. I had always keenly looked them up the birds in the battered book on the *Flora and Wildlife of Great Britain* that we had always carried with us on those Saturday afternoon trips. A list of familiar plants came into my head: primrose, celandines, toadflax, meadowsweet, ragwort, cow parsley and the ubiquitous rosebay willow herb. How comforting these links with my childhood should have been and yet I was in no mood to be comforted.

I ran along the damp lane, avoiding the numerous large puddles while trying to blot out the faces of April and Ben, both of whom seemed to be looking at me with strange and slightly menacing smiles. April was a little girl again, about eight and wearing a mauve party dress with her hair done up in ribbons and curls. Then she was twenty again and dressed in a black skirt, a long sleeved top and with a velvet choker around her neck.

With the heavens lashing down upon me I began to hum to myself the tune of The Black Velvet Band and had got as far as singing, 'Her eyes they shone like diamonds...' when I cursed myself for letting the taxi drop me so far from the house. I shook the rain from my hair and then I saw an image of Ben in his late teens, dressed in his cricket whites and holding a ball as if he were about to bowl into the teeming black night.

Was this really the same lane in which I had picked blackberries and had clutched the neat little greaseproof paper packages containing cheese and pickle sandwiches that my mother had made? Was it here that I had happily chatted to Dad while Meg had trotted behind, wagging her tail and looking out for the scattering rabbits that enlivened the simple rhythms of her uncomplicated life? If it was, then it had all happened in a different age, far away from the present.

I went on and could see the tasteful and discreet painted metal sign which proclaimed 'Clay Moss Farm - Strictly Private.' Bracing myself against the squalls of rain which tasted salty as if they had blown in straight from the ocean, I continued to run up the curving drive towards the small stand of trees which formed a windbreak of sorts and emerged beyond there at the house itself.

Battling against the now strongly rising and relentless wind and the driving rain, I looked around to see if there was anyone around. But there did not appear to be and the house seemed to be deserted and in darkness apart from the metal lantern hanging under the porch. I pulled desperately at the bell handle next to the door.

There was no reply. Perhaps I was too early and Ben had come to his senses and had gone back home. I was relieved, but in an echo of that other fateful evening in Blundellsands forty years or so ago, something compelled me to go round to the back of the house and look for myself.

The storm seemed to reach a new ferocity and pitch and I winced as the struggling trees huddled behind me, swaying and creaking as the wind tore through their limbs and scattered branches, breaking off twigs that fell on top of the leaves of last autumn. It was, I thought, that on a night like this, with the wind howling like a demented dog and the rain falling like a rippled sheet of glass, that the world would probably end.

I went round the gable end of the house and found myself in a neatly paved courtyard. An old iron pump set beside the glistening cobbles and a car was standing there. With a sinking feeling I recognised Ben's Audi, which I had last been in on the way back from Gerald's funeral a handful of months ago. A barn, obviously used as some sort of garage, faced the yard and I could just make out in the gloom of the open door a dark coloured Range Rover which I assumed to be Toby Ainsdale's.

A faint light drew me towards an uncurtained window next to the back door. Standing on tiptoe, I managed to see in to a kitchen of painted wooden cabinets, neatly arranged copper pans and old-fashioned storage jars. Of any inhabitant of the house I could see no trace.

I tried the next window which, due to the slope of the courtyard, was higher up the wall than the kitchen window had been. This time I could not reach up enough to see anything so I hunted in the barn, among debris and bags of rubbish until I discovered a couple of strong wooden boxes that had once contained a croquet set. I shuddered as some small beast, a mouse rather than a rat I hoped, scuttled away into the darkness. I dragged the boxes across the yard and placed one of them below the illuminated window.

As I stepped up I could now see that there was a passageway at the side of the room and, through a partially obscured doorway, a dining room. But I could make out little more than a peepshow made up of odd and disjointed shadows.

For a moment I thought I could hear voices, raised and angry, but I was not sure if it was just my imagination playing tricks against the noise of the wailing wind in the trees.

The back door of the house was firmly shut and although I banged on it a number of times there was no response. Then I saw Malcolm coming out round from the front and I launched myself at the door in an attempt to smash it off its hinges and dislodge the heavy mortice lock but my attempts to gain entry were futile.

'Is anything happening in there, Chris?'

'Nobody's answering the door but I think they're in there.'

'Well Ben must be – his car's here.' And after a few seconds I heard him mournfully add, 'I hope that he hasn't done anything – anything bad, I mean.'

I agreed and regained my stance on the old wooden box and I started to bang on the glass as hard as I could without breaking it. Even though there was a lull in the storm, nobody appeared.

'I can't actually see anything, but I'm sure that I've just heard voices.'

Malcolm dragged the other box beside me and clambered on to it to peer inside.

Then distant figures came into our view and we could pick out Ben and, rather more indistinctly, another person, just recognisable as Toby. I could tell from their wild gestures that they were shouting at each other although we could not pick up what they were actually saying. To my horror I saw that Ben was holding something in his hand.

'It's a cricket bat – his favourite one, too', said Malcolm.

It was only then that we saw the glint of light on the barrels and saw that Toby had a shotgun cradled in his arms and he was pointing it straight at Ben and trying to make him back off with the bat. But Ben was undaunted and continued to approach him.

'Oh, my God – he's going to use it and shoot Ben. Look out Ben!'

But the noise of the storm prevented our sounds carrying inside so Malcolm desperately yelled at me, 'Do something, Christopher!'

I jumped off the box and ran over to the kitchen window. Spotting a heavy glazed plant pot, I picked it up and shouted, 'Stand back', then I hurled the pot through the window and the small panes disintegrated. I reached my hand in, oblivious of the lacerations which I received from the web of shards still sticking to the frame, opened the casement and carefully heaved myself over the broad stone sill.

'You bastard, you complete bloody bastard! You're still denying it but we both knew that you did it.'

'Did what? You're mad and you've completely gone off your head! You don't understand what you're saying.'

'I know what I'm saying all right. You're the sick one. You had sex with my sister and then...'

He hesitated, suppressing a swelling up of tears, before adding, 'And then you killed her. And you haven't even got the guts to admit that.'

'It wasn't like that, I swear it wasn't!'

'Bullshit! You slept with her and then you killed her because you were jealous.'

'No, you've get it wrong, completely wrong, Ben, I only...'

'And you had the gall to claim that you loved April! You're nothing but a bloody hypocrite and a rapist.'

As I sprinted towards the room I heard Toby's voice raised in a high-pitched call of terror.

'Listen to me, Ben. You've got it all wrong. I wouldn't dream of doing anything like that. Not to April. I loved her dearly but not in the way you thought. I wouldn't have dreamt of having...'

But Ben wasn't listening any more.

'Lying bastard!'

Seeing us there, Toby looked momentarily relieved but as Ben continued to scream whilst wielding the bat around, he started trembling with terror. 'Oh for God's sake, Ben, put that bloody thing down! Oh my God don't make me use this.'

Malcolm shouted, 'You've heard him – don't do it, Ben! You'll spoil everything that we've worked for together. He isn't worth it!'

And, as if in slow-motion, I watched everything happen. Toby, incandescent with terror, swung round and there was a dull flash and bang as the shot-gun roared and something flew past my face. Malcolm and I dropped down to the floor and we saw Ben slowly raise his arm then there was a loud crack and a piteous scream – a sound like an animal in pain.

'Please, please, for pity's sake, Ben! I think that you've just broken my leg! Put the bat down.'

What followed was an epitaph from Ben.

'You are nothing but scum! A murderer and rapist! I will never, ever have any pity to waste on the likes of you. You killed April and destroyed our family and you deserve everything you will get.'

Toby whimpered and Malcolm and I were not sure if he was motioning to drop or to raise the firearm but before he could do either, Ben lifted the bat high and swung it down again, methodically delivering the same decisive stroke with which he had once scored the runs on the sunlit playing fields at school while the younger boys looked on him with admiration.

There was a brief rasping sound from Toby and then Malcolm screamed, 'Stop it, Ben. You'll...'

And then all was silent except for Malcolm's sobs and the incessant pounding of my almost ruptured heart.

Paralysed with fear, I managed to croak out a few words but they were too few and much too late in the day.

'But Ben, Toby didn't...'

But I couldn't finish the sentence. Ben was miles away, absorbed in the rapture of the moment. Slowly he turned towards me, a satisfied smile on his perspiring face, and dropped the blood-stained bat, its last innings having been scored. I did not look down at Toby's body because I had no need to and Malcolm turned away as well. He was beyond any help – a lifeless shape lying on the floor, just as I had seen April so many years before.

There was a long silence until, above Malcolm's sobs, Ben spoke.

'That piece of shit deserved to die – he had April and then finished her off. You told me yourself, Chris. And now the bastard's dead. He deserved it!'

Then, without further comment, he dropped down onto his haunches and repeated the same words, over and over again. 'Thy will be done, Thy will be done.'

*****

By the time the authorities were on their way I had managed to calm Ben down by getting him to drink a cupful of the whisky that I had taken from the sideboard. He'd put his arm around Malcolm and kissed him gently. I looked down at Toby's lifeless body and then picked up the telephone and made the call. I knew that it would only be a matter of minutes before the ambulance and police cars would arrive and transform the sombre courtyard into a fantasy of blue lights flashing like a bizarre and out of sequence futuristic ballet.

Then the lawyer in me kicked in.

'Say nothing, Ben. Tell them nothing until the solicitor arrives. It was self-defence. We saw that he was pointing a gun at you.'

What he might have been going to say I had no idea, but in the circumstances, 'say nothing before the solicitor arrives' seemed an appropriate piece of advice. Ben continued to look at me with an almost condescending air and he, unlike me, seemed to be have everything well under control.

'You understand why I had to do it, don't you, Chris?'

I was tempted to say that I did but I knew that Ben didn't want to hear anything further. Besides there was nothing I could say now that would change things.

'The bastard had to die. I've got no regrets, none at all. He got exactly what he fucking deserved.'

And as Malcolm turned away, unable to look him in the face, I saw that Ben had started to reverently pray in this, his hour of need. And then the irony struck me, that after all I had done to uncover the truth about one killing, Ben's only hope of salvation was if I, like Toby, helped to cover up another.

27

That night I eventually fell into a troubled sleep and dreamt of many things. Most of all of April still lying there on the Minton tiled floor and of Toby gently turning her over so that she would cease to stare at him with uncomprehending eyes, Ben fussing around with an old Mini that he would probably never drive again and of Maura weeping for a past that she wished had never happened in the way that it turned out. And then I dreamt of a smiling girl, a girl wearing a new straw hat and a green necklace, an almost mythical girl who I had once been in love with, had lost and had found again. But this time I had managed to lose her for good. And amongst all of these jumbled images, nothing seemed to make sense any more and I thought of Kirsty and of Jess and the future.

I went back to sleep in the dark of the hotel room and it was just before nine and the sun had risen on a bright morning when I awoke to the buzzing of my phone and struggled to answer it. It was Gavin Teviotdale of all people. At that moment he was the last person that I wanted to talk to.

'Hi, Gav!' I tried to sound less half-hearted than I felt though in reality I was less than half awake and certainly much more than half asleep.

'Chris, is that you? I've been trying to get you since Thursday evening. I've had great trouble in tracking you down. You never seem to have your phone switched on. What the hell have you been up to?'

'What the hell' was in fact pretty much exactly the right expression for what I had been up to. I tried to remain calm and even-tempered. 'I've been really busy.' An understatement if there ever was one.

'You sound tired, Well never mind, you're there now. Look I've got some great news...'

I began to say, 'Gavin, I really need to speak to you right now. It's really important." but he didn't seem to have heard me and went on regardless.

'Well what I have to tell you is really important, too.' I wondered if Gavin ever really listened to anyone other than himself.

'It's all decided.'

'What's all decided?'

'We had a meeting, you see...'

'Who are these "we" and what the blazes has this got to do with me? Look I need to talk to you about something urgent.'

'Just listen, Chris.'

I sighed, realising that I didn't have a choice.

'Well, it was Michael Shalday who suggested it really.'

Gavin was so excited that I resisted the urge to ask him any questions that would string the matter out even longer as I feared that I would never be able to get him off the line.

'So what I was saying is that...'

'Just get to the bloody point.'

I was beginning to lose my cool now as I surely had far bigger problems than whatever Gavin had been discussing in some pointless bloody meeting, but he merely continued, oblivious to my impatience.

405

'The point is that we, I mean those of us in our Chambers who actually matter, you know, excluding the half-wits, have made a decision about what we want to do once Henry has been put to pasture in the high court. The decision was unanimous.

He paused as if 'unanimous' would underline the importance.

'Gavin, what the hell are you all talking about? Just tell me what it is that you have decided.'

'We've decided to have you as our new Head of Chambers, of course.'

I was so dumbfounded that I couldn't think of what to say.

'Chris are you still there? What do you think – say something!'

I should have said, 'I'm very appreciative, thank you. It's a great honour to be recognised by my colleagues', or some other wet response like that. But instead I just retorted angrily, 'Look, nobody's decided anything because I haven't put myself forward for the job.' All I could think about was what had happened at Clay Moss Farm last night, the fact that Toby was dead and that Ben had been arrested. I had not had time to think it all over yet, and everything Gavin wanted to talk about was, to my mind, wholly irrelevant.

'Gavin, I need to talk to you about something else. It's really important and I need your help.'

He interrupted me again.

'If it's about the others, don't worry. All that silly in-fighting amongst the factions in chambers and all, meant that you were the clear choice. The obvious choice I would say. As soon as Jennifer suggested you, Jack and Tom were both keen to stand down.'

Bloody Jennifer – who would have thought of Jenny two-shoes as a fairy godmother – more of a lumbering and interfering, if well-meaning cow. So I was the compromise candidate was I? The one no one really wanted, except that my election would neither frustrate nor mollify both sides at the same time. Well they could wait for my answer, if and when I was ready.

'Gavin, it's good of you all to feel that way but I don't want the damn job! Look, I need to talk to you...'

'There's no need for an immediate answer – Monday will do. You know that all of us think that you're the best person for the position? Even Henry thinks that.'

A damning indictment if ever there was one.

'Anyway I'm off to buy some Easter eggs for those damn kids of mine, though frankly they're too old and fat for them now. Oh, and by the way, the job's off with Vi at the moment – she's got a boyfriend in Putney.'

'He's no boyfriend – he's her husband. And I hear that he's got a bit of a temper so you'd better be careful!'

'Oh well, nothing ventured nothing gained. You know what I always say about women being like buses. If you miss one, there'll be another two along in a few minutes.'

'Great advice, Gavin. But before you go...'

Anyway, cheerio again and bon chance.'

And with that he rang off before I had the chance to ask him the one important thing that I had been trying to get out.

I could hardly think straight and decided I needed something to eat before trying to sort out any more of this nightmare with Ben. My nerves were still shattered and with the loss of sleep I felt too tired to cope with anything. I checked Twentyman's watch – breakfast was still being served and as I hurried down for coffee and toast I was beginning to feel more upbeat, more in control of my own life again.

I managed to speak to Gavin again after I had left the breakfast table. Keeping his attention for the best part of an hour, I told him all about Ben and Toby and how I needed his immediate help. For once he didn't try and sideline me but said that he would come up to Liverpool immediately after the bank holiday and that Ben and I were not to worry any more as he would be prepared to represent my unfortunate cousin in court himself.

At last the gravity of the situation had been understood and he made none of the wisecracks about being found not guilty by Liverpool juries or anything else equally daft that I was half-expecting him to come out with. I finished, sure that he had taken it all in and told him that I would phone the family solicitors without delay. I felt relieved and ready to calm myself down. I had now been up with the police until four o'clock and was quite frankly dog tired.

But there was still one thing to do and after much trouble, I managed to get hold of L. Rupert Dewfold, the solicitor who had sent me the Liverpool Packet in the first place. I felt, perhaps unfairly, that he was responsible for the whole of this tragedy in the first place. Dewfold listened as I told him what had happened but he said that the duty solicitor had already phoned him last night because he knew of the family connection. He couldn't get hold of me but I told him not to worry. I could tell that, like me, he knew nothing about where a solicitor with a criminal practice would take the case from here. I told him that I had already found – good counsel – to represent Ben and that I wanted his firm to instruct this very morning even if it was a Saturday.

After an anxious pause on his part, I reassured him that it wouldn't be on Legal Aid or an insurance job or anything like that, but that our family would be paying for it ourselves. He relaxed and promised that he would contact Gavin this very day and he set up the necessary meeting on Monday, despite it being a bank holiday. I thanked him and felt that I had done everything I could possibly have done for Ben and Malcolm, who had already arranged to see him at Walton later in the day.

I rang off. What was that bit of Candide that we learnt at school that Doctor Pangloss used to say? Something about everything working out for the best in the best of all possible worlds? But how could it ever be like that for Ben? He had killed Toby and it was all my fault, whatever the law might say.

Of course nobody else but Maura knew that Toby was innocent of April's murder. Maybe it would be better to remain silent and leave the assumption of guilt lying with Ainsdale who could no longer speak for himself – he had after all been implicit in covering up the crime. Even if it got out that he was April's real father it wouldn't preclude him from being her killer – in that case the blackmailing scenario could still be assumed.

Besides if a jury were to believe that Ben acted in self-defence and Toby had taken the first move, surely it would be more plausible for a murderer to raise his gun to silence somebody who had discovered his crime than it would be for an innocent and wrongly-accused man to decide to commit his first murder if he was hoping to clear his name. To say nothing might save Ben, both from serving a lifetime in prison, and from the awful truth that he had killed the wrong person and for the wrong reasons, all based on false information that I had given him.

I'd set out to discover the truth about April, but to what end? Her mother had killed her and now her real father was dead as a result. Would she now want her brother to serve a life sentence for avenging her, even if it was on a false premise? A narrative seemed to be building inside my mind to justify my silence but what if I was simply deluding myself? Playing a game of logic to direct attention away from the part I had played in all this. Toby's only crime had been to lie to protect somebody he cared about, and he had paid the ultimate price for it. And now I was treading a very dangerous, and not dissimilar path myself. What would happen if this truth ever emerged?

My mind turned back to Aunt Maura. Should she simply be allowed to get away with it all or should Ben and her go down together, in a final act of destruction for the Kingston family? Maybe spending the rest of her days in a sad, lonely, guilt-riddled, alcohol-numbed existence was punishment enough? But not for murder, surely. Shouldn't she face the impartial judgement of the same legal system that I had dedicated my entire career to upholding?

And what of Gillian? Would she now be left to believe her father had murdered her best friend. There was simply no longer an easy way out of all this. Maura and Ben had made sure of that. Why had I ever jumped in to defend him? Was it simply my own guilt or sense of loyalty? Was it too late to turn back now?

Even though the whole thing was my fault, it was no longer my responsibility. It was now a matter for Gavin and Rupert Dewfold to decide what to say that would convince a jury. Ben was an adult and he and Malcolm would have to live with the consequences of what he had done. The rest was now in the hands of fate. But God, what a sanctimonious arse I sounded these days.

And tomorrow would, after all, be Easter Day and, with luck, I would be back in the best of all possible worlds, back home in time for lunch. Kirsty would be waiting for me and Jessica would be there, too. I wondered how everything was going to work out from now onwards.

Soon I would have to face my son and daughter and tell them everything that had taken place in the last few days. After all, they have a right as they are as much a part of the Kingston family as I am. But what was I supposed to say exactly? I couldn't help thinking that our family history was decidedly better off when it only contained one unsolved death. Now another innocent person lay dead and a second member of the family could be set to get away with murder.

I went upstairs, crawled back in to my unmade bed and slept fitfully for what remained of the morning and much of the afternoon for that matter.

*****

When I woke up again it was beginning to get dark. The more I thought of everything, I realised that there was nothing more left to keep me here in Liverpool. I picked up Seb's book, opened it at the last page and read the final sentence:

So in conclusion the author now bids farewell to his fond readers and, for the moment at least, to this blessed township of Crosby, placed on the shores of the majestic river which flows ever onwards through to the great sea of life itself.

I rapidly got dressed and knew that I still had one more journey to make, one last thing to accomplish before I finally left my home town.

I stopped at the foot of the stairs only to mutter something to the girl at Reception about how I was going down to the beach to get a breath of fresh air before catching the train for London first thing tomorrow morning. She looked surprised and said that she would have the bill ready for seven thirty a.m.

After thanking her and turning away, I narrowly managed to avoid getting accosted by the woman to whom I had purported to have been an architectural historian. As I hurried past I heard her indignant call of, 'Oh, Mr Hawkshaw or whatever your name is...' But, I thought to myself, you'll never know as, with any luck, you and your brats will never see me again!'

And, as I hurried through the front doors, the soft lights and subdued chatter of the hotel were behind me. For a moment I felt isolated and vulnerable again, even though it was still early in the evening and the street-lights were on, bathing me in their reassuring presence. I listened out for any sounds but all I could hear were the muffled echoes of my own footsteps on the well-lit pavement following me along the deserted road.

I was determined to reach the sea. Slowly, almost painfully, I picked my way across the worn grass and passed through the dunes and the spiky marram until I stopped at the very margin of the land itself. There I stood still and took in the cool sea air while I carefully held April's tiny gold cross and chain in the palm of my hand. I breathed a sign of relief and felt that, despite all that had transpired, I now felt strangely at peace with April. I looked round and smiled. All I wanted now was to take in the sound of the gentle wind and the lapping waves as darkness engulfed the lonely strand.

I looked around once again to make sure that there were no late lovers or dog walkers on the cold beach but there were none and I had the shore to myself. The lamps of New Brighton twinkled in the distance and I thought of how I would be returning there in a week's time to attend Twentyman's funeral. Somewhere, far out to sea, I could hear the steady beat of a ship's engines and I thought of the Aggelos and her human cargo passing by just before the world had been plunged into chaos. Then I turned and faced out towards the open sea and, with all passion spent, I raised my right hand and hurled the little cross and chain as far as I could, far out into the dark and swirling waters. More words came into my head – 'Earth to earth, ashes to ashes, dust to dust, in sure and certain hope of the Resurrection to eternal life'. Tomorrow, all over the world, the candles would be re-lit to celebrate the coming of the new era but what did any of that mean to me now and what right did I have to be making this gesture on April's behalf?

I wiped my eyes and looked up. Everything had changed in the last few days and yet, paradoxically, nothing had really changed at all. It was the same sea and the same beach that I had known all of my life. When we were children April would bring Ben and I to this same stretch of windblown sand. It was here that she showed us all of the mysteries of the sky at night – the stars, the planets and the constellations. Names like Betelgeuse, Aldebaran, Sirius, the Pole Star and the Pleiades now meant little to me. I could still recognise some of the more obvious ones on the rare occasions when I looked up and summoned up the courage to look at the what April had always archly described as 'The Heavens'.

I held my hands out to shield my eyes from the bright lights of the Seaforth docks and began to range my vision out over the water to the west. Quite low and almost directly ahead was the dim form of Orion, the primeval hunter with his belt and sword, while overhead was the unmistakeable and immutable line of the Plough, always reassuring and easy to find. But where was the one that I was looking for?

I began to scan the sky to the north in a concerted attempt to find it, and I did. There, barely standing out in the early evening, was the one formation which seemed to have meant more to April than any other – the great 'W' of Cassiopeia, the Queen of Ethiopia and the Mother of Andromeda.

I remained standing there without moving for several minutes, thinking of my long-dead cousin. However long that I lived, I was sure that she would always be a part of my life and that I would never forget her or this place in my dreams. I shivered and then, slowly but distinctly, her voice came back to me. In my imagination I could almost hear her speaking the same dreamlike incantation that had haunted my sleep ever since that lost summer day so many years before.

'Look up at the stars', she would say. 'Make sure that you remember them properly. You know that the stars will always be there, to the end of our time and beyond.

Remember that the stars blindly run. They always have done and they always will.'

I closed my eyes and could hear in my mind her softy spoken words mingled with the music of that song as if it were yesterday. 'Let's sing a song for Hazey Jane' indeed. She was definitely back into my mind again as if the long string of years when I first heard Ros sing it had never really happened. But the years had definitely passed and I had to face up to the fact that time was continuing to run, however I might try to stop it from doing so. I would now have to go back to the hotel and start packing my bag ready for the journey. Whatever I had already made of my life, it was the result of my own choices and there was no point in regretting any of them now. I was back in the present and could no longer dwell in the past, however much I may have wanted to.

Then I became aware of the presence of someone walking towards me along the deserted sands.

'Chris? They said that you weren't leaving until early in the morning and that you had just gone for a last walk before your supper. I kind of thought that you might be here at this spot. I'm really glad, because I didn't mean for you to go before...'

She never finished the sentence.

And I knew that Hazey Jane herself had come back like the return of the flood-tide of the Mersey on a moonless night.